THE QUICKENING AND THE DEAD

Charles Dickens Investigations Book Four

J C Briggs

SAPERE
BOOKS

THE QUICKENING
AND THE DEAD

Published by Sapere Books.

11 Bank Chambers, Hornsey, London, N8 7NN,
United Kingdom

saperebooks.com

ISBN: 978-1-912786-89-3

THE PAST

October 1840

The Burial of the Dead

This was the marsh country, a flat, desolate wilderness, dark under the shifting clouds from behind which the moon appeared fitfully like the face of a corpse in its winding sheet. The thin wind was from the east, slicing, blade-sharp, making its eerie hissing through wind thorn and reed. Somewhere out of sight, a night bird gave a harsh cry and the two men heard the leathery flap of its wings in the sedges. Away in the distance by the river were the faint lights of the Hulks; at another distance were the lime kilns where the gleam of the banked fires lent a lurid low-lying light. Nearer lay the squat form of a church and the outline of the castle's bulk. They had walked there one summer. The church was a cheerless grey structure, its tower a lonely beacon on the level marshes. The churchyard they had found bleak, with its curious cylindrical graves looking just like coffins awaiting burial. But they remembered the bleakness and the isolation the next winter.

The two men stood still for a while, waiting for the silence to settle again. The moon came out, silvering the edge of the spade as the heavier of the two took it from the cart and began to dig. The other slighter man, held the horse's head, soothing it with low words for it had whinnied nervously at the sound of the bird. He made himself keep his eyes fixed on the horse and his hands on the warm head. He felt frozen to his very bones.

The man dug on as best he could; the ground was clay, slime and swamp. They had chosen a spot within the reeds. No one would come there. The first man shuddered as he heard the slip and suck of the mud, and he heard the breathing of his partner, hot and heavy, as he struggled with the spade. There was the smell of sodden grass and mud — the smell of the grave. Neither man spoke.

A low whistle. Someone? A wild fowler? The digger stopped, holding his breath. They waited again, straining to hear. But there was only the wind rattling the reeds, the rushes murmuring their reply and the fluting whistle of the oozing mud as though the ground were a live, breathing mass. The smaller man glanced at the form which lay in rough sacking ready for burial. *It couldn't be done*, he thought, terrified, but they couldn't take it back. Then, to his horror, he saw that the sacking had fallen away to reveal the white face staring up at its twin, the dead moon. He made to cover that dreadful face, but the other threw down the spade.

'Your turn,' he said tersely. 'I've done my share.' He took a flask from his pocket and drank, but did not offer it to his companion.

The slight man said nothing, only took the spade and began. It was hard work. It was horrible work for he could not forget its purpose. He had seen burials before. He had watched his mother first, and then his father, go to their graves. Not in a landscape like this; not on a night like this; not brought on a rough cart like butcher's meat. It had been a bright spring day when they buried his mother. She had died in childbed and the child, a brother he had never seen, had been buried with her, and his father had sickened of grief. But there had been mourners: his uncles, their wives, cousins, friends. There had been ceremony. They had not been buried hugger-mugger in the dead of night, bereft of family and friends, bundled into a black hole by those who had a duty to take care of this dead one. Even the unknown drowned pulled from the river had shelter in the charnel house by the old church.

He stopped to get his breath and looked involuntarily up towards the lights from the Hulks; he thought of the prisoners there, men he had seen in the town, shackled together with irons on their legs, men degraded in their coarse suits of grey and broken shoes, men lost to the civilised world, men lost to hope and ambition. He began to dig again with a strength he had not known he had. They could not lose everything.

'Enough,' said his companion. 'Let's do it.'

The heavy man rolled the corpse more tightly in the sacking, covering the dead face, and securing the bundle with a rope round the feet and another round the neck. Sickened by that, the other helped him shove the sacking into the hole. It was light enough, light enough for a child. Only the head in its sack hood with the rope round its neck remained visible, flopped to one side. *Like a hanged man*, he thought, *like a man hanged for a crime he had not committed.* The heavy man used the spade to press the head down. The mud sucked it in. The other turned away.

They climbed into the cart. The slight man found he was sweating. Sickness came over him in waves. His companion stared ahead, his face carved stone.

'It'll not be found?' the sick man asked. He felt the dread of that, now it was done.

'Never,' said the other. 'If it's not deep enough, the flood will take it.'

Sure enough, the rain came; they heard the wind rising and rushing now, sounding like the winter water that would surge with the swelling river and take the dead to the sea. They rode away in the empty cart, the storm rack pursuing them through the thickening dark.

October 1850

The woman hurrying through the midnight street carried a parcel wrapped in brown paper. She turned off abruptly into an alley, arched like a tunnel, black as ink. No expected light showing. She stopped and seemed to stagger, leaning against the wall which dripped with water and slime. She was breathless after her long walk, and afraid. What if he wasn't there? She clutched the parcel more tightly to her breast.

As she waited, peering into the darkness, a flickering light showed at the end where a figure stood by an iron gate which was half open. He raised the lantern and she saw the stooped, elderly man she expected. She walked on to meet him. The man raised his lantern again to look at the woman's face. The face was white and drawn in the yellow lamplight. *She looked ill*, he thought, hoping she wouldn't collapse before it was done. A sick woman on his hands was the last thing he wanted. He nodded his recognition and let her through the gate.

There was a freshly dug grave away in the north corner. The woman followed the old man across the wet grass, past the angels, their stone eyes blind to her going. A weeping cherub looked down. At the grave, she peered into the open hole and saw a smaller hole dug in the centre.

'It's deep enough,' the man said gruffly.

'What will you do?'

'I puts the parcel down there in the little 'ole and I covers it with the earth and tomorrow the coffin's ter be lowered and it'll rest on top. Nobody's the wiser. There'll be no more burials 'ere. Tomorrer'll be the last one.'

'Who is to be buried there?' asked the young woman, staring down into the gaping blackness. It smelt of rain and something darker; something bitter caught at her throat. She drew back, but asked again, 'Who?'

She wanted to know who would lie with her dead child.

He was not baptised, though she had given him a name. She could not afford a grave for him, but this was consecrated ground. That's something, and when prayers are said tomorrow, they can be as much for her dead child as for whoever will lie here. Prayers can be for anyone. Jesus won't mind, surely, who suffered the little children. She remembered that from Sunday school.

It is better that he is buried in secret. Then she can go home, away to where they cannot find her. She won't tell. No one will ever know. She can find a job, earn some money, and come back sometimes, just so he will not be forgotten. Poor little thing. She hadn't wanted him. She had felt only terror and shame, but when she had felt the quickening in her belly, she had known that she could not do what they had planned, and he had looked so fragile when he was born that a great feeling of pity had swept over her. She would have loved him. She did love him, even in death.

'Yer don't 'ave ter know that. Yer can't be comin' back. Folk might wonder.'

'I must come sometimes. I'll be careful. I won't come near the grave if anyone else is here. I beg you, please.'

He saw the tears on the gaunt face glistening in the lamplight. *Half-starved*, he thought. She seemed to sway as if she might faint. Wouldn't matter if she knew. The next grave she visited would be her own.

'An ol' woman,' he said. 'Mrs Martin. That's all I'm sayin'. Now, let me get on.'

'A good woman?' she asked.

'Yes, o' course. Nice ol' body.' She might have been. He never thought much about his clients. Good or bad, he had no interest. The grave held no terror for him. He climbed nimbly down a wooden ladder. *He was like a gnome*, she thought, *a wicked elf from a story*. She wanted to run, but then she thought of the good woman with her boy.

Look after him, Mrs Martin. She uncovered a bit of the brown paper to reveal the waxen forehead and kissed the little head. 'God bless,' she whispered, and handed him to the sexton, never taking her eyes off her son while the sexton placed the parcel in the small hole and covered it with the rotten-smelling earth.

He brought nothing into this world. She tore a ragged little cloth flower from her bonnet and threw it down. The sexton shook his head. Her eyes pleaded in the lamplight. He placed it on the mound.

When it was done, she paid him the five shillings. It was all she had. He watched her walk away. Her gait was that of one exhausted. She paused to touch the hand of an angel. Its stone trumpet pointed heavenward. He felt anxious then, but she moved on, not looking back, making her stumbling way towards the passage, shrinking to a shadow as she went. Then she was gone, swallowed by the dark.

The sexton went back to the grave. He climbed down the ladder again, picked up the artificial flower and put it in his pocket. Risky to leave it. Then he flattened the earth, ready for the new occupant. He climbed back out, ready to make his way to the inn he knew would be open. Thirsty work all that digging. And she'd paid him. It was a nice little extra. He'd done it before. Others had. Pity, the graveyard was closing.

Rain came in the early hours, filling the gutters, streaming along the tunnel, swirling round the tombs, soaking the rank grasses, flooding an open grave.

And the dead shall be raised.

THE PRESENT

November 1850

On a smoking, sulphurous early evening in November, when wisps of fog wreathed round gas lamps and traffic slowed, and voices seemed to come at him from distant regions, Charles Dickens made his way home from the office of *Household Words* in Wellington Street. He was thinking about the oddities of life, how curiously ill-matched things were sometimes jostled together as if some providential hand were making a joke. What, for instance, was a notice for Madame Tussaud's, advertising the exhibition of the waxworks of that murderous pair, Maria Manning and her husband, Frederick, doing, nestled up against advertisements for the *The Wood Nymph's Polka*, flexible hose pipes and grey goose feathers which could be bought, apparently, for one shilling and sixpence? And the new fish carving knives could be had from the appropriately named Savory and company who *respectfully informed the public...* Madame Tussaud did not *respectfully* inform her customers that the murderers could be viewed for a shilling. She did promise a plaster head of the Mannings' victim, Patrick O'Connor, and, if that were not ghoulish enough, a plan of the kitchen wherein he was murdered. The head on a plate? Macabre thought.

Dickens stopped suddenly. Murder and carving knives had brought him unaccountably out of his way. Instead of turning into Devonshire Street from Portland Place, he had taken the earlier turning into Weymouth Street. The fog — and wayward thoughts. But then again, perhaps not, for this was the street in which, only the other day, a doctor had been stabbed to death — fish knife? He thought not. He could have turned round, but he went on to walk past the house. It was perfectly ordinary — well, except for the fact that a man had been murdered there. He remembered seeing Stanfield Hall, the scene of the murder of Isaac Jermy and his son — he had thought it had a murderous look that seemed to invite such a crime, but number 34 Weymouth Street looked innocent enough. And the street was perfectly ordinary, too, apart from a slight ghostliness supplied by the descending fog. There was a cab stopping opposite; a nurse with a little girl hurried by; the sound of a piano could be heard, the sweet notes dissolving into the misty green air; a boy with a little barrel-organ stood on the pavement.

An Italian boy looked up at Dickens, who saw a pair of wide brown eyes in a face of the kind that reminded him of his stay in Genoa, but there were plenty of Italian boys plying their trades in London: the barrel-organ players like this one; the ones with white mice to show; the ones selling artificial flowers, wax pictures; the harpists and flute players, all so often under the control of some gang master who put them to work and beat them.

The face that looked up at him was delicate, a sweet face, hopeful and innocent. And poignant, somehow, because of a little birthmark shaped like a tear under the left eye. Dickens gave him a sixpence and walked on. When he looked back, the boy was still standing, staring at the house with the drawn blinds. He was not playing his barrel-organ. But someone else had stopped — a tall, dark figure bending over the child. He had an impression of a long coat and low-crowned, dark hat, and the blur of a face looking at him for a moment. Another sixpence, Dickens hoped. Then they were lost in the fog.

1: Lost Girls

First: Annie

'Get undressed.'

The voice was not unkind, just impatient. The speaker gave the girl a little shake, but there was no response. The girl simply stood, passive, her head bowed.

'Yer need ter get undressed — now.' The woman spoke more loudly, more slowly. *Deaf, p'raps*, she thought. *Dumb, mebbe, or just simple. Yer got them all the time — poor simple girls knowin' nothin', jest scrapin' their way in the streets till they stole somethin' 'cos they was starving, or 'cos a man telled 'em ter.*

'Wot's she on remand fer?' The words were directed to a large, tallow-faced woman who stood at the door of the room which contained a boiler with a furnace and a large stone bath where tepid water waited for the girl who must be washed and searched before she was taken to her cell. Remanded for two weeks before her trial.

'Murder.'

'Niver — she don't look as if she'd 'urt a fly. She don't seem all there ter me. Don't seem ter understand.'

'Policeman said. She killed a doctor — stabbed 'im. They found 'er not far away. Blood on 'er 'ands, it seems, an' a five pound note in 'er pocket. Where'd a girl like that get a fiver? Still, not our business. Jenny, you'll 'ave ter get 'er undressed if she won't do it. Can't wait all day.'

Jenny, more kindly disposed to the prisoner, tried again. 'Take yer dress off, will yer.'

The girl heard the words, but they had no meaning. She understood them as individual sounds, like stones dropping one by one down a well, a well in which she was at the bottom, looking up to a circle of light. She knew that the cover would be put on, that the circle would shrink like the moon being covered by cloud. Then she would be in the dark. It was what she wanted — the dark.

She had been brought by the policeman from the court. He hadn't been rough, and she had walked, putting one foot in front of the other, watching her feet taking her along a passageway lined with heavy walls, sheer and black as cliffs. There were iron gates, gratings, locks, bolts, spikes, barred doors, opening and shutting, each slam of a door or gate a drumbeat taking her to the cell where she must wait for her trial. Voices came down the maze of passages, shouts reverberating off the stone walls, but they seemed far away, coming from a distant place.

Jenny Ince, a prisoner herself, but who had earned her position as a wardswoman, began to undo the buttons at the back of the girl's drab dress while the other woman, the Matron of the female remand ward, stood looking on, unmoved by the sight of the prisoner's starved frame emerging from the folds of the dress. Jenny helped the naked girl into the stone bath. The sight of the bony shoulders hunched over, and the way the girl flinched at her touch, made her gentle. Jenny noticed the dried blood on her inner thighs. She thought she knew where the blood on the hands, and what looked like a blood stain on the dress, had come from. But she said nothing, only watched as the water turned a faint, rusty red.

Something about the girl made her think of Miss Gray, the daughter of the woman for whom she had worked once — laundry she'd done. *Poor Miss Gray — there'd been an un'appy little girl. Still, Miss Gray was to be married, she'd 'eard. Not this girl, though. Shame.* She noticed the bruised ribs and knees and scraped hands. *Poor kid*, she thought, *beaten, p'raps, and starved.* She'd likely die afore the trial. She took up the bar of rough soap and began to wash her. The girl was rigid, but she made no sound — only endured.

The Matron, Mrs Betty Tode, picked up the dress, gave it a shake, looked in the pockets, and, satisfied that the girl had nothing valuable, put it on the chair and waited for Jenny to finish.

'She can keep 'er own dress an' things — clean enough, apart from some stains. Looks as if she's tried to wash 'em out.'

And they were, Jenny thought. *Kept 'erself clean enough somehow. Not like some that came in — all in rags, and filthy with it. Well, she'd been the same. Still, she'd not done murder. A silver box, from that sour mistress she'd worked for. Deserved it — mean old cat. But, murder. Well, she'd 'ave liked ter murder Mrs Gray, that she would. Called perlice, and she, Jenny, was convicted of theft. But, she liked it 'ere now — food an' clothes, an' a wardswoman, too. Funny 'ow things turned out.*

She dried the girl on the rough towel and dressed her. Just a kid, really.

They took her to the cell.

And Annie Deverall never spoke a word.

Second: Lavinia

The lilies on the altar seemed to give off a faint smell of corruption. The young man sitting alone in the first pew could smell it, he thought. Sickly. They were festering already. Lilies for the bride. The bride who had not arrived.

By half past eleven, Richard Farleigh had known that she would not come, and when the message came, he had not been surprised. The guests had departed. Under the feathered and flowered hats, the women's faces had looked incongruously solemn, that is those whose expressions were not of avid curiosity. The men had looked embarrassed, awkward now in their frock coats, as if they had found themselves in the wrong place, dressed for a wedding, and finding themselves at a funeral. They had all stood frozen for a few minutes. What was the etiquette for such an occurrence? Did one wait for the bridegroom to leave, to make his solitary way down the aisle? Surely, it would be unseemly to hurry away in a crowd. Someone had coughed discreetly, and then his Aunt Constance, a formidable woman, had made a move as if to leave her pew. And at this signal, others shuffled into the side aisles. Then he had seen no more for his father had taken him by the arm and had led him unresisting into the vestry.

And that was it. What had he felt then? The truth was — relief, and he had seen, fleetingly in his father's eyes, that he knew and understood. His father had offered to go to the bride's house to find out more, but Richard had gone himself. He wanted to see her mother, that grim-faced, miserable woman in black who had said she would not be well enough to attend her only daughter's wedding. The wedding breakfast was to be held at the bride's uncle's house in Manchester Square.

He thought now about the empty rooms where the guests would have mingled — the food that would not be eaten, the presents displayed which would have to be sent back — well, no doubt, they could be used again for some other bride and groom who would eat from the Crown Derby, drink from the crystal glasses, gaze lovingly at the damask cloths and the shining silver in place for their first dinner guests.

Stop this, he told himself. *Think of the poor girl who is missing. Lavinia Gray. Where is she? Had she gone in the night?* And though he had not believed in this marriage, he felt only pity for her. She had fled because she could not bear to marry him. Why hadn't she told him? He would have released her. He had wanted to, but he had not known how to withdraw.

Mrs Gray had refused to see him. Her message was that she had nothing to say to him. The housekeeper, kind Mrs Pook, had told him that Miss Lavinia's maid had gone to wake her in the morning. Miss Lavinia had not been in her bed. They couldn't understand it. They had waited. Perhaps she had gone for a walk in the garden of the square. Millie, the maid, had gone to see, but Miss Lavinia wasn't there. They dared not wake Mrs Gray — it was too soon. Mrs Gray had her breakfast in her room — always at eight o'clock. They waited for half an hour.

What then? Richard had asked. At which question, Mrs Pook had wiped her eyes. Mrs Gray had said to wait. That was all. Should Mrs Pook go to Mr Gray, Lavinia's uncle? Mrs Gray had only looked at Mrs Pook and the frightened Millie. Such a look, Mrs Pook had said, such a look. He could imagine. He had seen it himself — that look of contempt when he and Lavinia had discussed the wedding.

It was deliberate, he thought. She had waited until the last moment, when she knew the church would be full, and then she had sent poor Mrs Pook to tell him that there would be no wedding. That his bride had run away. And, Mrs Pook had said, not once had she expressed any concern for her daughter. 'She will be back.' That was all she had said. He could imagine the thin lips compressed into that line of disapproval he had known so well. Cruel, Mrs Pook had declared. She was. That was why he had not withdrawn. He had thought that he might have made Lavinia happy, at least to be away from that dreadful woman, though, in his heart, he had known it was no good. She could not bear him to touch her.

Richard had confided his fears to his father. Of course, Richard could not withdraw — a question of honour, certainly, and, he advised that, perhaps with patience and loving care, away from her mother, Lavinia might come to be less nervous. Might he, Mr Farleigh had suggested gently, might he consult Lavinia's doctor? It was clear that Mrs Gray would not help, and it was impossible that Richard's mother could broach such a delicate matter with Lavinia, and there was no one else. But the doctor — a medical man, surely, would be objective in giving Richard his view as to whether there were any reason that Lavinia should not marry.

And that interview with the doctor — painful — and embarrassing. The man was a pompous ass. Richard had disliked him. He must understand, the doctor had said, that young ladies were bound to be afraid of marriage, and Miss Gray was sensitive, of course — not necessarily more so than others, but with time, yes, time, she would come to terms with what was expected. In his experience, young ladies learned to submit to the duties expected of them.

And that was it, Richard had thought, *she would learn to do her duty...* God, it was insupportable, impossible that their marriage would be conducted in such a way. According to the doctor, thousands were. And he was trapped.

Richard Farleigh left the church. Why the devil had he come back at all? He went out into the fading day. Rain was beginning to fall. He looked at the flower on the lapel of his frock coat. A kind of revulsion filled him. He wrenched it from its pin and tossed into the gutter, and saw, regretful now, how it was dirtied in the mud.

A man passed by and looked at him curiously. Richard recognised him — Charles Dickens. He turned away. Perhaps he knew of the failed wedding, perhaps the whole town knew. The papers would get hold of it, he supposed. *Bride Missing* — he could imagine the headline. Well, he didn't care what people thought. What mattered was that she should be safe. Lavinia. Where could she be?

Third: Evie

Evie Finch stood in the narrowest of alleys, her feet in the mud and filth. Where should she, where could she, go? She looked up at the stars. They said it was 'eaven up there. She dint know. Too far away, anyways, for wot she'd done. They'd say 'eaven want fer 'er. In any case, her feet was in hell. She looked down at the mud. She wanted to bang her head against the grimy wall, to stop the thoughts. She thought she'd go mad. Head full o' things on little clawed feet, skitterin' round and round.

She put her hand on the front of her dress, feeling the stickiness there, and she knew, though she could not see, that it was blood. She could feel it dripping down her legs. And there were terrible crampin' pains. It oughter stop soon. Mother 'Ubbard had said not ter worry. That's what they all called her — 'cos of what she had in her cupboard. She'd paid up — even though the doctor hadn't come — Mother 'Ubbard had said she knew what she was doin', and Evie had no choice.

She had a few shillings left. Mother Hubbard had charged her ten pounds — a reduced rate. It would have been more if the doctor had come. A blessin', Mother Hubbard had said, seein' as 'ow Evie 'ad only ten quid. Evie had stayed one night, but she hadn't been able to bear the woman — those fat, prying hands. It had been worse than she had ever thought. She had gone to the house — a neat, little terrace off Barlow Street. Near the burial ground — she thought of that now. But the place was clean. Fresh sheets on the bed, and 'Ubbard's bustling kindness. But the pain and the matter of factness. Which was worse, she didn't know. She just wanted to get away, out of it, away from the kindness that ten quid had bought her.

'You'll need a nice lie down at 'ome, dearie. Pains'll come, then it'll be over. Just a bit o' blood and the nasty thing'll come out. Yer ma'll clear it up. She'll know what ter do. Right as ninepence in a day or two. Yer'll need a bucket.'

Evie had kept her eyes closed. Home — she couldn't go there. She'd find somewhere. Anything to get out of there.

Ten quid, thought Evie, *a year's wages*. Jem had given her five — all he could get, and the rest had been her savings. Jem. She thought of his face when she had told him. Frightened. No talk of love then, no talk of marriage. He was sorry, but he couldn't marry her. Married already. Wife in the country. And something else, besides fear — blame. Her fault. She'd been angry, but then came the sickening terror, and the cold, empty feeling that was loneliness. The illegitimate child would be her responsibility — there was no law that could make him pay. He'd told her that much when he'd seen the anger dwindle into terror. She could 'ave it if she wanted, but even the workhouse wouldn't 'ave ter take 'er and 'er bastard. Hers — not his, not theirs. He pressed home his advantage, and she had felt his power. Hatred in his eyes — eyes that had been hot with the lust she'd thought was love. But it hadn't been. She'd known it then, really.

In any case, he'd said, how did he know it was his? He'd seen her making eyes at Mr Roderick — master's son's bastard, he'd bet. And he'd squeezed her arm so hard that the bruises showed the next day.

And he'd gone. Told Mr Simpson that he had to go — his wife was ill. Oh, the talk in the kitchen. Kind of Mr Simpson, they all said, to let Jem go to Mr Simpson's brother's house in the country, get a job there. Evie had said nothing. No point. It wouldn't help.

Jem had found out about Mrs Raspin — Mother 'Ubbard, as Evie called her — she didn't know how, but he'd said she was respectable, and that a doctor would do it. Soon over, Jem had said — *for you, yes*, Evie had thought, but she was glad to see the back of him. She'd seen him all too clearly then — his black eyes darting away from her face. Licking his lips. And his mouth had revolted her suddenly when she thought of what she'd let him do. She was the fool. Underneath the bluster about Mr Roderick, she'd seen that he was still scared she'd tell. She'd taken the five quid, and she'd gone to Mrs Raspin's. That, or give birth in the street.

A sixpence would get her a night's lodgings — two maybe, if the place was dirty enough and no questions. *She had to lie down*, she thought. Her skin was on fire — sweating like a pig. She felt it under her arms, and on her face, and such a thirst. And the pain. She leant her head against the cold stone wall. When would that stop?

Then what? Who could help? Mollie Spoon — Rogers now. Lived at the stationer's in Crown Street. Fell on her feet, Mollie Spoon had. Evie had thought Alf Rogers not much to write home about, but good enough for little Mollie. Pretty enough, Mollie, and kind hearted. But where had Evie's looks got her? Into a stinking alley and nowhere to go. Mollie'd got sense — always had. They'd been in service together in Grosvenor Street, then Evie had moved on to work for Mr and Mrs Simpson, and Mollie had married Alf Rogers. But Alf Rogers was a policeman — she'd have to tell Mollie what she'd done, and Mollie would have to tell Alf, and then what?

Could she go to Effie Scruggs? She and her husband, Zeb, had an old clothes shop in Monmouth Street. Good people, but they knew Ma, and she couldn't go home. Not in this state. When she felt better, then she'd go. She could tell Ma she'd lost the job, that she'd not been needed any more — some story. Lodgin's then. In a day or two, she might go to Mollie's. Mollie would lend her something, surely.

Evie Finch went out of the narrow alley, into the teeming streets, where she found a stall selling tea, coffee and sandwiches. She felt a bit better after that — not so hot, and the blood seemed to have stopped. She walked on until she found a lodging house in a dank little street. The landlady, a scrawny hard-faced woman, looked at the sixpence in her hand and nodded. Then she took Evie down to the squalid cellar that was not worth tuppence a night, never mind sixpence.

2: In Newgate

Annie Deverall was in her narrow cell, imprisoned by great slabs of cold stone, pressed down by a low vaulted ceiling. A little light came through the grating of the high arched window. It was always twilight by day, and when she was locked in at night, she was in the dark. Not that she minded.

She did not mind the narrow bed, the coarse linen sheets, the jug and ewer with cold water for washing, the slop bucket, the gruel. Nothing mattered. A prisoner on remand, she was entitled to have her own food brought in, to have books and writing materials, but she did not want any of those things. She hadn't the means to pay for them anyway. All she possessed was her life — and she didn't want that now. A hopeless, ragged pauper of a thing, what use was it? She ate enough to keep alive — she did not want to be taken to the prison hospital. She wanted only to be tried and put to death so that it would be over, and it would be dark always.

She was entitled to visitors. The prison chaplain had come, but he had shaken his head because she would not speak. And there was a lady visitor who read to her. She was here now.

Lady Pirie read from the Bible. It was dark in the cell so she had requested a candle, and Annie Deverall had seen in one swift glance from under her lashes, her visitor's mild, kind face.

Annie had not spoken. Lady Pirie hoped the readings might prompt some response — tears, perhaps, which might herald a confession, or be a sign of innocence. But the girl's head remained bowed, the narrow shoulders hunched as if she expected a blow. *Perhaps that is what she has known*, Lady Pirie had thought when she first saw her. It happened. Cruel employers brutalised their servants; unscrupulous masters seduced their maids; callous mistresses put servant girls onto the streets for some petty misdemeanour. Lady Pirie understood very well what brought so many of these girls and women through the stern, black archway of Newgate.

It wasn't as bad as it had been — thanks to Mrs Fry. She who had ventured in to the old wards for women and had seen for herself the filth and squalor, the drunkenness, fighting, gambling, what she had called 'the abandoned wickedness' of the place where women had had to strip a dead baby to give the wrappings to a child that had not a cloth to cover it. It was from Mrs Fry's determined endeavours that reform had come, and had allowed women like Lady Pirie to follow her example.

There were women imprisoned here for all kinds of crime: theft, mostly — many driven by desperation for their starving children; deception; drunkenness and sometimes, murder — like Mrs Manning, executed a year ago for the murder of Patrick O'Connor.

Murder, though. Lady Pirie looked at Annie Deverall. Was it possible to forgive that? What had been done to this poor creature? Or was she as callous as Mrs Manning? Lady Pirie could hardly believe it, and unless Annie Deverall broke her silence, they would never know. Perhaps this silence bespoke such a weight of guilt that it was impossible to speak of.

She continued to read the verses from Saint Mark:

'While he yet spake, there came from the ruler of the synagogue's house one which said, Thy daughter is dead: why troublest thou the Master any further? As soon as Jesus heard the word that was spoken, he saith unto the ruler of the synagogue, Be not afraid, only believe...'

Annie could hear the words, and she knew their meaning. The story of Jairus's daughter was meant to comfort, to give the girl hope that she might be born again into a new life, but their meaning for her was very different from what Lady Pirie hoped.

If she concentrated enough, Annie thought, if she closed her eyes, the candlelight would be made to disappear, the cell would vanish, the noises would diminish and the gentle voice uttering the words she knew so well, would change into the voice of another. The voice of her father, just as gentle, but deeper — and that would be her comfort.

Annie Deverall had been born in Ireland. Her father had been a Protestant clergyman at Pallasmore in the county of Longford. His wife had died when Annie — not the name she was given at birth — was a little girl of five. Father and daughter had lived happily together, though the Reverend Henry Deverall had only about forty pounds a year from his stipend as village preacher and the few fields he farmed. He was a good man, simple in his tastes and wants. He educated his daughter, and she loved him as well as the books they read together.

When she was twelve, he thought to marry again — his daughter needed a mother, and, besides, he had succeeded to a better living at Lissoy in the county of Westmeath. An income of two hundred pounds, a respectable house and farm, made him attractive to a younger widow, Mrs Catherine Hodson — who had nothing much beyond the fifty pounds a year left by her husband, and a desire to be better off.

Annie's life was not unhappy with the new stepmother, but she remembered her own mother well enough to draw a contrast which was unfavourable to the new Mrs Deverall. For her father's sake, she tried to love her new mother. But she was glad to be of little account when a boy was born. She was sure of her place in her father's heart.

And then he died. Annie was fourteen. That was the beginning of her silence. Mrs Catherine Deverall lost her home and her two hundred pounds. What the Reverend left, she claimed for her son, of course. There was no special provision for Annie. Why should there be?

There was little room for Annie Deverall at the cottage where widowed Mrs Deverall took refuge, and no room at all for her at the house of the gentleman her stepmother took as her third husband. No room at all for a pretty stepdaughter. Mrs Deverall had been fond of the Reverend Deverall, but she would prefer to forget him. And her son had never really known him; he would find his father in Mr Michael Murray, the gentleman farmer. However, there was employment to be got for the pretty stepdaughter with the former Mrs Deverall's milliner cousin in London. There Annie was sent. No one asked if she wanted to go. Mr Michael Murray looked at her with some sympathy. Difficult to tell what she was thinking, she was so silent. Still, it wasn't his concern, and Catherine obviously didn't much care for the girl.

And she took nothing with her, except twenty pounds to be paid to the milliner for her apprenticeship and a little picture. And her father's voice. Now, she willed it to come, her eyes tight shut. But she could hear only the voice of the lady.

'*And he took the damsel by the hand, and said unto her, Talitha cumi; which is, being interpreted, Damsel, I say unto thee, arise. And straightaway the damsel arose and walked.*'

Lady Pirie stopped reading. It was time to go. She felt she had failed. She said goodbye to silent Annie Deverall, and made her way along the cold passageways. What could be done? And she thought of someone who might help, someone whose words she had read, who had written to the poor girls in the prison at Coldbath fields, words which she had remembered:

'*You will see, on beginning to read this letter, that it is not addressed to you by name, but I address it to a woman — a very young woman still — who was born to be happy, and has lived miserably; who has no prospect before her but sorrow, or behind her but a wasted youth...*'

Words written by a man who must have a fund of compassion for the girls to whom he was offering a second chance. She would write to him to ask him to come to see Annie Deverall.

3: A December Vision

I saw a poisoned air, in which Life drooped. I saw Disease, arrayed in all its store of hideous aspects, and appalling shapes, triumphant in every alley, bye-way, court, back street and poor abode, in every place where human beings congregated — in the proudest and most boastful places, most of all. I saw innumerable hosts, foredoomed to darkness, dirt, pestilence, obscurity, misery, and early death. I saw ...

Dickens put down his pen. *Powerful stuff*, he thought. The article was for *Household Words*, the weekly periodical he had established earlier in the year. Gloomy, though. Still, it could go in on 14 December, and he had an idea for a piece about a Christmas tree for the week after. *Brighten it*, he thought, *for Christmas.*

But it was what he had seen on his way home. Dark already. November dark, and bitingly cold. Cutting through Covent Garden from Wellington Street, he had seen savage-eyed urchins darting about on their naked feet, seizing what shreds of leaves, bits of offal and rotten potatoes they could lay their hands on.

He had seen a wretched girl sitting on the pavement, bare feet bruised and blue in the cold. The eyes were closed in the gaunt face and there was, in her attitude, such a look of exhaustion that Dickens stopped. Chalked on the pavement were the words: *I am starving*. The girl must have sensed his presence because the eyes opened and the girl looked at him. Was it recognition that Dickens saw then? He didn't know, but there was something — an appeal, something unspoken flashed between them. The girl saw two large and luminous eyes gazing at her which seemed to say, 'I know you, and your suffering.' And Dickens saw the tears welling from the exhausted eyes, which closed again. He found a half crown in his pocket, put it into the thin hand and went on his way towards Oxford Street.

He had seen faces, shadows in gaslight: an old woman with a face fallen in, dragging a little girl with her; a wretched woman with a child in her arms, attempting to sing some popular ballad in the hope of wringing a few pence from a passer-by; a young man with the thin-armed, puff-faced, leaden-lipped face of the gin-drinker; a muddy, wretched, slouching boy sweeping a crossing. An Italian boy, too, the other day, with a face like an angel, an angel in rags.

And he had seen a terrible face, a beetle-browed, hare-lipped youth clad in a bundle of rags, which it held together with one of its hands. It shivered from head to foot; its teeth chattered and it stared at him. *What am I*, thought Dickens — *persecutor, devil, ghost?* He put out his hand to stay it. It twisted out of its garment, and Dickens was left standing alone with the rags in his hands.

And in the shadow of All Souls Church in Langham Place, he had seen a young man toss a flower into the gutter. A glimpse of a troubled face — young and disappointed.

Then he had gone home to write his piece. And to read an interesting letter.

The letter was from Lady Pirie who was a prison visitor to Newgate. She wondered if he might visit a poor girl, Annie Deverall, who was on remand for the murder of Doctor Lancelot Plume. Lady Pirie had tried to help the girl, but the significant thing was that Annie Deverall would not speak, had not spoken since her arrest. Lady Pirie knew of his work for the home for fallen women which he had established in

Shepherd's Bush. Miss Coutts, with whom Dickens had founded the Home, had shown Lady Pirie the letter which Dickens had written to the female prisoners at Coldbath Fields, and Lady Pirie, much struck by the compassion shown by Dickens, thought he might be able to help Annie Deverall. No one else had been able to reach the girl, not any of the lady visitors, not the prison chaplain. She would be brought to trial in a few weeks, and the evidence against her was compelling.

Well, well, Doctor Plume of Weymouth Street, the street into which he had wandered and where he had looked at the house. *There's fate in this*, he thought. Inscrutable as yet, but fate, in the guise of Lady Pirie, required an answer. He wrote his reply. He would, of course, visit the young woman. Tomorrow.

Dickens studied Annie Deverall intently. She had been brought to the receiving room by the wardswoman, Jenny Ince. It had seemed to Dickens as though Jenny had been leading a blind girl. Annie Deverall made no sign that she knew or understood what was happening to her. She allowed herself to be pushed into the chair, her head bowed, and there she had sat, unmoving, never raising her head.

He looked at the narrow hunched shoulders in the dark dress, and at the thin hands tightly clasped so that they seemed all bone, the knuckles raised white into sharp peaks. He had seen her gaunt face only briefly when her head had risen involuntarily as she sat down. Just a glimpse of a pale oval. *A portrait in wax*, he had thought. A death mask.

He had spoken as gently as he could, asking her if he could help her, if he could do anything for her. If she would tell him her story, he would see that she had a lawyer to represent her. Was she guilty of the crime of which she was accused? She must tell the truth, and then she could be helped. If she were innocent, and he was sure she was, she must speak so that witnesses could be found to support her case. Would she look at him, let him see her face? If only she would look at him, she would see that he meant to help her.

Annie Deverall heard the kindly voice. She understood the questions, but they had no more meaning for her than the shrieks and yells that she heard from the corridors of the gaol. It was a man's voice, not the lady's. It meant no harm. But it was no use. She kept her eyes closed, listening, listening for the voice she wanted to hear. But, there was only the stranger's voice.

Dickens felt helpless. He knew that if she looked at him, he could gather all his power in his own eyes. He could will her to speak, but there was only a silence which thickened in the little room, wrapping itself round the girl like a shroud. *She will die,* he thought — *whether on the gallows, or here in the gaol. She is willing her own death.*

Jenny Ince felt the silence, and moved her feet to break it. Dickens looked at her. She shook her head. No use, she was telling him. There was nothing to do but go. He made a sign to Jenny that she should take the prisoner away. Jenny came forward to take the girl's arm and help her to her feet. Annie stood up, and as she did so, the chair tottered. Annie put out her hand to steady herself, and something dropped to the floor.

Jenny was quick. She picked it up. Annie gave a cry — the first sound she had uttered since the policeman had found her in a lodging not far from the doctor's house. Dickens saw her face clearly now. Her eyes were open, and in them he saw a look of such grief and loss, so fathoms deep, that he was shocked to his heart's core.

Jenny spoke. 'I knows, dearie, it's yours. You shall 'ave it back.'

Something unlocked in Dickens. This was a chance. 'Let me see.'

Hearing the command in his voice, Jenny obeyed and handed him the object. Annie stared at him with wide, terrified eyes, but she did not speak. He avoided those eyes and looked at the little picture he held in his hand. It was a miniature in a paste frame that had once been gilded, but was now tarnished and cracked. The subject was a girl of about seven years. A beautiful child with a delicately tinted complexion, bright eyes and dark, curling hair. He turned it over to find written on the back in faded ink the words: *My dear one, thee, my daughter.*

He spoke without thinking. 'Miranda?'

Annie Deverall covered her face and wept as if her heart would break. And Jenny led her, unresisting, back to her seat.

Dickens and Jenny waited a long time. And then the poor blotched face looked up into the eyes of the man who had spoken her name. The name that her father had given her, the name that her stepmother had taken away after his death.

'You are Miranda? Miranda Deverall, and this is your picture?'

She nodded.

'Tell me.'

'I ... cannot.' From somewhere deep within herself, a hoarse whisper emerged. It had, Dickens thought, the faintness of solitude and disuse. So sunken and suppressed it was, that it was like a voice underground, so expressive of a hopeless and lost creature that his heart contracted in pity.

'You did not kill the doctor?' Dickens was certain she had not. There was a mystery to be plumbed here.

But, she did not answer. She sat back in her chair and closed her eyes again. Dickens could see that she was exhausted, as though the two words she had spoken had taken her little strength.

'Jenny, will you fetch some water?'

Jenny went out. Should he persevere, or ought he to leave it? Come back again? But she might retreat into her silent world, and the connection would be lost. This was the moment. It might be the only moment in which there was chance to save her. He said her name again. 'Miranda.'

Her eyes opened. So dark with pain that it was impossible to say what colour they were, but there was something in the shape of the face that was a faint echo of the picture. If this were she, then, perhaps, her father had written the words. The words were Prospero's, addressed to his daughter, Miranda, in *The Tempest*. Try it. He weighed the risks — but swiftly — save, or destroy? Courage — persevere.

He kept his voice low, though his hand shook a little. 'What see'st thou in the dark backward and abysm of time?'

It was her father's voice she heard. Infinitely gentle, tender. She looked up into eyes that seemed so luminous that they compelled her to speak. And in that low, hoarse, unused voice, Miranda told Dickens something of her past.

Perhaps, Dickens thought as he listened, she had once been a beauty. Surely the girl in the picture would have become beautiful. He saw how life had wrecked her — some of her teeth had gone, and the dark, curling hair looked scanty now, dried out. The rosy-tinted skin turned yellow as wax.

Not wanted, she had been despatched like a parcel to the unknown cousin in London. Torn up by the roots. And, as if that were not violence enough, there she had been apprenticed to a trade which was not millinery.

4: A Life Thrown Away

Miranda Deverall had taken her last look at the quiet churchyard where her father had been buried with her mother. She had wept there. She had walked for the last time in the garden of the old grey house and looked at the pear trees with their blossom as light as a dusting of snow. She went down the green slope to stand beside the little River Inny where, with her father, she had seen otters play, and trout leaping in the summer, their scales shining in the dappled light. She dipped her handkerchief in the cool water and bathed her hot eyes.

She was put in the charge of a family going to London, Mr and Mrs Westcourt and their two children. Mr Westcourt was selling his land at Ballymahon. They were grand people by the new Mrs Michael Murray's standards, connected to the Edgeworths, titled people in the great house of Edgeworthstown, and they were willing to take Annie to London. Mrs Westcourt's nursemaid had gone home to Glassan — she could hardly manage the journey to London without a nursemaid. Of course, they would pay Annie's travelling expenses — it was the least they could do. She was competent with children, wasn't she? The question occurred somewhat belatedly to Mrs Westcourt, but Mrs Murray was able to assure her that Annie was very good with her own son.

It was true. Miranda was fond of the little boy who called her Ana — his version of Miranda. Mrs Murray took pleasure in turning it into Annie. Somehow, she felt, it put the girl in her place, in that uncertain region between poor relation and servant girl, which Miranda occupied for a very short time in the lovely old house that belonged to Mr Murray. So began the process of Miranda losing herself. Not to be found again until a stranger said her name in a little, twilight room in Newgate Prison.

The train took them from Athlone to Dublin where they stayed two nights in an hotel so that Mr Westcourt could complete his land sale with the solicitors. And Annie was found to be competent enough to take care of the little ones when the Westcourts dined out. It was very convenient, too, that Annie could sleep in the children's room so that Mrs Westcourt was spared the nuisance of feeding and dressing them.

They sailed from Dublin on the *Princess Alice*, a ship bound for Liverpool, and then New York, taking so many hundreds of emigrants away to America, away from poverty and famine. Then the train took them to London. It was on this last leg of the journey that Mr Westcourt, a kindly man, fond of his children, if wary of his wife whose fortune he had married, suggested, in his diffident way, that Annie might be engaged as their nursemaid in London. The children liked her and she managed them very well. Granted, she hadn't much to say for herself, but she talked to the children and that was what counted.

In the brief silence that followed, Miranda Deverall's life was poised between happiness and misery. Not that the three concerned knew that. But Mrs Westcourt had a girl's life in her hands. She threw it away.

Mrs Westcourt's narrow blue eyes looked at Miranda. Mrs Westcourt wasn't a beauty, but she had been brought up to believe she was — which is the next best thing, even better, perhaps. Her mirror showed that she was elegant; her dresses fitted perfectly; her fair hair was fine and shining and artfully arranged to make her small head look somehow fragile. She was pale with fine, delicate skin, but the blue eyes were too small, the lips were too thin, and already, there were faint lines traceable from nose to mouth. She would fade. Not that the short-sighted blue eyes saw those things in the glass.

She could see, however, well enough, the curling dark hair and the long lashes curved like a fan on the delicate, rose-tinted cheek; she thought about the curiously green-gold eyes and the surprised look of gratitude that Annie had given to her husband. A quick look before the eyes were lowered again, then the face resumed its usual submissiveness. Mrs Westcourt remembered her mother saying, 'Get a plain nursemaid. She'll be grateful and she'll do as she's told. Pretty ones are —' her mother had paused — 'unpredictable.' She looked at Annie again, a cold, appraising look. Mr Westcourt looked out at the passing landscape.

'No,' she said, 'we shouldn't interfere.'

Mr Westcourt didn't answer. It didn't really matter. Just an idea.

From Euston, the Westcourts went away with their children to the comfortable house in Tavistock Square. The children were put to bed in the charming nursery with its rocking horse and toy cupboard, its blue papered walls and white paint, the nursery where Miranda Deverall might have slept her innocent sleep, listening to the soft breathing of two little children who would have loved her.

The housekeeper put Annie Deverall in a cab for Amelia Hodson's respectable house in East Street, a stone's throw from the St Marylebone Workhouse, and just a few streets from Weymouth Street where Doctor Lancelot Plume's blood now still stained the paving stones which edged the grass.

5: The Death of Innocence

It was dark by the time Dickens came out of Newgate. He did not want to enter the wheeling, jostling life of the city; he stood reflecting on the passers-by rushing onward in one perpetual stream of life, utterly unmindful of the throng of wretched creatures pent up within the massive walls, perhaps not even knowing, or if they did, not heeding, the fact that they passed within one yard of a fellow creature, bound and helpless, whose hours were numbered.

He looked at the women and the girls; women in shawls and battered bonnets, carrying misshapen bundles; a wan-faced girl who looked consumptive; a woman with two children clutching her scanty dress, the little girl gazing about with round eyes that seemed to wonder at this whirling world and its strange doings. A girl selling some bunches of the old-fashioned sulphur matches, splints of wood tipped with sulphur at both ends, approached him. The family probably made them, sending out the children to sell them, two bunches a penny.

They all had stories. There were thousands of stories passing him by. Miranda's story had cut him to the heart — it was the death of innocence, the waste of promise, and what she might have been under her father's care and love. She should have been allowed to flourish, to have been loved, to have been first in someone's heart as, perhaps, was that pretty girl there in her dark green costume and matching bonnet, whose escort looked down at the smiling face with such tenderness. They were gone in a moment.

He thought of his own daughters, of Mamie and Katey, safe at home. Mamie at twelve was not much younger than Miranda had been when her father had died, and the long descent had begun, which had brought her here to this grim fortress, out of which she might never come. Unless he could find out who had murdered the doctor — and why. For, though she had not answered his question as to whether she had killed the doctor, he was sure she had not.

And that thought sent him plunging into the relentless stream of life which bore him on, whether he would or not. It was time to see his old friend, Superintendent Sam Jones of Bow Street, to find out where to start. He crossed the Old Bailey into Fleet Lane, up Grey Street by the Rolls garden and office, depository of the court records, all those parchments bound in red tape, sealed with wax like a drop of blood, stamped with heraldic devices, holding prisoner all those lives, parcelled, ticketed, and carefully put away on a top shelf out of human reach. Lives knotted up in red tape, strong as adamant or steel or iron. Like the life of Miranda Deverall, caught in the strangling ropes of the law. In the years that followed, the record of her case would lie forgotten, perhaps a footnote to history — a girl's life crumbled to dust. Not if he could help it. He quickened his pace to Bow Street as if, by walking faster, he could hasten the matter.

As he was speaking to Sergeant Alf Rogers in the corridor, a young man hurried by. Dickens caught a glimpse of the face he had seen yesterday — the young man who had thrown the flower into the gutter.

He went into the Superintendent's office, where he found Sam Jones gazing out of the window. Jones turned, smiling to see his friend.

'You look pensive, Sam. That young man I saw in the corridor?'

'Yes — his bride is missing — rather his bride-to-be. You don't know him, do you?'

'Slightly — Richard Farleigh. I know his father. I saw him outside All Soul's Church yesterday — he dropped a white flower in the gutter. It struck me. I wondered what the story was. He looked so — stricken.'

'I'm not surprised. The wedding was to take place at eleven. A message came to tell him that she was not coming — disappeared, it seems. So, she is a missing person. She was not in her bed on her wedding morning — no one seems to know when she went — or where. I can't do much about it — asked him if he'd spoken to friends, relatives — he had, but nothing. All I can do is ask the beat constable to keep an eye out, and alert the other divisions. Odd, though.'

'You don't think he —'

'No, no. But there's always something unsaid. No one ever tells the whole story — just what they think you need to know, which isn't always what you want to know. He didn't tell me why she might have run away, but it was clear that he had his own thoughts on the subject. I didn't press him, but I will when I see him again, unless she turns up, of course. But, what brings you here, apart from a desire to see me?'

Dickens grinned. 'Goes without saying, but —' Jones saw his face change — 'I wanted to discuss something with you. I've just come from Newgate. I was asked to see Annie Deverall — by Lady Pirie — she's a prison visitor.'

'The girl who stabbed the doctor — I read about it in the paper. What did Lady Pirie want you for?'

43

'Annie Deverall will not speak. She has not confessed nor has she protested her innocence. Lady Pirie thought she might speak to me.'

Jones smiled at him. 'I take it she did and you found out something which troubles you.'

Dickens told him all that he had heard about Annie Deverall's life, including her real name. 'I cannot believe she is guilty — there is something about her — the ghost of the girl she was.'

'Was, yes, but you do not know what she became — you don't know yet what her life in London has been, nor, from what you tell me, anything about her contact with the doctor. There must have been some. She can't simply have walked into a doctor's house and killed him.'

Dickens could see how unsatisfactory his account was. He had not pressed Miranda about the murder. It had been enough that she had told her story. 'You think I don't know enough; that my conclusion that she is innocent is too rash.'

'As a policeman, yes. However, as I know Charles Dickens and his understanding of the human heart, I give weight to your conclusion. You came to ask what might be done for her, and I say, regrettably, it is not my case. Plume's body was found in his house in Weymouth Street — that's D Division, under Superintendent Goss —'

'Could you not?'

'What? Barge in there and say he's got the wrong person because my friend, Mr Dickens, has seen Annie Deverall and knows she is innocent. No, Charles, I cannot, but you can do something. You can find out more from the girl —'

'That's just it — I don't know that I can. There has been damage done to that girl. When I asked her about her life in London with the milliner, she looked at me with such dumb helplessness and suffering, that I forbore to ask more. I wondered whether a woman might —'

'Elizabeth, perhaps?'

'Exactly — she has such tenderness in her for the helpless. She is patient and tactful. I wondered if you would ask her to go to the prison.'

'I shall. I'll tell her all you have told me. Elizabeth could go tomorrow. And, I shall ask Sergeant Rogers to have a glass of ale with Sergeant Watts of D Division. They are friends — Watts was a constable here before he was promoted. Rogers can find out more about the murder. Watts is shrewd, whereas Goss —'

'The Superintendent — you know him?'

'I do — irascible, touchy, and not a man who would welcome doubts cast on his choice of suspect. The newspaper report says that Miss Deverall was found nearby with blood on her hands and a five pound note. Five pounds was missing from an open drawer in the doctor's desk, and the girl did not deny it.'

'But she said nothing. In any case the evidence is only circumstantial.'

'The evidence for a murder usually is — unless, and it is very rare as you know, there is a witness who happens, conveniently, to be in the room at the time. The circumstantial evidence is carefully weighed, and if it is strong enough, then the jury will bring in its guilty verdict.'

'Mistakes have been made — look at the Eliza Fenning case. I know it was a long time ago, but she was young — and she was hanged — and she was innocent.'

'But there, the judge, Sylvester, bullied the jury. The circumstantial evidence wasn't good enough. Sylvester twisted it, but I take your point. The stumbling block, though, is her refusal, so far, to speak in her own defence.'

'I bet Goss intimidated her — glad to find a suspect so quickly.'

'He might well have — but not wittingly. From what you say, her silence is more than simply a frightened girl unable to speak up for herself.'

'That's true,' Dickens conceded. Jones was always perceptive. He understood the human heart, too. 'Motive? What motive could she have?' he asked.

'We won't know that until Rogers and Elizabeth find out more. And whatever they find out, I can't take it to Goss. You'll have to approach the Governor of Newgate — tell him what you have found out — you, I say. Keep me out of it. The Governor, Lady Pirie, you, can all use your influence to get the Commissioner to order Goss to have another look at the case.'

With that, Dickens had to be satisfied. He bade farewell to Jones and went out into the street. There was something comforting about Sam Jones, and he felt hopeful that Elizabeth would be able to find out more.

6: Fever in the Blood

'Evie Finch, you say?'

Mollie Rogers looked at the ragged little servant girl who had brought the message. Evie Finch, with whom she had once been in service in Grosvenor Street, was ill — at a lodging house off Compton Street. She couldn't understand it — Evie was in service now with Mr and Mrs Simpson in Duke Street. What was she doing in a lodging house? Sacked, perhaps — Evie was always a bit forward — but, why hadn't she gone home?

The child was staring at her. She'd answered Mollie's question and was waiting for the answer. She repeated it. 'Yers, Evie, she sed 'er name woz, an' she asked for Mollie in Crown Street — stationer's, she sed. That's you, innit?'

Mollie came to. 'Yes, yes. Wait — I'll get my coat.' It was time to shut the shop anyway, and Alf wouldn't be back for a while. Gone to see Billie Watts.

Mollie and the girl went down Crown Street and turned into Compton Street from where they turned into a nest of narrow alleys. The girl led Mollie into a little lane of the meanest looking houses crammed together like dirty old cards in a pack. The lodging house was a tumbledown affair. She took Mollie down a set of dilapidated stairs into a cellar where a hard-faced woman in an untidy black dress stood by one of the cots. There was a selection of wretched individuals lounging on some of the other beds. It was squalid in the yellow light of an oil lamp, and the smell was of unwashed bodies, damp and decay. Too close to breathe. Yet it was cold — some of the windows were stuffed with rags or tacked over with oil cloth.

The hard-faced woman looked at Mollie — a sharp, cunning look. *She'd pay*, she thought. *The girl on the bed wouldn't be able to tell 'er that the landlady had already received sixpence. You 'ad ter make wot yer could these days — an' it want right, anyways, that she should 'ave the trouble of a sick girl. Mrs Rogers could take 'er away.*

Mollie saw the hard look — she knew what it meant, but she was more concerned about Evie. She looked at the girl on the fusty bed with its straw mattress — no sheets, just a threadbare blanket. She looked at the face of Evie Finch, almost green in the light of the lamp, with what looked like red splotches on it, the tangled wet hair on the dirty rags which made the pillow, and she saw the blood on the skirt. Dear God, what had brought her to this?

'Evie, Evie, it's Mollie Rogers.'

The eyes fluttered open, but there was no recognition in them. The dry, cracked lips parted. The girl began to mutter. Mollie bent down to listen, but all she could make out was a confused jumble of words. 'Old Mother 'Ubbard — 'Ubbard,' she seemed to be saying. Delirious, Mollie thought — the hand felt so hot. She touched Evie's brow — burning. Some fever — must be. 'In the cupboard — 'Ubbard...' Evie tossed and turned on the bed, mumbling, breathing shallowly. 'No doctor, no doctor, no...'

Mollie took the burning hand. 'A nurse, then, Evie, a nurse can come.' Why didn't she want a doctor? 'A nurse — she needs a nurse,' Mollie said to the landlady.

'You oughter take 'er away — I don' want 'er 'ere — might be catchin' wot she's got.'

She caught it here, Mollie thought, looking at the filthy bed. She turned angrily to the woman. 'How can I take her anywhere? Can't you see she's not fit to move? I know a nurse. Send for her — Mrs Feak at 22 Earl Street. Send the girl.' She turned to the little girl who had brought her. 'D'yer hear what I say — go — tell her Mollie Rogers needs her — tell her it's urgent.'

The girl looked at the landlady. ''Oo's payin'? She owes me rent.' She looked down at the girl on the bed.

'I'll pay — an' for the lodgin's. Just send the girl — please.'

The landlady nodded and the girl went out.

Evie was quiet now, her eyes closed. Mollie saw the red weals on her arm. They were like burn marks, and the red seemed to be turning black. What the hell was wrong?

'Evie, it's Mollie. Hold on, Evie, I've sent for a nurse. She'll come. Then you'll feel better.' She said the words, knowing them to be untrue. But she had to say something. She wanted Evie to know that she wasn't alone in this dreadful place, that there was someone.

Poor Evie, so pretty, so smart. Men liked her, but she was choosy, Evie. She'd looked a bit mocking when Mollie had told her she was marrying the policeman she'd met at Grosvenor Street. Oh, Alf Rogers, she'd said when Mollie had told her. Police, eh — well, if 'e suits yer. And Mollie had said that Alf suited her fine. Evie had come to the wedding — *that'd impressed her*, thought Mollie — Superintendent Jones had come and his wife, and to cap it all — Mr Dickens'd come, too, an' he'd given them champagne because Alf had saved his life when they were after a murderer. Oh yes, Evie had not mocked then.

She looked again at the face all marked with red. What if Mrs Feak wasn't there? Oh God, what ter do? She'd have to send for Alf — he'd know.

The breathing seemed fainter now. Evie lay still — *still as death*, Mollie thought. *She's dyin' an' there's nothing I can do except see that she doesn't die without someone to care.* She stood at the side of the cot, waiting, holding Evie's burning hand. Time seemed to stand still.

Footsteps on the stairs. Mollie looked up to see Mrs Feak's kind face. Mrs Feak came to the bed and looked at Evie. Then she looked at the landlady who, seeing something that cowed her, moved away without saying a word.

Mrs Feak took Evie's wrist. The faintest fluttering pulse. She looked at the reddish-black stains that gave the arms the look of raw meat, and she looked at the blood on the dress. Then she lifted the skirt and looked at the mess between the legs, but she said nothing. The landlady looked, too, and Mrs Feak gave her a hard stare. She took the wrist again, but there was no pulse this time.

'She's dead, isn't she?' Mollie knew by Mrs Feak's face that it was so. She felt sick, seeing Mrs Feak's face turn so set and grim, realising what she had seen under the bloodied skirt.

'When did she come here?' Mrs Feak asked the landlady.

'Other night. Couldn't turn 'er away — she dint look well.' Mollie saw how she was suddenly all sympathy — hypocrite.

'How long's she been like this?'

'I dunno — one o' me residents, Martha there —' she indicated another bedraggled looking woman on one of the beds — 'come up ter tell me the girl was sick. I come down, and she told me ter get 'er friend Mollie from Crown Street so I sent for 'er.' She pointed at Mollie. 'Did all I could, dint I? Dint know wot woz wrong. Wot'll yer do now?'

'You didn't do this to her?' Mrs Feak pointed at the blood-stained dress.

'Wot d'yer mean? Don't know anythin' about it. She woz sick when she come 'ere. You can't pin anythin' like that on me.'

'Mollie — you go an' get Alf — tell him that Evie's dead. You know what's happened to her?'

Mollie nodded. Oh, Evie, bright, careless Evie to get caught like this. She knew now why Evie hadn't gone home. Her mother would have known what she'd had done to her.

''Oo's Alf? 'Oo yer sendin' fer?'

'Police.'

'Don't want no perlice 'ere — it's respectable 'ouse, this is — I don't 'ave whores 'ere — an' I ain't got nothin' ter do wiv this.'

'A girl has died, and you know what's been done to her. You saw the state she was in under that dress. It's a matter for the police.' Mrs Feak was implacable. 'If it's nothing to do with you, then you've nothing to worry about. Mollie, go now, and if he isn't home, you'll have to go to Bow Street and get one of the other constables. You can't do any more for Evie here.'

Sergeant Alf Rogers came. He looked at the body, and heard what Mrs Feak had to tell him, and sent two beat constables to Bow Street for the mortuary van. Mollie told him about Evie's last moments, wondering at the strangeness of Evie's rambling about Mother Hubbard — a nursery rhyme. It was so pathetic, she said, so childlike. Perhaps she was back in some childhood place. Perhaps she didn't know she was dying. Mrs Feak listened to all this. *Mother Hubbard?* She wondered.

Mrs Feak went on her way. She knew what had been done to Evie Finch. She had seen under the blood-soaked skirt the bloody misshapen thing, a lump of bloodied flesh between the legs. Someone had botched it. Mrs Feak had seen plenty of miscarriages. Women who had taken something to get rid of the child they did not want — couldn't afford to have.

Savin — the oil of juniper — could be got quite easily for a few pence. It was well-known. A remedy that had been used for years, centuries. An old midwife had told her some lines once — written hundreds of years ago, she'd said. Mrs Feak didn't know that the poet Dryden had written them, but she remembered them:

Help her make manslaughter let her bleed
And never want for savix for her need.

Mrs Feak knew very well the violent stomach pains, the vomiting, the flushed face and headache which preceded the burning pains and the outrush of blood. Pennyroyal was used, too, and gin. The secrets that every woman knows. And Mrs Feak had helped, but she'd never offered her services for that. She was sent for when something had gone wrong — and very often, too late.

She'd seen children, wide-eyed, staring at a mother on the bed. She'd seen a mother, helplessly watching as her daughter had bled to death. A mother who had only wanted to spare her daughter the disgrace of an illegitimate child, and who had paid too high a price at tuppence for an ounce of savin. But, she had never blamed them — the sufferers — the girl whose life had been ended because folk would blame her and not the man who'd left her. Probably what had happened to Evie Finch. And the women who lived in all those grubby cellars and tenements, who had seven or eight kiddies already — and couldn't afford another, didn't want to bring another to live in filth, and probably die in it. But, she did blame the so-called nurses or midwives who were no better than butchers in their dirty aprons and wielding their even dirtier instruments — she'd seen the bent spoons, the penholders with wires attached, and once, the "nurse" had left behind the curling tongs which had been altered to become forceps. And there were doctors, too — quacks a lot of them.

Mrs Feak had seen, too, how infection came on so quickly, so that a thin, starved body would be stricken with a burning fever and covered with those black patches that she'd seen on Evie's legs and arms — and the rest of her, no doubt. She'd known it was too late as soon as she'd seen her. Blood poisoning — no cure for that.

Someone had let Evie Finch go. She knew about girls who were taken in a carriage to a respectable house with a piano in the parlour. Girls who would come out again after a short time, who would have to be supported on the arm of a mother or a friend, and who would be taken home. But someone had let Evie Finch go alone. *Mother Hubbard*, she thought. *Not the woman from the nursery rhyme, I'll bet.*

She went home and scrubbed down her kitchen.

7: The Morgue

Dickens and Jones looked down at the body on the white marble slab in the cold, white-tiled mortuary. The flare of blue gas flame showed them the waxen pallor of the dead girl's face. Her eyes were closed and her head with the scraped back hair, looked all bone, as if she were an effigy, the colourless lips and the high thin nose drawn in stone. But her uncle had recognised her. She was Lavinia Gray.

The news that a body had been found on the muddy shore by Waterloo Bridge had come in the morning. Jones had gone with Rogers to look. He had wondered about the missing fiancée of Richard Farleigh. The girl stretched out on the watery edge looked very young, very fragile, and the white face seemed quite without expression. Not peaceful, just absent. He did not know if it were she, but when they had removed her to the mortuary, he had seen the handkerchief with the initials L.G. embroidered there, and had sent for Mr Gray.

Caught, he had thought, in a familiar snare — should you hope that the body were known to the person for whom you had sent? If it were, then you were the bringer of grief to someone whose life would be irrevocably altered. You would feel a kind of guilt that you were the messenger. Yet, if you were wrong, then you had made a mistake and had caused unnecessary suffering, and must go through it all again with someone else. But, Mr Gray had nodded. He had turned away then, his face, in the ugly light, stricken. He had gone away to tell his sister that her daughter was dead.

Jones had sent a message to Dickens at Wellington Street — he wanted him to go with him to see Richard Farleigh.

The sheet had been pulled down so that they could see the neck and shoulders — so thin that it looked as though, at a touch, she might break. Dickens thought about Miranda Deverall. Something linked these two, if only a sense that they had been worn to bone by some grief. Lavinia Gray had run away the night before her wedding, and she had cast herself away into the river. Why? Or had someone cast her away? Dickens stared at the head and shoulders. Above the collar bones, the hollows seemed too deep, and the skin looked almost transparent stretched across the too prominent bones of the chest. 'She is unnaturally thin — as if she were wasting away.'

'The doctor who examined her said that she can hardly have eaten anything for months — starving herself to death, he said. Perhaps she had hoped to do so before the wedding. Which adds to the theory that she was a suicide — according to the doctor, she went into the water alive.'

'How could he tell?'

'There was no evidence that she had struggled against any attacker — no bruising or contusions, and she had grasped in her hand a piece of rope which, he thinks, she had caught hold of unconsciously as she went in. It seems that this is not an uncommon occurrence and is one of the strongest proofs that the deceased went into the water living. But, for us, it's her state of mind that tells us she killed herself. She ran away from her wedding.'

'But wouldn't someone have noticed that she wasn't eating — her mother? Richard Farleigh — surely he saw that she was becoming thinner and thinner?'

'Well, that's interesting — I didn't notice that she was especially thin when I looked at her at the river, but the doctor directed me to look at her clothes. The jacket, the bodice, the skirt were all padded. Someone had sewn padded linings into the garments. She didn't want anyone to know.'

'But her mother? Did she never see her daughter undressed? She must have had a maid.'

'We shall have to ask, but first I should like to see Richard Farleigh. I want you to come with me. You know him — I thought it might make it easier. I shall have to ask some difficult questions.'

'And the other girl?' Dickens pointed to the sheeted figure on another slab.

'Evie Finch — you remember her? A friend of Mollie Rogers — she came to the wedding.'

'I do — pretty girl, as I recall, lively — and sharp, I thought. Good Lord, what's happened to her?'

'She and Mollie were in service with the Crewes in Grosvenor Street, but Evie Finch went on to work for a Mr and Mrs Simpson. It seems that she had left her employment. A message came for Mollie from a lodging house off Compton Street. The girl was dying when Mollie got there. She sent for Mrs Feak —'

'Your Sybil of Star Street.' This was what Jones had named the nurse who was a mine of information — and wisdom. Mrs Feak's son was one of Jones's constables.

'Indeed. Mrs Feak knew the girl was dying of blood poisoning, and it took only a look for her to know why. Evie Finch had been pregnant and someone had botched an operation.'

'Good God! Any idea who?'

'Not yet, but Rogers has gone to see Mrs Feak, and he is going to question the other servants at the Simpson house. I haven't much hope — it's not a thing that folk will talk about.'

They were silent then in that cold morgue. Water dripped somewhere. There was the smell of carbolic soap, and underneath it, the faint smell of corruption. Lavinia Gray slept, the life that might have been hers vanished like a dream. Death and the maiden. Too soon. *The pity of it*, thought Dickens. He looked at the covered form of Evie Finch who he had last seen glowing with beauty and smart ribands. Another wasted life.

'Let's go,' Jones said. 'Let's do something useful.'

At the Farleigh house, Dickens asked to see Mr Farleigh. They stood in the hall where Jones explained the purpose of his visit. Miss Gray had drowned, and it was his duty to discover any circumstances which might explain that death.

'She killed herself, you think?' Mr Farleigh asked. He looked anxious. Dickens wished for a moment that he had not come. Mr Farleigh had looked doubtful at his presence. He hoped they did not think that he had come out of curiosity.

'I do,' Jones answered.

The strained look in Mr Farleigh's eyes relaxed for a moment. He had wondered if his son might be suspected. If this policeman needed to find out about Lavinia Gray, then he would have to know about his son's relationship with his bride-to-be, and that would be difficult for Richard — to talk about what had seemed, to his father, the obvious thing wrong with Lavinia — she had seemed frightened about her marriage. He felt glad then that Dickens was there — he knew him. *Man of feeling, sensitive*, he thought. Richard might be able to talk to him. He looked at the shrewd grey eyes of the policeman. Perhaps that was why he had brought Dickens — sensitive, too. He looked like a decent man.

They went into the library where Richard Farleigh sat by the fire, looking like a man who would never be warm again.

'Richard, you know Mr Dickens, and this is Superintendent Jones of Bow Street, who has come to talk about Lavinia. She has been found — drowned.'

The young man's face turned white. He put his hands over his face. They waited. When he looked up, his face was wet. 'My fault,' he said. I should never...'

Mr Farleigh put his hand on his son's shoulder. 'I don't think so, Richard — you did what you thought was best. You could not have known.'

'If you feel able to answer some questions,' Jones said quietly.

Richard looked at him, surprised at the kindness in his voice. 'I will tell you all I can — it is not easy, but I suppose you must know — for her sake. Please do sit down.' If Richard Farleigh was surprised at the presence of Dickens, he did not show it, but he looked at him as if at a man throwing him a lifeline.

'I do not really know where to start...' he faltered.

'Just begin wherever you like — you do not have to tell us from the beginning.'

Dickens sat down opposite Richard. Jones sat a little away from Dickens so that he could see the young man's face. Mr Farleigh stood behind his son's chair. He put his hand on the young man's shoulder again.

'You need to know the truth — I wanted to get out of it. I know it sounds brutal, but increasingly, I felt that she did not want marriage. She seemed to be shrinking before my very eyes — I felt, somehow, as if I were sucking the life from her by my very presence. I asked her as gently as I could if she would prefer me not to come anymore — how else could I phrase it? But she looked terrified then — I couldn't understand it. I didn't know what she wanted from me. But, I couldn't face seeing that doctor again.'

'Doctor?' Dickens asked, puzzled.

'Plume,' Charles Farleigh said.

'Lancelot Plume, the doctor who was killed?' Jones asked.

'Yes,' Richard Farleigh answered.

'Why did you see him?'

'He was Lavinia's doctor. My father thought — he thought that Plume might be able to tell me if there were any reason that Lavinia should not marry —'

'Why did you ask?'

'Because —' he paused, and they saw how his pale face flushed, but he looked at Dickens straight, and at Jones — 'because she could not bear me to touch her — she tried, but even when I took her hand, she seemed to flinch. It was impossible —'

'Yet, she was terrified when you offered to stay away.'

'Exactly — I tell you, I couldn't understand it. I couldn't abandon her — it was a matter of honour. I was bound to her.'

Jones asked, 'What did the doctor tell you?'

'It was natural that she was anxious — that she would come round — young women usually did. She would come to understand her duty — as if that made it right.' Richard Farleigh bowed his head. They waited for him to master himself. 'He was so sure of himself, so patronising, so — knowing — he knew nothing. She wasn't Lavinia Gray to him — she was just a silly girl who would submit to ... and now she's dead because she thought I was the kind of man who would insist on...'

'Would the doctor have told her that?'

'I don't know — I don't know if she saw him...'

Dickens glanced at Jones. It was an idea — perhaps the doctor had told Lavinia Gray something that had pushed her over the edge. Pity he was dead. What kind of a doctor had he been?

Richard Farleigh looked up, his eyes bitter and despairing. 'Do you know, he recommended a book I could give her — *The Medical Synopsis of Married Life*. Apparently, there's a chapter on marriage and its obligations. As if I could ... it's a wonder he didn't suggest we read it together.'

'We should go to see Mrs Gray — surely Lavinia's mother might be able to help us?' Jones rose from his seat. They had put Richard Farleigh through enough. He was surprised to see an expression of dislike in the young face.

'She'll tell you nothing.'

'A hard woman,' explained Charles Farleigh, 'and, I think it is probably the reason that Lavinia seemed terrified that Richard would withdraw. She was frightened of her mother.'

8: The Hard Woman

They walked away from the house in Adam Street, through Manchester Square, noting as they went, the drawn blinds of the Gray house where the wedding feast had been dismantled, the presents packed up, and the arrangements for a funeral would have to be made. And that made him think: buried hugger-mugger in the deep midnight in some unhallowed corner of a dank churchyard? So often the case for suicides. He felt horror at the thought. Perhaps Mr Gray would find a clergyman to read the maimed rites, or perhaps there might be a family vault in which she could be quietly interred. He thought to speak, but Jones was hurrying on.

Mrs Gray lived in Queen Anne Street. They passed number forty-eight where the old painter Turner lived. Dickens had met him at a farewell dinner years ago before he went to Italy. It had been a sultry June night, but he remembered the painter with a huge red-belcher handkerchief round his neck. No one could persuade him to take it off. A quiet man — Dickens had seen him looking at the lights on the river. What had he been seeing? Something visionary there over the river where the sky was dark and louring, save where the glory of the departing sun had piled up masses of gold and burning fire, and the reflected light had shivered and splintered in the dark water?

Reality was the black painted door of number twenty-three where the blinds were drawn, too, and a red-eyed housekeeper, Mrs Pook, came to answer their knock. She wasn't certain that Mrs Gray would see them — she was not in good health, and her daughter — well, if that's what they had come about, she would see.

They waited in the darkened hall. It was cold. Dickens thought, *what a dead house it was, so still, so silent.* Oil paintings on the walls, so dark that you couldn't tell what the subjects were — vaguely brooding landscapes. Dreary. He thought of Turner's great canvas — *Rain, Steam and Speed*, an explosion of light and colour. No light, no colour here. If the mother matched her surroundings, no wonder Lavinia Gray had wanted to escape. And Charles Farleigh had said that Lavinia was frightened of her mother. Why? Well, they would see. Mrs Pook came back to tell them that Mrs Gray would see them.

Jones had told Dickens to keep well in the background — he had a feeling that Mrs Gray would not welcome Charles Dickens. He would be Constable Feak of the Detective Division. Watch, Jones had said, and busy yourself with a notebook. Keep out of her line of sight. Dickens, the actor, had arranged his face into an expression of gormless simplicity. Jones had grinned. 'No need to overdo it.'

'I shall be as invisible as the air — sir.'

The room into which they were shown was dark, too. The curtains were closed. There were oil lamps and a small fire smouldering in the grate. No modern gas light here. Heavy furniture, dark velvet that looked black in the dim light. More sombre pictures, except for the portrait over the mantel — a young man in the uniform of an infantry soldier. The tight red jacket with its white band across the breast, the gold-braided cuffs and epaulettes glowed in the dark. The young man with the eager blue eyes carried a sword. Dickens recognised the thin, high-bridged nose. Lavinia's brother?

The same nose, though sharper and longer, could be seen on the woman seated in a wheeled chair by the fire. She was dressed in unrelieved black, a black so dense that the material of the dress seemed solid. On her grey hair she wore a square of black silk. Dickens thought of the black cap placed on the judge's head when he passed a sentence of death. Apt image. There was something death-like about her, and he was sure it was not only to do with her daughter.

A stern, narrow face, the colour of parchment, with thin, pale lips compressed into a line of disapproval as she looked at the Superintendent. Jones mentioned the constable, but she did not glance at Dickens, who kept well out of the way.

Mrs Gray did not speak. Her eyes were pale ice. She was mistress here, and this large man, a policeman, Mrs Pook had said, must state his business and be gone. She had nothing to say about Lavinia, and what she thought was her private business. She waited.

She is all edge, Dickens thought, *and our presence here whets and sharpens her edges.* He wondered how Jones would deal with her.

Jones knew what she was, and he knew that she had something to do with her daughter's suicide, but he kept his feelings to himself. He saw how she thought to exercise her power over him. However, he didn't care. He had plenty of experience of those who looked down their long, supercilious noses at the police, whom they were the first to call when they were outraged by a crime committed against their person, and as important, their property. He looked at those icy eyes. He waited. After all, it was a matter of courtesy — the householder should speak first. Let her wait. The atmosphere congealed as if the very air were freezing. Dickens would not have been surprised to see icicles forming on her lips.

She gave in. 'Well?'

'Your daughter, Mrs Gray. I must ask if you have any idea why she should take her own life. There will be an inquest. Information must be given for a verdict to be reached.' Jones's voice was studiedly neutral, that of a rather dull man going about his duty.

'Must?'

He ignored the edge of sarcasm. 'I am afraid so, Mrs Gray.'

'My brother will attend the inquest. He will provide any evidence — if there be any. I am not well enough. You see that I cannot walk. You must see him.'

Jones forbore to echo the "must", though he was tempted. 'It would be helpful if you could give any indication of your daughter's state of mind. After all, it was the eve of her wedding. Was she anxious about it?'

'I have no idea. My daughter did not take me into her confidence. I will tell you this — I did not approve of the marriage.'

'Why?'

She seemed to recognise a sudden tone of authority in the tall, well-built policeman. She gave him a look. Something formidable in his face forced her to answer.

'I thought her unfit for married life. She was not fit to be a mother — too weak, too nervous, but the young man insisted. I do not know why — Lavinia was not a girl to be loved. She had very little character. I thought it would be disastrous.'

'Did you tell her so?'

Her glance showed that she thought the question impertinent. 'I said nothing.'

No, you wouldn't, thought Jones, *but your silence was, no doubt, eloquent enough*. He saw exactly why Lavinia had run away. Scared about the marriage, knowing what her mother thought, believing she was unfit, yet terrified of the long, relentless imprisonment that would be her future here. Not fit to be a mother. Ironic. Mrs Gray was not fit to be a mother. That prompted his next question.

'Have you other children, Mrs Gray?'

She saw him glance at the portrait, the only thing with any life in the room.

'My son is dead.' She closed her thin lips on the last word, and he knew they would get no more from her.

'Thank you. Your information has been helpful. We will go to see your brother. Good day, Mrs Gray.'

She looked surprised and a little puzzled. She thought she had told him nothing, yet he seemed satisfied. She did not know that she had told him all he needed to know about her. She inclined her head, and turned from them to the dying fire. They went to the door. Dickens looked back at the motionless black figure. Was she thinking about her dead daughter — or the son whose death had killed his mother as surely as the sword in his hand might have pierced her heart? Pity and revulsion. That's what he felt as he followed Jones into the hall.

'She hated that poor girl,' Jones said.

Dickens nodded. 'What now?'

'I am going to tell the housekeeper that we must see Lavinia Gray's room.'

'But, shouldn't you have asked —'

'I should, but I don't much care what Mrs Gray thinks. Anyway, she can't stop us.'

'A cat in gloves catches no mice, eh?'

Mrs Pook came into the hall. She told them that her mistress could not be disturbed until five o'clock when she would take in tea. The hours were strictly observed. She understood what the Superintendent wanted.

'Poor Miss Lavinia,' she said, 'she hadn't much of a life here, but she was gettin' out. Mr Farleigh was a nice young man — he'd have looked after her. I don't know. I can't understand it, but if it helps her then you can go upstairs. I won't say anythin'.'

Jones asked if they might speak to her later in the kitchen. Then they went upstairs, treading quietly, to see what Lavinia's room might reveal about her life — and death.

Absence. Dickens felt the sense of emptiness here. A room in which a girl had suffered so much that she had lain down in that profound black pit of water. He imagined her desperate footsteps hurrying past the scattered lights gleaming sullen, red and dull, as the torches that were burning there to show the way to death. What had she felt there in that leaden winter night?

Yet, it was an ordinary enough room: a brass bedstead with a white counterpane, an ebonised chair with a cane back, a wardrobe, wash stand with a marble top, a desk with some books held between a pair of cast iron bookends with a loving couple in relief on each, and an oil lamp. There was the faint scent of lavender — old already, Dickens felt. Ordinary — but, not a young girl's room. It was too dark. There was a brown carpet with a pattern of muddy flowers, and heavy velvet curtains, almost black like the parlour furniture.

A sad room — and most poignant of all was the white dress with its lovely Honiton lace gleaming faintly in the dimness. It was hanging on the wardrobe door like the ghost of a bride, still as death in the silent room. It would never be worn. It might be folded into an empty trunk to lie, yellowing, until it mouldered into fragments. Nothing left of the bride who was to wear it. *Ginevra* — the poem by Samuel Rogers — the poet whose breakfasts were legendary — Ginevra was the bride who had died, trapped in a chest — nothing left of her but the wedding ring, a few pearls and an emerald stone.

Jones was looking on the desk. 'See here — she had taken off her ring. She knew what she was going to do.'

Dickens went over to look. The emerald stone shone, green as clear water, but there were shadows in its depths. There was a string of pearls, too, left where they had been taken off by the girl who was disrobing for death. And a little watch which she had unpinned from her dress. It had stopped, its little ivory face mute witness to the scene.

Jones opened the drawer of the desk, but there was nothing. 'No letters, no diary — nothing to tell us about her secret life — the life she lived in this room.'

Dickens took a book from the row held by the bookends. 'Might be something in one of these.' He flicked through the pages of a volume of Tennyson's poems, noting the pencil marks where she had indicated something important to her.

He read some words aloud:

'Twilight and evening bell
And after that the dark…'

Jones looked up. 'What?'

'Tennyson — poor child, brooding on death.'

They riffled through the other books, but found nothing. There was nothing in the waste paper basket by the desk. Jones turned his attention to the fireplace where there were signs that someone had burnt paper. He used a pair of tweezers to extract a fragment which had not fully burnt. Dickens could see that there were words written on the charred piece:

flies in the night
In the howling storm.

'A poem?' Jones looked enquiringly at Dickens. 'Tennyson, is it?'

'I don't think so — doesn't sound like Tennyson — I don't know. Could be — something in my mind.' He thought for a moment. 'Crimson — something linked to crimson. Crimson petal — no, that is Tennyson. I'll have to think.'

'Never mind — it might come to you. We'll take it and the book.' He put the paper in his notebook. 'There's enough evidence in the watch and jewels to say that she intended to kill herself. I'd like to talk to Mrs Pook. See what she can tell us about Lavinia's life here.'

They left the room to its silence and went downstairs to the kitchen. It was a quarter past four. They had time before Mrs Pook had to take in the tea.

The kitchen was warm, warmer than anywhere else in the house. Mrs Pook and a maid sat at the table drinking their tea, and there was the smell of baking and a glow from the range. Jones wondered about the maid — could she have attended on Lavinia, and if so, what did she know about the padding in the clothes?

'I need to know about Miss Gray's life here, Mrs Pook, and —' He looked at the maid.

'This is Millie, sir. What can we tell you?'

'Did you attend to Miss Gray, Millie?'

'She never wanted much — just help with fastening her dress. I looked after her clothes.'

'Tell me about the padding.'

Millie looked anxiously at Mrs Pook, who spoke for her. 'We knew she wasn't eating — she said would Millie pad out the dresses. She didn't want her mother to know —'

'Didn't they eat together?'

'Not generally — Miss Lavinia had her meals on a tray in her room. That's how we knew. She hardly touched anything, but we were not to tell the mistress. I was torn, sir, it didn't seem right not to say, but Miss Lavinia was so … well, mistress could be so cutting, you know, so harsh. I didn't want her to get into trouble, but I was that bothered, and so was Millie. What was we to do? We thought when she was married…' Mrs Pook's eyes filled. 'Mr Farleigh was so kind, we thought she'd be better — he'd see that she'd eat, we thought.'

'Was Mrs Gray always so harsh with her daughter?'

'Well, I've been here about ten years. Mr Godfrey was always the favourite — Mrs Gray loved that boy. She didn't pay much heed to Miss Lavinia — but when he was killed, well, that's when it started. Miss Lavinia was about fifteen then — about four years ago. Mr Godfrey was twenty-three, a good bit older, but he was always kind to her. I wondered sometimes —'

'What?'

'I shouldn't say it, but I wondered if Mrs Gray never wanted her — p'raps she wanted another boy — I don't know, but, when Mr Godfrey died, Mrs Gray went into herself, sort of silent, but disapproving — she seemed to be irritated by Miss Lavinia — not that she did anything, you know — but it was like she couldn't stand her daughter.'

'Then, you'd think she'd want her to marry, if only to get rid of her.'

'I know, sir, but nothing pleased her. Even when Miss Lavinia was poorly —'

'She was ill. When?'

'About eighteen months ago — before Mr Farleigh met her.'

'What was wrong?'

Mrs Pook looked uncomfortable. 'I don't really know, sir — something private, I think.'

'Millie?' Jones looked at the young maid.

'I wasn't here then. Miss Lavinia had a maid then — Susan Carter, but she left.'

Mrs Pook explained. 'A nurse came to look after Miss Lavinia and Mrs Gray said Susan wouldn't be needed any more

— and she went. Quick, it was. Susan was upset, but she wouldn't tell me anything.'

'Where did Susan go?'

'Home, sir. She went home to her family in Chalk Farm.'

Dickens who had simply listened, spoke suddenly. 'Did Doctor Plume attend her then?'

'Yes, he did, but Miss Lavinia…'

'What?' asked Jones.

Mrs Pook looked uncomfortable again. 'She didn't like him. Susan mentioned it. She used to ask that Susan stayed when he came, but she couldn't. Mrs Gray didn't like it. Suppose she thought Susan had no right, being only a servant. Mrs Gray thought a lot of the doctor.'

Dickens asked. 'Did he come often?'

'Before her illness — Miss Lavinia was what you call delicate — she never would eat much — and Doctor Plume came when Mrs Gray asked him. After the nurse came, Miss Lavinia got better and she went to stay with Mrs Gray's brother in Manchester Square — that's where she met Mr Farleigh, and things seemed better for a bit, but when she came home, Mrs Gray was still nasty to her. Mr Farleigh came with Mr Gray, the mistress's brother — he seemed keen on the engagement. But, Mrs Gray didn't seem to like it an' Miss Lavinia — I don't know, sir, sometimes, I thought she was frightened. She wasn't like a bride —' Mrs Pook looked anxiously at the kitchen clock. 'I'm sorry, sir, but it's nearly time. I mustn't be late with the tea. I don't want Mrs Gray to know — p'raps I shouldn't have…'

Jones reassured her. 'Don't worry, Mrs Pook, we'll go now — out the back way. Thank you for answering our questions. We'll not trouble you again.'

9: The Invisible Worm

'Well, constable,' said Jones, 'a canny question of yours about the doctor.'

'I thought about what Mr Farleigh said — he didn't like Plume. I wondered if he'd treated her for this mysterious illness.'

'I wonder what the nature of his treatment was — was it some nervous disorder, what they call, hysteria? It would fit with what we know of her.'

'And her personal maid was sent away — the one she trusted.'

'Something to hide then. I'm a bit at sea here, Charles, but something tells me that our murdered Doctor Plume is linked to this suicide.'

'And, don't forget, Miranda Deverall, another young girl, is accused of his murder.'

'Quite — very suggestive. And we want to know the connection between Miranda and the doctor. Elizabeth went to Newgate today. I suggest we go to Norfolk Street now to see if she has anything to tell us.'

It was tea time in another warm kitchen, in a warm house where the sounds of happy children could be heard, and a dog barking. Dickens saw how Sam's face relaxed and how he smiled, hearing the noise of his family. Sam and Elizabeth had adopted eleven year-old Eleanor Brim and her brother, Tom, aged six, and Poll, their dog. Their father had died of consumption earlier in the year. Elizabeth and Sam loved those children as if they were their own. Edith, their only daughter, had died some years before, giving birth to her dead child, leaving a space in their lives that they had never thought could be filled, but it had been. Scrap was there, too — a street boy who had run errands for Mr Brim and who had assisted Dickens and Jones in their earlier cases. A boy who was part of this family now. *This was a mother*, thought Dickens as he watched Elizabeth bending over the little boy, Tom, to tie his napkin. Poor Lavinia Gray.

Jones and Dickens sat with them until Elizabeth had served the food, though she had waited patiently until Eleanor and Tom, and Poll, had got over the excitement of seeing Mr Dickens.

'Poor Jip,' Eleanor said. 'Poor, poor Jip — our special dog.' When he had first met these children in their father's stationery shop, he had promised to create a nice dog for them in his new book — *David Copperfield*. Passionate dog lovers, they had not cared for Bull's Eye, Sikes's dog, though Dickens had explained that poor Bull's Eye, ferocious as he was, had been made that way by the criminal Sikes. Still, he had promised them Jip, Dora's dog. Now, he had to face the fact that he had killed him. He was, he thought, in his own way, a murderer. Oh, the unforeseen consequences of Jip's death, which he had thought so aptly pathetic. Jip dies, almost at the same moment as his mistress. He'd killed Dora, too. What to say?

Scrap, ever watchful of Eleanor Brim, spoke up. 'Jip ain't real, not like Poll's real, Miss Nell. It's only a story.'

Oh, thought Dickens seeing his life's work dismissed in that little word "only", but the literary critic continued.

'An' stories 'as ter 'ave sad an' 'appy bits, yer know. Makes 'em seem real — ain't that right, Mr Dickens?'

Sad and happy bits, forsooth — just what he thought himself. 'Streaky bacon,' he said. It was his theory — the alternation of tragic and comic scenes were the layers in streaky, well-cured bacon.

''Xactly,' said Scrap, approvingly.

'No bacon,' said Tom. 'Eggs and no bacon today.'

They laughed, seeing Tom looking puzzled at his plate.

'And Jip was very old, Eleanor, and he would have missed Dora,' Elizabeth observed. 'Now, Poll, here, is too young for such ideas. She looks a bit worried — she might like a biscuit.'

Eleanor smiled and gave Poll her treat, but Dickens saw that there was a gravity about her eyes. Elizabeth glanced at him. She had seen it, too, and knew that the same look was still there sometimes when Eleanor thought of her father. Not your fault, her eyes said to Dickens. But he felt guilty all the same.

They went into the parlour, leaving the children in the care of Posy, the servant girl whom Dickens had sent to them, having found her on the streets offering a pitifully shabby bunch of artificial flowers for sale. She had been apprenticed to a flower maker whose business had failed, leaving Posy on the street.

'I'm sorry about Jip,' said Dickens as they sat down.

'We cannot protect her from everything, Charles. She is bound to think of her father — it's still a vivid memory. Most of the time, she is happy — and carefree, but she'll always be a serious little girl. Tom fares better — he is so young, but Eleanor has her own thoughts.'

'What secrecy there is in the young — the secret agony of the soul.' Dickens looked at the fire. They wondered what he was thinking — what had been the secret agony of the soul of the boy, Charles Dickens? How much of the suffering of the child David Copperfield had been his? Elizabeth had wondered about this to Sam — the boy, David's suffering at his work in the bottle factory had seemed so real.

'But, she has you two now — she can tell her secrets to you, Elizabeth.'

'Unlike Lavinia Gray,' Jones said, glad to change the subject. Eleanor's too young gravity pained him, more than he liked to say. He loved the little girl, as much, he thought, as he had loved Edith. He wanted her to be happy.

'Lavinia Gray?' asked Elizabeth.

'The girl who drowned before her wedding. Suicide, we believe. And that reminds me, I wonder if this means anything to you?' Jones took out the piece of paper and handed it to her. 'We wondered what it might mean, if anything.'

Elizabeth read the words. 'William Blake — *The Sick Rose*. I have a copy of his poems.'

'Crimson joy,' said Dickens. 'I remember that bit — that's why I thought of Tennyson's crimson petal.'

Elizabeth found the book. 'Shall I read it?'

'Do.'

She read aloud:

'O rose thou art sick.
The invisible worm,
That flies in the night
In the howling storm:
Has found out thy bed
Of crimson joy:
And his dark secret love
Does thy life destroy.'

She handed the book to Jones. Dickens looked over Jones's shoulder, and they read it again. 'The last two lines,' said Jones, 'do they mean what I think they mean?' He looked at Dickens.

'A lover — who destroyed her life — that would account for her state of mind. Not Richard Farfield. A secret. That's why she was afraid of marrying him. I wonder if Mrs Gray knew.'

'Or Doctor Plume — that mysterious illness Mrs Pook talked of — a pregnancy?'

'What?' Elizabeth sounded startled. 'Plume was her doctor?'

'Why? What are you thinking?' Jones looked at her.

'About Miranda Deverall — I saw her today, and she told me about him —'

'She told you — you got her to speak about him. How?' Dickens looked at her with admiration.

'Well, you had prepared the way, Charles. I told her you had sent me, but, at first, she wouldn't speak — I think she is so depressed that she wants only to be released from the world. I don't think she cares about anything. I called her Miranda and she wept. I held her then. She has not been held in a mother's arms since she was five years old. No one has held her to comfort her, to wipe away her tears, to murmur that sorrow will pass, that tomorrow will be better. No one has kissed that child's eyes as she was falling asleep —'

No, thought Dickens, *no one has done for Miranda what you have done for Eleanor Brim.*

'And when I first touched her, she flinched. She was rigid —'

Dickens glanced at Jones. *Lavinia Gray*, they both thought.

Elizabeth continued, 'And I knew then that something had been done to her, something so dreadful that the touch of another human being, however gentle, appalled her.'

'You found out?' Jones asked.

'I did and it connects to what you have just said.'

'Miranda Deverall and Lavinia Gray are connected — the link is the doctor?'

'I would say so — shall I tell you what I found out before you tell me about Lavinia Gray?'

'Yes.'

Elizabeth told them how Miranda Deverall had found her way to the milliner's house. Mrs Amelia Hodson was not unkind, merely indifferent. There was not much hat making — just Miranda and two other girls. Neither of them stayed long. There was one called Kitty, who was kind to Miranda but she left suddenly — and Mrs Hodson gave no explanation.

But the doctor came, and Mrs Hodson explained to Miranda that he was a kind man who treated poor girls, mostly the Irish girls who live in and about the cramped streets in the shadow of the workhouse. He couldn't treat them at his surgery, so Mrs Hodson allowed him to use her house — she was sorry for the girls, too. But, Miranda had seen that they were not always poor girls. Some came in carriages, always heavily veiled, often accompanied by an older woman. Sometimes they stayed overnight; sometimes they left after an hour or so, and Miranda had seen how they had been helped to the carriage. Sometimes another woman came — a nurse, she thought. She came at night when, perhaps, one of the doctor's patients was ill. Miranda had heard the screams and cries — she had been frightened then, hearing feet on the stairs below and the door slamming. And the doctor would come the next day. And then the undertaker would come. Mrs Hodson would tell her how the doctor, for all his skill, could not always save his patient — it was a great pity, but there it was.

Sometimes, in the night, she might hear a baby crying, Miranda thought. But there were no babies in the house. Once, however, she had seen a lady leave the house, carrying a bundle, holding it as a woman might hold a baby.

'And Miranda didn't ask Mrs Hodson about what was going on?'

'No. I don't think she spoke very much at all — silence is her habit. She was simply passive. She had been torn from her home, planted in this foreign soil, and there was nothing to enable her to grow. She was simply neglected. Then she was ill. She suffered from dreadful headaches — not surprisingly. She was depressed and terribly lonely. Mrs Hodson thought she looked thin and asked the doctor to see her. Doctor Plume, his name was. She remembered that. He was kind and said she should eat more. He advised Mrs Hodson about what she should have. The headaches ceased, but Mrs Hodson was still concerned about her. Miranda was told that the doctor needed to examine her —' Elizabeth stopped. 'You can guess the rest, I think.'

'He seduced her, using the pretext of the medical examination.' Jones sounded angry. He thought of Eleanor Brim, orphaned by her father's death. What might have been if she had ended in an orphanage, or on the streets? He knew only too well.

'He did — again and again. If you had heard that poor girl — it was horrible — and she hardly had the words to tell me. She was so innocent and so young, and he hurt her. I could hardly bear to listen.' Elizabeth wiped her eyes. 'There is worse — he told her she must have an operation. He must have known she was pregnant — Miranda did not. She understood nothing of what had happened to her. But there was pain and blood. I guessed what it must be. And he started again. He drugged her, I think, though she could not tell me precisely — only that the medicine made her drowsy —'

'Chloroform, perhaps? It's new, but he'd know about it in his fashionable practice. Know how much to use, to sedate her rather than —'

'Rather than render her unconscious,' put in Jones. 'Laudanum, brandy, even — there was a case a few years ago in which the defendant was convicted because he had got his victim drunk. Good God, he's supposed to be a doctor. To use his position like that on an innocent girl. Mrs Hodson must have known — she's almost worse. Supposed to have been her guardian. I need to see her.'

'I know, Sam,' said Elizabeth, 'to think of a woman so callous. You can understand why Miranda ran away.'

'And the murder? Did she speak of that?' Dickens asked.

'She had nothing when she ran away. She lived on the streets — an Irish girl took her in, Kitty Quillian, who had worked at the milliner's and who had been kind to her. I asked Miranda where she lived. I thought you might need to know, Sam. It was in an alley, off Paddington Street — Dab Lane. It was Kitty Quillian who told her to go to Doctor Plume's house and ask for money — Miranda thought she would go back to Ireland. She thought that she could go back to Pallasmore — the village where she was born. That was it — just home. She'd no more idea than that. I think Kitty, Irish herself, had the idea the doctor might give her the money to get rid of her. I think Kitty Quillian probably knew all about the goings on at David Street where Mrs Hodson lives. Miranda went. Doctor Plume gave her the five pounds. Miranda left through the garden — that's all. I couldn't press her any more. She was exhausted. I could only promise that I would help, and that Mr Dickens, the gentleman who had sent me, would help, too. She wasn't alone now.'

'You don't think she knows anything about the murder? Goss said she had blood on her hands,' Jones pressed.

Elizabeth looked grave. 'I don't know, Sam. As for the blood, I think we can guess where that came from — when you think what had been happening to her before she ran away.' Her eyes filled again. 'It might have been a miscarriage

— and she wouldn't understand anything about it. Oh God, the poor child — it is vile what is done to young girls.'

There was nothing they could say. Jones thought that he and Dickens could be outraged at what was done, but, perhaps, only a woman could fully imagine the horror of it. Still, for better or worse, as men they could act, and act they would.

Elizabeth continued, 'I didn't think it right to ask about the actual murder. I was there as someone who would help. I'll try again, but I don't want to seem as if I suspect her — she has to trust me.'

'Yes, I see that. What about Kitty Quillian? Did she go with her to the doctor's house?' Jones asked.

'I assume so because someone must have seen her, recognised her, because the police found Miranda at Dab Lane.'

'Was Kitty there when the police came?'

'No, she'd gone out.'

'She'll have kept her head down, I'll bet. Moved to different lodgings. She won't want to talk to the police. Still, it'll be worthwhile looking for her.'

'Tell me about Lavinia Gray,' Elizabeth said.

Jones told her what they had found out from Richard Farleigh and Mrs Pook. Given the suggestiveness of the poem, it seemed possible that Lavinia Gray had suffered similarly at the hands of Doctor Lancelot Plume.

'Will you be able to take the case now?' Dickens looked at Jones hopefully.

'Well, I'll have to see the Assistant Commissioner — I'll tell him that I want to investigate Plume's death on the grounds that I have information connecting him to Lavinia Gray whose body was found in my division, and that there are links between Lavinia Gray and Miranda Deverall. I'll stress the complexity of it — say it makes no sense to keep the cases separate but — and this is an important but — I'll tell him I'm satisfied that Lavinia Gray committed suicide. I don't want to drag her name into the murder case. What I want to do is to show the Assistant Commissioner that I think there is doubt about Miranda and that I wish to explore other possibilities.'

'But surely we should find out more about Lavinia's death for the light it throws on Miranda's case.'

'I agree, but it must be done unofficially, which is why I think you and Elizabeth should go to Chalk Farm to see Susan Carter. Remember, we have no evidence to support our ideas about Lavinia Gray — only the fragment of a poem. And to suggest anything at the inquest about Lavinia Gray's relationship with the doctor would only damage her reputation —'

Elizabeth interrupted. 'I agree. She would be accused of hysteria — the morbid imaginings of a diseased mind, and that would be proved by her suicide. But, oh, Sam, a verdict of suicide —'

'I know,' said Dickens, 'I thought about that when we passed Mr Gray's house. I thought about her burial. Could it not be accidental death?'

'I doubt it.' Jones looked at their stricken faces. 'The evidence of the doctor at the mortuary, Mrs Pook and Millie, Richard Farleigh's evidence and the fact that she left the house alone on the eve of her wedding, all point to suicide. I don't think we can alter that. But, I should think there will be a verdict of temporary insanity — not much consolation for her family.'

'I imagine that Mrs Gray will be well satisfied,' said Dickens bitterly.

'Plume caused her death — he was a monster. It is so unjust — his will be a proper funeral, and hers, some midnight affair, as if she were the criminal.'

'I know, Elizabeth, but there is nothing we can do. We can only try to help Miranda, and that's not easy, either. For, despite our belief in her innocence, think about how what you have found out could be evidence against her — she had a motive to kill him.'

They were silent then, thinking about Jones's words. *It was true*, thought Dickens, *it would be easy for her story to be used against her.*

'Then we need to find the murderer of Lancelot Plume.'

'And we can only do that by examining his life, and by looking again at the night of the murder — and there I hope Rogers will be able to tell us something. I've not had an opportunity to ask him about his meeting with Sergeant Billie Watts.'

'I can ask about if you like — see if any of the doctors of my acquaintance can tell me about his reputation.'

'Good idea.' And that was all they could do for now. At least, thought Dickens, making his way home, there might be a chance to save Miranda — if the real murderer could be found. And, given what they knew about the doctor's relationships with Miranda and Lavinia Gray, there must be others who might have a reason to kill him — the father, brother, husband, fiancé of a girl, perhaps, who had suffered and died because of Lancelot Plume?

10: Superintendent Jones Takes the Case

'No weapon?' Jones was asking Rogers about his talk with Billie Watts.

'No. They looked about the garden, in the back alley, in the room where they found Miranda Deverall, but there was nothing. Goss thought she would have chucked it away, and, he reasoned, someone could've picked it up — bit far-fetched, I thought.'

'Did the doctor who did the post-mortem on Plume say anything about the weapon — what kind of knife?'

'Single-bladed. Not very big — quite a narrow blade. Could be anythin', sir.'

'No knives missing from the house or from the surgery?'

'Nothing from the house — kitchen, dining room, but the servants couldn't say about the surgery. The doctor was found outside the French windows of his office. Billie said there was no way of knowin' if he and the girl had been in the surgery — that's a room off the office where Plume examined his patients. Nothin' disturbed there, apparently. Anyway, Goss was convinced the girl had done it. Miranda Deverall came in with the doctor — the maid saw her, so she was there.'

'What time was that?'

''Bout six, the maid said.'

'Did Doctor Plume say anything about the girl?'

'Just that she was someone who needed help — sent the maid away and took the girl into his office — said not to disturb him, and she didn't — until the maid wondered if the girl had gone — about an hour after, so she knocked. No answer. She went back ter the kitchen and told the cook. They waited another half hour and sent the knife boy ter knock. No answer.'

'No one else in the house?'

'No, that's the thing — Mrs Plume was away vistin' relatives in the country.'

'Go on.'

'Well, they all went and listened at the door — couldn't hear a thing. Tried the door — it was locked — key in the keyhole — they tried to look through it, but couldn't see. So, they troops round the back. The garden door's open, and they finds the doctor dead on the terrace. French windows to his office open, and that's it. They sends the boy for a constable, who fetches Billie and Goss.'

'How did they light upon Miranda Deverall?'

'The maid, who's an Irish girl, saw another girl on the other side of the road — an Irish girl, she knew —'

'Kitty Quillian.'

'How d'you know that?'

'Trick o' the trade.' Jones tapped his nose. He couldn't help teasing Rogers who was gazing at him as if he had performed a conjuring trick.

'Get away with you, sir. Someone told you.'

'They did, it's true, but tell me all.'

'The maid told them where Kitty lodged. They found Miranda Deverall there — took her back ter the doctor's. The maid recognised her, told the story, and that was it.'

'What was said about the blood on her hands?' Jones remembered what Elizabeth had surmised about the blood. He was interested to know what Goss thought.

'Now, that's a facer — she did have blood on her hands, and she wouldn't tell them about it — in fact, she's never said anythin' at all. So, naturally, Goss takes it as evidence she stabbed him.'

'And what did our friend, Billie Watts, think about it all?'

'Well, the evidence is there — but, o' course, they don't know what the motive could be.' *I do*, thought Jones, but he didn't say so. He wanted to hear the thoughts of Billie Watts, a man who did not jump to conclusions. 'She had five pounds on her and Goss assumed she'd took it, but there's things that don't add up.'

'Such as?'

'The doctor was found outside the French windows. He was stabbed in the back. Now, Billie thought, how come the girl was sort of inside the room behind him? Which she musta been if she did it. What was the doctor doin' outside? Why would he leave the girl inside? An' he'd been smokin' a cigar — it looked, Billie said, like a man who'd just gone out ter smoke an' get some air, p'raps. It just didn't seem ter fit. What d'you think, sir?'

'I think Billie Watts is right.'

'Yet, there's the blood, sir, what about that? Can we —'

'We can, Rogers, we can do what we want. It's our case now.'

''Ow's that?'

Jones told him all that he had he and Dickens had discovered at the Gray house, and what Elizabeth had found out at Newgate, and about his visit to the Assistant Commissioner — and Superintendent Goss.

'You went ter see Goss?'

'I did — professional courtesy, Alf. Always better to do things openly — if you can, of course — no sense in my antagonising him or his men by going over his head.' Rogers thought about that — and tucked the advice away in his mind. His Superintendent was a wise man, and you could learn a lot about how to go about things. And Rogers was a willing pupil.' Jones went on. 'And Goss was quite willing to give up the case — easier that than to admit he was wrong. In any case, he said he had enough to do with the Thomas King murder.'

'The one who killed his father and attacked the housekeeper?'

'Yes, and he fled with a lot of valuable stuff so Goss needs to find him.'

'Gave him a good excuse then?'

Jones's eyes smiled. 'You might say that — I didn't, of course. However, it leaves us a lot to do — Mrs Jones has visited Miranda Deverall, but don't mention that to anyone. She thinks the blood is — well, natural causes, but I'll get her to try to find out more, and from the wardswoman at Newgate if Miranda Deverall can't or won't tell her. Mrs Jones and Mr Dickens are going to Chalk Farm this afternoon to interview Miss Gray's personal maid who left just after Miss Gray's mysterious illness.'

'You think she might have been expectin'?'

'I do — no proof, mind, unless the maid knows. I'm not interested in using this evidence at the inquest on Miss Gray — it would only harm her reputation. Suicide because her sin weighed so heavily on her. It would be her sin, of course.' Rogers nodded — he knew very well that the blame would be Miss Gray's and not a fine, upstanding doctor's. Jones went on, 'Mrs Jones thought, from what Miranda Deverall told her, that she had been pregnant, too, and that Plume had operated on her.'

Rogers's face flushed deeper red. 'Wicked it is, an' 'e a doctor. Makes yer lose any faith, sir. An' I've just thought. Evie Finch, sir. I wonder.'

'She didn't see a doctor —'

'No, sir, but Mollie said she kept sayin' "no doctor". Mollie thought Evie didn't want a doctor, but p'raps there should have been one. I went ter the Simpson house ter find out about Evie — one o' the maids said she was thick with Jemmy Pike, the coachman, but he'd gone home to his wife in the country — Mr Simpson got him a place at his brother's. Evie left soon after — said she was needed at 'ome, but the maid wondered.'

'So do I — I think you ought to get down to this country place and find out what Jemmy Pike can tell you about Evie Finch. We need to know if he found her a doctor and who the doctor was.'

'Mollie mentioned a Mother Hubbard — Evie kept talkin' about her — she thought it was the nursery rhyme, but Mrs Feak looked a bit thoughtful. We should ask her — she'll know who's performin' them sort o' operations.'

'Quite — we will. But, I was going to say earlier that, knowing the kind of doctor Plume was, it wouldn't surprise me if someone wanted him dead. And that someone, perhaps, was the person who walked behind the doctor onto the terrace where they were going to smoke a cigar together.'

'Unless it was a woman.'

'True, very true, Alf — but someone he knew, and a woman who didn't mind the cigar — a woman who knew him well.'

'A mistress?'

'Why not? And I'm beginning to think about a Mrs Amelia Hodson, the so-called milliner with whom Miranda Deverall lived, and who was, as you might say, very thick with him. I will go there today.'

'Right, I'll get off to the Simpson house again to get the address of Jemmy Pike.'

Rogers went out as Dickens came in, having returned from Chalk Farm. His eager eyes told Jones that something had been found out. 'You found her?'

'We found Mrs Susan Bliss, once Susan Carter.'

'Wedded bliss?'

Dickens laughed. 'Indeed so — bliss was it in that dawn. A happy young woman, but a serious one when she told us about Lavinia Gray — and her monstrous mother.'

'And Doctor Lancelot Plume?'

'Yes. Susan Bliss did not know that Lavinia Gray was dead. We told her about Lavinia's engagement to Richard Farleigh, said we were friends of his, and that he wished to know if she could shed any light on Lavinia's suicide. She told us about the death of the brother and about Mrs Gray, pretty much what Mrs Pook said. Then Elizabeth asked about Lavinia's illness and the doctor. Mrs Bliss looked most uncomfortable, but Elizabeth was gentle in her insistence. Susan Bliss knew that Lavinia Gray was afraid of Plume. Mrs Gray insisted that he treat her — Susan thought her cruel; she knew Lavinia hated his visits. It was a way of punishing Lavinia — Susan thought that Mrs Gray loathed her daughter because her son had died.'

'Did Susan say why Lavinia had to endure these visits?'

'Only that she wouldn't eat, had headaches —'

'Like Miranda Deverall.'

'Exactly. Susan said that Lavinia was depressed — Susan thought it was sheer loneliness — same as Miranda, I thought. Mrs Gray told Lavinia that if she wouldn't eat then she must be treated. Lavinia begged her mother to allow Susan to stay with her, but Mrs Gray refused — it wasn't appropriate that a servant should be present, and Plume said that his treatment must be private between doctor and patient.'

'I'll bet he did — did she say anything about the illness that precipitated Susan's leaving?'

'Lavinia got worse — not better. And more silent, Susan thought. She wondered what Plume was doing to the girl.'

'Any suspicions?'

'No — or, she didn't say, but she wondered about the bouts of sickness. She thought that if Lavinia ate anything, she was perhaps making herself sick afterwards. She had to eat sometimes because Plume and Mrs Gray made her. Then Plume apparently told the mother that he would need to examine Lavinia and it might be necessary to perform an operation. This was done — Susan knew nothing about it except that she was ordered to burn the bloodied sheets. And this is a significant point —'

'They wanted it all kept secret?'

'They did, of course, and I'll bet Susan had her suspicions, but, what's important is that Susan didn't burn the sheets because the washerwoman took them away — Susan thought it a waste when the poor old washerwoman could have used them. The washerwoman's name is Jenny Ince.'

'She'd know something then? Where do we find her?'

'Newgate Prison.'

'Very convenient. Rogers can —'

'I've met her.' Dickens couldn't help smiling at Jones's surprised face.

'Already — time traveller are you?'

'She was the wardswoman who brought in Miranda Deverall when I went to see her.'

'Well, constable, you'd best get back there and find out what she knows about the Gray family. Anything else from Chalk Farm?'

'Just as Mrs Pook said. A nurse was engaged by Plume, and Susan was told she wouldn't be needed any more. She didn't see Lavinia again.'

'And then Lavinia met Farleigh, and perhaps believed that she might escape, but when she thought of what marriage would mean, she couldn't go on with it. There was no way out for her but death.'

'Which is what Miranda Deverall believes — Elizabeth said that Miranda doesn't care what happens to her. What has this man done, Sam, what has he done?'

'Well, we can't prove that Lavinia Gray was pregnant back then. I doubt Jenny Ince would know, but it's worth going back to see her — just in case. However, it's time we looked into Plume's life. We need to find out about other patients — is there someone who killed him in revenge for what had been done to a daughter, a sister, a wife, even?'

'The case is yours now?'

Jones told him of his visit to Superintendent Goss and his conversation with Rogers about the anomalies in the case as described by Sergeant Billie Watts.

'You think someone else was there, someone he knew.'

'I do and my thinking leads me to Mrs Amelia Hodson — was she his mistress as well as the provider of young women for his so called benevolent ministrations? And, had she a reason to kill him? We can do nothing for Lavinia Gray now — the evidence at the inquest will simply focus on her depression and nervous temperament. Suicide, whilst the balance of her mind, etcetera. What we know we will keep to ourselves. It is more important that we should try to save Miranda Deverall. And to that end, I am going now to Mrs Hodson's. Will you come?'

'Barkis is, as ever, willin'.'

11: In Bones Alley

Dickens and Jones took a cab to David Street, a short thoroughfare just across the road from the Marylebone Workhouse — not so far from Devonshire Place where Dickens lived just by the York Gate, which led into Regent's Park and its wide, green spaces. David Street lay in the shadow of the workhouse walls, looming as dark as Newgate itself. Nevertheless, the street was respectable enough with its terrace of eighteenth century houses, the kind of street and houses that Dickens had lived in as a boy — many houses. John Dickens, his father, had been a spendthrift — was still — and his debts had led them all to the Marshalsea Prison. There had been a dingy terrace in Bayham Street, a shabby genteel house in Somerstown, lodgings in Margaret Street, Norfolk Street, George Street — John Dickens like some shabby Pied Piper leading his creditors a dance all over town. If only he would heed Micawber's advice: *Annual income twenty pounds, annual expenditure nineteen and six, result happiness. Annual income twenty pounds, annual expenditure twenty pounds ought and six, result misery.* John Dickens spent twenty pounds and the sixpence — and the rest. But his son paid his debts. Dickens remembered the houses as all the same: narrow hallways, cramped rooms, airless attics, careless housekeeping — and all mean somehow.

Not that number 13 David Street looked mean. It looked respectable, neat, the home of a quiet, respectable woman, earning a respectable living — not that the respectable woman was at home. That was obvious. The blinds were down. Windows like eyes over which the lids were closed, and quiet, too quiet. Jones went up the three clean steps and knocked.

There was no answer, just the sense of an echo in an empty hall where the silence was stirred, and dust motes shivered in the stale air. Amelia Hodson had gone.

'I wonder,' said Jones. 'Is she our murderer? How convenient for her that her cousin's stepdaughter should be the one accused — even if she had to give evidence, her story would be of a difficult young woman whom she had charitably taken in, who was depressed and silent, given to hysterics at times. A jury might well believe it. But, to be on the safe side, she's gone — but where?'

As if in answer to the question, a woman came out of the next door house. 'Mrs Hodson's away,' she said. 'Gone to Manchester to stay with a cousin who's ill. Said she didn't know when she'd be back. No one's there now.'

Jones went down the steps. 'She didn't leave an address or name?'

The woman looked at him curiously, wondering who he was. 'No, but there was a girl, a servant, May Brady — Irish kid. Nice little thing — simple, though. Lives down by the burial ground — Bones Alley, just off East Street before you get to The Neptune Public House. She might know.'

'Thank you,' Jones said and the woman walked away, her brisk footsteps pattering on the stone pavement.

'The aptly named Bones Alley then?' Dickens asked.

'Yes. I'd like to know what May Brady can tell us about Mrs Hodson, and about Miranda Deverall.'

They walked down East Street and found the narrow alley which led into the old burying ground which had been used for the workhouse poor. The sort of place which was the resort of typhus, dark, stinking with horrible odours and bad water. Dickens had read the report on the state of the city's graveyards sent to him by his brother-in-law, Henry Austin.

He'd dreamt of putrefaction then, and here it was again — an overcharged mass of corruption, the ground greasy with the putrid discharge of bodies whose coffins had decomposed, skeletons dug up, bones left to rot, the dead rising from their graves, diseased ghosts in the foetid air. Someone had observed in the report that one wouldn't bury a favourite dog in these places — apparently a favourite cat named Ralph had been buried in the more genteel south graveyard on the other side of Paddington Street, but it had been dug up. According to the report, there were dead dogs, rats, offal and refuse of all kinds in such graveyards. And people lived in this sewer where two grim nurses, Poverty and Sickness, presided over birth and death, death which would bring them to burial grounds such as this.

'Vile!' he said to Jones. 'Poor May Brady — she'd be better off in the workhouse.'

'Well, let's ask if anyone knows of them.' Jones didn't respond to Dickens's exclamation — his face reflected what he thought.

These were not the neat houses of David Street — these were ancient places, probably old stables or mews once attached to better houses, long gone. There would be old cellars, home to too many families. Mostly Irish — refugees from the famine of the 1840s. There was a large Irish population. That was why Amelia Hodson had come to the area, perhaps. A couple of boys sat on a broken bit of wall, throwing stones across the street.

'Know the Bradys?' asked Jones.

One of the boys looked up, a wild-haired savage, thought Dickens, observing the beetle brows and jutting chin, the bare feet, ragged trousers, the whole wretched appearance which denoted hunger, bad air and ignorance. Not that this boy looked hungry — he looked tough and aggressive. Dickens saw how his hands curled into fists. There was something hardened about him. The other boy looked hungry, thin as a rail and crooked with malnutrition.

'Jimmy Brady — wot yer want?' Black eyes, hard as bullets, took in Jones's authority and his height.

'We want to see your sister, May. Is she here?'

'Down there.' The dirty hand pointed to a ladder which led to a cellar.

I don't want to see this, Dickens thought. He could imagine it. He'd seen it — families crouched like subterranean troglodytes in the cellars of Seven Dials. He had written of the bare and miserable room, the pale and emaciated children, the room, once, where a naked child lay dead, the family too poor to bury it. He looked at Jones and saw the same feelings in his face. In any case, they could hardly climb down a ladder.

Jones took a penny out of his pocket. 'Get May, will you?'

The boy snatched it and vanished down the hole, negotiating the ladder like a monkey. His friend looked at Jones. Red hair this time, a wizened, old man's face, but an expression of such longing in the pale, lashless eyes that showed the child he really was. Jones took another penny from his pocket. The boy grabbed it. The child, they saw, now had a pair of makeshift crutches. *Tiny Tim*, thought Dickens. Or not. No Bob Cratchit to love him. The boy manoeuvred himself onto his sticks and scuttled away, crab-wise, two thin legs dangling uselessly, and disappeared down a little passageway.

They waited without speaking. Dickens had said what he thought to the inaugural meeting of the Metropolitan Sanitary Association. Pity some of those who denied the problems were not standing in the filth of this dank passage. Then they would see.

A face appeared from a hidden doorway. It seemed to hover uncertainly, looking like some animal emerging from its underground hole. Then the rest of May Brady came up with a crawling motion, little mole-like hands levering her up the steps.

She was tiny and misshapen, one shoulder higher than the other, and she stared with uncomprehending eyes at the two men. An unfinished sketch of a girl with a tiny snubbed nose and a little pair of twisted, colourless lips. All the vitality given to the black-eyed boy.

'May?' asked Jones gently. She might dart away, he thought, back down the hole.

She nodded.

'Can you tell us where Mrs Hodson has gone?'

'Away. Gone away.'

'To Manchester?'

'Manchester. Gone to cousin.'

'Do you know the cousin's name?'

'Cousin Lizzie Josser in Chorlton. Mrs said.'

'Mrs Hodson?'

'Mrs Raspin — the nurse.'

'Where does she live?'

'Dunno — somewhere.'

'Do you know Kitty Quillian?'

The little face looked sad. 'Friend. Kitty gone. All gone.'

And that was it. She could tell them nothing more, Jones realised. He gave her sixpence. She looked at the silver coin and back at Jones.

'Mine?'

'Yes, for you.'

They walked away quickly. As they turned the corner, Dickens glanced back and saw her still standing, watching them. A vision from another world, its meaning never guessed at. *May*, he thought, *May, fragile as the blossom which came and went in the month of that name.* Not that this May would bloom. She wouldn't make old bones.

12: Portrait of a Doctor

Bones Alley was left behind. They walked swiftly away down Paddington Street into Weymouth Street. Jones knew where he was going, evidently. When they stopped opposite Dr Plume's house, he spoke at last.

'Chorlton. An idea occurs to me — Inspector Hardacre.'

Dickens nodded. Hardacre was the Manchester policeman whom they had met when investigating the murder of a man named Clement Bell. Hardacre, a dogged, straightforward Manchester man. 'He might find Lizzie Josser and Mrs Hodson?'

'I can ask — needle in a haystack, I know, but Josser's an unusual enough name.'

'If May got it right.'

'True, but it's worth a try. Our witnesses seem to be vanishing — Kitty Quillian gone, Mrs Hodson gone, Mrs Raspin, the nurse, God knows where.'

'Raspin's not a common name — you might find her. In the meantime, are we standing opposite Plume's house for a reason?'

'We are. I thought I might ask a few questions and look at the scene of the crime. Perhaps the widow is here — I'd like to see what kind of wife he had.'

Mrs Plume, they were informed, was not available. Too poorly, the maid said. Jones explained who he was and that he would like to see the doctor's office. Something in his firm tone told the maid that she must let him in. He noted her Irish accent — he would question her later.

There were two rooms. One was well-furnished and very much what one might expect of a doctor's consulting room: a handsome desk with a leather chair and another straight-backed chair for the patient, a sofa, bookshelves with reassuringly serious-looking volumes of medical works, a table with decanters and glasses — handy for the patient with a tendency to faint or for the patient who had just received bad news. And a chest of drawers, the kind of chest in which a man might keep his papers. And a portrait over the mantelpiece, showing a broad-shouldered, handsome man with fair curling hair and blue eyes. Thick lips — *sensual*, Dickens thought, curved in a slight smile, but the face was bland somehow. A mask — that was it. The artist got the surface. It was competent — just the sort of portrait which would please the sitter. Because it revealed no secrets. The subject of the portrait was seated in the leather chair. At his side was the top of a table on which a thick white hand rested on a leather book. A stethoscope lay coiled on the table. The portrait of Lancelot Plume — prosperous, apparently benevolent, the trusted doctor. *An irony*, Dickens thought — he had been sitting for his own portrait and had called it off because the artist had made him look like the murderer, Greenacre, James Greenacre, the Edgware Road murderer who had cut off the head of his fiancée. A grocer, forsooth. And here was Plume, looking like everyone's idea of a doctor.

They opened the French window and looked out to where the doctor's body had lain. Dickens imagined the man standing, smoking while someone stood behind him with the knife. He looked again at the man in the picture.

'She couldn't have done it,' he said.

'What are you thinking?'

'You've not seen her. She's small and as thin as Lavinia Gray. Just a child. Look at his broad shoulders. He was a big man — and the maid told Goss that Plume took her straight into his office — now, was he wearing a coat? If so, then she wouldn't have had the strength — she couldn't possibly have stabbed him through it.'

'He might have taken it off,' Jones pointed out.

'No — he brings her in, hears what she has to say, gives her the five pounds and lets her out the back way. The murderer, whom he knows, comes in. Then he takes off his coat. He's comfortable with this visitor. They talk. Plume offers cigars — he goes to the open door. The visitor follows and does the deed.'

Jones looked at the portrait. 'Hm, plausible.' He looked back at Dickens. 'All right — very plausible.'

Dickens grinned at him.

'I need to ask the servants if he took off his coat before he went in to his office, and if not, what happened to the coat. We might as well question them now.'

They went to find the servants, the maid who had seen Miranda Deverall and had identified Kitty Quillian, the cook and the knife boy who had found the body of the doctor. None of them had anything new to add. No one else had come to the door that evening after Miranda Deverall.

Jones asked, 'Did Doctor Plume take off his coat when he came in with Miranda Deverall?'

The maid thought about it. 'No, sir, 'e just went in with the girl.'

'And when you found him, was he wearing his coat?'

'No, sir.'

'What happened to it?'

'After the — er — doctor was took away and perlice went, Mrs Plume come next day — I went in with her an' she told me to put the coat away.'

'Would you bring it to me, please?'

The maid looked puzzled, but she went upstairs and came down with a heavy greatcoat.

'This is the one he wore on that night?'

'Yes, sir.'

Jones carried the coat back into Plume's office, away from the maid's curious eyes. He examined it. There was no blood or any tear where a knife might have gone in.

'Circumstantial evidence. Miranda Deverall must say whether he kept his coat on while she was there. It's only her word, but a jury might believe her if she comes to trial.'

Dickens regarded the coat. A thought struck him. 'He was a big man — I honestly doubt that Miranda Deverall would have had the strength. Where was the wound on his back?'

'I see what you're getting at — was she tall enough to stab him? Billie Watts told Rogers that the knife had pierced the heart. That would have required strength and height on the part of the murderer — unless Plume was bending over to get his cigar.'

'Which is highly unlikely — he kept his coat on because he wanted her out of his way. Why would he light a cigar? A man who does that is at ease with his visitor.'

'And, I doubt if she would have taken the knife with her. No, you're right, Charles. She didn't do it. The evidence is against it, but I would like to produce the real murderer — then she won't have to come to trial at all.'

'Much better for her, so…'

'Let's see what we can find.'

In the second room, there was a couch covered in a white sheet, a sink where the doctor might wash his hands and an apothecary's chest with many drawers with brass plates containing cards. They looked at that, opening the various drawers in which were glass bottles of different coloured liquids and powders. Laudanum, opium pills, tincture of morphine, some with patent labels: Dover's Powder, Sydenham's Laudanum, but others with handwritten labels: tincture of opium, paregoric, savin and chloroform.

'Savin powder,' said Jones, 'used to bring on a miscarriage — it can kill.'

'Dear Heaven — it ties in with what we know of Miranda. He was taking tremendous risks. He could have killed her.'

'And got away with it — with Mrs Hodson's help. He'd have signed the death certificate.' Jones looked at some of the other bottles. 'Know anything about homeopathy?'

'Many say it's quackery. I have faith in hydropathy myself — drink cold water morning and night and pour it down my back besides — and look at me, Sam, a picture of wholesomeness.'

Jones laughed. 'I look and I marvel, but you've not tried homeopathy?'

'I'm not against it. I know Doctor Frederick Quin very well — he's the leading practitioner of homeopathy and I'd trust him, but Plume — the trouble is that he could take it up without any real skill just because it's fashionable, and it would attract the ladies of fashion.'

'And the chloroform is telling when you think of what Elizabeth told us. Just enough to render his victims sufficiently drowsy.'

'It is. Sickening to think how he might have used it. There's a paradox for you — it should be a benefit. Last year, when Henry was born, I insisted on chloroform for Catherine. The doctors were dead against it, of course, but I had my way and it worked. Catherine was up and eating mutton chops within hours. Yet, Plume, a doctor, uses it for his own sordid ends. Foul.'

On top of the chest were a mortar and pestle and the stethoscope from the picture, a device with an ebony cup, a flexible tube bound in silk attached to an ebony ball on top of which was an ivory plate.

'Very professional,' said Jones, 'and modern.'

'This is where the fashionable patients were treated — he must have been making some money. This is all very impressive, especially if you were a patient.'

They went back into the first room. Jones looked round and said, 'If he was up to no good here, what the hell was he doing in David Street, seducing servant girls? It doesn't make sense.'

'Power? Think of it Sam — all doctors have it. The patient is in their hands, and they have to submit. We all have to submit. He is our greatest master on earth. Why, even the tyrant crouches before him like a hound. And when a man with that power has no real benevolence, and is motivated always by self, then those who are helpless — and alone for some reason — become easy victims. Women, and girls, in his case. A double life, I'd say. Outwardly, the prosperous, fashionable doctor, but there was another, darker side.'

'Then we need to know more about him — there must be fashionable people who knew him. That chest of drawers will give us some names. Someone you might know.' He went over to the chest. It was locked. 'The keys. Let's have a look in the desk.'

The keys were there, and Jones found the right one which opened the drawers where the patient files lay. They looked through. And when Dickens breathed sharply, Jones knew they had found a name.

'Margaret Lawson.'

'What do you know of her?'

'I know that she is in an asylum.'

'So, it says here. Treatment for hysteria and depression — ah, stillbirth.'

'Yes, it was known that the child had been born dead, and that Mrs Lawson had not recovered. I know of her husband, Edward Lawson — he is a writer and journalist, a friend of Thackeray's —' Dickens paused. Jones wondered what he was thinking as his face looked downcast suddenly. 'They have that in common — Thackeray's wife is mad, too. It's a terrible thing — madness. No hope of a cure, in either case, and for the husband, well…'

There was nothing to be done. Two widowers with living wives. Thackeray's wife lived in seclusion at Epsom. It was said that Thackeray did not visit — Isabella Thackeray was entirely indifferent to her husband, but Thackeray at least had his two girls, Annie and Minnie, but Edward Lawson had no child.

'I wonder…' Dickens began.

'What was the nature of Plume's treatment?'

'Yes, though I can't think that he would risk treating a married patient in the way he treated Lavinia Gray. Lavinia Gray was friendless — she could not have told her mother, and there was no one else, it seems. In any case, a single young woman — how could she tell? In what words? But a married woman — she had a husband.'

'True — but Lawson might have blamed Plume — might have a grudge against him. Is there any way you could find out more?'

'You mean go to see him? I suppose I could ask him for another contribution to *Household Words*. We published a poem of his — a rather melancholy thing, I recall. *An Old Haunting*, it was called.'

'Suggestive title.'

'Yes, I'll have to look at it again. But, if I see him, I can only introduce the subject of Plume very carefully, and only, if the opportunity arises. In any case, it's all very slender, Sam.'

'I know, I know — I may be clutching at a straw. Let's have a look for other possibilities.'

'Such as?' Dickens sounded despondent.

'Any other female patients who have been treated for hysteria, depression, headaches —'

'That'll be a long list — I'll bet that's how he made his name.'

'I was thinking about narrowing the names down to those that have died, say in the last year — though, there may be others like Lavinia Gray, but we will never know.'

'Plume was a menace — I cannot feel sorry he's dead, and that a man like Lawson, say, might go to the gallows for doing a public service.' Dickens was angry when he thought of the women who might be dead or, like Margaret Lawson, in an asylum. 'If it were someone like Edward Lawson, I'd leave well alone.' Dickens walked to the French window and looked out at the place where Plume had died. No, he couldn't feel sorry, and he felt reluctant to go to Edward Lawson — a betrayal of trust.

'That's our dilemma — we bring a man to probable death, and we feel for him, and, as in all murders, we lay bare the details of innocent lives to a salacious public in the papers, yet—'

Dickens turned round. 'Miranda Deverall is in Newgate.'

'Exactly — and, in any case, I could not turn a blind eye, I've taken the case. But, I don't want you to do anything against your conscience — leave Edward Lawson to me.'

Dickens was silent for a moment. What — pick and choose the cases he wanted to investigate, then when his own delicate conscience was involved, abandon Jones because Jones couldn't afford a delicate conscience? Get involved in murder, he told himself, and take the consequences, or leave it alone.

'No, Sam — I shouldn't pick and choose. I should know as well as you that murder's a nasty, unclean business. And those who meddle in it cannot avoid some of the contamination. Why should I think that my hands ought to be cleaner than yours? As for Edward Lawson, I might be able to eliminate him. I might find out that he was out of town on the night of the murder. I might simply tell you that he could not have done it.'

'If you're sure?'

Dickens grinned. 'No, I'm not, but neither of us ever is — I saw your troubled face when we stood in that graveyard looking at the murderer of those boys last year. I tell you what, I'm at the *Punch* dinner tonight — there might be gossip. That lot always know what's going on. Thackeray might be there — not that I could speak to him about Lawson — or his wife. Too close to home, but I might hear something about Plume. I could ask Mark Lemon — he knows about thee and me. He'll understand what I'm getting at.'

'Good. Let's see what other names we can find.'

They worked in silence on the doctor's files, and found that two of Plume's female patients had died in the last year: Miss Emily Dixon and Mrs Sarah Wilkinson. Jones made a note of the addresses. The electoral register would tell them if a father or brother still lived there. Jones felt as Dickens did — horrible to have to pry and peer into their lives for the sake of a man who might have caused the deaths of those they loved. He would send Inspector Grove to ask some questions — Grove could be trusted to be careful and discreet.

They went outside and made their way to the garden door, which opened just as they reached it. A man came in, a man whom no one had mentioned before.

A man in the garb of a labourer, a gardener, perhaps, or general handyman, which he proved to be. One John Bark — *apt*, thought Dickens, noting his sinewy, brown face which had the appearance of some gnarled root, and the strong, thin brown hands with black nails. He lived, he told them, in rooms above the stables situated across the alley. He had not been there on the night of the murder, having left about five thirty to see his sister. His wife had gone with him. Superintendent Goss had not questioned him at all, but Jones asked if he had seen anyone at all in the alley during that day.

'All sorts o' people comes and goes, sir, but I knows most o' them. People wot works in the 'ouses and stables. No one comes down 'ere unless they 'as business with servants or cooks or the like. I didn't see anyone different.'

'Was there anyone in the alley when you left to go to your sister's?'

'There was the boy.'

'What boy?'

'Italian lad — 'e was often about — 'e 'as one o' them barrel-organ things.'

'What was he doing down here?'

'Well, 'e played fer us sumtimes — I don't know 'ow 'e come to be 'ere first, but the wife give 'im somethin' to eat once an 'e played fer them as wos about — servants an' that — takin' little lad — face like an angel, the wife sed.'

Jones glanced at Dickens, whose sudden intake of breath suggested some idea. It would keep for the moment. He made a slight motion with his hand.

Bark continued, "E came back o' course 'cos o' the food an' the pennies — we all give 'im somethin'. Come ter think o' it —' Bark scratched his head — 'I ain't seen 'im since — never thought of it before.'

'Did you know his name?'

'Joe — Joe Seppy, 'e sed — foreign o' course. We called 'im Joe.'

'Do you know where he lived?'

'No, sir — the wife asked 'im, but I don't think 'e understood — 'e dint speak much English — jest smiled an' played his little barrel-organ.'

Dickens, who had waited patiently, asked the question that had sprung to his lips earlier. 'Has he a birthmark shaped like a tear under the left eye?'

'Yes, he has. My wife said it made him look sad at times — made her feel sorry for him.'

Jones thanked John Bark, and he and Dickens went out into the alley.

'Well?'

'I saw the boy in Weymouth Street. He was standing opposite Plume's house — just looking. I gave him sixpence. He had, as Bark said, the face of an angel. I noticed the birthmark under his eye. I remember thinking that it was odd that the boy wasn't playing his instrument. And —' he broke off, his face suddenly anxious.

'What?'

'I saw someone else stop by him — a man, I think. I supposed just a passer-by like me. Then they vanished — into the fog, I thought. I hope.'

'Another possible witness — you're the conjuror, Charles. Get them back, will you.'

'I wish it were as easy as conjuring a guinea pig from a box of bran — I did that once. Alas, the guinea pig is dead. He left in his will that he believed the conjuring had done it.'

Jones grinned, 'You had my watch, too, out of my pocket.'

'Deformation o' character, sir. I give it back, yer honour. Temptation, it was to an 'umble man. The 'umblest person going, I am, Mister Jones.' He rubbed his hands together so much in the manner of the writhing Uriah Heep, that Jones had to laugh.

'Get away with you, Heep — and writhe somewhere else.'

Heep vanished and Dickens and Jones walked from the alley into Weymouth Street, making their way towards Wimpole Street from where Dickens could walk up Devonshire place to his home.

'Another needle in a haystack,' said Jones.

'The Italian boy?'

'Yes. I think I'll ask Scrap to have a nose round Bones Alley — he might find out something. Sharp ears, he has, and better than sending a constable. He might hear of John Bark's "Joe Seppy", as he calls him.'

'Oh, those children, Sam — little May, the lad on crutches … sometimes…'

'I know.'

They looked up. It was a clear, cold night with a little half-hoop of a moon and points of icy stars. And infinite, silent, scentless blackness beyond, mysterious and unknown — and somehow impassive. The stars look down. And if they do, thought Dickens, it is coldly. 'The universe makes rather an indifferent parent, I think,' he observed.

'That is why our children need us. I need an hour with little Tom Brim and a spinning top, or a toy train.'

'I, too, after such a blue-devilous day — a bit of toy-soldiering with a regiment of boys. Home, then?'

'Yes, I'll go back to Bow Street later and talk to Rogers about Jem Pike, and I need to ask Elizabeth to find out more about the blood on Miranda Deverall's hands.'

'Oh, yes, I remember. Elizabeth thought it might be a miscarriage.'

'I think she was right, but Billie Watts told Rogers that the blood was part of Goss's evidence against Miranda, so we need to be sure that there is something she is still not telling about the night of the murder.'

'But what? She can't have been there when Plume was murdered, surely?'

'We don't know. The door to the hall was locked, but the glass door to the garden was open. Did she see something, go back and touch the dead man? Does she know who the murderer is? Is she protecting someone?'

'I can't see that — it doesn't fit what we know of her — her loneliness seemed so absolute.'

'But, there was Kitty Quillian, a friend, it seems.'

'Who is missing — that's a thought. Kitty Quillian was there. She worked at Mrs Hodson's then left. I wonder why.'

'We'll have to find her — Dab Lane, Elizabeth said.'

'Listen, tomorrow I'll go to see Jenny Ince, then I'll go to see Edward Lawson and ask him for something for *Household Words* — see what happens.'

'And I shall have to come back to talk to Mrs Plume — I wonder what she knows about his work with the poor.'

Jones went on towards Portland Street and then to his house in Norfolk Street. Dickens went up to Devonshire Terrace. He let himself in. There was a very little boy on the stairs, seated in such an attitude of dejection that he wondered what calamity might have befallen. The Ocean Spectre, it was, who turned those unusually far-seeing, wondering eyes.

'Pa!' Sydney Dickens, aged three and a half, exclaimed. Then the eyes filled with tears.

Dickens went over and sat on the stairs. 'Sydney, my boy — what on earth is it?'

'Alley said I couldn't play — said I'm too little. He only wants Frank. Not me — no one to play with.'

Alley, five, and Frank, aged six, thought themselves too grand to bother with poor Sydney.

'Then you shall play with Pa — that you shall.' Dickens held the little boy to him — he thought of that poor boy with the useless legs, and held his own more tightly.

Later, he thought, *I did not take off my coat. Because Sydney was there. Plume did not take off his coat.*

13: Mr Thackeray's Advice

I woo'd the fair, and won the sweet consent.
But brief, alas! the spell, for suddenly
Peal'd from the tower the old familiar chimes,
And with their clear, heart-thrilling melody,
Awaked the spectral forms of darker times ...

An Old Haunting. Dickens read the words again from Edward
Lawson's poem. Regret, loss, disappointment. Could the man
who had written these words be a murderer? The poet as
murderer? It seemed a contradiction. Yet, King David
murdered the messenger who brought the news of the deaths
of Saul and Jonathan, and he wrote his psalms. And Thomas
Wainewright, whom he had seen in Newgate years back, had
been an artist and literary man. The painter of *The Milkmaid's
Song* had poisoned three members of his own family.

Anyone might be a murderer, given the right combination of
circumstances. Murder was so often the crime of someone
who, before the deed, had never been a criminal — the serving
maid with an illegitimate child; the jealous husband, lover, or
wife. Someone to whom opportunity presented temptation —
the temptation, perhaps, to kill a man who had wronged you,
to rid yourself of the corruption that the hated one bred in
your blood.

Time to go and see what could be heard at The Crown in
Vinegar Lane where the Punch club gathered. His way took
him back to Bow Street and into Catherine Street where,
opposite the Drury Lane Theatre, there was a narrow court in
which lay The Crown next to The Whistling Oyster — a place

of legendary fascination. Mr Pearke, the landlord had heard an oyster whistling. He had identified the phenomenal bivalve which had been given its own tub of brine and oatmeal on which to feast, and to captivate the crowds that came to witness its fluting. Douglas Jerrold had said that it was, no doubt, crossed in love and whistled to keep up appearances — to show it didn't care. What its fate had been, no one knew and Pearke could not say. Eaten, Dickens supposed, or turned into sauce. A lesson of life — the wheel of fortune could turn even for an oyster. It was easy to fall.

He looked at them in the window — they looked tempting, laid one deep in circular marble basins, if rather brooding like so many haunted eyes — what, he wondered, did oyster sellers do when oysters were not in season? Did they commit suicide in despair, or wrench open tight drawers and cupboards and hermetically-sealed bottles for practice?

'Crossed in love?' a voice observed.

He turned to see the diminutive Douglas Jerrold, who was just about to go into The Crown, when he had seen Dickens looking meditatively at the window of The Whistling Oyster.

Dickens looked down from his modest five foot nine to Jerrold's five foot. What a pair Jerrold and the six foot three Thackeray made when you saw them together, Thackeray looking like a giant in the company of a gnome.

'Does your mother know you're out?' he asked smiling down.

Jerrold laughed. How could he not, the author of so many witty squibs at his friends' expense? It was he who had named the untidy journalist, Stirling Coyne, "filthy lucre".

'Just a lone lorn creature — in the manner of your Mrs Gummidge.'

Hm, Jerrold thought, when Dickens did not answer. *Something on his mind, I daresay.* For all his high spirits, there was sometimes a melancholy about Dickens. You caught it occasionally when he didn't know you were looking. That finely cut face, mostly all light, made of steel, Jane Carlyle had said, had a — lostness — that was it. He wondered — how much of the boy, David Copperfield, was in him? That bitter toil in the bottle factory — was that Dickens's own experience? Well, one couldn't ask. 'Coming in?' he asked. 'Or is the oyster to be the subject of a Christmas story?'

'I once thought of a title for a comic novel — *Oysters in Every Style* or *Openings in Life.*'

'Or, *When One Door Opens*,' laughed Jerrold, turning to the door of the inn.

They went in to the warm room where Dickens saw Thackeray's unmistakeable towering height. He sat next to Mark Lemon with whom he was always at ease, close friend and editor of *Punch*. There were familiar, good-humoured faces: Hal Bayliss, president of the Punch Club; his old friend, Clarkson Stanfield, the painter; and Edwin Landseer; Ebenezer Landells, the engraver; and Jerrold, of course, already showing off his sparkling wit.

The talk turned to William Macready's recent *Hamlet* at the Haymarket, his penultimate performance of the role. Dickens had thought it very fine and he said so. It had been a good house and an enthusiastic audience, some for whom it would be the last time they saw the greatest actor of his age. George Lewes said he had preferred Macready's *Macbeth* which he'd seen in October.

'Nothing,' Lewes argued, 'could be finer than the indications he gave of a conscience wavering under the influences of superstition and fate.'

Thackeray agreed and quoted: '*Now does he feel his secret murders sticking on his hands* — an image that makes you feel that blood.'

They talked about murder, speculating about the murder of the fashionable Doctor Plume. Mark Lemon turned to Dickens, saying in a low voice, 'Do I see by your face that you are involved in this — with the good Superintendent?'

Dickens nodded. He did not like to make public his work with Jones, but he saw Thackeray looking at him with speculation in his eyes — or so he thought. Thackeray's spectacles glinted in the candlelight. It might just have been a trick of the light, but Lemon had seen something in Dickens's face when he asked about the murder. Perhaps Thackeray had. Sometimes, Dickens thought that Thackeray watched him with unusual intensity. John Forster, Dickens's close friend and a friend of Thackeray's, maintained that Thackeray studied him because he wanted to know how Dickens did it — how he managed to produce so many best-sellers.

Towards the end of the evening, those at table broke into smaller groups. Dickens could hear snatches of conversation about Plume. He was wishing he could hear more clearly when Thackeray came and sat by him.

'You are concerned in the matter of the doctor's murder?' he asked. *He has seen something*, thought Dickens. *I ought to be more careful.*

Dickens told him about Lady Pirie's request that he should see Miranda Deverall, how he was convinced that she had not killed him, and that he had been to the police to report what he had found. He did not mention Jones.

'Were the police interested?'

'They want to know more about Plume.' He took the plunge — might as well ask. 'Did you know him?'

'No, but Edward Lawson did.' Thackeray's voice had a grim edge and Dickens knew why. *Soft you now*, he said to himself.

'His wife was Plume's patient?' He framed it as a question. Everyone knew about Lawson's wife and the asylum, but Dickens wanted to be careful. It wouldn't do for Thackeray to know that Lawson might be a suspect.

'Yes — he couldn't stand the man — blamed him for...' Dickens saw the pain in his eyes. There was a silence and they could hear the laughter. Jerrold had no doubt made a joke, judging by the roar of amusement.

Dickens waited. It was the nearest he had come to real intimacy with the man he had known since 1836, when Thackeray had come to show him sketches that might serve for *Pickwick Papers*. Dickens had not liked them. Thackeray had praised his work and they had become friends of a kind, but each was secretive in his way. Each had secrets, and each, perhaps, feared that the other with his novelist's acuteness, might divine them.

Thackeray saw how his rival waited, and he came under the spell of those deep, searching eyes. 'I know what he feels,' he said. 'You understand me?'

Dickens nodded, but did not speak.

'You should see him. Lawson can tell you what kind of man Plume was.'

'I don't know him well enough.' Dickens felt again that sense that he was betraying a trust — Thackeray's this time.

'Tell him I sent you — he'll want to tell you. And he won't want an innocent girl to be hanged. He's a good man.'

With that they parted and Dickens went away, somewhat easier in his mind. Thackeray had given him his blessing, as it were. He had an entrée to Lawson's house, but he was conscious of deception, too. Thackeray had not known that Lawson might be accused — or had he? Dickens stopped by the window of the oyster shop again and looked at the eyes shining in the gaslight. He thought of Thackeray's eyes behind the lenses of his spectacles. Perhaps he had seen.

Then he felt guilty — and sorry, for, in that moment of intimacy when Thackeray had referred obliquely to his wife, Dickens felt he had betrayed him. Murder did that.

He would get a cab, he thought, walking out into Catherine Street, feeling suddenly weary.

Murder was a betrayal of trust: the lover with his hands round the slender neck of a woman who leant against him, or twisting the loop of hair three times around the little throat; the poisoner holding the cup to the tired man's lips; the man who came into the room, and with one hand accepted the cigar while the other concealed the knife — or the woman. The missing Mrs Hodson. Would she have accepted a cigar? Hardly. Though, when he thought about it, he remembered a time in Geneva when he had smoked cigars with a collection of ladies. Lady Walpole, he recalled vividly, smoking away like a Manchester cotton mill. He had never seen a woman smoke before. So, perhaps Mrs Hodson might have been a smoker. He imagined Inspector Hardacre offering her a cigar as he questioned her. She'd turn up, no doubt, if the Inspector in Manchester had anything to do with it

The cab dropped him near Devonshire Terrace. He went in through the iron gate. He stopped for a moment before putting his key in the lock. *Air*, he thought, *let me have air*. He could smell the cigar smoke on his clothes. He looked up into the night sky, but there were no stars. *Husbandry in heaven, their candles are all out.*

He thought of Thackeray quoting from *Macbeth*, and the talk of murder.

Now does he feel his secret murders sticking on his hands. Somewhere, but where — and who? Nemo — the man with no name. Yet.

14: Plain Clothes

Scrap was a master of disguise. When Dickens had first encountered him, he had been a thatch-haired urchin of the streets with an engaging smile and ragged trousers. But, he was a friend of the Brim children by that strange alchemy which draws children together, however wide the social gap. He was their unofficial protector, having rescued their dog, Poll, from a potential dog-snatcher. He had always been about the stationery shop, especially when Mr Brim had been confined to his bed with that creeping disease of consumption which had eventually killed him. Scrap worked at the shop which was managed now by Mollie Rogers.

Dickens was fond of Scrap. He was smart and brave and utterly loyal, and he worked for his money. Virtue showed quite as well in rags and patches, as she did in purple and fine linen. That was Dickens's belief. And, he was, as all the other boys Dickens came across or assisted, his other self, the shabby boy who had laboured in the blacking factory and had thought he would never be rescued: the crippled boy for whom he had found employment at his publisher's; the shoe-black boy placed in a ragged school; Davey, the mute boy whom he had taken to Mrs Morson at the home for fallen women; Kip Moon, whose parents and sister had died; countless others to whom he had given so many sixpences.

And now Scrap was in search of an Italian boy and glad to do it for Superintendent Jones. He went from Norfolk Street to the stationery shop in Crown Street, where Mollie watched him searching through his box.

The box, or rather, THE box — a receptacle for all those things which Scrap treasured. Not that there were many: a few shells from the sea shore where he had been with the Superintendent, Elizabeth and the Brim children. There was a rusty pen knife, a ball of string and a tarnished silver button he'd swapped once for an apple. There were some instalments of Mr Dickens's *David Copperfield* which he had bought out of the money Mr Dickens had paid him — not that Mr Dickens knew. He could read a bit — he had learnt from bill posters and scraps of newspaper. He had told Mrs Jones what he wanted to do, and she had begun to teach him properly. One day — soon — he was going to surprise Mr Dickens.

There was a little earthenware pot of Warren's shoe-blacking, the use of which would be divulged shortly to Mollie, and a miscellaneous collection of articles of clothing: an old cap, a canvas waistcoat and a shirt the colour of strong tea — it might have been white once, and a grimy, threadbare woollen scarf.

'What are you doing, Scrap, with these old clothes? You don't need them now,' Mollie observed.

'Disguise. Wot Mr Jones ses is undercover work — it's wot's called plain clothes. I can't go searchin' fer clues lookin' like this.' He gestured to his neat suit and shiny boots. 'Gotter blend in, yer see, Mollie.' He took the top off the blacking pot. 'Bit dry, but it'll do.'

'You're never goin' to black them new boots!'

He looked at her pityingly. Mollie woz awright, but she dint know much.

'Nah, course not — just yer watch.'

He dipped the fingers of one hand in the paste and rubbed it over both hands, making sure that the nails were sufficiently encrusted. Mr Dickens would have recognised the paste and the black nails. His own hands were like that once — he'd scrubbed at them, but the blacking would not come off. Scrap, too, had discovered he preferred to be clean. But, work was work, an' Mr Jones needed 'im. He sniffed at the shirt — not too bad — and exchanged his jacket for the canvas waistcoat and the scarf. He blacked parts of his face and neck, tousling his hair into spiky points before arranging the shabby cap.

Mollie laughed — he was every inch the street urchin except — 'What about your trousers?'

'I's'll ave ter go ter Zeb's fer them. Me old ones woz nothin' but rags — I use 'em fer polishin' me boots. I'll get some boots off him — old ones.'

Zeb Scruggs was an old clothes dealer in Monmouth Street, the place which Dickens had called "the burial place of fashion".

'Don't forget to pick up your better ones on your way back.'

'Right. I'll be off then.'

Scrap made his way up through Seven Dials to Monmouth Street and Zeb's shop. There were places far worse than Zeb's where Scrap might have found a set of stinking rags, but he'd have had to pay. Zeb would let him borrow, or, more probably, give him the worst pair of trousers he could find in the rag heap in the yard. The second hand clothes shops were usually foul-smelling, greasy, dirty places, the rags for sale often infected with fever or pox. But Zeb and his wife, Effie, were a superior sort of dealers — the shop was clean and well-aired with a breeze passing through the open front and back doors. Zeb's old clothes were wearable, and he gave fair prices to the sellers who were so often in desperate straits, having to exchange a usable cloak for a bit of sacking. Money for the rent — or for a loaf. It was frequently that bad. Zeb was also a translator, meaning that he and Effie were skilled at refashioning the better parts of discarded coats, dresses, skirts, trousers into something wearable — the skirts of a coat might make a child's cape; a little dress might emerge from a larger one; the decent back of an otherwise useless shirt might make a baby's dress.

When Scrap arrived, Zeb was paying a haggard-looking woman for a child's dress which looked in unusually good condition. It looked almost new — *poor little girl who'd had to part with this*, Zeb thought.

'She don't need it now, Mr Scruggs. She won't need nothin' — not now, not ever —' She burst into tears. Zeb waited until she wiped her eyes and was able to continue, 'I ain't niver goin' ter see my girl agin. This dress woz given me by Mrs Greenaway wot I did laundry fer. It woz too small fer 'er girl. I'd like ter keep it, but yer know 'ow it is.'

Zeb knew. He knew that Mrs Larks had spent much on her sick daughter, and he had guessed when she had produced the dress that little Lucy Larks was dead. He gave her two shillings. She'd be able to pay the rent, at least.

Scrap watched the haggard Mrs Larks go out of the shop. Zeb studied the little dress. Too many kiddies died too young. There were them as thought the poor 'adn't the same feelings as those with money and education. But it wasn't true — well, for most, at any rate. He'd seen many like Mrs Larks — good, 'ard-working women who did the best they could.

'Wotcher, Mr Scruggs.'

'Well, Scrap, what wind blew you here — detectin' are you?'

'Tha's right, Mr Scruggs. I needs some trousers. Yer got any rags? And some old boots.'

'Out the back — help yourself.'

Scrap came back with a garment that might once have graced a military parade — though, now, the trousers were cut down and the formerly smart red stripe had faded to a dirty pink. They looked just the sort of thing an urchin might have had from his superannuated ex-soldier father who had declined into drink and debt.

'Not bad at all,' said Scrap with satisfaction, having exchanged his own trousers for the ex-serviceman's leavings. He changed his good boots for some ancient, cracked things. They were too big, but he tied them with string. Wouldn't do to 'ave them fall off if he had to make a run for it.

Mrs Effie Scruggs came in. 'Who's this ragamuffin?' she asked, knowing well enough.

'Plain clothes, Mrs Scruggs — I'm on a job for Mr Jones — wants me ter find a witness — Italian boy wot 'as a barrel-organ.'

'But, there are hundreds of them,' Effie said doubtfully.

'Name o' Joe Seppy, last seen up Weymouth Street.'

'Where that doctor was killed?' Zeb asked.

'Right — Mr Jones wants me to search the alleys round there — see if anyone seen 'im.'

'Well, you be careful,' Effie said. 'Do you want me to take these trousers to Mollie at the shop?'

'Ta very much, Mrs Scruggs — save me comin' back.'

Scrap went out. He sniffed the air like a dog on the hunt. He liked his new life, but sometimes it was good to be out and about, looking and listening. You could take the boy from the streets, it might be said, but you couldn't take the streets out of the boy. He was like Dickens in that. Dickens who had wandered like a vagabond when he was the same age as Scrap; Dickens who had looked and listened, too; Dickens who walked and walked, and couldn't stop. The streets were in his very blood, the walking ground of his heart.

Scrap was off. Weymouth Street was not his territory, but, so what? 'E could look after 'imself. That's what he'd told Mr Jones, but Mr Jones had said that Constable Stemp would be in plain clothes, too, and he, Scrap must leave a message for his "uncle" at The Neptune pub on East Street if he found anything. Stemp would be about the streets, too. Scrap had wanted to protest further that 'e dint need lookin' after, but Mr Jones 'ad given 'im a look — an' 'is eyes 'ad slid ter Mrs Jones. Then Scrap 'ad understood. He saw her face, all creased.

So that woz it. 'E'd wondered when 'e went in the kitchen. Tension. A row? But Mr and Mrs Jones niver rowed — niver. Not like 'is own pa and stepma — always at it — 'ammer and tongs. That's why 'e niver went there now. Not that they cared a farthin'. But, and his mind filled with wonder at the thought, Mrs Jones woz worried about 'im — she cared wot 'appened to 'im, she really did.

Another lesson learnt — yer couldn't always 'ave wot yer wanted. There woz others ter think about. Yer weren't on yer own.

15: The Haunted Man

Mrs Philomena Flutter sat by the fire in the house of her nephew, Edward Lawson. She was thinking about Margaret, his wife, who was in the asylum, and about Edward, and how he was lost in his grief for the woman he had loved so. She thought about the child that had been born dead — Edward would never get over it.

She thought about love. She thought about the Archdeacon whose relict she was, and who had made his flight heavenward a decade before. Once, when they were engaged, he had named her Philly, and in a moment of nervous ardour, he had kissed her. And she had felt — what was it she had felt? She couldn't remember now.

She had not known him — she had wondered sometimes about the stranger in his black suit who had stood by her hearth. He had been mostly silent, though he addressed her as "my dear". At the beginning she had thought, perhaps, that there might be children, a child, but, no — something, it seemed, had not happened. Something that had happened to Flora, her sister, who had three children. There had been a pretty little boy who had died, then Edward, and after, a little girl who was married herself now with two children of her own. But no one had ever told Philly what it was that had happened. And the Archdeacon had not kissed her again.

She had seen Edward kiss Margaret. She had seen Margaret smile then, a lovely, loving smile which had a secret in it. But that was before. When the trouble came, Philly had put her hands over her ears to shut out those terrible cries. The doctor had come down, and Edward had wept then.

Doctor Plume — he had been murdered. Edward had said nothing about it, but Mrs Flutter had heard the maids gossiping. Edward's face had been closed. He had seen the headline in the paper, but he had said nothing. She dared not mention it. And Edward became more silent than ever, retreating to his study where he sat for hours, locked in his grief. When he came out, his face looked like that of a man haunted by some memory, his face so white and set that Mrs Flutter was frightened of him. Edward, who had been once so kind to her. She knew she was silly at times. She knew she chattered too much, but Edward had always been patient — and Margaret, too. But, now — and there was no one to turn to.

The entrance of the maid interrupted her thoughts. Amy brought in a visiting card. Her face was shining with excitement.

'There's a gentleman to see Mr Lawson — it's Mr Dickens, ma'am — Mr Charles Dickens — the author, ma'am —'

'Mr Dickens!' Philly was astounded. 'Good gracious. Where is he?'

'In the hall, ma'am. Oh, ma'am, shall I bring him in?'

Mrs Flutter, as became her name, fluttered uncertainly, patting her lace cap, standing up then sitting down again. Edward had said he was not at home — no visitors except by appointment. He did not want to see anyone, but you couldn't turn away Charles Dickens. And Philly very much wanted to see him — the author of *Pickwick* — and dear Little Nell and, oh, poor little Paul Dombey, over whose death she had wept. How much she preferred Mr Dickens to Edward's friend, Mr Thackeray. *Vanity Fair* — so cynical, and Becky Sharp, that dreadful adventuress. Not that she didn't like Mr Thackeray — but he was so very large. Oh, and his wife so ill like Margaret.

Such a pity. But, she would receive Mr Dickens. She would be brave — but she hoped Edward would not be angry.

She stood up. 'Yes, Amy, show him in here, and then go and knock on Mr Lawson's door — tell him, ask him if he wishes to see Mr Dickens.'

Amy went out. Mrs Flutter composed herself and, remembering the dignity of the Archdeacon, commanded her scattered thoughts.

Dickens came in to see Mrs Flutter, a papery sort of woman whose black skirts rustled like dried leaves as she stood to greet him. She offered a little hand like a collection of thin twigs encased in lace gloves, which felt like paper to the touch. *She looked anxious*, he thought, smiling at her kindly.

'Mrs Flutter, I must beg your pardon for coming so unexpectedly. Mr Lawson has written for my magazine and I have come to ask if he can contribute something more.'

Before Mrs Flutter could make her reply, Edward Lawson came in. Someone said that every man's face contains his past and future. *And his miserable present*, thought Dickens when he saw the worn, white face of Edward Lawson. Richard Farleigh's face had been stricken when Dickens had seen him by the fire at his father's house, but he was young and the sorrow would pass. His face still had the roundness of youth. He would live and laugh again. The marks of his experience would fade. Not like this man whose face was so lined with grief — lines that could never be erased. The eyes were dark, dulled with despair. He looked older than his years. Dickens knew him to be about thirty, but his future had rushed to claim him. Was there something more, Dickens wondered then, than the grief for his mad wife? He ought not to have come. Suppose the man had killed Plume. What then?

Lawson spoke. 'What can I do for you, Mr Dickens?'

'I wondered if you might have anything to contribute to *Household Words* — I so liked the poem we published.'

Lawson's eyes brightened. 'Thank you. I'm afraid I have not been writing much of late — my wife is…' He faltered and his eyes clouded once more. He looked away into some unfathomable distance. Dickens felt pity for him. How could he help the man? Not by asking questions about Plume; that was certain. He ought to go, to give it up. Jones would have to —

The dark eyes were looking at him again, burning now with some question. 'I saw that piece in *Household Words* about prisoners, about Manning — should a man hang for murder? You don't think so?'

Dickens's heart turned over at the sudden unexpectedness of the question. He looked back at the man. 'I don't know now, but I do know that such a thing should not be a public spectacle, even for Manning — and his wife.'

'What if the victim were a villain as bad as the murderer? What then, Mr Dickens, what then?'

His voice was so harsh and loud that Mrs Flutter uttered something like a cry — a little sound of fear — or distress. Dickens looked at her. Her pale blue eyes were alarmed.

Dickens took charge. 'Mrs Flutter, I do need to speak to Mr Lawson privately. I wonder if you might leave us alone.'

Mrs Flutter looked relieved. 'Oh certainly, Mr Dickens, certainly. I beg your pardon. So pleased to have met you.'

Lawson did not seem to hear. He paid no attention as his aunt fluttered away to the door and vanished with a whisper of leaves and paper. *Poor bird*, thought Dickens. *I hope to God Lawson isn't the killer.* He turned back to the man with the burning eyes and led him to a chair. Lawson looked at Dickens now, as if seeing him for the first time.

'I beg your pardon. I am not myself. My wife ... that villain Plume —' He put his head in his hands. Dickens could hear the terrible, dry sobbing that seemed to wrack his thin frame. It was dreadful. *I shouldn't have come*, thought Dickens again, but he waited until the sobbing ceased and the gaunt face looked up at him.

Dickens sat down opposite Lawson. 'Can I do anything for you? Do you wish to tell me something of your trouble? It might help you if you were to speak.'

Lawson looked into the wide, luminous eyes that gazed back at him, so full of pity and understanding. Thackeray said he was a good man. The eyes seemed to say so and the sensitive mouth, well-shaped and expressive. Mesmeric eyes that compelled him to speak.

'Guilt, Mr Dickens — do you know how it grinds one down? How it eats away at a man's very soul?'

Dickens sat still. He felt his own heart quiver — was this to be a confession of murder? He continued to look at Lawson. He must not show any foreknowledge.

'You know it, of course you do. How well you know the haunted man, and how his mind fixes upon that one thought. Jonas Chuzzlewit has that body in the wood forever on his mind; Sikes is pursued by the eyes of poor dead Nancy —'

Dickens felt a sense of horror. Did this man feel the eyes of the dead doctor upon him? Was it the body of Plume that he saw? He had written of how his murderers were pursued by the phantoms of their victims — he knew it, of course he did. But to see it in the agonised eyes of the real man before him. It was very nearly unbearable — but he had started this, and he must see it out.

'Margaret's eyes. What terror was there. She knew. She knew what was to happen, Mr Dickens, she knew. When Plume and his associate came and took her to that place, she looked at me in such terror, and at the last, with such pleading — and I let them take her. For her own good, Plume said. Her own good! And now, she does not know who I am, and it is doubtful that she ever will.'

Lawson was silent then. *What am I to say?* thought Dickens. 'There is no hope for her?' he ventured.

'I think not — do not mistake me. She is not cruelly treated. She is quiet and calm — not raving as she was, happy in her own way, but she is absent. Margaret no more, but I cannot help wishing that I had not agreed. Perhaps if I had kept her here — but Plume…'

'You know he is dead?' Dickens had to ask.

'Yes.'

'And that an innocent girl is accused of his murder?' There it was. The word was out of his mouth, written on the air, reverberating, it seemed to Dickens, sounding in the glasses on the table, whispering in the leaves of the tree outside the window. Murder echoing from stone to stone, until the word rolled away with carriage wheels that passed by in the street.

Something cleared in Lawson's eyes. There was light now, as if the man had woken from some terrible dream. He hasn't done it. He could not look like that. His guilt is for his wife only, not for Plume.

'Innocent, you say?'

Dickens watched him keenly. A man like this would not let an innocent woman hang for his crime.

'Yes, I have seen her, and I tell you, Mr Lawson, it will be a monstrous injustice if she is hanged for it.' He allowed his voice to sound the anger he really felt about Miranda Deverall. Draw him out. Let's be certain.

'I had no love for the man — when I read of his death, I could feel no pity for him.' Dickens saw how his eyes took on the haunted look again. 'When our child was to be born, poor Margaret was so ill. Plume told me that to save her, I must lose the child. It was my decision, he said — and there would be no more children... I begged him to send for another surgeon, another opinion, but it was too late, he told me. I must decide immediately. And I could not think of the child, only of her, and now, I think, it would have been better to let her go. If I had known what was to happen to her. I lost both.'

'You think Plume was —'

'Incompetent — yes, I think he was. He should have brought in a colleague sooner. He must have known there was danger, but he said nothing — and then it was too late. And then I had to see him take her away. Oh, he had his colleague with him then.' His voice was bitter now. 'And I was glad, God forgive me, when I read that he was dead. What have I become, Mr Dickens, that I should be glad to hear that a man has been murdered?'

Dickens was sure now. The man was eaten up with guilt for his wife and dead child, and he loathed himself for his hatred of Plume and his satisfaction at Plume's death. Would it help him to know what kind of man Plume was, or would it make it worse for him to know that the doctor to whom he had entrusted his wife was a vile man? And, what if Lawson thought that Plume had seduced his wife? No, on balance, better to say nothing about it.

His voice was gentle now. 'I cannot blame you, Mr Lawson. You were faced with a decision no man should have to face. I do not doubt that Plume was at fault, but his murder is nothing to do with you. Think of him no more — of course, he did not deserve his death, but any man who has suffered as you, must feel as you do. It is only human. And, as for your guilt about your wife, I am not going to tell you that you should not feel it, but there is balm in the wound, perhaps. She is peaceful, you say, and the worst may be over for her to whom you were so devoted. You loved her. And that is what you must recall when you can. Not every man may say that, Mr Lawson.'

He could say no more. It was not much — not enough, no doubt, but Lawson looked calm and his eyes were more those of a man who was alive rather than those of a dead man. It was as if the light had come back, a candle flaring up again.

'When did he die?'

'Plume? On Sunday last — a week ago.'

'I went there — I did not realise. I saw the headline and thought only — you know what I thought. I did not think about who had done it. And you said earlier that a young woman is accused and that she is innocent.'

'She is. At what time did you go?'

'In the evening. I went round the back — I hoped to find him in his office. I knew that if I went to the front, he wouldn't see me. I'd been before. I wanted to — I don't know why I went — to force him to admit that he was responsible, I suppose. But, I could not do it. I hung about the entrance to the lane. I walked down and back again.'

'Did you see anyone?'

'A man passed me as I was coming back up the lane. I saw him seem to linger by Plume's garden door.'

'Can you describe him?'

'It was dark, but there was a gas lamp above the door.' Lawson closed his eyes, trying to remember what he had seen. 'Tall — taller than I am. He was wearing a hat — not a top hat — a low-crowned hat with a wide brim, and a heavy coat, black, I think, with wide sleeves. That's all I remember. There was nothing exceptional about him. Oh, I saw his spectacles glint for a moment in the light.'

That tall figure with the long dark coat and the hat — Dickens had seen a figure very like that description bending over the Italian boy before they were swallowed up by the fog — could it be? Coincidence? If so, a dark one.

'Did you see anyone else?'

'No.'

'What time was it? Can you remember? It is important — the accused girl was there at six o'clock and the body was found at about half past seven o'clock.'

'It was after six — a quarter past, perhaps, when I left here.' Lawson lived in a terrace of houses just off Wigmore Street. 'It takes about ten minutes. It was before half past when I stood in the lane. I suppose I was there about ten minutes before I saw the man go through the garden door.'

'You went away then? You saw no one else?' Dickens thought about the Italian boy.

'Yes, I came home. I didn't notice anyone else, I'm afraid. Is all this useful? I should like to think that I could be of help — I have been too much concerned with myself — I own it — if I had thought more about the murder, I should have given my evidence to the police, and the poor girl —'

'It is not too late, and yes, it will be useful. Now, I must go — I shall take your evidence to the police. Superintendent Jones may wish to see you, or send his sergeant. Can you deal with that?'

Lawson nodded. 'I must — and I must be kinder to poor Aunt Philly, and I must go out and begin life again — I ought to do my duty.'

'It is so often the case with all of us that, in our several spheres, we have to do violence to our feelings, and to hide our hearts in carrying on this fight of life, if we would bravely discharge our duties and responsibilities — that is what I believe, Mr Lawson.'

'You are right, Mr Dickens — and you have done me good. I thank you.'

'And you will have done some good for the poor girl in Newgate — I am much obliged to you. I hope we may meet again — and,' Dickens smiled at him, 'you might consider my request for something for *Household Words*.'

'I will — I will get back to my work.'

Dickens saw how Lawson's eyes filled. It was not over — yet. 'Courage. Persevere.'

With that, they parted. Lawson watched him step briskly, lightly, away down the street. He thought of the last two words Dickens had spoken. From another man, they might have sounded trite, but he had seen something in Dickens's face when he spoke them. He had to have courage and persevere. No doubt about that. Well, they were as good words as any — and true.

Lawson went back into his house — not to his study, but to take tea with Aunt Philly, who must not be so frightened again.

16: Something Remembered

It always seemed to Jones that Biddy Feak had come straight from an apple orchard rather than the smutty London Streets. There was something appley about those round red cheeks. If she were a character from a Dickens novel she would be Peggotty, certainly not Mrs Gamp whose calling she followed. Biddy Feak was a nurse, yes, but not one who would take a shillingsworth of gin. And there was no imaginary Mrs Harris. Biddy Feak's sturdy legs and feet were planted firmly on the ground — like ready money, as his grandmother used to say. And she was looking at him with keen, blue eyes. She had news. He hoped so.

Rogers had found out nothing from Jemmy Pike. Pike had denied everything. Yes, he was friendly with Evie Finch. No, there was no affair — Jemmy Pike had been indignant — 'e was a married man with kids. Anyways, Evie Finch had been lookin' elsewhere — makin' sheep's eyes at the master's son. Rogers had not believed him, but they couldn't prove his relationship with Evie — and Jemmy Pike knew it. Rogers had seen that in the little spark of triumph in the man's eyes when Rogers bade him good day.

Mrs Feak spoke, 'I found out who Hubbard is — real name Bertha Raspin. Profession midwife — at least that's what she calls herself — not what I'd call her.'

'I've heard the name — a servant of the woman Miranda Deverall lived with mentioned her. She is connected to this Mrs Hodson and therefore to the murdered Doctor Plume.'

'And to Evie Finch who muttered those words about a doctor that Mollie told me about. Perhaps he was to do Evie's operation —'

'But he could not — he was dead. And what does our Mrs Raspin know about that, I wonder? I need to see her — unless she has vanished like Kitty Quillian.'

'Kitty Quillian?'

'She was there the night of the murder. The servant at Plume's house saw her. She didn't go in with Miranda Deverall, but she worked at Mrs Hodson's, knew Plume, and I want to find her.'

'You think she might have killed the doctor?'

'It's possible if he'd seduced her, too, which is more than likely. Anyhow, I've got Constable Stemp looking for her. Did you find out Mrs Raspin's address, by any chance?'

'I did — but, you know, Mr Jones, she won't tell you about Evie — she'll deny it. And, though I can't approve of the way she treated Evie, I have to say that some of these girls have to go somewhere. Settin' aside what happened to Evie, I can understand why she went. No man to support her — he's got off scot free — and the workhouse, she'd not want that. In any case, she might not have got in. She had no choice, and neither do hundreds of others. I don't like it, Mr Jones, course I don't, but there's many women, single or married, that can't support a child. I know abortion's illegal — but I can't help thinkin' that it's a law made by men.'

Jones heard the indignation in her voice. The law was all very well in theory, but he had seen as well as Mrs Feak, the cellars where emaciated women eked out their existence with too many children to feed. He had seen the utter despair of a woman of whose seven children, three had died, and yet there was another to come. He remembered when he was a young policeman, how a mother whose daughter had been a suicide had asked him why the girl should have been forced to bring another slave into the world. He remembered her defiant eyes and her angry grief for her daughter. He had slunk away, unable to answer. He had been taught that children were a blessing, but he had learnt a different tale then. He looked at Mrs Feak, who saw the bleakness in his eyes. Of course, he knew.

'I know. I know what desperation leads women to. Well, I shall concentrate on Mrs Raspin's link to Plume and Mrs Hodson. There's nothing I can do for Evie now, but I have to solve the murder — whether I approve of the victim or not, and if I can give Mrs Raspin a bit of a scare, she might think a bit more carefully about her patients in future. So, tell me where I might find her.'

'Fox's Lane, off Northumberland Street — you know, by the workhouse.'

'I know.'

'Well, I've to go.' Seeing Jones's face, she added kindly, 'You can only do what you can, Mr Jones. This is a hard world and no mistake. And you've chosen a hard path, but I daresay you wouldn't choose another — you're a good man, I know that.'

She stumped away then. He felt the better for her words. A good woman who did the best she could, too. Now, he thought, I need to find Mrs Raspin. And Kitty Quillian. Had she done it or had she seen something? The murderer? Had she seen Mrs Hodson at Plume's house or someone else? A memory came to him suddenly. Something that Dickens had said about the Italian boy — he had seen someone approaching the boy in Weymouth Street. Dickens thought the passer-by might have stopped to give the boy something, but the boy wasn't playing his barrel-organ. He had seemed to be looking at the house. And Dickens had used the words "I hope", as if he were afraid. A man, Dickens had thought. Somewhere, perhaps, there was a man who had murdered Plume, and who had seen Kitty Quillian and the Italian boy. Kitty Quillian — not the killer, then, but someone in danger from the killer. It was time to look. Raspin could wait. He thought about Scrap — what danger had he sent him into?

Dickens came in then to relate what he had found out from Jenny Ince and about Lawson.

'Jenny Ince couldn't tell me much more than we learned from Mrs Pook and Susan Bliss. She confirmed what we know about Lavinia's illness and about the sheets she was given, which she washed and gave to her son and his family. But, she did wonder, of course, about the blood, but she didn't dare ask.'

'Anything about Plume?'

'No, she knew that a doctor came, but nothing about him.'

'And Edward Lawson?'

Dickens told Jones about the man's grief for his wife and his loathing of Plume, whom he held responsible for his wife's condition.

'Yet, I do not believe that he killed Plume. It is true that his grief has driven him almost to madness. I pitied him.'

'I do, too. You are sure that he did not kill Plume?'

'Had you been there — had you seen him, heard him, you would have known it, too. There is something else. Lawson was there on the night of Plume's murder — and he saw someone going in — at about twenty minutes to seven.'

'Not the boy?'

Dickens told him about the man in the black hat and coat, and his remembering the figure with the Italian boy. He saw how Jones's face betrayed a sudden apprehension.

'What? What have you thought?'

'I remembered your saying that you hoped the figure was giving the boy sixpence, as if you were uncertain, and I think about the missing boy and the missing Kitty Quillian. You say Lawson saw a man entering Plume's garden at twenty minutes to seven or thereabouts. Where was our Italian boy then? Bark saw him at about five-thirty. Suppose our man saw the boy when he came out of the house. He might have been hanging about, hoping for food or something.'

'But what about Kitty Quillian? If our man went in at twenty minutes to seven, then Miranda must have gone. Why would Kitty Quillian be hanging about to be seen by him when he came out? It doesn't make sense.'

'Whatever she was doing, she was there, and she may have been seen by our man in black. Now she is missing and that concerns me. We need to find both of them before our killer does. And, I need to find Scrap. I worry that I have put him in danger. I'm going to Kitty's lodgings now — there'll be a landlord who might know something. And I'll leave a message for Stemp at The Neptune pub, telling him to look out for Scrap and bring him home.'

'I'll come with you.'

17: A Fiend in Human Shape

Mary Brady was frightened. In her head, she had a list of things of which she was terrified. The lump in her breast was not at the top. *Death*, she thought, *would be a blessed sleep.* That sleep she longed for, anything to escape the feverish nights of pain and terror. At the top of the list was poor little May. Not that she was frightened of her, but for her. May, left to the mercy of her brother, Jimmy — and her father, Paul Brady. And of those two, it was Jimmy who was the worse.

Jimmy, her first born at her breast, his hard, greedy, little black eyes staring at her. Even then he hated her. She remembered his fierce little mouth sucking the life out of her, biting with his tough gums. He had exhausted her, and she wasn't surprised when May came, unfinished, into the world. Jimmy had done that. He had taken all the life from her. After May, there had only been miscarriages or dead babies. Not that she wanted to bring any more children into the dank cellar where Jimmy terrorised her and May. He flew into rages, broke things, beat and bullied them both. Paul encouraged him — little man, he called him, but she knew that his favouritism was born of fear. Sometimes, even Paul beat him, but the boy didn't care. He was a fiend in human shape. He was capable of any vile thing — and it was her fault. She must have done something to deserve him.

In the early days, she had still prayed. There had been a little statue of the blessed Virgin. Many a time, she had fallen on her knees, begging the Virgin to intercede. Paul had laughed at her, but Jimmy, at five, had swept the statue to the floor and had ground it under his heel. Paul hadn't dared do that. May had collected the pieces. They were still in a drawer, and sometimes she looked at them hopelessly, knowing that there would be no intercession. But, perhaps, that was what the lump was — a punishment that she must endure for her sins — until she was taken to the rest she craved. If it were not for May, she would welcome death now.

And Paul? What was he up to? He had money. Where from? Workin', he'd said. None o' your damn business. And he had money for drink. He'd given her some, though — guilty about something. Then he'd gone. But, she'd heard tales, strange tales. They said the alleys was haunted. *Kids' talk*, she thought, but Jimmy said it was Satan. 'We works fer Satan,' he'd boasted, 'me an' Pa. We does 'is work.' Mary half believed it. They'd work for anyone. There was an Italian family living not far away. Annie Leather said that there was someone called the gangmaster who the Italian family had to pay money to. 'Rich, 'e was, but 'e dint live in the alleys,' Annie said. 'No one 'ad ever seen 'im, but 'e 'ad 'undreds under 'is control.' Mary couldn't make much of it all, but somehow the money and Jimmy's boasting and Paul out all night, merged into one sense of danger. The danger was like some dark, cloaked figure stalking her dreams, coming nearer so that she woke in terror, listening to May's soft breathing and biting on the rough blanket so that she wouldn't cry out.

She slept with May now in the little dank room, the size of a small pantry. It was cold as the grave, but she could keep May safe. Paul didn't want his wife now. There was someone else, she could tell. He was never in. Keepin' her somewhere, she supposed. Paul was still handsome with flashing black eyes and he could talk when he wanted something. And he hated the disease, he was frightened of it — *perhaps he thought it was catching*, she'd wondered bitterly. She wished it was. No, it was the idea of something eating away at her that revolted him. He avoided her eyes. Let him have who he wanted. More fool her — the girl, whoever she was. But if she died and Paul left with a new woman? *If?* When — for it would come. Would May be left with Jimmy? Oh, please, God, let May be safe.

Jimmy had seen her and Paul in the days when Paul wanted her. She'd seen him watching, black eyes gleaming in the dark. And she saw now how he watched May. She knew what he was thinking, what he wanted, and that frightened her more than anything. Jimmy was angry with Paul, too, angry that Paul wouldn't take him with him to wherever he went — to his fancy woman's, she supposed, leaving her to deal with him. If only Mrs Hodson had not gone away. If only Kitty Quillian was not missing. Surely Kitty would have looked after May. She would have found her a place somewhere. Mary had kept the most of the money Paul had given her. She would have given it to Kitty. But now? To leave May with Jimmy. God forgive her, she wished him dead.

But he was very much alive. She could hear him out in the street shouting at someone. She went up the ladder to see what he was up to.

Scrap found himself in Bones Alley. He'd heard on his searches that an Italian family lived somewhere in the lanes off East Street. Maybe the Italian boy lived hereabouts. He saw a boy a bit older than him — thirteen or so. Rough looking and tough, but Scrap knew his way about — and he had money. The lad was lounging against a tumbledown wall. Occasionally, he looked up and down the alley. Waiting for someone, perhaps.

Scrap approached him. The boy looked him over with hard black eyes. Scrap saw how his hands curled into fists. Well, two could play at that game. He stared back. But he noticed that the boy was thickset and there was something in the eyes, something expressionless. Scrap had seen a lot. He could hold his own in a fight and his quick tongue and fast feet got him out of most trouble, but, here he sensed something different, something inhuman almost, and for once he felt a prickle of fear.

'Wot d'yer want 'ere?' Stone hard voice. Older than the boy's years.

Scrap wanted to run. Pride kept him where he was. *Never failed Mr Jones yet. Told 'im I could look arter meself. Bloody fool, I am. Gettin' soft.* He folded his arms. Forced himself not to look behind. 'Lookin' fer someone.'

'Well, 'e ain't 'ere, nancy boy.' A coarse laugh.

Scrap kept his temper. 'I'm payin' fer information.'

'Oh, perlice are yer? Dint know they 'ad kids in the force. No wonder they don't catch no one.'

'Dint say that, did I? 'Im wot I works fer wants ter find a lad — Italian.'

The boy's eyes seemed to gleam suddenly. *Found 'im,* thought Scrap.

''Ow much yer payin'?'

Scrap calculated. A tanner wouldn't do. 'A bob.'

'Deuce. Now, or yer can whistle fer it.'

Scrap gave the two bob. He knew it was a risk — the lad might not tell him, and he worried about the way those hard eyes seemed to see right through him.

'Italian lot live down Beggar's Lane — yer go down them steps.' Jimmy pointed to a narrow opening. 'Do 'e 'ave a name? I might know 'im.' Suddenly Jimmy seemed almost friendly.

'Joe Seppy.' Scrap, usually so canny in reading character, made a mistake.

The eyes were blank again. 'Nah, niver 'eard of 'im. Now, get lost.' Jimmy picked up a large piece of brick.

Scrap went without another word. Beggar's Lane then.

Mary Brady had listened. She watched as Jimmy spoke to the other lad — *nice lookin' kid*, she thought. And she thought about the Italian boy and the talk about Satan. She saw Jimmy pick up the brick, and she saw his face, calculating and sly. He knew something.

18: Brimstone and Treacle

Mrs Brimstone, Kitty Quillian's landlady at Dab Lane, had a face the shape of a flat iron, narrow at the brow and broad at the chin, and as featureless. There was a nose, but nothing to speak of, and a grim crease for a mouth. The eyes were oddly mud-coloured and opaque. If the eyes were the windows of the soul, then hers were closed. She was solid — the wash tub on which was perched the iron. House-proud, too. There was a smell of carbolic and vinegar — and something sulphurous? The room in which Dickens and Jones stood was clean, if sparsely furnished.

Jones was surprised. Somehow, he had pictured Kitty Quillian — and Miranda Deverall — in miserable lodgings. Kitty Quillian had left Mrs Hodson's employment, yet she had been able to afford a room at Mrs Brimstone's. *Interesting*, he thought — where did her money come from?

Mr Arthur Brimstone was tall and thin and yellow with dark brown eyes — dosed, thought Dickens, with sulphur and treacle, perhaps. He imagined Mrs Brimstone as Mrs Squeers, stirring her immense basin of brimstone and treacle, and her husband with a wide open mouth ready to receive the wooden spoon and taking the whole of the bowl at a gasp. He didn't look to have much of an appetite; perhaps Mrs Brimstone's philosophy was that of Mrs Squeers: brimstone and treacle spoils the appetite and comes cheaper than breakfast and dinner. Interestingly, he seemed much younger than his wife — perhaps thirty or so to her forty or more years. How had he fastened himself to this plain, stout woman? Not that he was what one might call attractive. His face was too long.

'Kitty Quillian,' repeated Jones. 'Have you any idea where she is?'

Mrs Brimstone regarded the policeman impassively. 'No, I don't — never heard a word of her since that night the police come for that murderess. Friend of Kitty's, supposed to be — I didn't want her here. Kitty said she was going back to Ireland so I let her stay. Few nights, Kitty said. Then the murder happened and Kitty disappeared. Hope she wasn't mixed up in that business.'

Jones ignored the reference to Miranda Deverall as a murderess. 'Did she have any friends around here that she might have gone to?'

'Friendly with Mrs Brady down Bones Alley — Irish, of course. They stick together.'

They knew she wasn't there. May Brady had said that Kitty had gone. Still, it was worth asking Mrs Brady if she knew anything. She'd know more than poor little May.

'How long had Kitty Quillian lived here?'

'About six months.'

'Why did she leave Mrs Hodson's?' Jones hoped the suddenness of that question and the revelation that he knew something of Kitty Quillian's past might sting Mrs Brimstone into some unguarded comment. He was wrong. Her expression remained unmoved.

'I've no idea.'

'Did she have employment?'

'No.'

'How did she pay her way?'

'Savin's, she said. It wasn't my business. As long as she paid.'

Impasse, thought Jones. *She won't tell me anything.* He thought about the money. 'Her room — I'd like to see it, please.'

Mrs Brimstone made no sign of assent or denial of his request. Dickens glanced at Arthur Brimstone. He saw how the man's eyes darted to his wife, and how he licked his lips nervously. He noted the feverish hands coming in and out of the pockets. Something to hide here.

Just at that moment, they heard the sound of a baby crying. It came from upstairs. Again, Mr Brimstone looked uneasy. Dickens thought he saw a sudden flicker of alarm in his eyes, but the man looked down quickly, furtively. He said nothing. He hadn't said anything at all.

Mrs Brimstone looked up to the ceiling. 'I was just about to say. My niece is in Kitty's room now — with her baby. Arthur, you'd best see if she's all right. Teethin', I think, an' Bessie — that's my niece — gets a bit anxious. Arthur's very good — he has a way with little ones.'

Arthur Brimstone went off. They heard him going upstairs. A door opened and closed. Then the crying stopped.

'What about Kitty's possessions?'

'Took 'em.'

'When?' Jones's tone was sharp. Mrs Brimstone had not heard of her since the night of the murder and Billy Watts had said Miranda was alone when the police came.

Mrs Brimstone remained unmoved. 'I don't know. In the night, I suppose — after they'd taken that girl away. Next morning, no Kitty and her things gone.'

It was possible, thought Jones, *but altogether too pat, somehow. Something not right here, but what?* Mrs Brimstone looked at him steadily.

Jones gave in. He wasn't prepared to waste any more time on her. 'Well, if you hear from her, you must let me know at Bow Street. It's important that I find her.'

'I will.' That was all she said. Her thin lips closed on the last word. Dickens thought it curious that she did not ask why they wanted to find Kitty. Either she simply didn't care or, more likely, she knew something that she was not telling.

Dickens and Jones went out into Dab Lane, making their way north up East Street towards the workhouse and Fox Lane, where they hoped to find Mrs Raspin. Perhaps she knew something about Kitty Quillian. They walked in silence for a while, thinking over the interview with the Brimstones.

Jones broke the silence. 'Well, what do you think?'

'Samivel —'

'Mr Weller?' Jones looked down at Dickens.

'I think he's the wictim o' connubiality — a dilluded wictim o' a designin' female, that's wot, 'e is.'

Jones laughed. 'Odd pair, weren't they. She's the power there.'

'I tell you what I noticed while you were talking to Mrs Squeers there. I noticed how Brimstone looked uneasy — I thought he looked frightened when the baby cried. They're hiding something.'

'I thought so, too — they know something about Kitty Quillian.'

Dickens thought for a moment. 'That baby — Kitty Quillian left Mrs Hodson's about six months ago and, now there's a baby. Suggestive, ain't it.'

'So, you think she was pregnant when she left Mrs Hodson. So, who paid for her to stay at Mrs Brimstone's?'

'Plume? Blackmail?'

'That might explain why she thought Plume would give Miranda something to get rid of her. But why should the Brimstone woman tell us it was her niece's child?'

'That's what worries me — what do they intend to do with the baby? Sell it? Or worse?'

'The first, I'd wager. It happens. She's just the type – greedy, I thought. But, we need proof that it is Kitty Quillian's child.'

'May Brady's mother?'

'Mrs Raspin. We'll go there first. And we can ask about Evie Finch. On the way, though, I'd like to look in at The Neptune — see if Stemp's there. I want to know where Scrap is.'

Constable Stemp was standing outside The Neptune as they approached. He was looking up and down the street as a man might who was trying to make up his mind what to do or which way to go. When he saw the Superintendent, he looked somehow relieved.

'Have you seen Scrap?' Jones asked.

'No, sir — I was just decidin' what ter do fer the best. Whether ter go back ter Bow Street or go lookin'. I ain't seen 'im all day. I come back 'ere ter see if 'e'd left any message.'

'What's worrying you, Stemp?'

'Let's go somewhere else, sir. I don't want them in there seein' me with you — perlice ain't their favourite folk.'

'Right.'

'There's a chop house, sir, on South Street — 'bout five minutes away.'

'We'll go there. We can get a bite to eat while you tell us.' Jones was concerned. Stemp was a tough, practical man, taciturn and imperturbable. And there weren't many villains who frightened him. Jones often wondered what went on behind that unreadable face. He'd seen Stemp angry once after they'd found the body of a little girl who'd been abused. Stemp had hung on to the man they'd arrested, Jonas Finger, a brawling brute of a man. Not that Stemp had cared about

Finger's violence. Stemp had children of his own — and for some reason, he was worried about Scrap.

The chop house was a shabby affair with its sanded floor and straight-backed chairs, lit by some sickly gas lamps, but it was warm and there was food — of sorts. It would do.

The hot pies weren't bad. They looked to have meat in them, and the pastry was crisp enough. Whatever was inside tasted like meat. And the tea was hot.

'Well,' said Jones, 'tell me.'

'It's them alleys, sir — I knows my way about. I've seen a lot, you know that, sir. It don't bother me, but I dunno, sir, it's 'ard ter say. There's somethin' not right. A feelin' — lot o' frightened folk and queer talk, sir.' Stemp looked at them, his expression pained. Stemp liked certainties, hard facts, hard villains who deserved what they got, but this sense he had of menace, it was very difficult to put into words.

Jones was patient. 'Talk?'

'O' Satan, sir. I know it sounds daft, but that's what I 'eard. Folk — an' not jest kids — sayin' they've seen a ghost — figure in black with a black face an' a long nose. Not human, they say. Satan's in them alleys — that's what they're sayin.'

'And Scrap?'

'It worries me, sir. I felt it meself — as if someone's be'ind you, but when yer turns, there's nothin' there — 'cept, well I thought I saw it — somethin' black — I can't say more than that. Coulda bin just a person, but it vanished. Like a ghost, I thought. It's a rotten place, them lanes, an' that burial ground, no wonder. Anyway, I think I should try ter find 'im. It ain't right fer 'im ter be there, an' when 'e dint come I was worried.'

'So am I. You need to get back to The Neptune. Leave a message for Scrap, telling him to come here. Say that Mr Jones wants him. Then go and look. I'll send a constable to Bow

Street to get Rogers to come and help. Don't put yourself in danger. In the meantime, Mr Dickens and I must go and see a Mrs Raspin — about Evie Finch and Kitty Quillian. No sign of her or the Italian boy?'

'No, sir — will yer come ter The Neptune?'

'No, we'll meet you here with Rogers — in an hour — I don't want us all to go in just yet, but if you haven't found Scrap by then, I'll get more men — armed.'

'Right, sir. In an hour then.'

Stemp went off. Dickens and Jones hurried away to Fox Lane. On the way, Jones found a constable to send to Bow Street for Rogers. The word "armed" echoed in Dickens's head, and he thought of Stemp's talk of Satan. Dear God, where was Scrap?

19: Wherefore to Dover?

In that scrubbed clean house in Dab Lane, Arthur Brimstone eyed his wife nervously. 'They'll come back,' he said.

'Don't you think I bloody know that, B.A.' B.A., she called him, somewhat humorously — a reversal of the initials A. B. and reference to his learning. She was not without pride in her husband's education when it suited her — for example when she recommended him to Doctor Plume. It was true that Arthur had studied for his degree. That he had failed his examinations was nothing to her. Whether it was art or science was nothing to her. He had studied to be a chemist — and that's what he was. Good job the police hadn't known that.

'But we'll have gone out, won't we? Just a little errand. I've a parcel to deliver.'

'But, the baby?' He was worried. He never quite understood her. Had never. Nor had he understood how he had married her. Mr Tony Weller could have given him the words of wisdom he had shared with Mr Pickwick about the mysterious machinations of women: *You're never safe vith 'em, Mr Pickwick, ven they vunce has designs on you; there's no knowin' vere to have 'em; and vile you're a considering of it, they have you* — but Arthur Brimstone hadn't read *Pickwick Papers*. Mrs Brimstone didn't hold with fiction — real life was enough for her. Poor Brimstone was none the wiser. He had married her — and she frightened him.

'The parcel, Arthur. We'll be deliverin' —' she smiled at her joke — 'that baby to Mrs Jocelyn Cartwright. You'll be tellin' her to meet me at St Pancras Church, and you'll be tellin' her to be sure to bring the money. And with that nice little bit of money, you and me'll be takin' a little holiday an' when we come back — whenever that's to be — Mr Policeman will be long gone.'

Arthur knew better than to ask where they might be going. He didn't much care — he just wanted to get away. This baby business — he hated it. Not that Mrs Brimstone would do harm to the kiddies — she only sold them — to better lives she said. But, he felt sorry for the poor girls who left their babies. Some were brazen, it was true, and glad to get rid of an unwanted burden, but some wept and held them, and looked back longingly until Mrs Brimstone closed the door and shut them out for good.

Kitty Quillian had said she was keeping her baby. Mrs Brimstone had said that, seeing as Kitty had left it, the baby was theirs to do what they liked with. *What she liked*, he had thought bitterly. Mrs Cartwright wanted a baby. Mrs Raspin had promised her one — but it had gone and died. And now, said Mrs Brimstone, they had one. A bit older than had been agreed, but it was small enough — and no doubt Mrs Cartwright would manage. She was desperate enough.

So desperate that she had agreed to come to Mrs Brimstone who would, for a fee, arrange the "birth". Arthur knew what she and Mrs Raspin did — bottles of bullock's blood were obtained from the slaughterhouse. Sometimes, even a placenta could be got by Mrs Raspin. The "mother" was encouraged to make as much mess and noise as she liked. Her companion in the outer room could well believe that a birth had actually taken place.

But, Mrs Brimstone said, all that wouldn't be necessary — they'd deliver the child to Mrs Cartwright. She was hardly likely to say no, was she — and her husband was in on it anyway.

'Get the carpet bag, B.A. and put the baby in it. A touch of laudanum'll keep it quiet. You know what to do. On your finger — not too much, mind — well, you're the chemist. I'll leave it to you. Five minutes, no more.'

Arthur Brimstone went upstairs to Kitty's room. The baby was asleep. He had given it a little laudanum when his wife had sent him upstairs while the police were there. Hungry, he supposed. Mrs Raspin had sent a girl to feed it — some poor kid who had a baby of her own and needed the money. He looked at it — poor little thing. Kitty had loved it — him, a boy. Kitty had named him Billie — as good as gold, too, until Kitty had gone. Well, perhaps it was for the best. But, if Kitty came back? He didn't want to think about that. He liked the babies. He'd thought once that Martha might... When they married, he was twenty-two to her thirty-two, but he hadn't known that. Well, he'd better be quick — she was an impatient woman. He put the sleeping child into the carpet bag as gently as he could.

Mrs Brimstone would take a cab to St Pancras Church with the baby. She'd wait for them by the colonnaded entrance to the Church. Arthur was to go to Mrs Cartwright's in Montague Square and then make his own way by cab to Euston Station, where Mrs Brimstone would meet him at the bookstall. She didn't want him spending any time with the Cartwrights — he might let something slip about Kitty. All Mrs Cartwright needed to know was that the baby's mother had died. Mrs Brimstone preferred to talk to the Cartwrights herself — she could tell the pathetic tale of the poor dead mother, an orphan herself, who'd only wanted a loving home for her child. It had been her dying wish — that Mrs Brimstone would find somebody to be a mother to her child. It's what Mrs Cartwright would want to hear — and why not? Kitty might not be dead, but she'd want a good home for her child.

When Arthur came down with the carpet bag, Martha Brimstone was ready. She was taking nothing with her — except money. It didn't do to let Arthur know how much, which was why she had sent him upstairs. There'd be plenty with the Cartwrights' money. And there was Kitty's money, too — no sense in letting it go to waste. They could stay away for good if they needed to.

Arthur left her. Montague Square wasn't far. He went down East Street, past The Neptune pub and then into Dorset Street. He was glad it was dark. The visit of the policeman had unnerved him. Everything seemed, suddenly, bafflingly complicated. And it had all started with the murder of Doctor Plume. That girl, Kitty's friend, Annie Deverall, hadn't done it. It was impossible — a skinny, silent thing like that. And Kitty disappearing. And Mrs Hodson. Now the baby to be sold. He had to admit it — good homes or not, they were trading in babies. And something else — something he hadn't dared tell his wife — the man who had asked for Plume. Arthur had come out of the garden door at the doctor's where he'd delivered medicine — stuff he made up himself. Plume used him as his chemist. Arthur was cheap and asked no questions. Chloroform, laudanum, paregoric, savin, slippery elm, tonics, cordials — his own mixtures, all sold to Plume who asked no questions either, only suggesting the increase of tincture of opium in some of the remedies, for coughs, he said, or to soothe the restless patient. A little less treacle and a little more morphine in Godfrey's Cordial, or, perhaps Arthur could make up his own. Brimstone's Cordial, Plume had joked, it had a ring to it — Brimstone's Cordial with treacle. Arthur had not laughed, but he did as he was asked. Mrs Brimstone said it was a nice little business. They were all in it — Mrs Hodson, Bertha Raspin, Martha, him. He wanted out.

Because that man worried him. A man in a low-crowned hat and a long, dark coat who he'd seen with Kitty Quillian and, what was worse, who had been in the alley some nights before Plume was murdered. And he, Arthur Brimstone, had told him that it was the doctor's house. Had he seen a murderer, or, more terrifying, had a murderer seen him? He thought of the accused girl again. She hadn't done it. But, he couldn't tell the police. They'd find out about it all — the babies, the drugs, Plume. He thought of Martha's furious face. He couldn't face that, either.

He stopped suddenly in the crowded street. He could go. After seeing the Cartwrights. He needn't go to Euston. He could go anywhere. He could sneak back through the alleys to the back of the house in Dab Lane. No one would see him in the fog that was coming down now. He could pack a bag, take his medical case with the bottles of laudanum, paregoric, tincture of opium, cocaine, arsenic, all the things which might interest the police and he could dump it in the river. Then he could go — where?

Martha wanted to meet at Euston — she was going north then. He could go south from London Bridge Station to — to — Dover? Wherefore to Dover? He'd read that somewhere — at school, perhaps. And he thought of an odd thing. Once, when he'd been in Weymouth Street at Plume's, he had met Mrs Plume and she had asked him if he knew the work of Mr Dickens. He did not. She gave him one of the numbers of the serial *David Copperfield* — just published, she'd said — number five. She was following the story avidly. Take it, she'd said.

And he'd read the number in a pub over his lunch. He had never forgotten the story of the little boy's journey to Dover on foot, selling his jacket to a mad old man, sleeping under haystacks, washing his blistered feet in a stream — a lonely, outcast child. When he'd read it, he'd left it in the pub, not daring to take it home. And he never encountered Mrs Plume again, nor had he ever found out what became of David Copperfield.

Had the lonely boy become a lonely man? Lonely — like him. He suddenly felt it — the real loneliness of his life in that roaring city. It had always been so. Tears pricked at his eyes. Dover then. If a little boy could walk it, so could he. He would never come back — never.

20: Mother Hubbard

Someone was hammering on the door.

'No need to knock the 'ouse down — I'm comin' — Bloody 'ell,' Bertha Raspin said under her breath. She shouted again, 'Give us a minnit, will yer.'

She was alarmed. She had a patient upstairs and she was struggling — so was the patient. 'Stay with 'er and don't come down fer anythin' — keep 'er quiet.' She addressed her words to the servant who looked back at her with terrified eyes. She pointed to the knotted cloth. 'Put it in 'er mouth.'

Outside, Superintendent Jones continued to bang on the door. This one wasn't getting away.

'Here's a knocking indeed,' murmured Dickens, unhelpfully. Jones gave him a twisted smile, but continued to thump the door — a quite respectable door, in fact, not unlike Mrs Hodson's, or, indeed Mrs Brimstone's. Not, it must be admitted, as smart a door as Doctor Plume's in fashionable Weymouth Street, *but*, Dickens thought, *they all had this in common: secrets*. Every house encloses its own secret; every room in every one of them encloses its own secret, and these doors had the ugliest of secrets behind their painted respectability.

The door flew open, but before Mrs Raspin had time to do more than open her large mouth in indignation, Jones was through it, followed by Dickens.

'Police. Evie Finch and Kitty Quillian — I want information.' Jones looked down at the woman who stood before him, her face red, her breath coming in little gasps. She was unable to speak. Jones pointed to a half-open door. 'In there.'

Mrs Raspin obeyed. She sank like a spoiled loaf onto a sofa.

Upstairs, someone screamed.

'Upstairs, constable.' Jones looked at Dickens meaningfully.

In the room above the parlour, Dickens' eyes took in the exhausted figure on the bed, the blood, the terrified eyes of the servant and the bloodied lump she held in her hands.

'Where's the doctor?' he shouted. 'The nearest doctor.'

'Work'ouse 'ospital — Northumberland Street.' The girl knew it. It was where she had been born.

'Stay with her — there's a policeman in the house.'

He clattered downstairs. Shouted to Jones, 'A doctor — I'm going for one.'

Mrs Raspin's red face turned to the colour of purplish liver, then to a yeasty grey.

'Get upstairs to your patient — do what you can until the doctor comes.'

She staggered away. Jones followed her as she stumbled up the staircase. Evie Finch would not have recognised her — nor would any of her other patients. Gone was the beaming, red-faced, seemingly kindly old nurse who told them all: 'I'm a jokeler person, I'll cheer yer up. Don't fret none — I'll see yer awright. I'm the old original I am.'

The old original looked a hundred years older to the servant, but she took the thing from the girl's hands and put it in the bucket, and then she sat down by the bed to bathe the patient's head. Jones stood at the door and felt sick.

Mr Sydney Fuller, the medical director of the Marylebone Workhouse Infirmary looked in astonishment at the man in the doorway of the dispensary, who looked — and sounded, by his breathing — as if he had run a mile race and been pursued along the way by Furies. That, in itself, was surprising.

Astonishing was the fact that he recognised the man.

'Mr Dickens?'

'Yes —' Dickens exhaled a long breath — 'Mr Fuller, is it not? We met when I came here in May. I need your help — I'll explain on the way. I'm with Superintendent Jones of Bow Street. There is a young woman — Fox's Lane — Mrs Raspin —'

'The midwife?'

'Yes — will you come?'

Doctor Fuller turned to the nurse who was with him, and who was gazing at Dickens as if he had dropped from a faraway planet. 'Miss Andrews, would you get my bag from my office, organise a stretcher and follow us to Fox's Lane. What number?'

'Number ten.'

The nurse nodded and went out.

Dickens and Doctor Fuller went out into Northumberland Street, turned right by the northern burial ground and into Fox's Lane. The Doctor went upstairs to find the large policeman by the open door. Inside, he saw the girl on the bed. The bucket told him what he needed to know.

'You did this?' he asked Mrs Raspin.

Good question, thought Jones, *and one to which I would like the answer.*

'Yes — that is, I — she — a miscarriage.'

The Doctor insisted. 'You aborted the child?' He didn't need an answer for he saw what Jones had not seen. On the table by the bed was a set of curling tongs, altered to resemble forceps. And the blood on them told the truth. Doctor Fuller picked them up and held them before her. 'Answer me.'

Mrs Raspin nodded and whispered, 'Yes.'

Jones turned to the servant. 'Get me some paper.'

From a cupboard in the room, the girl retrieved some brown paper — the sort in which a parcel might be wrapped. He wondered about that. There had been a story in the paper back in October, the story of a parcel found in an open grave which had been flooded in heavy rain before a funeral. There had been a dead baby in the parcel. The sexton had said he knew nothing about it, but Jones knew that such things happened. Mothers who couldn't afford a funeral. Enough, however, for the time being.

The Doctor turned back to his patient. 'She's alive. When the stretcher comes, I'll have her taken to the infirmary. If she recovers, you can question her there, Superintendent.'

'Thank you. Mrs Raspin, you must come with me. You will be charged under the 1837 Act which says that anyone intending to procure a miscarriage, who unlawfully uses any instrument —' he looked at the curling tongs — 'shall be guilty of felony. And, if she dies, it'll be murder.'

If anything, she looked sicker than ever. 'I niver meant — I was just —'

'Save it for the magistrate,' Jones said curtly. He took her downstairs. Dickens watched her as she stood in her neat parlour, gazing at her sofa, her chairs, her two china shepherdesses on the mantelpiece and the waxen cherubs under domes like little cupping glasses. They looked like miniature dead babies. Perhaps she thought that they might offer the consolation of angelic resurrection to the bereft mothers.

Jones took Dickens into the hall. 'She confessed. I'll have to find a constable — keep your eye on her. I'll want someone to take her to Bow Street. Then we must go to that chop house — it's nearly time. When the doctor comes down, tell him I'll contact him at the workhouse infirmary. I'll be as quick as I can.'

Dickens waited, contemplating the varnished door. *No varnish can hide the grain of the wood.* How true. Plume, for all his fine shirts and expensive coats, was a sordid seducer, and this house with its pretty parlour, was a sink of vice.

The nurse came, and two men with a stretcher. In a while, they came down again with the patient.

Doctor Fuller stopped to say goodbye to Dickens, who gave him Jones's message.

'A bad old woman,' Fuller observed.

'Will she live?'

'If blood poisoning doesn't set in, there might be a chance. I can't say. You can't blame the girl — not married, I daresay. No one to turn to. The father nowhere to be found — he'll know that there's no law that could have made him responsible. Thanks to the New Poor Law — but, you've said your bit on that, Mr Dickens. I read your piece in May about the Itch Ward Nurse at the workhouse.'

Dickens had entitled his article *A Walk in the Workhouse* and had described the nurse's grief when a little child she had looked after had died. The dropped child, she'd called it, because it had been found in the street.

'Perhaps children wouldn't be dropped in the street or young women butchered if the law made fathers responsible — as it used to.'

'No, indeed,' Dickens replied. 'I've heard of three cases now — one young woman missing, one dead, and this poor girl.'

'Missing?'

'A girl called Kitty Quillian — you've not heard the name?'

'No, but I'll ask about. We have plenty of Irish girls in the workhouse. You never know.'

'If you hear anything, send to the Superintendent at Bow Street.'

'I will, and I'll go now to see what I can do about my patient. Good day, Mr Dickens.'

Dickens watched him go. A decent man — and a caring one. There were as many as three hundred patients, he knew, in the Workhouse Infirmary. Fifty pounds a year in salary and he had to pay for medicines. So much did the Poor Law Guardians care for their charges. And that nurse — a pretty young woman. Good people. To set against the bad old woman within. He heard her crying. For her lost cherubs, he'd bet, and her china ornaments. Bah! Humbug!

He heard the sound of a cab. Jones jumped out, followed by a uniformed constable to whom he had already given instructions to take Mrs Raspin to Bow Street. The constable was to speak to Inspector Grove and the woman installed in a cell.

Mrs Raspin was allowed to put on her bonnet and cape, and, unaccountably, she took an umbrella from the stand in the hall. It wasn't raining. *Mrs Gamp*, thought Dickens, watching the dumpy figure totter down the steps. The constable helped her into the cab, and away she went to her cell.

Jones went upstairs again to speak to the servant. He did not suppose she was any more than a wretched instrument of Mrs Raspin — she had looked about fourteen. But the room was empty. An open window showed an iron staircase leading down to a yard, the door of which was ajar. *Poor kid*, he thought, hoping she had a home to go to. He didn't even know her name.

He came down the stairs. 'We must hurry, Charles — it's been more than an hour. Let's get to that chop house — and quick.'

21: Until Death Us Do Part

In the safe darkness of the closed carriage, Mrs Jocelyn Cartwright listened to the story of 'Patsy Molloy' and her baby. Patsy was, of course, a good girl — Martha Brimstone could vouch for that — her bein' as much as a ma to her as ever Patsy had. A good girl, seduced by a young man of means — in the bankin' way, it seemed. Good family. Handsome, too.

Good, thought Mr Eldred Cartwright, looking down involuntarily at the sleeping baby, though he couldn't see much of it in the dark. Good blood. The fact that the entirely fictitious father might have been a debauched young man whose blood was as bad as could be was an irony that escaped him. A good family mattered.

Patsy was Irish and Catholic, continued Mrs Brimstone, warming to her theme. She did not hold with fiction — unless, of course, the tale was of her own devising.

Irish and Catholic — not so good, reflected Eldred whose Anglo Saxon name was a source of pride — it had been his father's and grandfather's. It meant "wise counsel". Whether it was wise to be here at all, he had wondered, but, a son — to be called Eldred, too. He hoped the child wouldn't look Irish. He thought about asking the woman what the father looked like, but thought better of it. No one need know.

The rusty whisper went on. Poor Patsy had died as she had lived, friendless and alone — well, except for Martha Brimstone who had, out of the goodness of her heart, taken her in.

Get on with it, you old witch, Eldred thought, but he saw in the shadows how the set of his wife's head showed her listening intently. He stilled his impatient foot.

Patsy's last words were repeated — how she'd begged Martha Brimstone to find a good family who would love and cherish the child, and how she'd be glad that Mrs Cartwright was the woman — p'raps she knew already — you never knew, did you, what went on in heaven?

That was enough for Eldred Cartwright. He was a man of the world, read the papers, knew what Martha Brimstone was. His voice was curt like a blade in the darkness.

'Your payment?'

Martha Brimstone was unmoved by his sharpness, but she took the hint without changing her tone. Take no chances — concentrate on the wife. She wouldn't change her mind.

There had been Patsy's funeral to pay for, the wet nurse for the baby and the clothes. Little Billie Quillian had been carefully dressed by Mrs Brimstone — good investment, she'd told Arthur. And it was. Mrs Cartwright had noted the frills and spotless linen in the brief flaring of the Lucifer match held by her husband, which had illuminated the child's sleeping face. Her son — hers — at last.

Money changed hands — fifty guineas. Mrs Brimstone liked the sound of guineas — *more professional*, she thought.

Little Billie Quillian was taken away to a house in France where he would be born again as Basil Archibald Cartwright, who would, in due course, come into his inheritance. In the event, Eldred Cartwright could not give his name to the child — neither could he love him. But, he died when the boy was five — and Mrs Cartwright had enough love for a regiment of parents.

He would never know that his auburn hair and brown eyes came from his mother. Fortunately, Jocelyn Cartwright had brown eyes. The auburn hair, she said, came from her dead cousin Archie who had been a Fraser, family legend had it, from the Highlands of Scotland.

He would never know — no one yet did, except the murderer — that Kitty Quillian lay dead in an unused privy behind a house in a wretched alley off East Street. She lay where she had fallen, her head stove in, her right eye destroyed, her head split by some blunt object. Blood had poured inside her skull, drowning her brain. She had died within minutes. One amber eye was open, looking up to the pitiless stars.

Martha Brimstone hurried into Euston Station. Arthur was to meet her by W.H. Smith's bookstall. She was surprised that he wasn't there. If he had come straight from Montague Square, he should have been waiting for her. She'd told him to get a cab. Twenty minutes, surely, at the most. The Cartwrights' carriage had come quickly enough — she'd been standing by the porch of St Pancras. How long had she been with them? That didn't matter. Arthur should be here. Surely the fool hadn't gone back to the house.

She scanned the faces sweeping into the Great Hall from the portico outside. The place was crowded. No use lookin'. He knew where to find her — if he was comin'. She thought about that. Arthur was easy to read. He was a worrier — always had been. But — and that gave her a sudden, nervous feeling — Plume's murder had shaken him for some reason. He had been badly frightened when the police came — afterwards, she'd told him it wasn't anything to do with them. And, they'd taken that girl away — so why worry? Arthur had remarked that such a skinny, silent creature couldn't have done it. Not to do with us, she'd told him — again and again.

He wasn't coming. She knew it. She'd waited — an hour. Time to go. There was a train to Manchester at nine o'clock — the last one. And she was going. She'd plenty of money and somewhere to go. Amelia Hodson was living in Chorlton with cousin Lizzie Josser. Time to go, Amelia Hodson had said after the murder of Doctor Plume. They didn't want police askin' too many questions. Think about it, Martha, we could start a nice little business up there — you and me.

And Martha had thought about it. She had made her plans. When the arrangement had fallen through over the last baby, she'd thought then that it might be worth moving on. But when Kitty left her baby behind, she'd thought about the money — fifty guineas, a nice little nest egg worth waitin' for. There was plenty in the bank, too.

If Mr Dickens had asked the question he always asked about his characters: *What's his motive?* The answer would be simple. Money. Born greedy she was. She wouldn't have killed for it. In a way, she was worse than that — she just didn't care for any living thing.

The house was clean. Rent paid for the next month. The landlord couldn't complain. She'd told him they were goin' away for a while — Arthur's health. Kitty's stuff sold as well as some of hers and Arthur's. The few bits she wanted in the carpet bag at her side.

She went to the booking office. She bought a first class ticket to Manchester. Might as well travel in style.

22: A Long Black Nose

At Bow Street, Jones's office seemed a bit crowded. Dickens sat on the desk, Stemp and Rogers took the two straight-backed chairs, and Jones stood by a fire of rather miserable coals. Brandy and warm, Dickens had said, darting into his office at Wellington Street to get a bottle of brandy, and now they felt the benefit of it — warmer than the fire, at any rate.

Scrap was looking at the feeble flames while he sipped his drink. The rest were waiting. Scrap had been found by Stemp, coming at a run from the alleys that led off Dab Lane. Rogers had met them at the chop house — he, too, had experienced the eeriness of those alleys. As he had observed trenchantly to Stemp, 'Give me the creeps, I'll tell you.'

Dickens and Jones had been mightily relieved to find Scrap unscathed, if somewhat subdued. Back to Bow Street, Jones had decided. He wanted to question Mrs Raspin — though she would keep for a while. *Let her stew*, he thought grimly. First he wanted to hear Scrap's tale for, he thought, seeing something curiously sombre in those eyes which usually sparkled with confidence, *there was a story to be told*.

'I dint find the boy, Mr Jones, but I found some Italians — livin' in Beggar's Lane. I asked 'em if they knowed of Joe Seppy. I think they did, but they don't speak much English. Jabbered a lot, they did, 'ands flappin' an' that — all talkin' at once. Got the impression they woz frightened.'

'What kept you so long? Constable Stemp was worried about you.' Jones's tone was mild, but he wondered about the expression in Scrap's eyes — something had happened, other than his discovery of the Italian family.

Scrap looked at Stemp. 'Sorry about that — I woz follered. Dint see no one, but I knowed it.'

'How?' asked Jones.

Scrap thought. 'Felt it — yer knows. Yer senses someone — a footstep, p'raps, a sound o' somethin'. Yer looks back, but nothin' ter see. But, 'e's there. An' it's queer, Mr Jones, there ain't no one about — not like the Dials — dead quiet — as if folk are hidin' indoors. I dunno — it's 'ard to explain.'

'Just wot I felt,' Stemp offered.

'Any idea who followed you?'

'There was a lad — in Bones Alley. 'Ard case — black eyes. Nasty look in 'em. Dint trust 'im, some'ow.'

Dickens looked at Jones. *Jimmy Brady*, they both thought. 'I think we met him,' Jones said, 'and you're right — a nasty piece of work. Go on.'

'Well, 'e told me about Beggar's Lane and them Italians. Said 'e 'adn't 'eard the name Joe Seppy, but I don't know. Picked up a brick so I went off. Anyway, I went ter see if I could find Beggar's Lane. Met a woman an' a little girl — queer-lookin' like she was only 'alf there. I dunno — jest — innocent — some'ow.'

May Brady, Dickens thought. He wasn't surprised. Scrap was a perceptive reader of human nature. Some sense, he had, about people. Intuition. He thought of how Scrap had tried to comfort Eleanor Brim after her father's death. Scrap saw into people, and he felt for them. He thought about the difference between Scrap and Jimmy Brady — and why Jimmy Brady might have followed Scrap.

Scrap continued his tale. 'The woman told me where Beggar's Lane was. She said it was dangerous down there — told me to be careful. While she was talkin', I saw the lad across the street. An' she saw 'im, too. Then she hurried off an'

I went down the alley. I dint see 'im, but I knew 'e was there. I lost meself, tryin' ter shake im off, yer knows. Dint know where I was. That many twists and turns, but I found Beggar's Lane. When I came out o' the Italians' place, I thought —' he stopped again, and Jones saw how his eyes took on that unusual darkness.

'What?'

'It's 'ard ter say, Mr Jones. I dunno wot I saw, really.'

'Not the lad?'

'Nah, it wasn't 'im — it was a sort o' figure — it woz dark down in them alleys — jest a bit of a gaslight, an' I saw a shape, but the thing wot scared me woz that when it turned my way, I saw jest a nose — a long black nose — then it was gone —'

Scrap paused as they all heard Stemp's quick breath. 'Wot I saw, sir.'

'So you did, Stemp — and whatever, or whoever it is, may account for the fact that there's no one about. Not a ghost, I'll bet — someone up to no good. What then, Scrap?'

'I ducked into a doorway, an' I waited — I thought the lad might think I'd gone, an' then I thought I'd make a run for it. Dint know which way I woz goin, neither, but I met Mr Stemp — an' that's it, really — 'cept, there's somethin' wrong in that place, Mr Jones. Wot about that Italian boy?'

'I'm sure you're right, Scrap. And we need to find him. But not tonight. In daylight. There might be people about then. And we can ask questions. Rogers can take you back to the stationery shop, now — you've done enough for one day.'

Scrap looked up at Jones, a challenge in his eyes, 'I'd rather go ter Norfolk Street if yer don't mind. Mrs Jones'll wanter know.'

Jones nodded and Dickens saw him smiling at the boy — some secret understanding they shared. *The cherishing of Elizabeth Jones, that was it*, he thought. Something lovely to set against all this darkness.

'Right — tell her —'

'We're awright — nothin' ter worry about.'

'A cab, then, Scrap — it can drop Mr Rogers at Crown Street. Mollie will want to know that all's well, too. Alf, I'd like you to go to Mrs Brady's in Bones Alley in the morning. Ask about Kitty Quillian and see if you can find out about her son. The boy you met, Scrap, I think he's a lad called Jimmy Brady. Stemp, you can go back to The Neptune tonight. Just keep your ears open. We'll meet you at the chop house at 12.30 tomorrow. I'll need to get to court with Mrs Raspin — I want her out of our way. Scrap, you meet us at the chop house, too — you can show us the way to the Italians' house.'

Scrap went out with Rogers and Stemp.

'How's your Italian?' Jones asked Dickens.

'Good enough, I think. Shall I come here to meet you before you go to the chop house?'

'Yes. In the meantime, would you care to sit in while I question Mother Hubbard?'

Mrs Raspin sat in her cell, wearing her respectable black coat and bonnet, and clutching her umbrella. She looked like a woman waiting for a train, a perfectly ordinary middle-aged woman who had nothing on her conscience but a few sharp words, perhaps, to a little servant or to an ordinarily irritating husband.

She looked up at Jones. Dickens saw that her fright had passed — there was a calculating look in the little, hard eyes. *Goat's eyes*, he thought, yellowish, with a curious black line across the pupil. He suspected that she had one of those adaptable natures — she'd make the best of it. In prison, she'd work her way up to wardswoman or the prison hospital, where she would jolly along the female patients with common sense and handy tips.

But Jones was speaking. Dickens made himself concentrate.

Jones had seen her eyes, too. Time to give her a bit of a jolt, take her by surprise. And he needed to know if their suspicions about Kitty Quillian's child were right.

'Kitty Quillian's baby — where is it?'

She was surprised into the truth which was never her first instinct. 'At the Brimstones' house.'

'I know that. I want to know what they've done to Kitty and what is to happen to the baby.'

'I don't know what's 'appened to Kitty. Martha Brimstone said she'd gone — left 'em 'oldin' the baby —' she attempted a chuckle, but seeing Jones's face, decided against it. 'Martha said she'd gone off with a fancy man —'

Jones glanced at Dickens. Martha Brimstone hadn't told them that, but then she'd tell a different story to whoever was listening — she was clever enough. Still, it was worth pursuing.

'What man? Or just gossip? The truth, if you please. Lying won't reduce your sentence. You look stout enough for a transport ship.' It was unlikely she'd be transported, but she didn't know that. She flinched and Jones saw that he'd hit home.

'Someone give 'er that baby — an' she 'ad money to pay Martha Brimstone. An' I saw 'er meself with 'im — a gent.'

'Describe him.'

'Only saw 'em once — I can't remember much.'

'Try.' Jones was implacable, his voice iron.

'Tallish, spectacles, big 'at, dark coat — that's all I can remember. It's the truth, sir.'

Another fleeting glimpse of the man in the dark hat and coat — *a shadow*, thought Dickens, darkening all before it, a silent something, a muffled human shape, passing under a gas lamp behind Plume's house. And in the alleys, perhaps, seen by Scrap and Stemp.

'When?'

'Week or two ago — I dunno, sir, but I thought that she musta gone with 'im like Martha said.'

'And the child — what are Martha Brimstone's intentions? You must know.'

'Mrs Brimstone wanted a baby, sir, for a rich lady — don't know who. I —' she broke off, understanding that she must incriminate herself.

'Your part in this?'

'There was a girl 'ad a baby — couldn't keep it so I was ter give —'

'Give?' Jones was contemptuous.

'I was ter — ter arrange fer Mrs Brimstone ter tek it ter the lady, but the baby died so I think Martha'll give —'

'I think you mean sell, as you were going to sell the baby that died — buying and selling babies, abortion — that's your trade, is it not, Mrs Raspin?'

She had to admit it and she had to tell the frightening policeman everything. It all came out, water out of a tap you couldn't turn off. She couldn't stop herself. She told them about Doctor Plume and how Mrs Amelia Hodson, who was his fancy woman, employed her to assist in the abortions, and how, when he wasn't there, she and Mrs Hodson managed it themselves, and how she delivered the babies of young women who were accommodated with her or Mrs Brimstone, and given a percentage of the fee to be paid by those who adopted the babies. Good 'omes, they went ter, she tried to justify herself. No 'arm done.

'Evie Finch.' Jones leapt on her last words. 'No harm, eh?'

'Said she was goin' 'ome — told 'er ter stay, but she wouldn't. What was I supposed ter do? 'Eadstrong that one.'

There was nothing more to be said. They knew enough — not that they hadn't guessed it all. They left her, sitting on the rough cot in the cell. When Dickens looked back, he saw that she still held on to her umbrella, waiting for the train that would never come. A police van would take her to Newgate where she would wait for her trial. And they must find the man in the dark coat so that Miranda Deverall could be brought out of Newgate into the light.

23: A Shadow As Yet

'Soup?' Jones asked, peering into a pan on the kitchen range.

'An honest and stout soup, it smells to me — rice and barley, perhaps?' Dickens suggested.

Jones tasted what was on the spoon in his hand. 'You're right — it tastes very good, too.'

'Then I will — it might put some heart into us.'

'And fresh bread, and a nice bottle of claret here, I see.'

Jones brought over the bowls of soup and Dickens cut the slices of bread.

'There now, we look compact and comfortable, as the father said ven he cut his boy's head off, to cure him o' squintin.'

'Thank you, Mr Weller, I'm obliged,' Jones said, raising his glass to his guest.

They had walked from Bow Street to Jones's house in Norfolk Street. A light supper, Jones had offered — before they discussed the case.

'Or cases,' Jones observed when they had finished the soup. 'There are separate matters here, I think. Raspin, Brimstone and Mrs Amelia Hodson are all connected by the trade in abortion and live babies. And Plume was in it, too. But I don't think any of them killed him — they fed off him. We've got Raspin, Plume is dead, Hardacre will find Hodson, I'm sure, and we can go back to Mrs Brimstone's now we have the evidence from Mrs Raspin. We can close down their operation, at least. And that leaves us clear to pursue the murder of Plume.'

'The stranger in the low-crowned hat seen by Lawson in the alley and seen with Kitty Quillian, and by me with the Italian boy. What do we make of that?'

'Well, the stranger is seen at Plume's — Plume dies. The stranger is seen with Kitty Quillian — she vanishes. He is seen by you with the Italian boy — the boy disappears. That's what worries me.'

'It answers my question as to what Kitty was doing in the alley after Miranda Deverall had left the house. She was waiting for him — because she knew him.'

'Very likely, but we don't know him — that's our problem. I sent Inspector Grove to the houses of the patients whose names we found in the records. I hadn't time to tell you.'

'What did he find?'

'Miss Emily Dixon's mother is a widow living with two unmarried daughters. The brother is a clergyman living in Devon with his wife and six children. In fact, Mrs Dixon and her daughters were just back from Devon themselves. Mrs Sarah Wilkinson's husband has married again.'

'The funeral baked meats —'

'Exactly — he married six months after his wife's death. He had no complaints about Doctor Plume's treatment of his wife. She died of a heart attack — nothing to do with the doctor. She was a frail woman, apparently, always ailing, weak heart which killed her.'

'I wonder — convenient for him if he had someone else lined up.'

'Grove was suspicious, but since the matter has no bearing —'

'What if he killed Plume because Plume knew he wanted his wife dead? What if — I see it, Horatio, in my mind's eye — what if Plume arranged it —' Dickens was off in pursuit of murderous Mr Wilkinson, a gentleman who, if not entirely innocent of a certain relief at his wife's death, had not, in fact murdered Plume, though it might be argued that Plume's overlarge prescriptions of morphine had killed her. It hadn't suited Mr Wilkinson to ask too many questions. Besides, the young and lovely Selina Dean was waiting.

'He was on his honeymoon at the time of Plume's murder. Sorry to disappoint you.'

'I had it wrapped up then, Sam — damn the fellow. Honeymoon, indeed. Where, I'd like to know.'

'Paris, I'm afraid.'

'I might have guessed.'

They drank their wine in silence for a while until Dickens spoke up again. 'Motive? What's his motive?'

Jones thought. 'I don't know. Money? Did Plume have debts? Gambler?'

'I wonder he had the time — he seems to have been very busy with his assortment of patients. Someone he knew something about? Someone to whom he was a danger? Someone whose good name he could injure?'

'Plume the blackmailer — to add to his other sins. What else?'

'Jealousy, perhaps — some woman he'd betrayed, or some man —'

'Something in the past, maybe. Suppose our dark stranger is from Plume's past — about which, I may say, we know nothing. I should have gone back to Mrs Plume. Well, I shall. There must be someone who can tell us about him — even if his wife isn't yet fit to speak. Solicitor, maybe.'

'The past — it never goes away, Sam. It's always there, behind, or in front of you like your shadow or the shadow of your shadow, creeping silently with you like a thief in the night

— like our murderer. I think of him shadowing that poor boy and Kitty Quillian.'

'Plume had a secret life, we know that. Suppose there was some secret in his past, something or someone he thought he had left behind.'

'Someone with a grudge — someone who hated Plume for something he had done. Someone who got to know Kitty Quillian.'

'Someone who offered her money.'

'I assume so —'

'My God — that's it. That's what Elizabeth said.'

'When? What did she say?' Dickens was baffled.

'When she was telling us what Miranda Deverall had told her about Kitty Quillian and the night of the murder, I asked her if Kitty Quillian went with her, and Elizabeth said "I assume so" because the maid recognised Kitty, but, and I'd forgotten this detail because it didn't seem important at the time, Billie Watts told Rogers that the Plume's maid saw Kitty Quillian — on the other side of the road. She didn't see her with Miranda.'

'So, what if?' Dickens thought for a bit. 'What if she went there on behalf of the murderer to find out if Plume was in and saw that Miranda was there? Our stranger is round the back. Kitty goes to tell him, tells him about Miranda. They wait, see Miranda come out. Our man goes in. Kitty waits for him and off they go.'

'Then Kitty learns about the murder and Miranda's arrest. He'd realise she knew so —'

'You think she's dead?'

'She had a child — she wouldn't have just left it. Think about it. We think it must be Plume's child. If so, why wasn't she persuaded to get rid of the child? She must have wanted it — she left Mrs Hodson's. She lodged with the Brimstones — they

176

knew Mrs Hodson. Why didn't she go elsewhere? And where did her money come from?'

Dickens thought about the questions. 'Suppose the child wasn't Plume's. It makes sense. Plume would have made her abort the child. He's done it twice before — at least — Lavinia Gray and Miranda Deverall. Why should Kitty be different? Because there was someone else — someone who supported her and her child.'

'Mrs Brimstone might know, or Mrs Brady. I'll get Rogers to go to the Brimstone house before he goes to Mrs Brady's. In fact, I'll send Feak as well. The two of them can get some answers. Mrs Brimstone told Raspin that Kitty had gone off with her "fancy man", so she knew about him. And I want to know what she knew.'

'He'll be easier to crack — the husband. He looked very shifty to me, frightened of something — and not just his wife.'

'Good idea — Rogers and Feak can bring them to Bow Street — interview them separately.'

'And the boy?'

'I can't help thinking of your seeing him in the street — that was days ago. He wouldn't keep him alive.'

'Unless the boy got away — he might have done. Our man couldn't have taken him off the street without a struggle. There were people about. In any case, the boy would have known him if he was in the alley that night — surely, he'd have run away.'

'He might. I hope…' But Jones didn't sound very hopeful as he stared into his empty glass. 'Perhaps he's still about those alleys — and that's another thing. All that talk of Satan. Something criminal going on there, but I'll pass all that on to Goss. It's his patch. We'll have a word with that Italian family — they might know something about the boy.'

'We'll go to the alleys at 12.30?'

'Yes, but I must go to Plume's house first. You might come with me — observe. You could be a lawyer for Miranda Deverall.'

'I've a very convincing false beard — and a wig, if you like. My own mother wouldn't know me.'

Jones laughed. 'I was thinking more of a dark suit and spectacles — something simple that would prevent her from recognising you. I don't want to complicate the matter by having Charles Dickens with me.'

'It shall be done — not even a moustache — a small one? I had one in Italy — glorious it was, trimmed at the ends. Very shapely and charming.'

'I'm sure it was, but no, if you please — I don't want to spend my time worrying that your moustache might fall off.'

'No faith, Samivel, you're a disappointment to me. However, I shall go home and find me a suitable suit and spectacles.'

They stood at the door, looking out at the fog descending. The opposite side of the street was fading away and the gaslight looked green and eerie. *Jones looked weary*, Dickens thought. 'Worried?'

'In a fog, that's what I feel, Charles. Suppose this, suppose that — I'm like a man stumbling around in the fog, reaching for something to hold on to, only to find that the thing has vanished. I don't want to fail —'

'We'll not fail,' Dickens said with more confidence than he felt. Lady Macbeth had failed for all her vaunting words. 'Tomorrow then.'

Dickens went home. The house was quiet. *Bed*, he thought. He would sleep in the dressing room. No sense in disturbing Catherine. He hoped she would be asleep. She had not seemed well since the birth of Dora, born in August 1850. Catherine complained of headaches and sickness, and she was nervous and unwilling to stay at other houses. The baby, too, was delicate. Poor little Dora, whom he had named in honour of Dora Spenlow in *David Copperfield*. Thank goodness for Georgy. Georgina Hogarth was Catherine's sister who had lived with them for eight years, taking over the running of the household from Catherine. He could count on her good sense and loyalty.

He went upstairs. Halfway up he felt a sudden weakness, a kind of giddiness overtook him so that he sat down on the stair, listening to the silent house, strange in the dark. Stillness and solitude. *Something awful*, he always thought, *in being surrounded by familiar faces asleep — in the knowledge that those who are dearest to us and to whom we are dearest, are profoundly unconscious of us.* He listened to the ticking of the clock in the hall. Time going on. Time ticking on for Miranda Deverall, whose trial would come on soon, and who had every reason, a jury might find, for murdering Plume, unless the murderer be found.

He thought of Sam in the doorway of his house, peering into the fog, looking for the answer. Sam, who was never afraid, who looked the world in the eye, whose face had nothing to hide, but showed himself exactly as he was, every inch of him an honest man. They were alike, he and Sam, wanting to make sense of things, wanting to create order, to see justice done, to put things right. In a novel, the writer could put things right — the lovers could be united, the child could find its home, the parent could find the child, the wrong-doer could be punished, the murderer brought to justice.

And murder's a tale, he thought. Its beginning lay in the early chapters of Plume's life, perhaps. But the ending was, as yet, unwritten. And the characters' destinies were obscure. Miranda, Kitty Quillian and the Italian boy. He had said to Sam that the boy might have run from the man in the dark coat. Joe Seppy, as Scrap had said. Guiseppe. That led him to Guiseppe Mazzini, the Italian politician. He wondered about the Italian school in Clerkenwell. It would be worth asking there — Dickens had visited the school with John Forster. Mazzini, who had established the school, had taken them. Mazzini was back in Italy now, but Dickens knew James Stanfield, the brewery owner who was looking after the school. He would go there after he had been to Mrs Plume's with Sam. There was a chance, perhaps.

24: Written in Blood

Bertha Raspin was on remand in Newgate, her case having been heard by the Bow Street magistrate, who was satisfied with Jones's evidence that she had committed an indictable offence. Doctor Fuller had sent word that the girl he had taken to the infirmary had died. When Jones had dealt with that, he went back to the police station to meet Dickens. They were to go to Mrs Plume's. It was time to find out about the doctor's past.

Dickens was waiting in Jones's office. In his spectacles, his hair smoothed down with bear's grease, and wearing a long black coat, he looked, Jones thought, like a particularly unctuous undertaker. He saw, too, the neat moustache. Dickens had not been able to resist. Jones wasn't surprised, though he raised his eyebrows.

'Nothing shall move it except that I be torn to pieces by some whirlwind.'

'You're sure it won't come off in the rain?' Jones glanced towards the window where the rain ran down the panes.

'Sammy, Sammy, you speak to the man who has taken theatres by storm, wearing mustachios which would not have disgraced Don Quixote. And have they fallen? Never. A dot of spirit gum and the thing is safe.'

'I believe you, and, despite your looking to me very like an undertaker, you'll do very well. Just keep in the background.'

'Dumb as a drum with a hole in it — from this time forth I never shall speak word as Iago said when he was asked why he had ensnared Othello. Though, I did want to tell you a thought I had about the Italian boy. I —' Before he could begin, the door opened to reveal Constable Feak who was to have accompanied Sergeant Rogers to bring the Brimstones to the station. He looked like a man who had come in a hurry.

'Feak — I thought you were at the Brimstone house. Something happened?'

'We went there. No one answered the door so we went round the back and found a body.'

Kitty Quillian? Dickens thought.

'Man or woman?' Jones asked.

'Man, sir — stabbed.'

On the way out, Jones called Inspector Grove and two constables, Semple and Johnson, to come with them to the Brimstone house.

A ten minute cab ride brought them to Dab Lane, where they stood in the rain looking down at the corpse of Arthur Brimstone who lay on the flagstones, his eyes staring up at the louring clouds, and his shirt front stained with blood. His face was bruised and there was blood on his mouth. His coat was half off and wet; his hat had fallen some distance away and there was a case that looked like a medicine bag, which looked as if it had been flung away. Little bottles had smashed from which the sweetish smell of cordials spilled. Some wooden boxes had been toppled over. It looked as though a struggle had taken place. Arthur Brimstone had lost the fight.

'No sign of his wife?' Jones asked Rogers.

'No, sir. I went in, but there's no one there.'

'No sign of a child or a young woman?'

'No, sir, the house is empty.'

Jones turned back to the body. 'Turn him over, will you, Feak.'

Feak did so and they saw that underneath the body the ground was dry.

'It rained in the night,' Dickens said. 'I heard it — about midnight.'

'So, he was killed before then.'

'Door was open, sir, and the key on the floor at the bottom of the steps. Perhaps he was locking the door when he was attacked. His back to the murderer. He turned round, they fought and Brimstone was stabbed in the chest.'

'Hm — someone came in from outside. Not his wife — the evidence of a fight suggests a man. Brimstone knew Plume — perhaps he knew Plume's murderer. Brimstone was stabbed — a link to Plume's death. It could be that the killer of Plume is the killer of Brimstone. That'll be our thinking until evidence proves otherwise. But, we need to find the wife. Feak, you'll go back to Bow Street for the mortuary van. Grove, I'll need you to ask the neighbours, find out where Mrs Brimstone might be. Take Semple with you. Rogers, Johnson, you stay here with the body.'

Dickens examined the broken bottles. The handwriting on the labels was familiar as were the names: tincture of opium, morphine, savin pills. He picked up a bottle and showed it to Jones. 'He was deep in it. He supplied Plume.'

'Made up to his own recipes.'

'Or Plume's, perhaps — a little more opium and a little less water.'

Semple who was standing by the door from the alley to the yard, spoke up. 'There's blood here, sir, on the door — handprint, sir.'

Jones went over to look. There on the inside of the door was the clearly discernible print of a hand. Not likely Brimstone's blood, he thought, looking back at the body which lay at some distance from the door. It could be the murderer's. He might have been injured in the fight.

'Semple, have a look down the alley — see if there's any more blood — our man might have been injured. Rogers, you go with him.'

Dickens came over to look at the mark. It was large enough, he thought, to be a man's hand. That was something. He was real: that spectral black figure he had seen bending over the Italian boy. His signature. Written in blood.

'He's real, then,' he observed to Jones.

'I think he is, but where is he — that's the question.'

Semple shouted out, and Jones, Dickens and Grove went out into the alley, leaving Johnson and Feak to guard the body. Semple was looking at another handprint on the wall. It looked as if the murderer had leant there for a moment.

'Injured, do you think?' asked Dickens.

They walked further along and they saw at intervals the handprints. He had been resting then moving on. They came to the end of the alley which then turned into another. There was another handprint on a door which was ajar. They went into a yard to find themselves at the back of a house. The door was open. There was no sound at all, only their breathing. Jones looked up. There was no light, just a few broken windows. That didn't mean the house was uninhabited. People lived in worse places. Jones pointed, telling Semple and Dickens to stay at the door of the yard and indicated to Grove that he should take out his wooden truncheon.

Grove went first, followed by Jones. They were in an old scullery. There was a sink where a tap dripped. Black stains covered most of the distempered walls. They could smell the damp and mildew. There was a rusty bucket with no bottom and a collection of cracked and broken bottles on the floor where the stone flags were damaged and split. But there was blood, a few spots on the floor. They stopped and listened. They heard the tap dripping — one drop at a time. Jones looked in the sink. There was water which had not fully drained away — blocked probably. But he thought that someone had used it recently. And he could see that the water was faintly pink and there were splashes of red on the edge of the sink.

The scullery door was hanging off its hinges. Jones walked on tip-toe to peer into the next room. It was in half darkness, but he could make out the shape of a table and some chairs. But he could not see what was to the left of the door. There was a human smell — the smell of old clothes and sweat — and worse, the smell of excrement and urine. He listened again. Someone was in there — someone was breathing, a regular, rather hoarse, whispering sound. Breathing in. Breathing out. Someone asleep?

He pushed at the door which fell at his touch and crashed to the ground, creating a plume of dust. He picked up a piece of wood as he stepped into the room. Grove was after him in a second with his truncheon.

'Police,' Jones shouted.

At the noise, the man on the rough bed sat up and the sickening stench of an unwashed body and mouldy bed coverings and gin swept at them like a wave of filthy water.

'Holy Mother o' God!' They saw a grimy face framed by a matted thatch of long black hair and a pair of indignant eyes glaring at them. 'Can a man not be left to sleep in peace?'

'Police.'

'Ye don't need to knock the door down. Faith, if an English man's home is his castle, can't a poor Irish man have a miserable feckin door to call his own? And, mebbe ye'd care to open that curtain so's I can have a look at ye.'

An Irish man — no doubt, a rogue, probably a thief, certainly a drunk — but not the murderer, Jones was sure.

'And ye can put that lump o' wood down — no need to murder me as well as frighten me to death.'

Jones felt a bit of a fool, brandishing his piece of wood. He dropped it. And he opened what the man had called the curtain — a ragged affair, dangling from a piece of string. 'We're looking for someone. Someone came here last night — someone with a bloody hand. I want to know about him.'

'Clever, ain't ye. And are ye after payin' for this information?'

'Never mind that. You can tell me now — or at the station.'

The man fumbled around the bed clothes. He found his bottle and took a long swig of whatever it was — the gin, Jones supposed, but he waited. He didn't want to be bothered with taking the man in.

''Tis a terrible thing. A man's willin' to cooperate with the authorities — a poor man an' all, but where's the gratitude? 'Tis the way o' all this miserable world.' He sighed and drank again.

All I need, thought Jones, *a loquacious Irish philosopher.* 'You'll get your bob when you've told me.'

The man took another deep swig. 'Well, what is it ye're wantin' to know?'

'All about him.'

'He came creepin' in here — what time, I can't say. I haven't me time piece about me these days. Dark, though, except for me little candle. I was about to say me prayers to the Blessed Virgin and the Blessed Saint Margaret — herself the patron of the gentlemen of the road. Well, in he comes, the poor divil. Said he'd hurt his hand and could he stay till he was feelin' a bit more like it. To be sure, I didn't mind. Open house, this is.' He gestured to the hole where the door had been, chuckling at his own wit, and took a swig from his bottle.

'So I see,' Jones said drily. 'Go on.'

''Tis all. He came. He went away. Gave us a couple o' bob, mind. Said I should get a good meal and give up the drink. A real gent — two bob for nothing but a sit down, whereas —'

Blood and stones and drawing teeth came into Jones's mind. 'What did he look like?'

'A gent — not a gent of the road, o' course, like meself. Clean except for a bit o' mud. Fell p'raps. Shockin' state o' them streets. Black coat and hat an' a ruddy great cut on his hand.'

'Hat? Spectacles?'

'Black hat — quare thing, that — all muddy like he'd dropped it. Specs — yes, he had.'

'How long did he stay?'

'Don't know. Rainin' when he went. Invited him to stay, o' course, but he wrapped his hand in his handkerchief an' said he had to be off.'

'Did he say where?' Useless question, thought Jones, but he might as well ask.

'No. Just went. Didn't look so good, to be sure. Went out the back the way he came.'

'He didn't give you a name?' One could always hope.

'I introduced me self — Michael O'Malley, I said —'

'Bridie —' The word was out before Jones could stop himself. Not that this could be the Michael O'Malley who was Bridie's husband, last heard of — God knows when. Bridie O'Malley at whose house Jones had lodged all those years ago, and who was still a good friend — despite the fact that her house now was not entirely respectable. Bridie O'Malley who looked after her girls — and an assortment of waifs and strays.

Michael O'Malley was staring at him. It was the eyes that Jones recognised now. Green, so deep that it was like looking down into the sea — the very eyes that Bridie had sworn had ensnared her, though she had known very well what he was. Light-fingered Michael O'Malley who'd left her, giving his emerald eyes to someone else.

'Sammy? Sammy Jones?' Michael O'Malley laughed, a great-hearted, deep laugh, and Jones remembered that, too. 'The divil, it is. Sammy, the policeman. Did you marry her then?'

'Who?'

'Bridie, the light o' my life — but she had a fondness for you, me boy.'

'She was married to you, as I recall, Michael — she wasn't free to marry anyone else.'

'Ah, to be sure, I ought to have told her — you see, Sammy, my lad, although my heart was Bridie's, I didn't like to mention that I'd married before — in Ireland. 'Twas —'

I haven't time for this, Jones thought. Dear Lord, Michael O'Malley and his talk of love and bigamy when he was looking for a murderer.

'Michael, I'll tell you about Bridie another time. I'm looking for a murderer — and you have met him. I need to get you out of here — into lodgings. I'll give you some money, but for God's sake, tell me about the man — did he give his name? Don't give me the full narrative, just tell me.'

'Bedad, a murderer and I —'

'Michael, please.'

'Well, I introduced meself, o' course. Michael O'Malley at your service, says I —' Michael saw Jones's face. 'Then, "Will", he says.'

A name. A name. A cut hand bound in a handkerchief. A low crowned black hat. A black coat. Spectacles glinting in gaslight. He was coming into focus. Jones had seen a daguerreotype being developed. He had seen the image take shape on the silver plate, a man emerging from blankness, blurred to begin with, but finally he was there. "Will." Or was it? 'Michael, are you certain?'

Michael O'Malley screwed up his green eyes and thought. 'Sure, I don't know, Sammy. I thought it was his name, but o' course, you're thinkin' why would a murderer say his name? But, I heard the word "Will" — an' then he said no more — finished wrappin' his hand and went.'

Jones turned to Inspector Grove, who was still standing with his truncheon ready.

'Get Mr Dickens, will you. He can stay with Mr O'Malley while we work out our next moves.' Grove went out. 'Michael, I want you to wait with Mr Dickens. I've got some things to organise.'

'You don't mean —'

'I do, but I can't explain now.'

Dickens came in. Michael O'Malley looked at him. 'Deed, Mithter Dickens, you're not like your picture, sir — I'd a thought you was an undertaker come to measure me up for me coffin.'

Dickens laughed. 'In disguise, sir.' He looked at Jones.

'This is Mr Michael O'Malley —'

'Not —'

'Deed I am, though I'm ashamed to say it. I left a beautiful woman, sir — to me lastin' regret.'

Jones went out to confer with Inspector Grove and Semple. Dickens would have to manage — if he could get a word in.

'Now, Mithter Dickens, I'll tell ye what I think — them tales of yours is very fine things. When I was a readin' man, I did like that tale of Oliver Twist. 'Tis a lesson to us all — and I should know. Too fond I've been of askin' for more —' Dickens thought of interrupting, but it was clear that the critic had not finished — 'an' the Carol — yes, sir, sure we could do with a bit more benevolence in this world. However, I'm bound to be honest with you —'

I'm sure you are, thought Dickens. Some adverse comment was coming — it was usually prefaced by the speaker's earnest resolve to be honest.

'Ye'll not be offended, now —'

'No offence in the world,' Dickens said. He longed to know what truth would be unfolded. Michael O'Malley was not a man to be hurried.

'Well, bein' an Irish man o' the world, a trampin' man, you might say, an adventurer of the road, I'm bound, now, to tell ye, the grandest book of all is — no offence, now —'

'Indeed, no — I am all agog.'

'Barry, sir, Barry Lyndon — *The Luck of Barry Lyndon* — an Irish wanderer like meself. Mr Thackeray had it right there. A grand man and a grand writer, to be sure.'

Dickens couldn't help laughing. What a story for Thackeray — how Charles Dickens met an Irish man in a filthy room who told him that Thackeray had written the best book ever. It made him feel better — something to chuckle over with Thackeray. He still felt uncomfortable when he thought of their conversation about Edward Lawson. More amusing still was the fact that Thackeray didn't much care for the book.

Jones came back. He had sent Grove back to the Brimstone house to make sure that the body had been taken away. Then he and Feak were to question the neighbours, to ask if they had seen or heard anything, to ask about a man who might be called Will. Johnson and Semple were to search the alleys near the empty house for any further trace of the murderer after Semple had taken a message to Stemp at the chop house, telling him to wait with Scrap until he, Rogers and Dickens should join them. It was well after 12.30, the appointed meeting time. But Jones had thought it out. He longed to go to see Mrs Plume, but the murder of Brimstone sharpened his fear about the Italian boy. It might be too late. But they had to try. Mrs Plume would still be there later and she might know something about a man called Will.

He heard Dickens laughing as he went back into the room — that was Michael O' Malley. An incorrigible rogue, but you had to laugh. Bridie O'Malley said that his silver tongue and his eyes were what she had missed.

'I've a murderer to catch, Michael O'Malley. If you've any idea of seeing Bridie, then I suggest you take a bath. There's a bath house just along the New Road opposite Lisson Grove. You know it?'

'I do.'

'Tuppence for a first class hot bath with towels. Get yourself some new clothes from somewhere. Here's a half sovereign. Don't spend it on drink, or Bridie will show you the door. The door is at thirty-three Back Lane, the first left turn off Shorts Gardens, just above Brown Street where the old house was. Do you remember?'

'Engraved on me heart, Sammy. Do ye think I'd forget where Bridie O'Malley, the dream of me life, was livin?'

'Right. Get out of here — you've met a murderer and he might be back. Tell Bridie you saw me.'

'Deed I will, Sammy, and may God give ye a bed in heaven — sure why should he not?'

'I can't think, Michael — let's hope that Bridie'll give you a bed at Back Lane.'

Jones went out. Dickens turned back to Mr O'Malley. 'I'm obliged to you. I'll tell Mr Thackeray what you said about Barry Lyndon.'

'Tell him all the best from an Irish reader. Grand to have met ye, Mithter Dickens, grand.'

They went into the lane and made their way back to the Brimstone house.

'Michael O'Malley — who'd have thought it? I wonder where he sprang from?' said Dickens.

'As your Mr Peggotty would say, I'm gormed. Lord knows and he won't tell us. I wish I'd had time to see Bridie — to warn her, but we've too much to do now.'

'*She'll* be gormed,' Dickens said, grinning.

'She will — not that I want to be there to see it. Let's get off to the chop house to meet Stemp.'

'Not Mrs Plume's?'

'No, we'll have a try at finding that boy. It's not what I wanted — getting dark already, but it's more than urgent now. I'm not hopeful, Charles, after seeing what was done in here.'

They went back into the yard. Arthur Brimstone had been taken away to the mortuary. Rogers and Johnson were waiting for them.

'Rogers, I want you to come with us to the alleys. Let's have a look for that poor Italian lad. Johnson, when Semple comes back, you and he can search these alleys for any trace of our murderer. Name of Will, so Michael O'Malley tells me. Any news, get back to Bow Street — I'll be back later.'

Dickens and Jones stood at the yard door, Jones contemplating the handprint.

'Will?' said Dickens.

'I don't know. Michael O'Malley — fuddled with drink and sleep, I daresay. Perhaps the man was just going to ask a question, as in "Will you tell no one I've been here."'

'He didn't say anything else?'

'No — just went.'

'Then, perhaps he regretted saying his name — wanted to get out of there.'

'Could be — well, they'll ask about. We might have a piece of luck.'

'The luck of the Irish, Sammy Jones, is what's needful — will I ask Michael O'Malley for a piece of shamrock?'

Jones laughed. 'I think I might be avoiding Bridie for a while. What she'll say when she sees him I don't want to think about. Now, let's get on.'

25: Labyrinth

It was after three o'clock and the November dark was descending. You could see the darkness staining the walls of houses, pouring down, creating shadows which unrolled in front of them, pointing the way, leading them on. Their own shadows unfolded, grew monstrous at their sides, strangers to them, sometimes leaning down as if to smother them.

Jones and Scrap led the way, followed by Rogers with his bull's eye lamp. Dickens, then Stemp. They had passed the burial ground as they had gone through Bones Alley, descending some steps, down which Dickens and Jones had seen the crippled boy disappear, and which Jimmy Brady had pointed out to Scrap. It was if they had gone down into the underworld. No light came here. The air was thick and the ground wet. And there was a stench of cess pit. The houses huddled together in the shadow of the taller buildings which imprisoned them.

They moved out of the court into a winding labyrinth of more passages. Scrap stopped at various corners, looking this way and that, getting his bearings. *It was odd*, thought Dickens. Scrap and Stemp had been right about that unearthly quietness. The alleys were narrow and the houses and buildings loomed over so that it was like walking through tunnels. He noted the crazy leaning buildings and patched windows where sometimes a light flickered. Occasionally, a face appeared pressed up against dirty glass, distorted and flattened like a thing from a nightmare. There was a sense of eyes watching, and sometimes, glancing down an offshoot, he thought he saw a shadow darting — some watcher vanishing into the thick darkness.

There was clotting mud beneath their feet and foul vapours seemed to wind round them so that the three figures in front of him seemed to shiver and dissolve, and he hurried forward, terrified of losing them, but reassured by the sound of Stemp's breathing behind him and the little streaks of light that came from Stemp's bull's eye lantern.

Deeper and deeper into blackness they went, turning back on themselves. Sometimes it seemed that they were just going round in circles. Every alley looked the same. Dickens fancied that even the grotesque faces were the same. He looked at a doorway and something looked back — a mask with a horrible long nose. He almost cried out. He looked back for Stemp with his light, but there was no light, only darkness and a sense that something had moved behind him. He looked ahead and thought he saw a figure disappearing round a corner. Rogers, surely. He hurried on, his feet sticking and sliding in the treacherous filth. Follow, follow. Which way?

Stemp kept his eye on Mr Dickens's back. He could see him in the light of his lamp and further ahead were Mr Jones with the lad and Sergeant Rogers. He felt uneasy, though. Somethin' not right. Too quiet. He saw Mr Dickens turn his head and seem to recoil. Then something, a black shape seemed to slide from a doorway. He couldn't see Mr Dickens. He held up the lamp and all the shadows reached for him. He made to hurry forward, his mouth opening to cry a warning.

Too late. He felt the strong hand over his mouth and his arm was wrenched, twisted up his back. He saw the shape in front of him. And the nose. Then it vanished and he was dragged into another tunnel — before he had chance to make any noise.

Rogers thought he heard something. He whipped round. A face, a terrible thing with breath so foul that he jerked his head back. But he felt the nose on his mouth and the breath in his throat. Suffocating. He couldn't make any sound, could hardly breathe. It was forcing him against the wall and down, two hands pressing on his shoulders and still that foul nose in his face. When he was down on his knees, a hand grabbed at his lamp. Then it was gone. Only its rancid breath seemed to hover in the air.

Light extinguished, as if a hand had closed the bull's eye lamp. It was so sudden. Then Jones heard the retching sound and turned. Rogers was down. 'Scrap, stay —' but Scrap was gone.

'Alf, what happened?' Rogers was getting to his feet.

'Dunno — thought I heard something. And then a face came at me — great big nose. Pushed me down — an' took me lamp.'

'Stemp?' Jones looked back down the alley, but there was no sign of Stemp. He looked to the place from which he had come. There was no one, only the fleeting impression that the darkness had stirred, that something black, a cloak, perhaps, had fluttered away, leaving just this deadly stillness and silence behind.

'Mr Dickens, Scrap, where are they?' Rogers squinted into the darkness beyond.

'Vanished like Stemp. What the hell is happening?'

'What'll we do, sir?'

'Stay together, Alf, that's what — wait until we get our bearings. Still got my lamp on my belt.'

Rogers lighted the lamp with a lucifer match struck on sandpaper. At least they could see a bit more now. They walked back down the alley a few paces and saw the narrowest of passages leading off. They looked down into the pitchy black — nothing to be seen.

Rogers thought for a moment. 'Suppose in the dark, Mr Dickens turned down here by mistake — mebbe that thing that came at me got between me an' Mr Dickens an' he turned off — lost his bearings like.'

'Makes sense — what about Stemp? I wonder if the same thing happened. Let's go back a bit, see if there's another passage.'

There was. On the other side of the alley, another narrow passage led into equally pitchy darkness.

'Shall I use my rattle — might bring a constable from his beat.'

'No, I'm thinking we'd better do this quietly — if we bring more police, we don't know what might happen. We might make it even more dangerous for Mr Dickens —'

'And Scrap.'

'That Jimmy Brady is the only person who knew Scrap was looking for the Italian boy. There was something about that lad — something very nasty. Has he a master? Has he told whoever it is?'

'The one they call Satan, sir — sounds like some sort of gangmaster. He'd not want strangers on his patch — mighta guessed we were police.'

'Then they are in danger. Let's have a look down here for Stemp — but we need to be quick. Dear God, Alf, we could do without this — we're supposed to be investigating Plume's murder, not getting caught up with some criminal gang.'

They went down the narrow alley, but there was no sign of Stemp. Jones could only hope that he had simply lost his way, and that he would find his way back to the chop house. He'd know to meet them there. Stemp was tough. Dickens and Scrap were more vulnerable, but he'd bet on Scrap to run for his life — if it were not for Jimmy Brady. Still, Scrap had sharp wits. No, he was most worried about Charles — and he didn't want to think about what might have happened to him.

26: Satan

Lightless like the end of somewhere — life itself. Perhaps the end was just this void, this silence, this darkness so suffocating that it seemed to be crushing him like the clamping on of an iron mask. Tightness in his chest. He wasn't breathing. He turned round. Got to get out. But there was only a blank wall. He looked up but the thick roof of the night pressed down. He turned again, putting out his hands like a sleepwalker. He felt like one who had risen in the night and found himself in a room made strange by the dark.

Dickens peered into the darkness ahead. It seemed to move. It was as if someone behind a stage curtain had parted it to stand suddenly, as if by magic, upon the apron of the stage. Someone was there. He could hear a noise like hissing — a sort of whistle — *s-s-s-s-s*, came the sound. A light leapt up that made darkness visible, and he saw again the mask and the nose. The plague doctor's mask he had seen in Venice once, its wearer flitting through a gloomy archway. Darkness again and that dreadful whistling.

This is hell and I am in it, he thought. *This is the Satan of whom they spoke. Hell to pay. The devil to pay. Am I to sup with the devil? Devilish sharp, then.*

Flames flared up again and another figure stood there. The gleam of a knife. The flames died down to a red glow and he saw that the figure was standing in front of some kind of brazier. By some devilish magic, he had caused the flames to leap up and die down. Beyond the red glow, the figure was still in shadow, but he could see the thin silver of the blade cutting the darkness over and over again. It was like watching the blade being sharpened, and that whistling hiss went on.

The figure came nearer the fire and Dickens could see that it was a gypsyish, young man with a face dyed red by the glow of the coals like the devil in a pantomime. But frightening. He saw the glint of an earring and a jewel flashed on a finger. But there was no sign of injury on either hand. Not Will, then.

'S-s-s-s,' the voice hissed. Then, 'Signor.' It was human. Dickens breathed, he thought, for the first time since he'd seen the mask in the doorway. Italian. No devil, not the murderer — a lad in a pantomime of his own devising. Ask then.

'*Prego* — I —' he struggled to find the words. He'd practised what he was going to say to the Italian family, but now, he could hardly remember — '*cercando* — *un ragazzo, un ragazzo che* —' He wanted to say that the boy played the barrel-organ, but the words wouldn't come. Instead, he just said the name — 'Guiseppe —'

A glitter like lightning. The knife came through the air, the hissing, swishing sound of something wet on hot coals.

Something, someone pulled at him. He felt the knife — it passed like a wind. He heard the thud as it embedded itself in something wooden. He was being dragged into a tunnel.

'Gotter gerrout, Mr D.'

Scrap.

He blundered after the boy into all sorts of ginnels, alleys, tunnels, courts — through the maze. He thought they'd never get out. He didn't know if Scrap knew his way. Perhaps he was just improvising. But he followed, and they ran, skidding on the thick mud, turning round corners into impossibly narrow passages, bouncing off walls; Dickens catching his scarf on a piece of jutting iron, tossing it away; Scrap tripping, falling, scraping his knees, but up again, shaking the water off him;

doubling back when they came to a dead end; stopping for a moment in a broken down doorway; glancing back to see if they were followed; pushing through a door ajar, and finally coming to rest in what seemed like an old stable where they flung themselves into a loose box, where something very large and warm seemed to fill the space. It moved in the dark and they shrank back against the wall, their feet finding straw. And then it let out a low, mooing noise. A cow — just a cow. Dickens could see it looking at them with mildly inquiring eyes.

'Blimey,' Scrap said. 'If it ain't an old cow.'

'Blimey, indeed,' Dickens whispered back, sharing Scrap's relief.

They stayed where they were, crouching by the wall, listening, hoping that no one had followed them. The cow shifted again and they heard its feet on the cobbled floor. But there was no sound of anything human.

'Do you know where we are?' whispered Dickens.

'Not a clue,' Scrap answered.

'Well, we can't stay here all night.'

'Nah, but I don't know which way ter go — don't wanter go back where we came from. Yer coulda bin killed, Mr Dickens.'

'I know — you saved me. In the nick of time. My thanks, Scrap.'

'We're quits now, Mr Dickens — you saved me last time.'

'But how did you come to be there? I don't know what happened. I thought you were all in front then I was somewhere else entirely and Stemp was gone, too.'

'Dunno — lost Mr Jones an' Mr Rogers — it's like they just vanished — creepy it woz. Thought somethin' moved down the alley so I went that way. Thought there woz a light. 'Eard yer speakin' an' then I looked round the wall an' saw the knife. Gawd, Mr Dickens, 'oo woz it?'

'Italian — I asked about the boy and then I saw the knife coming at me. But it's worrying — where are Mr Jones, Mr Rogers and Stemp? They can't have vanished — it's impossible.' He said so, but he felt a chill of terror. Down there in the alleys — like no place he had ever been, and he'd been in plenty of slums. A nightmare place, unreal, a place you fell into from out of the world.

Scrap echoed his thoughts. ''Orrible place, Mr Dickens — like something yer'd dream of, a place where anythin' could 'appen.'

'Well, I think we're out of it now — that cow somehow reassures me.' They looked at the cow and the cow looked back, its warm, low breath like a sigh. 'Just a minute, I'll have a look over this wall.' Dickens peered over. He was looking into another sort of loose box. Two more cows. It was a dairy then. Probably safe to have a look. 'I'm going to have a look round. More cows next door. Wait here.'

Dickens crept out into the yard and followed the line of the old horse boxes where more cows moved restlessly as they sensed him. High up on the wall of a taller building there was a gas lamp and he could make out the words painted on the wall: *Jos. Evans Dairy.* He knew where he was. It was where his milk came from, brought on the cart to Devonshire Terrace. The front of the dairy was off Paradise Street — down a lane where other passages led to the burial ground and Dab Lane. Somehow, they had woven their way to safety. If they turned left when they went out of the yard, they would get into Paradise Street and thence into the busy High Street. What then? He thought of Jones, Rogers and Stemp — and a man with a knife glittering in his hand.

Jones and Rogers turned into the alley down which they thought Dickens must have gone — and Scrap. Jones had stopped just a few paces beyond the opening of the alley. Scrap had been a step behind him. Then the light went out and Scrap had disappeared. He could only have gone down the passage. Jones would have felt it if Scrap had passed in front of him.

The alley seemed to be a dead end. They could see a blank wall ahead, but Rogers saw the little turning which brought them into a yard of some kind where there was a smoking brazier with the embers of a fire glowing in the dark. Behind the brazier they could make out a shed of some sort. They went to look but there was no one there. On the floor there was something black. Jones picked it up. It was mask, black with a long nose.

'What Scrap and Stemp saw, and what came at me,' said Rogers.

'Not a ghost then — whoever's in these alleys, whether they call him Satan or whatever, he's real and he went off in a hurry.'

'With Scrap and Mr Dickens?'

'Maybe not — if he was cool enough to take them, he wouldn't have dropped this, and, why not keep them here? It's secret enough — we wouldn't have found it if we hadn't had a light or if we hadn't been looking for someone. Let's have a look round — I want to be sure that our friend, Will, hasn't been about.'

'You don't think that Will's the one that's hauntin' these alleys?'

'No, I don't — what's going on here is separate, I'm sure, apart from the Italian boy, but I just want to be certain there's no tell-tale blood from his injured hand.'

They made a careful search, but there was nothing to see that suggested that Will had been here.

Jones was satisfied. 'So, let's work our way back like policemen rather than two children lost in the dark. Let's assume that they — or, I admit — one or the other — saw the blank wall here and turned back. We are looking for traces of them going through these alleys — and as quickly as they could. So, we go slowly and we use our eyes.'

They went back the way they came. There was another turning before they got to the end.

Jones looked down the turning. 'Let's suppose they took the first turning — it would be natural. They'd want to get away from the dead end — they'd not want to be trapped.'

And so they went on, picking their way through the refuse and puddles, using the lamp to light up the walls and the ground.

'Look, sir — someone's passed by — look at that mark, as if someone banged against the wall. Looks like the shoulder rubbed against the wall and smeared the mud.'

Jones looked. 'The height tells us it was probably a man — bit smaller than you.'

'Mr Dickens?'

'Let's hope so.'

Rogers shone the light on the ground. Before the mark on the wall, they saw a long print in the mud as though someone had skidded and there was another footprint where the runner had put his right foot down. A man's foot — not a big man. To the right of that print, further away on the other side of the alley was the print of another foot — a boot, this time, a man's boot.

'Two people — two men. It might mean that someone was with Mr Dickens.'

'But, they wouldn't be running, surely,' Jones said. 'And why so far apart? The man on the left here — if it was Mr Dickens — was running free. He skidded in the mud, banged into the wall, righted himself and went on. The one on the other side was too far away to be holding onto a prisoner.'

'But it's not a kid's boot — too big for Scrap.'

Jones had a sudden vision of Scrap sitting in his office by the fire with his feet on the fender — feet in boots too big, boots tied with string that he'd got from Zeb Scruggs. Scrap in the disguise he had been so proud of — plain clothes, he'd said. Let him be safe. He looked again at the boot mark. 'Scrap was wearing a man's boots. I saw them. Let's go on.'

In another alley, they found the scarf, caught on the jutting iron. Jones recognised it, and they saw, further on, the way in which the gravel had been scattered where someone had tripped over a big stone and fallen. Muddy water had been splashed onto the wall. And there were more footprints, signs that two had run together through these alleys.

'They've escaped, surely. There's no sign that they were followed. If they've got out of this maze, they'll have gone to the chop house, surely.'

'Yes, and we've ter get out yet — I still don't know where we are.' Rogers looked about him, shining the light into the blackness ahead.

'No more do I — we'll just have to follow the signs so conveniently left by our friends.'

Threading their way through more twisting alleys, patiently following the signs left by the runners, they eventually found themselves by an open doorway. The lamplight showed a muddy handprint on the door — small, a boy's hand. Dickens had been wearing gloves.

'Scrap?' whispered Rogers.

Inside the yard they saw the old stables where the cows were kept. In the first one, they saw the cow. It sighed again — more visitors. And, they saw that two people had sat in the straw by the wall, but they had gone now. The only sound was the cow's breathing.

Outside in the lane, they looked left. A gas lamp flickered at the corner. Two women hurried by, one with a bundle and the other with a basket. They went down to the ordinary street. Rogers looked up at the sign.

'Paradise Street.'

'So, it is — Paradise, indeed,' said Jones.

Stemp lay still in the foetid cellar to which his attackers had brought him. He could feel the wetness seeping through his jacket — pity he didn't have his uniform coat — but the thin jacket and the canvas waistcoat were his plain clothes, the clothes of a labouring man. One eye was closed and the other seemed so, but through the slit he was aware of the flickering of his lamp held by the boy.

They'd thrown him down some steps. Nothing broken — he hoped. There would be bruises, but he could put up with that. He wondered what they were going to do with him.

There were two — a man and a boy, muffled up to the eyes in scarves. The man had grabbed him from behind and the lad had snatched the lamp. Then they'd dragged him down the alley. He'd not resisted — *more use to Mr Jones alive*, he'd thought. He'd relaxed his body so that when they'd thrown him down the stairs, he'd fallen like a sack of spuds. Then he'd lain quite still — hoping that they'd think him unconscious. When the boy had opened the cellar door, he'd caught a glimpse of two hard, mad eyes, greedy with excitement — the boy wanted to hurt him. *Wicked little sod*, Stemp had thought, but he gave no sign.

A shadow loomed over him, blotting out the light. The figure gave Stemp a kick, and then another.

Stemp didn't move, though he felt each blow. He wasn't an easy man to frighten, but this lad — he was capable of anything. He wondered about the man. The boy picked up a large stone, ready to bring it down on the policeman's head.

'No killin' — for fuck's sake, Jimmy, come away. Yous'll ave the whole feckin' police force down 'ere if you kill 'im — police know you. You said yourself. Come away.'

Irish, thought Stemp — and he caught the name. Jimmy Brady — it must be — the lad Scrap had seen and Superintendent Jones and Mr Dickens. Well, if I live, I'll find 'em again.

'Leave 'im be — sure, you've done enough. If yous wants to please Satan, let's find that Italian kid — Satan wants 'im back.'

Stemp felt the last vicious kick to his head. Sickened, he heard them going up the steps, the key in the lock and then silence. But he couldn't move. The darkness seemed to swim about him as he tried to sit up. He felt himself drifting. Then there was nothing.

27: Conversation with a Philosopher

'See, Mr Dickens…' Between mouthfuls of hot pie, Scrap was responding to Dickens's speculations regarding the whereabouts of Superintendent Jones and Sergeant Rogers. 'Mr Jones'll deal wiv ol' Satan an' 'is knife. See an' Mr Rogers — they'll be tergether an' they'll come 'ere ter find us.'

'I don't doubt you're right,' Dickens answered, feeling, however, more anxious than the sanguine Scrap — those alleys. And Stemp — where was he?

'Mr Jones ain't afraid of nothin' — I seen 'im — villuns is more afraid of 'im. Ol' Satan's got no chance.'

It was true. Dickens had seen all kinds of villains quail before Sam Jones, and in all sorts of miserable cellars and thieves' dens. He had heard the steel in his voice and seen the flint in his eye. And Stemp was tough, too. Nevertheless, he worried about that dark, secret place where eyes watched and shadows flitted in the darkness in which a man might vanish out of the world.

Scrap was speaking again. He seemed to have read Dickens's thoughts. 'Mr Stemp, 'e's tough that one. 'E'll find 'is way — we did, dint we?'

'So we did.'

'Eat yer pie, Mr Dickens — gotter keep yer strength up.'

Dickens obeyed, laughing inwardly. It wasn't bad, either.

'I wouldn't mind…' Scrap began. He stopped and ate another mouthful of pie. Dickens waited. Scrap looked at his plate. 'I wouldn't mind bein' a policeman — later o' course when I'm older.'

And a bit bigger, Dickens thought. He looked at Scrap. He was bigger than he had been — good food, light and air did it — but he was still small in stature for his age. He'd be about twelve, he supposed. 'You would?'

'Plain clothes, o' course — I'd like ter be one o' them detective perlice. I could work fer Mr Jones, I daresay — jest as I does now, but mebbe I could get ter be a sergeant like Mr Rogers. Excitin' life.'

'You might need to go to school, perhaps.'

'Don't fancy it, Mr Dickens — Mrs Jones is teachin' me. That's enough, I reckon. Did yer go ter school yerself?'

'For a couple of years when I was your age.' Dickens had spent two years at Wellington House Academy after his removal from Warren's blacking factory — but it wasn't much. As his father had once said when asked where his son was educated, Charles could be said to have educated himself. And he had. His real education, like Scrap's, had been in the streets and alleys.

'Yer not tellin' me that yer learnt all them things yer know in school fer two years. Nah, Mr Dickens, yer woz out an' about like me.'

'I was — out and about, as you say…' A memory came to him of his twelve year old self wandering about the darkness of the Adelphi arches, lingering by a little public house to watch some coal-heavers dancing, pacing the stones, counting the dull chimes of the clocks, feeling more utterly alone and cast away than in a trackless desert.

Scrap waited, wondering at the change in Mr Dickens's face. Somethin' sad there — memory p'raps. Scrap knew about that — he remembered his ma, and how when she had died, no one had told him anything. There was just a big hole in his life that had never been filled until — and he thought of Mrs

Jones's crumpled face the other morning — until Mrs Jones, and o' course, Mr Jones and Eleanor and Tom, and Sergeant Rogers an' Mollie, too. An' Mr Dickens. *Rich, I am, rich as — as a king.* He smiled at the thought.

Dickens saw him smile and looked at the boy's black hands — blacking. Well, John Forster knew. And the readers of *David Copperfield* knew the bottle factory where the boy, David, had laboured but not that it was his own blacking factory at Hungerford Stairs. 'I worked before I went to school — in a blacking factory.'

Scrap nodded. 'Just the way o' things, I serpose. Still, funny way round,' he observed, 'folk gen'rally goes ter school before they goes ter work.'

The great secret, thought Dickens, half-laughing to himself, the secret so old that it seemed to have grown into him so that the writing of it had seemed to tear his very fabric. And to Scrap, it was just the way of the world.

The philosopher had not finished. 'All that stuff yer knows now, wot yer put in the books, where's that from?'

'Well, being out and about, and reading, too. I read a lot when I was a boy.'

'There yer are then, s'wot I says — Mrs Jones is teachin' me. She reads yer books ter me and Eleanor an' Tom — an' I reads for meself, o' course. I'm readin' ... well, I'm not sayin' yet. But it stands ter reason. I don't need no school.'

The argument won, the great writer trounced by ineluctable logic, the young Socrates finished his pie and began on the rest of the pie that Dickens couldn't eat.

How long should they wait for Jones and Rogers? He could not really believe that they were swallowed up in that terrible darkness. People didn't simply disappear. But if they'd been separated? Then again, as Scrap had reasonably pointed, they had found their way out — and in the dark. Rogers had his lamp, but so had Stemp and he had vanished. His thoughts went round and round. They should go to Bow Street, surely and report that the Superintendent was missing. He half rose from his seat, ready to act. Anything was better than this infernal waiting.

The door opened and he saw Sam come into the chop house, carrying the scarf. He sat down. His heart seemed to lurch in his chest. *I was terrified of losing him*, he thought. Scrap put down his fork.

'Well, you two look all right — good pie is it?' Jones asked, but his swift glance at Dickens showed his relief.

'It was,' said Scrap. The plate was empty.

'Bruised, bloody, battered, squelched — but ne'er undone,' said Dickens.

'Your moustache is unharmed, I see.' Jones smiled at him.

'What did I tell you? Neither tempest nor hurricane can move it. You found my scarf, I see.'

'Yes, we followed the trail you left and saw that you'd been at the Dairy. We came out in Paradise Street.'

'Out of Inferno.'

'Quite. We saw the brazier and we picked up this.' He took the mask from his pocket. 'You saw him.'

'I saw a young Italian man — not Will — he had no injury to his hands — one of which, incidentally, he used to throw a knife at me.'

Jones raised his eyes. 'He missed, clearly.' Not the moment to discuss the fact that Dickens might have been killed. Later, when they were alone, his eyes said to Dickens.

'Scrap grabbed me — saved my life. He threw it when I asked about the Italian boy.'

'Hm — the gang master, we think. The boy is one of his, perhaps, and he wants him back. No sign of the lad?'

'No — nor of Stemp.'

'We didn't see him, either. However, there was no one about. Before we discuss anything else, Rogers and I must go to the Marylebone Police Station. I want to get a search party to look for Stemp. He may be injured somewhere.' *Or worse*, Jones thought, but there was no use in saying it. By their faces, he knew that the others had the same thought.

28: Mog Chips

Something woke Stemp. Some sense of change. Light, and something, he was sure, had tapped his face. Something like a little hand, gentle and cool. Stemp opened his eyes and looked into two little brown ones which were gazing at him with a mixture of curiosity and concern.

The eyes were in a little, wrinkled brown face, and it was a little brown paw that had tapped softly at his face — a monkey's paw. That's what his visitor was — a monkey in a red jacket. Stemp stared back and the monkey cocked its head. It looked at him as if it understood all that had happened. Human eyes, wise eyes, kind eyes — so kindly that tough Stemp could have wept.

Then he realised that a light was coming from above. He looked up. Someone was shining a lamp down.

A voice said, 'That's Pete — follow him up if you can.'

There was a ladder leading up to some kind of trap door in the ceiling of the cellar. The monkey looked at him, its human eyes asking. He nodded and the monkey climbed lightly up the ladder.

Stemp got to his feet, swaying rather. *Stiff as a corpse*, he thought, *but I'm alive and that's somethin'*. He could feel the stiffness in his jaw where Jimmy Brady had kicked him and he was aware of the sore places where the vicious boots had landed their blows. But there was a way out. He looked up to see Pete peering anxiously down at him.

'Can you manage it?' the voice asked — *a London voice*, he thought, *not Irish. Warm not cold. Well, let's see who it belongs to.*

'I think so.'

Stemp climbed gingerly up the ladder — he hoped it would take his weight. But it wasn't far up — six or seven feet. He wormed his way through the trap door and found himself in a loft — a clean and tidy loft where there was a makeshift bed and a sailor's box serving as a table upon which Pete now sat. And there was a man, a man who was undoubtedly a sailor with a brown face, tight grey curls, wearing a peacoat, and looking at him out of brown eyes as kindly as the monkey's.

'Mog Chips, sir, and Pete, you've already met.' The sailor held out his hand, warm as the voice.

'Frank Stemp, sir. I'm more than glad ter meet yer, Mr Chips — and Pete, too.' Stemp gave a nod to the monkey, which bowed to him. 'I don't know 'ow as I'd got outer that there hole.'

'Take a seat, Mr Stemp,' said Mog Chips, pointing to one of two rough packing cases which served as his chairs. 'You'll take a glass of rum? I'm afraid I've no warm — Pete an' me's off this day.'

He poured two measures of rum into two tin mugs and they sat. Mog Chips lit his pipe.

'I heard somethin' of what went on down there — terrible boy, that. Heard 'im say you're a policeman.'

'That's right. The boy and his pa jumped me — thought I'd 'ad it at one point.'

'Yes — I was ready to jump down. Thought at first it was a row between thieves. Then the dad pulled him off an' I waited till the coast was clear and sent Pete to have a look.'

'I'm obliged to yer, Mr Chips.'

'Mog's fine.'

'Mog?'

'Aye — short for Mahogany. That's what they called me — on account of me darkness. Father black, mother white — not that I ever knew him. Gone afore I was born — by the docks. Went to sea when I was but twelve. It ain't a bad life, Mr Stemp, for a man whose got no one — 'cept Pete, o' course. Had a sister — younger than me — different father. When our ma died, I went to sea and she was taken by our auntie. Not me — not Mahogany — too dark.'

'Goin' back ter the sea?'

'Don't know yet. Came back to find my sister. When a man's out there in the dark, lookin' at the stars an' the moon ridin' there like a great silver dollar — millions o' stars out there, Mr Stemp — he gets to thinkin' about the meanin' o' things. Just wanted to know for sure that there was no one but me and Pete.'

Stemp looked at Pete who was watching his master with the same look of concern he'd shown to Stemp. *Worried about 'im*, he thought. *Why, that monkey knows more and feels more than most human beings.* He thought of Jimmy Brady's hard, greedy eyes. *No more feelin' than a snake.*

'Did yer find 'er?'

'No — I came this way because I knew that Penny lived with our auntie in Dab Lane, but it was too long ago — course it was. I should 'ave known, but a man gets an idea an' he has to follow it. Who were you followin'?'

'I was lookin' fer an Italian lad — witness, maybe, to a murderer. In danger, my chief thought.'

'The Irish man mentioned an Italian boy — I wondered about that. Saw a little lad up near the workhouse. I went there to ask about Penny. Curled up in a doorway — I stopped to have a look. Could have been dead, I thought, so I spoke to him. You'd 'ave thought I was the devil himself, the way he stared at me. Terrified. Then he ran off.'

'Into the alleys?'

'No, I was on Northumberland Street. He shot across the road — into Nottingham Street, I think it's called. The Irish man said Satan wanted him. And he was terrified. What do you make of that?'

'Interestin'. I dint 'ear that bit. I need ter get back ter meet the chief — 'e'll want ter know about that if 'e 'asn't found the lad. Satan'll be some kind o' gangmaster, we think. 'Ow long yer been 'ere? Queer sort o' place.'

'Only a few days, but I know what you mean — too quiet. Sinister. I'll be glad to get out. Folk are frightened hereabouts. Of your Satan, p'raps?'

'Should think so. If yer leavin', mebbe yer could come with me to meet the Superintendent. Tell 'im what yer 'eard an' about the boy. We meet at a chop 'ouse — could treat yer — an' Pete.'

Mog nodded. It took only a few minutes for the rum and tin mugs to be stowed in the chest, which Mog stowed on one shoulder. Pete perched on the other and out they went.

Jones gave Dickens his scarf. 'You two get off home — Charles, you could drop off Scrap at Norfolk Street, if you will.'

'What about Mrs Plume?'

'Too late, I think. I don't want to go knocking at her door in the dark, and anyway, I need to try to find Stemp first. Then to Bow Street to see if Grove has found any trace of Will.'

'Hospitals,' said Rogers. 'He might want to get the hand seen to.'

'Good idea — we'll get a couple of constables from Goss's division to make enquiries.'

'He'd perhaps go to the Workhouse Infirmary — worth trying Doctor Fuller,' Dickens said.

'Yes, I'll tell them to mention my name. Mrs Plume tomorrow?'

'I'll come round from Wellington Street.'

'Right. Let's go.'

Jones turned back to the door just as it opened. Stemp came in, accompanied by a man with a sea chest on one shoulder and a monkey on the other.

'This is Mr Mog Chips and Pete — got me out of a cellar, and 'eard some interestin' things, Mr Jones. I thought you should know about.'

Stemp told his tale of the assault by Jimmy Brady and his father and Mog Chips added what he had heard about the Italian boy.

'You saw him run off down Nottingham Street?' Jones asked Mog.

'That's right.'

'When was that?'

'Two days ago.'

'Which explains why Satan still wants him —'

'And that our murderer might not have found him,' Dickens interrupted. 'He was running away from the alleys.'

'Let's hope so.' Jones looked at the red mark where Jimmy Brady had kicked Stemp. It would ripen into a bruise by tomorrow. 'Anything broken, do you think?' he asked.

'I don't think so — I'll be bruised about the ribs I expect. Nothin' too serious.'

'Still, you ought to see Mrs Feak — you could call there on your way home — you might have a cracked or broken rib. I was just about to organise a search party from Marylebone Street. It'll be a search for Jimmy Brady and his father now. Rogers and I will need to go to Marylebone Police Station. It's their patch and they need to deal with whatever's going on down there. I'll try to see Inspector Cuff — sensible man. Rogers and I know him. Mr Chips, where are you going now?'

'Not sure. I'll try to get a lodging at the docks — I might go back to sea.'

'I would like to stay in touch with you — witness against Jimmy Brady and his father. Is that possible?'

'Yes, I've some thinking to do. I can let you know where I'm staying.'

'If you need lodgings, we've got room at the shop,' Rogers offered.

'Good idea,' said Jones. 'That way, I can reach you quickly. Scrap, while —'

Scrap wasn't listening. He was engaged in communion with Pete. Scrap had seen plenty of monkeys on barrel-organs, but had never met one like the courteous Pete whose bow had enchanted him and whose handshake he was now returning with a look of wonderment on his face. The monkey turned to Dickens, offering another handshake.

'A most engaging little fellow, Mr Chips,' he said. 'I am glad to make your acquaintance, Mr Pete.'

The monkey examined him gravely, and being satisfied with what he saw, bowed.

'Sorry, Mr Jones,' said Scrap, 'you woz sayin' somethin'.'

'I thought you might take Mr Chips and Pete to the shop before you go on to Norfolk Street. Explain to Mollie about Mr Chips — and Pete.' *I hope Mollie doesn't mind the monkey*, he thought. Too late, now. Rogers had committed her to two house guests.

'Right,' Scrap agreed.

'Take a cab then, all of you — Stemp you must go to Mrs Feak's — and then home. Charles, you should go with them.'

Dickens agreed. He could tell that Jones was anxious to be off. He had wanted to tell him about his idea of going to the Italian School, but it would keep. *In fact*, he thought, *he could go now*. He had looked at his watch to discover that it was only half-past five. Their sojourn in the alleys had seemed to last an age. Time had seemed very long there. In that ink black, Old Time had slept, and the world had stood still.

Well, time had restarted — Jones was safe, and Rogers, Stemp was all right, Scrap and he were delivered from danger. Time for action. Clerkenwell.

29: The Italian School

In the cab, Dickens bethought himself to take off the moustache and to comb his hair into its more natural style. He couldn't see, of course, but he thought he might look more himself than the undertaker to whom Jones had likened him. He got out of his cab at the end of Field Lane, from where it was a brief walk up to Charles Street and thence into Greville Street. He knew this area well. Near Field Lane was the house to which the Artful Dodger had brought the unsuspecting Oliver Twist, the house from where Fagin had slunk, on a chill, damp, windy night not unlike this one, through the black mist and thick muddy streets to meet Bill Sikes in Bethnal Green.

Dickens knew the seething streets off Field Lane and Saffron Hill, the countless dreary little shops, the filthy odours, the mud, the grimy public houses, the drunks, the fighting men and women, and the heaps of children screaming and shrieking, all the teeming life of the place. It was filthy and crowded, but it was alive — unlike those silent, dark, underworld alleys where a lad with a face lit by lurid flames had sent a knife whistling through the air.

Had the boy meant to kill him? Perhaps not — if he had, the knife would have entered his heart, not hissed by his ear to end with a thud in the door beside him. Perhaps. Well, no need to dwell on that. He wasn't afraid of this place. In his way, he owned these streets and alleys.

Up beyond Saffron Hill was Clerkenwell Green where Mr Brownlow's pocket was picked and Oliver Twist arrested. Hatton Garden was the site of the police court where Oliver's case was tried by the magistrate Fang. The Three Cripples Inn in Bleeding Heart Yard where Sikes, Fagin and the villain Monks, Oliver's half-brother, conspired the boy's ruin. Along the way in Ely Place, David Copperfield had visited Agnes Wickfield. From where he stood he could look down to Snow Hill where Squeers had collected his boys at The Saracen's Head. And he knew the Field Lane Ragged School well — and the Italian School.

He went up Field Lane, turned left into Charles Street, bypassing Bleeding Heart Yard and went on into Greville Street where he went into the school to find a young Italian man in the hall.

'Mr Dickens?'

'Yes. I've come to enquire about an Italian boy — Guiseppe — I don't know his other name.'

The young man smiled. 'It's a common name around here.'

'I know, but he is quite distinctive. He has a birthmark like a tear drop under his left eye. He might have come here a couple of days ago.'

'I know him — he is here. Why do you want him?'

'It's a long story, Mr —?'

'Bellini — Salvatore Bellini.'

'The story concerns a murder and your boy, Guiseppe, might have seen it happen in an alley behind the house where it took place. The police are looking for him — they are afraid the murderer might have seen him, that he may be in danger. I thought of your school and wondered if he might have taken refuge here.'

'He has not said anything about it — but he is frightened. I thought he was afraid someone was after him, but he would not tell me who.'

'There is something else — when we — I mean I was with the police — when we were looking for him in the alleys near the workhouse at Marylebone, I came across a young Italian man whom we found out was after the boy, too. I don't know his name, but I know he is dangerous — we think he may call himself Satan.' Dickens saw the man's face change to something like anger. 'That means something to you?'

'It does — there is a young man — a bad young man who was here a long time ago as a boy. He was bad then. He is called Saturnino Betti.'

'Whom people called Satan — it fits.'

'It is another long story. Have you time to hear it?'

'Yes, indeed. The policeman, Superintendent Jones of Bow Street, will want to know about him.'

'Then, come in to another room.'

They went into what was a classroom of sorts where Mr Bellini motioned Dickens to sit.

'You know our work here, how our noble Signor Mazzini started the school in 1841 because, when he talked to the little boys with their barrel-organs and their mice and rats, he found out about the masters who made them slaves. He found out about how the poor peasant boys were brought to England with promises of pay and good living, and how they came here to be beaten and starved. Signor Mazzini went among those men and some were brought to justice. But he wanted those boys to have a better life, so they come to the school in the evenings to learn to read and write, and to learn Italian history. He is most loved by all those boys — except a few — and most particularly Saturnino Betti, who even our noble Mazzini could not help. He was a cruel boy who sought to influence the others and Mazzini expelled him from the lessons. Then we heard no more of him until Mazzini went away to fight for the cause. Saturnino came back and took some of our boys away — he promised them riches, no doubt. Guiseppe Betti is his brother, and in the mind of Saturnino, he belongs to him to do with him what he will — to slave for him, I do not doubt. So he took him, too, for there is no father or mother to guard the boy.'

'So, Guiseppe ran away — from the murderer and his brother?'

'I would think so. He is a good boy — about ten years old, I think and not corrupted — yet. I hope.'

'Will Saturnino come for him, do you think?'

The Italian smiled. 'Not now — for our hero is back. He has come secretly from Switzerland. You know that the French have defeated the republican Rome — Mazzini has fled for his life, but he is here, and when Saturnino Betti knows that, he will not dare to come here. Will your policeman need to speak to him about the murder?'

'I do not think so — we have other witnesses and we are close on his trail, I believe. We just wanted to know if he was safe from Satan.'

'We will take care of him, do not fear, Mr Dickens.'

'May I leave something for him?' Dickens held out a sovereign.

'It will help us. I thank you, Mr Dickens. I will tell Signor Mazzini that you came.'

'Give him my regards. Now I must go to give my news to Superintendent Jones.'

Dickens went back to Bow Street. Sam might be back and he would want to know about Guiseppe. At least he was safe now and Jones could go or send someone to see Mazzini to find out if anyone else knew anything about Saturnino Betti.

Jones was in his office with Rogers. They had seen Inspector Cuff and Sergeant Billie Watts, who had recruited more men to search the alleys for the Italian and Paul and Jimmy Brady. Inspector Cuff was in charge for the time being. Superintendent Goss was out of action, it seemed. He had found Thomas King who had murdered his father. In the struggle to force King up the steps from the cellar where he had been hiding, Goss had slipped and broken his ankle. Inspector Cuff had delivered this piece of news with a straight face — the straight face of a man who was trying not to laugh.

'Not pleased — the Superintendent. I was sorry to have to leave him down in that dirty cellar, but I had to get King to the station. It took a while, too, before I could send someone back for him.' His eyes seemed to shine with that suppressed amusement. 'An hour or more, I'm sorry to say. Still, we'll have to manage without him somehow, Mr Jones.'

Cuff knew about Satan, and about Jimmy Brady and his da. Paul Brady was a petty kind of thief — not known to be particularly violent. One for the ladies, apparently, but the lad — well, he was a little brute. Cuff said they'd bring in both of them. And he'd been wanting to get in those alleys and flush 'em out. He heard the tales about Satan. He had been waiting for the go-ahead from Goss — he needn't wait now. The attack on a policeman was enough.

Jones told him that he believed that Arthur Brimstone had been murdered by the man who had killed Plume. He would investigate those two murders together and while Cuff was searching the alleys; perhaps he could keep an eye out for Kitty Quillian who seemed to have vanished.

Jones and Rogers had come back to Bow Street to find out what Inspector Grove and his constables had discovered about Will. Nothing. He had vanished, too.

'My hope now lies with Mrs Plume,' Jones was saying to Rogers as Dickens came in. 'Charles, I didn't expect you here. I thought you'd gone home.'

'No, I went to the Italian school. I was going to tell you that I'd thought of it, but events overtook us. But I bring glad tidings. The boy is safe.' He told them about his talk with Salvatore Bellini. 'I thought you might send someone to talk to Mazzini. He knows all about the one they call Satan, and he might know who knows him. If the boy was running away from Satan, it explains why he was hanging around the alley at the back of Plume's house. Perhaps he thought he might take refuge with Mrs Bark — she'd been kind to him.'

'And they were out — at his sister's, so maybe the boy was waiting for them to come back and, unfortunately for him, he saw our murderer.'

'I'll send Grove to see Mr Mazzini. In the meantime, Inspector Cuff and Billie Watts have taken some men to search the alleys. Cuff said he'd send news when they found Jimmy Brady and his father. I asked them to keep an eye out for Kitty Quillian. And to enquire at the hospitals in case Will asked to have his hand seen to.'

'I thought I'd go ter Mrs Feak's,' said Rogers, 'see how Stemp is, make sure he's all right.'

'Good idea — then go home. You ought to see Mollie about that monkey.' Jones gave Rogers a knowing look.

Rogers grinned back. 'I'm not puttin' it off, sir, well not for a bit. Give 'em a chance ter settle in.'

'Well, tell her Pete's an important witness — with my compliments for her hospitality.'

'I'm sure Pete will charm her — a very gentle beast and of a good conscience.'

'If you say so, Mr Dickens. I'll be off then.'

When the cheerful Rogers had gone, Dickens saw that Jones was looking at him with a sombre face.

'Thy thoughts, most reverend and grave elder?'

'That I am glad not to find thee a grave man.' Jones smiled, but Dickens knew he was thinking of the Italian and his knife.

'Saturnino Betti?'

'And his knife. That was a near thing.'

'I was thinking about it. He could have killed me — if he'd wanted to. I'm certain of it, Sam. The knife went into the door frame. He wouldn't have missed. He could have aimed for my heart, but he didn't. Still, I'm much obliged to Scrap. Not that I wasn't terrified out of my wits. Like Mrs Gummidge, I felt a visitation in the back — the creeps up the spine. Ugh —' he shivered at the memory — 'I was very glad to see that cow. I shall double my order from Mr Josiah Evans, the dairyman.'

'You're probably right — about the knife, I mean. Still, it was a nightmarish experience down there. Cuff will sort it out, I'm sure. Goss is out of commission — broken ankle in pursuit of a murderer. He should have dealt with that place sooner. Cuff wanted him to, but Goss is touchy about his rank.'

'Are you going home soon?'

'For an hour or two. I shall come back here by nine o'clock when the beat constables change over to see if there's any news. Inspector Walklate —'

'Walklate — never! Night Inspector, is he?'

'He is, appropriately. He takes over from Inspector Jolley. Don't —' Jones saw Dickens's eyes light up — 'a more lugubrious individual, you could not hope to meet. I'll introduce you. He looks like a parson. But, he knows to send a reserve man for me if there's anything urgent. You coming my way?'

'I am, indeed — after I have met the melancholy Mr Jolley. Pity I can't wait until nine to see the spectral Walklate glide through a solid wall into the station.'

'Solid is the word. Big man is Walklate. Could knock a wall down with one meaty fist.'

They went out into the Inspector's office where Jolley stood at his window to hear the charges. He was as Jones had described him. There was an atmosphere of gloom about him; he looked like a man who knew the end of the world was coming, but out of pity for his fellow men, was keeping it to himself. He was about thirty-five with a thin, worried face, a long nose and dark hooded eyes, which were at present gazing with a kind of weary patience at a swarthy man who was enquiring if a gypsy woman had been taken in charge. There was a queue of other supplicants reporting on lost, stolen or otherwise misappropriated possessions, among which curious selection were a horse and cart, a small dog, a brooch, and a firkin of butter.

The swarthy man had lost his gypsy woman — he couldn't recall where. *Gone off in her caravan*, Dickens wondered. Nothing so picturesque. She was drunk when he'd seen her last. Jolley assured him that there was no gypsy woman in the cells — no dark one, no fair one, no tall one, no short one, no gypsy woman of any kind. The swarthy man retreated, rather crestfallen — she would turn up, he supposed.

While Jones was speaking to one of the constables seated at a desk, Dickens slipped out into the barrack-like room beyond into which bustled a stout, livid-faced woman and her gaunt companion. Between them they had a shaggy-looking individual as their prisoner, holding on so tightly to his canvas coat that it took on the appearance of a straightjacket. His feet did not touch the ground. When the two women dropped him,

Dickens could see that he was a small, handsome, curly-headed boy of perhaps seven. The boy looked quite unconcerned when the stout woman explained in shrill tones that he had robbed her shop. The policeman took him away to the cells, telling the woman that she must appear before the magistrate in the morning to substantiate her charge.

Jones came through and they made their way out of the station.

'That child —' Dickens began.

'The Artful Dodger — not that he dodged this time. Nor a few times before. The number of children brought here, either as prisoners, or as having been lost, is between five and six thousand a year. And how many do we save? Very few, too few. It's depressing. Talk about progress.'

'I know — is there any earthly thing that boy can do when his new sentence is served, but steal again, be imprisoned again and again flogged? There are six hundred and fifty-six gentlemen in the House of Commons. I wonder, do none of them care to walk these streets to see and hear what such childhood is and what escape it has from being what it is — it's enough to break the heart and hope of any man.'

'I've never seen 'em, but they act fast enough when they're robbed and complain if we don't catch the thief. Write it all down, Charles — pitch it to them, strong as you can in that magazine of yours.'

'That I will — a nice little piece about Bow Street might make a few folk sit up and take notice.'

They walked out into the street, crossing over Long Acre to make their way to Oxford Street.

'I meant to ask about Miranda,' Dickens said as they approached Jones's house in Norfolk Street. 'What did Elizabeth say about her?'

'She went to Newgate yesterday and intended to go today. Mollie was going to look after Eleanor and Tom at the shop. Elizabeth says she has eaten. She says nothing about Plume, or of what happened, only of her childhood, her father and mother. It's very sad — she talks as if she might go back there — home, she says, she wants to go home. She talks as if her father is still alive. Elizabeth daren't contradict her — she's afraid she might retreat into silence again. And Elizabeth is worried about what we might do with her when we get her out of Newgate.'

'She must have a home — not the home at Shepherd's Bush. The girls there are very different from Miranda. I'll write to Miss Coutts — she might know of someone, someone who would give her a proper home, who would understand what she has suffered. Tell Elizabeth, I shall do all in my power.'

Jones was sure he would. Charles Dickens kept his promises.

30: Enter a Partner

Rogers had gone to Euston Station to catch the early express for Manchester. Inspector Hardacre had telegraphed. He had found Mrs Hodson and Mrs Brimstone, and he would bring the women to London Road Station where Rogers would take charge of them. They would get the very next train back to London. As far as Jones was concerned, they were both suspects — Mrs Hodson for Plume's murder and Mrs Brimstone for her husband's. Not that he thought either of them guilty, but there was reason enough to have them in custody. There was also the question of Kitty's baby and the evidence against them provided by Bertha Raspin. *The three witches*, Jones thought grimly.

The dependable Inspector Cuff had been to see Jones at nine o'clock after Rogers had gone. There was no news from the hospitals that Cuff's men had been to — a glazier had gone to the Workhouse Infirmary with a cut hand, but no one had heard of anyone resembling Will. Two other constables had found Paul Brady — at home, in his bed with a drink or two inside him. Jimmy Brady had run off when they came out of the cellar where they had left Frank Stemp. Paul Brady hadn't been able to stop him and the family hadn't seen him since. It was Cuff's opinion that they were all frightened of Jimmy — mother, father and the odd little daughter who had a black eye. Mrs Brady would have helped him, Cuff had been sure, but she had been wary of her husband. Paul Brady had been brought to Marylebone Police Station and charged with the assault and kidnap of a policeman. He'd be up before the magistrate later that morning — in Newgate by dinner, Cuff had said with satisfaction. Cuff intended to go back to Mrs Brady's later to see if she could tell him where Jimmy might be. And the Italian had disappeared — with his masked accomplice.

'I've a name for him,' Jones had said. 'Saturnino Betti.' He gave Cuff the details he had learned from Dickens the night before. 'The creature in the mask was probably one of the boys he'd lured from the Italian School. I've sent Inspector Grove there to see if he can find out any more. I'll let you know.'

'I've got my men knocking on doors and telling folk we're after him. People might start filling those alleys and lanes again. They'll feel safer now. Not that they like us much down there, but they probably like even us better than Satan.'

'I think I'll go to see Mrs Brady,' Jones said. 'I want to ask her about Kitty Quillian — the girl who we think was seen with Plume's murderer, and who was near Plume's house on the evening of the murder. I'll ask about Jimmy, too.'

Cuff agreed and went on his way. Jones sat thinking while he was waiting for Dickens. On his way home he had been tempted to call on Bridie O'Malley to see whether Michael had turned up. But he had thought better of it — Bridie might not be too pleased to see him. Thinking about Michael had made him remember something odd — something that he had paid no attention to because the name O'Malley had distracted him. It was what the murderer had said to Michael when he gave him the two shillings. The two shillings were odd in themselves. A cold-blooded murderer give a tramp two shillings? Why? And stranger still were the words that had accompanied the shillings. "Get a good meal and give up the drink."

Kind words of advice and money for a meal — those two things did not square with a man who had murdered Doctor Plume, Arthur Brimstone, possibly Kitty Quillian, and who had been after the Italian boy. Plume had known his murderer. They were sure of that. Someone from his past. Someone who had killed Plume, but who, perhaps, had not intended to — and then, as often with murder, had found that he had to go on — or give himself up. And that led to Arthur Brimstone? What had he known? Had he met the murderer? That was something to find out from his wife.

And there seemed to be still in the murderer — Will, perhaps — some reserve of his old self — the self that gave his name politely — even to a tramp, the self that cared enough about that same tramp to give him money for a meal. A gentleman then, whose old self elbowed aside the murderer, and saw a man in need. Someone whom Plume knew. "Give up the drink."

Another doctor? That was a possibility. Mrs Plume ought to know if there were any doctor in Plume's past who might have a grudge. Dickens should be here soon.

Jones made to go up the steps of number 11 Weymouth Street when the door opened and a tall young man came out. He was wearing a black coat, gauntlets and carrying a travelling bag in one hand and a top hat in the other.

'I am here to see Mrs Plume. Superintendent Jones of Bow Street.'

'Oh — about Doctor Plume.'

'Yes, is Mrs Plume well enough to see us?'

'I'd say so — she's out of bed. A bit — er — delicate, but I'm sure she can talk to you. Brought the undertaker, have you,' the young man said, glancing at Dickens who had come in his disguise, albeit with a new moustache. The other, he had assumed, must be lying on the floor of the cab he had taken to the Italian school. The new one was a little larger, to be sure, but firmly attached to his upper lip as he had assured Jones who had merely looked at it with an eyebrow raised. Dickens bowed his head in what he thought was a suitably sombre manner. It wouldn't do to laugh.

'No, this is Mr —'

'Vholes,' said Dickens, seizing inspiration. He had seen the name on a passing cart. 'Solicitor for the young woman accused of Doctor Plume's murder. Recent evidence suggests that she is not the guilty person.'

'Oh, I see — well — er —' The young man seemed at a loss. 'You are?'

'Martin Brooks.'

'Of —' Dickens nearly said "Sheffield", but he stopped himself in time — suppose the young man had read of David Copperfield whom Mr Murdstone had, for reasons of his own, named Brooks of Sheffield.

'Manchester — but I'm on my way back there. My train leaves in thirty minutes.'

'And your business here, sir?'

'I am Mrs Plume's stepson.'

Jones was astonished. No one had mentioned a stepson. That fool, Goss — he wondered whether Goss had withheld that information wilfully. How like him. 'Stepson,' he repeated.

'Yes, not his son. Thank the stars. I'll let you in.'

'I'm sorry, Mr Brooks, but I will have to delay you. I shall need to ask you some questions.' Jones was firm.

'I see. I just came to see my stepmother — I suppose I can take a later train.'

They went into a well-furnished drawing room where a good fire was blazing. Dickens glanced up at another portrait of the doctor — that smile again, as if he knew something others did not. Killed for what he knew? What he knew about the murderer? That was a thought. Well, the murderer had wiped the smile off Plume's face. Uncharitable, I am. But he could not like the man, could not feel pity for him — he thought of poor Miranda Deverall and Lavinia Gray. Oh, Plume had secrets — perhaps this young man knew something.

Martin Brooks stood uncertainly in the centre of the room. He had left his travelling bag in the hall, but he had not taken off his coat or gloves. Jones eyed the gloves — did one of them conceal a cut hand?

'Do you wish me to fetch my stepmother?'

'Not for the moment, Mr Brooks. I should like you to tell me something of Doctor Plume — your history and so on.'

Brooks motioned Jones to sit and he sat down opposite. Dickens remained standing nearer the door, behind Jones so that he could see Brooks's face. The young man had forgotten him.

'Where to start? I'm not sure what you want to know.'

'About your family and Doctor Plume, if you will.'

'My father was a brewer — in Rochester — in partnership with his brother. I had a happy childhood. But my mother died when I was eight — it's a long time ago. Seventeen years, but I haven't forgotten her. She was lovely — all sparkle, full of life and funny. My father loved her — and so did I. It was as if the light went out of our lives when she died. When I was ten, my father married Mrs Plume — Miss Julia Lamb, she was then. She was a cousin of my aunt's — he wanted someone to look after me, I suppose. I didn't mind. I knew her and she was kind. A little woman, silly and affectionate. My father was fond of her — now, I think that … she wasn't my mother. He was busy and, well, she was there. I had my aunt and uncle, too, and cousins. And then my father died — a riding accident.'

Enter Plume, thought Dickens, *to comfort the grieving widow, I'll bet.*

'Was Plume your family doctor?' Jones had obviously had the same thought.

'No, he was my stepmother's doctor — his practice was in Chatham. I don't know why — something about nerves, I remember. My father didn't care for him, but he indulged her — because he didn't love her, I suppose. Felt guilty. I went away to school. When I came home for the holidays, she was to marry him. My uncle frowned a lot — whispers in the parlour with my aunt — that sort of thing — money talk. My father left her twenty-thousand pounds and Plume was a doctor with not much of a practice.'

'What did you feel about it?' Jones had his eye on the gloves.

'Not much — I had my mother's money and the rest of my father's. And anyway, I was fifteen. I had my horses, my cousins. I just hoped that I could stay with them.'

The room was warm. Martin Brooks was sitting near the fire. He began to take off the left-hand glove. There was something awkward about the movement of is right hand. He winced as if it were painful.

'You've hurt yourself?' Jones asked.

Dickens held his breath. Surely this open-faced young man with the bright blue eyes who had loved his mother and spoke with a kind of tolerant affection of Mrs Plume, could not be the murderer. But, what was it he had said? He was not Plume's son, thank the stars — he hadn't much liked the doctor, that was clear.

'Sprained my wrist.'

He peeled off the left hand glove and then the right — there was no bandage, no sign of injury. Dickens breathed again.

Martin Brooks put the gloves on a side table and resumed his story. 'I stayed with my uncle and aunt. Then I came to London to read for the law — at Gray's Inn.'

'Did you see much of your stepmother and Doctor Plume?'

'I made a duty call now and then — for her sake.'

'You didn't like him.'

Martin Brooks smiled. 'I suppose I gave that away. No, I didn't. I realised that this house and the fashionable practice were built on my father's money — not that I minded for her, but he was so complacent, so patronising. It was as if he had got it by his own efforts, and he didn't want me here. Didn't want people to know that he'd had nothing until he married a wealthy widow.'

'What was he like with your stepmother?'

'She didn't complain. I don't know. There was a kind of contempt sometimes for her. He'd be sharp. I could tell she was hurt. She didn't deserve that — she's silly, not very bright, but good at heart. I didn't come very often, only when I thought he'd be out. And he often was.'

'Did she know where or why?'

'I doubt it — he was master here. She'll be better off without him. I'm sorry — shouldn't have said that. The man was murdered after all, and she is upset.'

'You don't have any ideas about the murder?'

'Well, it wasn't me, and it wasn't my stepmother. I was in Manchester and she was visiting my aunt.'

'I rather think it might be to do with something in his past. Do you remember anything about his life in Chatham that could shed light on this matter. Any enemies there?'

'I really don't know. Plume left his practice when he married my stepmother. There was a partner — don't know what happened to him. He might still be there.'

'Do you remember his name?'

'No — my stepmother will probably remember. She went to the surgery in Chatham.'

'I ought to see her now.'

'I'll take you to her. I'd better stay with her — to reassure her. I'll get a train later.'

Martin Brooks led them to another room where the widow was seated on a velvet sofa before another fire. A small, rather faded woman — about forty, Dickens guessed, her faded prettiness not enhanced by the hideous widow's cap and the unrelieved black of her gown. She looked bewildered and lost in the weeds like a child in clothes too big for her. And she looked afraid when Martin came in with the two strangers.

'Ma,' said Martin gently, 'nothing to worry about. This gentleman is a policeman and he wants to know about Doctor Plume's old partner in Chatham. The other gentleman is a solicitor. Nothing to concern you.'

'But why? That girl did it. Lancelot tried to help her and she stole his money. The policeman said.'

Jones sat down. 'I'm sorry, Mrs Plume, but we now know that the girl didn't kill your husband. I need to know about the past.'

'The past — so long ago. It can't — Lancelot left it behind him. He wanted to start afresh here in London.'

'What did he want to leave behind?'

'A quarrel — Mr Sefton was angry. He said Lancelot should pay, but Lancelot said he owed him nothing. Mr Sefton said that he couldn't afford to keep the practice on his own, but Lancelot told me that Mr Sefton had no right to any money. We should forget him.'

'Who is Mr Sefton?' Jones knew he must be patient.

'Frederick Sefton — Lancelot's partner.'

'Is he still in Chatham?'

'I don't know. We never spoke of him. I don't know anything about him.'

Jones saw the tears running down her cheeks. She wouldn't know anything, he thought. But there was certainly something — except his name wasn't Will. But then, Michael might have been wrong. Sefton was a doctor — with a grudge.

'Can you remember the address of the practice in Chatham?'

'Clover Lane.'

'Thank you. We will try to find him.'

Martin Brooks showed them out. Jones asked him the address of his old home in Rochester.

'The Brewery was at Restoration House, but they're not there now. My uncle died and his widow, my aunt, lives with her daughter at Strood — at the vicarage there. Agnes married the Reverend Henry Stevens.'

Restoration House, thought Dickens. He remembered it. He'd last been in Rochester two years ago. He remembered the house of old red brick, built in the time of Charles II, and he had seen the empty brewery buildings. Perhaps someone else lived there now. But, he knew Chatham and Rochester very well. It was where he had spent a happy childhood — before his father had brought them to London, before his father had been imprisoned in the Marshalsea, before the blacking factory.

On his last visit, he had stayed at The Bull in the High Street and he had been to see the Reverend William Drage in Minor Canon Row by the Cathedral. He might know about Sefton — he'd know of the doctors in Chatham as well — that is, if Sefton were still there. He could have gone back after the murder of Brimstone, and if he were not there, someone might know his history.

They stood in the street looking at the opposite pavement where Dickens had seen the Italian boy and the man in the dark coat bending over him, and where the maid had seen Kitty Quillian.

'There's a gleam in your eye, Charles. What have you thought?'

'About someone I know in Rochester — who might know something about Sefton. It would be somewhere to start — discreet, too. I mean, that's if Sefton is in Chatham —'

'Which seems unlikely to me. It seems odd that Sefton should come up to London after so long just to murder his former partner. He had to be here — perhaps he found out something about Plume's activities and went to see him. A quarrel that ended in murder.'

'True, but I think it's worth a visit to find out about their partnership — it's only half an hour by train. We could be there and back in no time. At least we'd know something about this Frederick Sefton — he might be dead for all we know. Then we could cross him off the list.'

'And what list would that be?' Jones grinned at him.

'Metaphorically speaking, Sam, of course, but you know what I mean. You said when we were on our way here that you thought that Michael O'Malley's "Will" might be a doctor — so here's a doctor with a grudge against Plume.'

'But not called Will — though, I admit, Michael could have been wrong.'

'To be sure, he could, Sammy, and he with the drink taken — Rochester, then?'

'Somewhere, at any rate. Standing here's not doing a lot of good. Let's find a bite to eat, then you can tell me about your man in Rochester. I told Cuff I wanted to see Mrs Brady about Kitty Quillian — we could go there after we've eaten.'

The Angel on Carburton Street was snug after the cold standing in Weymouth Street. They found an empty booth and ordered chops and mashed potato from a waiter whose face contorted itself into a variety of expressions, but from whose mouth no sound came. They assumed that the waiter had understood their request for, with a violent nodding of the head which seemed in danger of parting from the shoulders, he went off at a run.

'The Face-Maker, himself — I swear I saw him at Astley's Circus the other night, exhibiting all the contortions, energetic and expressive, of which the human face is capable, and all the passions of the human heart — love, jealousy, revenge, hatred, avarice, despair — the last words in capitals on the poster: *A Thousand Characters in One Face.* Perhaps this is his day job.'

'Disguised as a waiter. Talking of which — disguise not waiters — you might abandon your role as undertaker now, Mr Vholes. Where did you get that from? Smith would have done.'

'Lawyer, Mr Jones, if you please. Saw it on a passing cart — Vholes with an H — odd, ain't it. Good name for a lawyer — sounds a bit rodentish, I thought. Vholes creeping about his dusty office, nibbling at his deeds and parchments. Well, if you think I don't need it, I shall take off my moustache and put it in my pocket.' He took out his comb and rearranged his hair. 'There — I am myself again. The Inimitable, at your service. I never shall desert Mr Micawber.'

'Revenge as motive?'

'Very likely. It strikes me as not entirely unnatural that someone should murder Plume. When I think of what he has done to those girls — and to Mrs Lawson — it makes my blood boil.'

'Mine, too, but we have to find Sefton. We want Miranda Deverall released before she comes to trial and I want to know why he did it — if he's our man.'

'You're thinking whether Sefton wanted revenge because Plume did him down over the money. But, it's a long time to wait — unless Sefton had fallen on hard times and went to Plume for money, was refused, and stabbed him in a fit of rage.'

'I can certainly see Plume refusing. But I was thinking that if our murderer is Sefton, is a doctor, then perhaps the motive lies in Plume's life. And I thought about something Michael O'Malley said. His visitor gave him the money to get a good meal and he told Michael to give up the drink.'

'You mean that doesn't square with our idea of him as the murderer of Brimstone and possibly Kitty Quillian.'

'I suppose I do. I wondered about Plume's past — we know what he got up to in London. What did he get up to in —'

'Suppose,' Dickens interrupted, 'Plume was up to his tricks in Chatham and Sefton knew something, somehow found out about Plume's doings in London and went to confront him.'

'But, it would be more likely that Plume would kill him to stop his mouth. There were no signs of a struggle — had there been, Goss couldn't have believed Miranda Deverall had done it. Plume refused him something — the money perhaps.'

'Or, Plume refused to cease his activities. There was something between them — something old that had been eating away at Sefton for years.'

Jones considered Dickens's words. 'You could be right. You said that the past doesn't go away. And it's true — murder happens so often because the past catches up with the present, somehow.' His eyes gleamed. 'You've got it. Something in Plume's past that is linked with the present. Something that

Sefton knew — something tipped the balance, something he found out.'

'And that ties in with Brimstone — we said he was deep in it, supplying the drugs to Plume. Suppose Sefton found out about the Brimstones and went to threaten Brimstone —'

'But, why after the murder of Plume? He's surely not intending to bump off the whole lot of them.'

'I suppose not, but I'd like to know why he went to the Brimstones.'

'I shall be asking Mrs Brimstone if they knew of any Doctor Sefton — unlikely, I know, but there must be a connection. I don't think she did it — not that I'll tell her that.' Jones frowned. 'Of course, there may be no connection at all — it's possible that Brimstone's murderer is someone else entirely.'

'Then Sefton is not Will, and to eliminate Sefton we need go to Rochester.'

'You're right — we'll go after we've seen Mrs Brady. Now tell me about your friend in Rochester.'

'The Reverend William Drage — I knew him years ago. He was a curate in Chatham, lived at Ordnance Terrace next door to us when my father was a Navy Pay Clerk. I was in Rochester in October 1848, and called on him about the daughter of one of his parishioners. He wanted a place for her at the Home — we got her in, and she's done well. Anyway, he lives now at Minor Canon Row by the Cathedral. He'd know the doctors and lawyers, the professional men. I thought he might know of Sefton.'

'And, if he doesn't, we can go and find Clover Lane.'

'Oh, I know where that is — I was at school there. The school of William Giles — he's not there now. He gave me a copy of Goldsmith's *Bee* when I left — I still have it.'

The waiter brought their chops and beer — the mouth worked hideously and a mysterious voice from the interior announced sepulchrally, 'Two chops and mash, two beers, number four.'

'Throws his voice as well,' said Jones as the waiter ran off.

Dickens laughed. 'Run off to now to catch it, perhaps, or skimmed. Have you noticed that peculiar and mysterious power that waiters have of skimming out of rooms which other mortals possess not?'

'Born to waitering — bred to it. Runs in families, I daresay.'

'Or skims.'

'Very droll. Never mind waitering — it's doctoring, we're concerned with. Do you know any doctors in Rochester or Chatham?'

'I knew Doctor Matthew Lamert — he married my aunt Mary, my mother's sister. They went to Ireland where she died in 1822. He died two years ago in Cork. His son, James, used to take me to the theatre. I remember the smell even now — orange peel and lamp oil. I remember being terrified at *Richard III* — and *Macbeth* — thrilled, too, at the wonder of it all. Ah, memory, memory, Sam.'

Dickens was silent then. It was James Lamert who had employed him at the blacking factory. His own mother had been eager to send him back there when his father had quarrelled with Lamert — he could never forget that.

Jones watched a shadow like a flitting cloud darken the bright eyes. What was he thinking about? Something from the past, something upon which he brooded sometimes, something untold?

'Well, let's hope that someone remembers Plume and his partner,' Jones said.

Dickens looked at him. 'Yes, indeed. Doctors, you said. There's a Doctor Steele who lives in Strood — Chairman of the Liberal Association. We might see him, if we've time.'

'Time we went. Let's pay up and go to see what Mrs Brady can tell us about Kitty.'

31: Mother and Son

Mary Brady was shoving a few things in a bag. Time to go before Jimmy came back. And he would come, and he'd be in one of his furies. She knew that. Crippled Bobby had seen him and told him about Paul. Jimmy would blame May. She couldn't protect May now. Jimmy was too strong. You couldn't reason with him. You couldn't fight him off — not now. When he was smaller, Paul had been able to subdue him. Sometimes, even Mary had soothed him, but that was a long time ago when he was small enough — not much more than a baby and she'd given him a cordial, rocked him and said his name, over and over: *Jimmy, Jimmy, hush now, hush.* Not that the peace lasted. He'd cry, a terrible sound like howling. His arms and legs would thrash, he would beat at her with his little fists and those black eyes would stare at her, wild, angry eyes. God forgive her, she'd not been able to love him.

Get out, she told herself. She had some money in the tin. Where to go? She could have wept. In all this city of millions of souls, she had no one to turn to. No use going to Annie — too near. Jimmy would find them. There was only the church — but she hadn't been in a long time. Hadn't dared. Confess — all her sins. She couldn't. She didn't love her son. She didn't love her husband. She didn't care that he had another woman. She'd brought a fiend into the world. But May was innocent. Surely, they'd look after her. The priest at Our Lady in Lisson Grove might find somewhere for May. The Sisters of Mercy might give them both sanctuary. She'd have to try.

No use thinking about Paul. They wouldn't be seeing him again. He'd told her about Kitty Quillian. Kitty Quillian — his lover. And there was a child. His child — dear God, the fool. He didn't know where Kitty had gone. The child was at Mrs Brimstone's — looked after, Paul said. Well, Mary had thought, I hope Kitty's somewhere safe. She hadn't answered him. Only May mattered.

The pain came suddenly. She felt as if an axe had cleaved her in two. Her breath stopped and she sat suddenly. May stared at her with uncomprehending eyes.

Mary waited until the agony subsided and she was able to breathe. 'May — there's drink in the cupboard. Get the bottle.'

Paul had had some brandy from somewhere. He'd drunk most of it before the police came, but there was some left. It'd bring her round — enough to finish the bag and get going.

May brought the bottle and Mary took a few sips. 'Just a minute, May, till I get me breath back.'

She felt her eyes closing. Just to sleep, she thought — and not to wake up. She opened her eyes and there was poor May. She looked frightened. Mary saw the tears well up.

'Just sit with me a minute, there's my good girl. Ma'll be right as rain.'

They sat on the bed, half asleep, their eyes closed.

Then in the silence, Mary heard the scraping of boots on stones. The sound came from the little room beyond where she and May slept. There was a coal chute leading from the alley behind and whoever was sliding down could get in if the little door was open. She'd put the bolt on, hadn't she? She felt terror then. Jimmy.

The door which separated the main room from the little room burst open. He was there, black as the devil, those terrible eyes burning and half a brick in his hand. She pushed May behind her.

'Goin' somewhere, ma? Leavin' me, woz yer?'

From somewhere she found the strength to get up to face him.

'Yes, Jimmy. And you'll have to kill me to stop me. I'm dyin' anyway so I don't care. And while you're killin' me, May can get out.'

Jimmy stepped back. She wasn't his ma anymore. He didn't know this woman whose eyes blazed back at him. She seemed bigger, somehow.

Mary saw his hesitation. He was frightened of her. She saw his hand drop, the one holding the brick.

'Well?' she said.

He didn't answer and the silence seemed to swell in the room.

'Jimmy, Jimmy, oh, Jimmy, hush, hush.'

He seemed to shrink, to dwindle to the child she'd lost somewhere along the way. She took a step towards him. Then came the sound of knocking at the door.

'Police, Mrs Brady, open up.'

Jimmy dropped his half-brick. He gave her a look. There was something — a half-longing, perhaps. Then he was gone. She heard him scrabbling up the chute. She never saw him again.

Mary sank onto the bed. The knocking continued. 'Open the door, May. Let them in.'

Dickens stood at the open door. Sam was on the ladder behind him. Dickens saw the frightened face of the girl at the door and, stepping in saw the woman on the bed. This is a sick woman, he thought, looking at the grey face with its sheen of sweat and pinched nostrils.

'Don't be frightened, May,' he said gently to the child. 'She'll be all right in a minute.'

He saw that there was some brandy left in a bottle. He took his handkerchief and moistened it then dabbed at the

247

colourless lips. Mary's eyes opened and he saw how they were black with pain in the deep, dark sockets.

'Can you get some water, May — for her to drink?'

Jones eased himself quietly into the room and waited for Dickens to feed Mrs Brady with the water.

Mary Brady looked at the face bending over her and the kindness in the large eyes. Not police, surely. And how gentle was his touch. Then she saw the other man standing at the door — he looked more like a policeman. She drank some of the water and eased herself into a sitting position.

'Are you able to speak?' Dickens asked her.

The pain had eased a bit — but she could feel it. It was her constant companion, sometimes like a dull burning as if a knife were lodged in her breast, at others like the cleaver splitting her in two, but never absent. An always sullen, sometimes violent lover who would kill her in the end.

'Yes. What do you want?'

The taller man spoke. 'I wanted to ask you about Kitty Quillian.'

'Why?' She couldn't understand. What had Kitty to do with it all? She'd gone off somewhere — she couldn't have been with Paul last night.

'Do you know about the doctor who was murdered? Doctor Plume.'

'I heard somethin' — Mrs Hodson — who May worked for — was friendly with him. Kitty worked there.'

'We think Kitty had met the murderer — someone saw her with him and she was outside the doctor's house in Weymouth Street on the night of the murder. I think she may be in danger. Do you know where she might have gone? She left her baby at a Mrs Brimstone's.'

'I don't know.'

'You don't know who the baby's father is? Might she have gone to him?'

Mary Brady made a sound that might have been a laugh, but she might have been just getting her breath. Jones waited for her to speak again.

'May, lovey, will you take the bag into the other room. Take the things out and put them on the bed — laundry, sir,' she said to Jones. May took the bag away. *They were leaving*, Jones thought. He wondered about Jimmy Brady. He'd ask about that later.

'I didn't want May to hear. Kitty hasn't gone to the baby's father. He's in prison. You might as well know it — the father is my husband, Paul. Not that I cared. I don't care about anythin' — only little May and what's to happen to her when I'm gone.'

'Gone?' Dickens asked.

'I'm dyin', sir — cancer, here.' She pointed to her breast. 'I thought Kitty would look after May, but then she disappeared. I didn't know then that she and Paul... She's a good girl, an' Paul, he could be charmin' when he wanted to be. He told me before the police took him. But, now — I was goin' away — the bag — but —'

'What about your son, Jimmy — you know the police are looking for him. Has he been here?'

She closed her eyes. 'I haven't seen him.'

Jones knew he could ask May. She would tell him, he had no doubt. She would not lie, she was too simple, too innocent and he would not take advantage of that. And he had seen the half brick on the floor. He remembered that Stemp had told him that Jimmy had been going to finish him off with a brick or stone. Hm. It didn't matter. Cuff would find him. The important thing was what to do for Mrs Brady and May. He looked at Dickens.

'Mrs Brady, you need to see a doctor — I know Doctor Fuller at the Infirmary. He can give you something for the pain. I can ask him to come.'

'I can't go to hospital, sir. I can't leave May, but she can look after me — and my neighbour, Annie will come.'

Dickens understood that. What would May do if her mother was in hospital? They couldn't abandon her. He thought about the boy, Jimmy. May couldn't be left here, alone. Suppose the boy did come back.

'I'll see Doctor Fuller for you.'

'Thank you, sir. It's good of you.'

They left her then and climbed the ladder up into Bones Alley.

'Too late for Rochester, Charles. I'll have to see Paul Brady at Newgate. See if he knows where Kitty is. And I have to meet Rogers from the train with Hodson and Brimstone. I'll see what they can tell me about Kitty — and her baby.'

'I'll go to the Infirmary to see Doctor Fuller, and then I'll go home. Tomorrow, then?'

'Yes, but I'll have to get Mrs Hodson and Mrs Brimstone before the magistrate in the morning.'

'We could get the train from London Bridge at one o'clock. I'll come to Bow Street at noon — from Wellington Street, where I shall be doing some work for *Household Words*.'

'Writing on the plight of child criminals?'

'Something on those lines. I've a piece for 14 December — *A December Vision* — thirty thousand children, hunted, flogged, imprisoned, but not taught. Disease, triumphant in every alley — a few darts at the noisy fools and greedy knaves who talk about it and do nothing. Don't get me started again — I'm off to the workhouse to find Fuller. And so, farewell until I meet thee next.'

Jones smiled as he watched him walk away with his familiar quick, light strides. He'd read what Dickens had written before about the orphans, the ragged schools, the workhouses, Newgate — all the ills of society. What a passionate man Dickens was — such fire, such tremendous energy, and yet such tenderness. He thought of him moistening Mary Brady's lips with the brandy. Poor woman. Newgate, then, to see her husband.

Dickens made his way up East Street, turning right into Paddington Street and then into Northumberland Street and the Workhouse Infirmary. Doctor Fuller was in his dispensary. Dickens told him about Mrs Brady and the doctor said that he would see Mrs Brady as soon as he could — tomorrow morning. He would give her something for the pain. There was not much else he could do.

'Did you find your missing girl? Kitty Quillian?'

'No, we did not. Superintendent Jones is following a possible lead. You didn't have a man come in with a cut hand yesterday or this morning?'

'I'm afraid not. A constable enquired last night. We don't get many accident cases. Half our patients are children with chronic diseases, and the other half are adults with the same. TB, other lung disease, skin diseases, lepra — all the consequences of poverty and hunger. And I must get back, Mr Dickens. I'll do what I can for Mrs Brady.'

Dickens went away across Nottingham Street where the sailor had seen the Italian boy. He had liked the look of Mog Chips. He wondered whether he would go back to sea. If not, then Dickens thought he might send him down to Devon with a message for a certain Captain Pierce. Captain Pierce was the grandfather of the mute boy, Davey, who had been employed at the home for fallen women in Shepherd's Bush — Dickens had rescued him from the street. He ought to write to the Captain — perhaps Mog Chips would take the letter. Somehow he thought Mog and the Captain would get on well. It was an idea.

A few minutes from Nottingham Street and he was in Devonshire Place and walking up to number 1 Devonshire Terrace. He thought how quickly the workhouse and its attendant slums were left behind. Here was quiet and comfort, warmth and ease. *Double city*, he thought, *double lives*. There was harassed Doctor Fuller, doing what he could on a pittance; there in Weymouth Street had been Doctor Plume, whose well-furnished house sheltered a blackguard.

And are we not all two — he reflected, coming to the iron gate behind which he led his private life — the private one and the one our public life calls forth? He thought of Jones and the secret sorrow of the death of his daughter, Edith. And himself? A man might keep secrets even from himself, so deeply buried were they. But secrets came to the surface, unbidden sometimes. A wave of something like sickness would sometimes assail him — the old, unhappy want of something, something that even his wife and nine children could not supply.

And this other doctor, if doctor he be? What secret had he kept? Had it been a fever in his blood, at last running so high that he came to confront his enemy?

32: Trapped

Paul Brady was a man who lived in the moment. He took his pleasures without much thought of the consequences. He liked a drink, he liked a talk at The Neptune, he liked a game of cards, and he liked the company of a young woman. He had liked Kitty Quillian — lively, good-humoured and willing. She made him feel — well, like a man again. A man who could please a woman. Mary was …

Well, sure, Mary was sick, but what could he do about that? It wasn't his fault. Jesus, he gave her what he could — sure it was as much as a man could do. He knew that Satan — whatever they called him — was a bad 'un, but, Christ, he needed the money. There was Kitty and her baby to think of. What was a man to do?

Jones watched him as he listened to the man and his excuses. Not a bad man, weak and wanting a good time, heedless of his sick wife and that poor child. And careless of the son whose badness he pretended not to see, but Jones didn't want to hear anymore.

'I'm not interested in your doings with Satan — that's for Sergeant Cuff to deal with, though it was my constable you attacked — and you'll go down for that. I want to know about Kitty Quillian.'

'Kitty?' Paul Brady looked confused.

'Where is she?'

'I don't know and that's the truth, sir. I've been lookin', but no one's seen her. I can't understand it — she — we — I was goin' to marry her after…' He looked down. *Guilty about Mary*, Jones thought. Paul Brady shook off the thought of his wife.

'She was a good girl, Kitty, and she was fond of little May. It would have been all right except —'

'Jimmy?'

'Ah, well — there was a bit of difficulty, to be sure. Jimmy is — Kitty was — she said he frightened her. She said she'd seen him followin' us. I didn't see that, but sure — it would have been all right. I'd have seen to that.'

Jones didn't ask how. He very much doubted it. He could see that Jimmy would be too much for Kitty to deal with. Perhaps she had vanished because of Jimmy. But, then she wouldn't have left the child.

'What about the child? Your wife said you were the father.'

'Sure, 'tis true, sir. An' I can't understand it — Kitty loved that little boy. That's why I needed the money, sir. I was a desperate man. I —'

Oh, stow it, thought Jones. He was curt. 'She was seen with a man by several people — a man I want to find in connection with the murder of Doctor Plume. What can you tell me about that?'

'She told me that some fella had asked her about the doctor — asked where he could find him. He had business with the doctor so he told her, an' he offered her some money for information — for your baby, he said. He was all right. She said he was all right. She told him what she knew about the goings on. And, then, after the doctor was killed and that girl was taken by the police, Kitty disappeared —'

Paul Brady stopped suddenly. Jones saw the sudden fear in his eyes. He had realised the significance of Jones's statement, that he wanted to find a man in connection with Plume's murder.

'That girl didn't do it?'

'No.'

'And you'll be thinkin' that the murderer is the man Kitty met? And that could mean… Oh, Jesus.'

'Exactly, Mr Brady.'

'But, she said he was all right — he was interested in her and the child. He gave her money — said it was for the baby. Hoped she'd be happy. It doesn't make sense, sir. Why would he kill Kitty?'

It didn't make sense. Once again, the murderer confounded Jones. The man who gave money to Kitty for her baby was the man who had given money to Michael O'Malley and told him to give up the drink. Jones didn't answer. Paul Brady didn't know where Kitty was. He couldn't waste any more time.

'The baby — you know that Kitty didn't take him? How?'

'I saw Mr Brimstone. He said they'd look after him till I could make some arrangement. Sure, I would have — I was going to when —'

Would have. Would have. Too late, Jones thought, but he didn't say it. No point. It was time he went to meet Rogers. He could find out about the baby from Mrs Brimstone.

Sleek. That was the word. Sleek as a cat, Mrs Amelia Hodson. At Bow Street, Jones regarded the woman who had left Miranda Deverall to face a charge of murder.

There was something polished about the smooth, dark green velvet pelisse and the matching bonnet which she had taken off. He saw the dark, shining brown hair and the deep blue eyes. Yes, she was very attractive, indeed, and she knew it. He could tell by the way she looked back at him with the suggestion of a smile on the full lips — assessing him, wondering if she could charm him.

He let the silence continue while he read his notes. She could wait. Silence might unnerve her. It often did with suspects.

They wanted you to be the first to break it so that they could feel that they still had the power of their secret. Not that the secret meant guilt, not always. But murder had a way of uncovering the secrets of all those who were linked to the act itself. Murder was the stone cast onto the waters, the sudden, violent smack rending the placid surface, but then the ripples rolled outwards to the very edge of the lake, and even those at that edge felt the cold touch of the water.

The secrets might not be germane to the case, but they rose out of the dark water, and hitherto ordinary, unremarkable lives were never the same again.

But, he knew her secrets and she didn't know how much he knew, and that gave him the power. He knew that she hadn't killed Plume. But, she didn't know that. More power to him. Rogers had told her that she was wanted in London in connection with the murder of Doctor Lancelot Plume.

Jones had written down the evidence he would put before the magistrate: Mrs Hodson had left London immediately after the murder. The accused, Miranda Deverall, had lived in her house. Mrs Hodson was concerned in the case of the missing Kitty Quillian who had worked for her. She was associated with Mrs Martha Brimstone whose husband had been murdered, too.

Jones had laughed to himself while he was writing. He could see very well how he might portray the two of them. Harpies. And he could add the association with Mrs Bertha Raspin, already on remand in Newgate, accused of procuring abortion. Mrs Raspin, it was alleged, had been frequently at Mrs Hodson's house to treat young women… He could pause there, he had thought. Let the magistrate draw his own conclusions.

There was plenty against Martha Brimstone, too — she had left London to take up residence with Mrs Hodson. She had left just after the police had visited her house in search of Kitty Quillian. Her husband had been murdered. He, Superintendent Jones, had reason to suspect her.

Besides, he would tell the magistrate, there was the disappearance of Kitty Quillian's child. He had spoken to the child's father who had told him that Mrs Brimstone had promised to take care of the baby. When the police searched the house, the baby was missing and there had been no baby in Manchester where Mrs Brimstone had been discovered with her associate, Mrs Amelia Hodson. Associate — nice word. Very suggestive.

The evidence would serve, he thought, keeping his eyes down. They wouldn't be found guilty of murder. But, they might be brought to trial on other grounds. Brimstone implicated in abortion and the stealing of a baby — not that he thought Kitty's baby would be found. There might not be enough evidence to convict Mrs Hodson of anything — but, for now, he would be glad to see her on remand, if only for what she had done to Miranda Deverall. And that's where he would begin.

He looked up. She sat perfectly still. Unmoving and unmoved. Time to set the ripples rolling.

'Annie Deverall?'

She was surprised. She hadn't expected this. There was the hint of a flush at her jawline.

'Miranda Deverall as I know her now. You didn't stay in London to help her. Why? She had been sent to you by Mrs Catherine Murray, your cousin who was her stepmother. You were responsible for her, were you not?'

She was annoyed. He saw the thinning of the generous lips and a flash of fire in the blue eyes. A glimpse of what she might be when charm failed her. 'I couldn't do anything with her. She was so sulky and awkward. It was hopeless, and she didn't want to be a milliner. I would have sent her back to Catherine, but she went off. There was nothing I could do about it. I was sorry for her, of course.' She tried a smile which was meant to tell him that she had done her best. He ignored it.

'Why do you think she killed Doctor Plume? You must have thought so since you made no attempt to defend her — the girl who had been put in your charge.'

'I have no idea — he tried to help her. She wouldn't eat. I asked him to see what he could do for her. But she wouldn't co-operate. Sullen and silent. Doctor Plume couldn't understand her. God knows, he tried.'

'He seduced her. I know it. I found it out, and you knew it. Was that your motive for killing him?'

She was rattled now. 'I didn't kill him. There was no reason.'

'But you were his mistress.' She opened her mouth. 'No need to deny it. Surely, you were angry, distressed, to realise he had betrayed you?'

'No, I —'

'What? You knew about what he had done to Miranda — seduced her, aborted her child and you felt nothing. You just accepted the situation — let the girl go and carried on your affair with him?'

She was trapped. To save herself from a charge of murder, she had to condemn herself as an accessory to abortion and to the ruthless abandonment of a girl for whom she had been responsible. And to being a pandar for her lover. She couldn't answer. It suited Jones.

'You can work out the answer to that one when you are on remand. I shall be putting my evidence before the magistrate tomorrow morning. As far as I am concerned, you are a suspect for the murder of Lancelot Plume. I have no doubt that you will be remanded in Newgate along with Mrs Brimstone who is suspected of the murder of her husband. I am sure the magistrate will be interested in the fact that both of you fled London after the murders, and that you were found together in Manchester. And Kitty Quillian, who worked for you and lived at Mrs Brimstone's, is missing. As is her child.'

He left her then. He wasn't sorry that he'd trapped her. He thought of what Elizabeth and Charles had told him about Miranda Deverall. Amelia Hodson deserved all she got. Now for the grieving widow.

He watched Martha Brimstone before he went into the cell. She looked insignificant, a dowdy nobody compared with the smoothly polished Mrs Hodson, but he knew what she'd done. That expressionless face, the colour of stale lard, gave nothing away, and she was sly — slyness hung about her like a smell of old cooking. She wouldn't be easy to crack. Perhaps he should try the deceptive mildness. Softly, softly.

He went in and stood before her. She looked up at him with little, black opaque eyes, behind which, he thought, she would be thinking how to free herself.

'I didn't kill my husband. You can't say I did.'

'But you left London and he was found dead in your back yard — you need to explain.'

'We were to meet at Euston after —'

'After what?' Jones kept his tone mild.

'Just a few erran's.'

Jones merely nodded. 'But, you didn't wait for him — your husband.'

'I thought he'd get a later train.'

'You were not worried, alarmed, that he didn't come?'

He saw her think about this. 'No, I —'

'Of course, you wouldn't be,' Jones's voice was reasonable. 'You knew he was dead.'

'I didn't know. I didn't kill him. I didn't.'

'If you want to avoid a murder charge — and your situation is a grave one — then you must tell me what you did on the evening of the murder. What errands did Mr Brimstone carry out that night?'

Like Amelia Hodson, she was in a trap — the trap in which she had ensnared herself — and she knew it. Jones watched her eyes darting to the bars of the cell and back to the policeman. Jones waited, never taking his eyes off her, a cleverer cat than Amelia Hodson.

'He went to see a Mrs Cartwright — she wanted to adopt a baby. Well, I had one spare. Kitty Quillian left it — didn't care tuppence, that one, so I thought it best to find it a new home — a good one, too. Cartwrights are well off folk. They'll look after it. Better off.' She looked at him defiantly.

It was probably true. If Kitty were dead — which seemed more and more likely — the baby would have ended up in an orphanage. He thought about Eleanor and Tom Brim — but he and Elizabeth hadn't paid for a child. Mr Brim had asked them to take care of his children. And they loved them as if they were their own. But, so would Mrs Cartwright, perhaps. However, it didn't make Brimstone's conduct right — she couldn't know that Kitty wouldn't come back. And that word "spare" told him that, for her, it was business. He wouldn't debate the matter with her.

'The address?'

'They aren't there. Gone to France. You won't find 'em.'

'Someone there will remember your husband — if you want a witness, that is — it's up to you.'

She was sullen, hearing the sarcasm. 'Montague Square, twenty-eight. Rich folks.' As if that made it right.

'And the arrangements were?'

'He was to tell the Cartwrights to meet me at Saint Pancras Church. I gave 'em the baby —'

'How much?'

She didn't want to tell.

'I said, how much?'

She heard the iron in his tone. 'Fifty guineas.'

'And then?'

'I went to wait for Arthur, but he never came so I went. That's it.'

'And your husband — who else might have reason to kill him? Any other doctors you were dealing with?' That was as far as Jones wanted to go. The name Sefton would warn her that there might be someone else he suspected.

'What d'yer mean "else"? I had no reason —' she thought of herself first — 'an' I don't know who might have done it —'

'A pity that — useful for you if you could point the way to someone else.'

It wasn't, but he didn't need any more. He'd have to decide what to do about the baby later when they knew for sure what had happened to Kitty. He had enough evidence from the three witches. What he didn't tell Martha Brimstone was that he intended still to make much of the murder to the magistrate tomorrow morning. Let her sweat.

33: The Voice of Old Time

Brooker and Briggs, Burgess and Bailey, Budden the fat boy and one eyed Sparks, Dartle and Edwards, Parsons and Pordage, Tapley and Tupman and Weller and Wren. Weller and Wren, Weller and Wren…

Dickens could hear the names in his head beating in time with the sound of the train which was taking them to Rochester — names he had stolen from neighbours and shops and gravestones to give to characters in his works. Mary Weller had been his nurse when they lived in Chatham, at Ordnance Terrace, then St Mary's Place, where, from an upper window at the side of the house, he had looked upon an old graveyard. All the childhood days — the river where he had sailed on the Medway with his father in the Commissioner's yacht, the ships, the military parades on the lines, the windmills, the woods, the fields — had all vanished like a dream to be replaced by the dreary reality of Bayham Street, Camden Town.

'I left Chatham by coach when I was nine years old,' he said to Jones who was gazing at the unfolding landscapes as they chugged past the Elephant and Castle, Camberwell, and through Dulwich where Mr Pickwick had retired to his white house. The train gathered speed, taking them on to Penge, then Bromley.

'On your own?'

'Yes, packed like game — forwarded, carriage paid, to the Cross keys, Cheapside.'

'A parcel to be collected?'

'I suppose I must have been collected. I can't recall, but I've never forgotten the smell of damp straw — it rained all the way.'

'Kitty Quillian's baby.'

'What about it?'

'Passed around like a parcel — Mrs Brimstone said it was going spare. Dear God — she got fifty guineas for it — him, I should say.'

'A son — someone wanted an heir, I daresay. Moneyed folks?'

'So she said. Name of Cartwright.'

Dickens looked thoughtful. 'Any address?'

'Montague Square.'

Dickens whistled. 'Eldred and Joyceln Cartwright. Well, I never.'

'You know them?' Jones's eyes were eager.

'He's a stockbroker — I met them at some dinner. My wife told me that Mrs Cartwright was expecting a child — the interest being that they had been married for six years without any sign of a child. Great happiness, apparently, at the prospect of a son. He hoped for a son, of course.'

'Perhaps they'd ordered one from Mrs Brimstone,' Jones said drily. 'She said they'd gone to France.'

'To put you off the scent. But, they'd go somewhere — then come back with a few months old child. What can you do about it?'

'That's what Elizabeth asked when I told her. And the answer was that I didn't know. She only pointed out what I thought myself. Drag them through the courts — disgrace them, and what happens to the baby? The father is Paul Brady who will be in prison for a long time.'

'Orphanage. We know he would be better off with the Cartwrights, but — oh, I don't know, Sam — what did you say about the baby to the magistrate?'

'Only that he was missing and that I was pursuing enquiries. Not that he was interested in the child.'

'Who was the magistrate?'

'Old Snapper.'

'Ah.' Dickens knew Julius Snapper, beak-nosed, irascible bachelor whose outbursts of temper were legendary, and whose disdain for any woman brought before him meant that, innocent or guilty, she was sure to find herself in Newgate.

'It suited me that he ignored the fate of the child in this case because I wasn't ready to mention the Cartwrights — Mrs Brimstone could have told me a pack of lies. But now — well, I'll wait until we know for certain that Kitty is dead.'

'You think she is.'

'I do — Paul Brady told me how she loved the child. She wouldn't have left him.'

The train slowed as it approached Strood Station. They went out to take a cab which, after a few minutes, took them over Rochester Bridge where Mr Pickwick had dallied, contemplating nature and waiting for breakfast, and over which David Copperfield had trudged, footsore and tired, on his way to Dover.

The cab deposited them at the Bull Inn where Jones looked through the covered gateway as if he hoped to see Pickwick or Jingle, or best of all Sam Weller.

That gentleman seemed, after all, to be beside him. 'Business first, pleasure arterwards, old 'un, as King Richard said when he stabbed t'other King afore he smothered the babbies.'

Old 'un — impudent blighter, thought Jones, laughing, as he turned to follow Dickens marching on down the High Street towards the Cathedral and Minor Canon Row.

They went through the quiet precincts where the only sound was of the rooks hovering about the cathedral tower. Passing through Prior's Gate, they found themselves in the Row — a terrace of houses with red-brick walls toned down in colour by time and clinging ivy winding its leaves around the latticed windows, and odd little porches over the doors which Dickens always thought looked like the sounding boards over old pulpits.

A maid opened the door and they were shown into a panelled room where the windows showed a stone-walled garden with bare fruit trees. The Reverend William Drage stood waiting for them.

He was delighted to see Mr Dickens — and the Superintendent, of course. He asked about Mrs Dickens, the children, Mr and Mrs John Dickens whom he had known at Ordnance Terrace in Chatham; enquired about the girl he'd sent to Mr Dickens's home at Shepherd's Bush; praised *David Copperfield*, remarked on David's passage through Rochester and Chatham and the appearance, as the ugly old man to whom David sold his jacket, of Old Charley, a Rochester dealer in second hand clothes, a notorious drunkard who, legend had it, had sold himself to the Devil; invited them to take tea and plum cake, and after it was served, gazed at them benevolently with a question in his kindly hazel eyes.

'There is something with which I can help the Superintendent?'

'You have read of the death of Lancelot Plume?' Dickens asked by way of preparation.

'Indeed. A most shocking affair. A young girl, the newspaper said — dear me.'

Dickens explained his visit to Miranda Deverall in Newgate, and told him of their conviction that she was innocent, their certainty that the reasons for the murder lay in the past, and their desire to know something of Plume's former partner, Doctor Frederick Sefton. Could Mr Drage remember anything of them?

'Not a great deal,' William Drage responded. 'I know that not long after Doctor Plume's departure for London, Doctor Sefton gave up the practice and took a post at the hospital at Fort Pitt. Then, he went to London...' He paused there, and they saw him frown. He resumed after a few moments' thought. 'An odd young man — I met him once or twice — he came to the cathedral sometimes. Very reserved, lonely, I would say... *Something in his soul o'er which his melancholy sits on brood.*'

Dickens was quick. He completed the quotation from *Hamlet*. '*The hatch and the disclose will be some danger.*'

William Drage stared. 'You do not think he —'

Jones interrupted. 'We have no evidence, sir, but Mrs Plume told us of a quarrel. Had you heard of that?'

'Doctor Plume became a wealthy man upon his marriage. Sefton gave up his failing practice. It was said that Plume was better liked, and that Sefton failed for lack of funds as well as popularity. That was the talk, but I hardly think...'

'No,' said Jones, 'but I should like to find him. Would anyone at Fort Pitt know of him? He must have had a recommendation for a post in London if that is where he is.'

'I should think he will be remembered. Perhaps you should try Doctor Piper there.'

'We will. We ought to go now. I need to get back to London this evening.'

William Drage stood to escort them to the hall, but as they prepared to leave the room, he said suddenly, 'There's something I've remembered. Of course, it may be nothing of moment, but it's an odd little story connected with the two doctors.'

They sat down again and waited for William Drage to collect his thoughts.

'The story concerns a young servant girl whose mother was in service with the doctors — not a housekeeper, exactly — a woman who cooked and cleaned for them. She lived in her own house, but her daughter, Rose, helped her.'

Dickens glanced at Jones. A young servant girl. Something, perhaps. At last.

'How old was the girl?' Jones asked.

'Fifteen or sixteen — her mother's pride and joy. A beauty, they said. An only child. A sad tale. She disappeared on a bleak winter's day. It was thought she had drowned out on the marshes.'

'What was she doing out there?' Dickens knew the marshes well — not the kind of place you would take a stroll on a cold winter's day when the light faded fast and the water might rise. Where it was easy to lose your way.

'There was a sick aunt lived over at Hoo — Rose was to go to see her and stay overnight. She knew her way, having walked often, but the marshes can be treacherous. That is the only explanation. I don't know that it has anything to do with Plume or Sefton. The mother left their service. She died not long after.'

'No one connected either doctor with her disappearance?'

267

'No, Superintendent. It came into my mind because it was such a tragedy — the daughter, the mother and the father all dead so very quickly. It's the only odd thing connected with the two doctors that people remember.'

But, it's more than odd, thought Dickens, *if only you knew*. He thanked Drage for his help and they left him in front of his warm fire, musing on the death of the pretty little girl.

Their returning steps took them to the great west door of the cathedral. Somewhere quiet to reflect on what they had heard. They went in to the soaring space where shadows were deepening in the corners, and jewels cast upon the pavement of the nave from stained glass by the declining sun, began to perish. There was a smell of dust and earth. *And something indefinable*, thought Dickens, *the smell of age*.

'It's like looking down the throat of old Time,' he murmured.

'The past again. What did Sefton brood on when he sat here for those years after Plume was gone?'

'The story of the servant girl? Rose. What did you make of that?'

They sat down in the gathering twilight. The jewels faded to darkness. Someone came out of shadows near the altar with a taper shivering in the dark.

'A little light in our darkness,' whispered Jones, 'that's what I think of it.'

Candles flared up. The darkness was dissolving up there, at a distance. They caught the gleam of light on the brass eagle holding the sacred book upon his wings.

'A beauty, they said. Young — innocent, probably. A girl who vanished, a girl who worked in the house of Doctor Lancelot Plume,' Dickens whispered back.

'I wonder — did he seduce her? Did she run away — to her death, out on those marshes?'

'With child, perhaps?'

'And Sefton knew.'

'That's what he brooded on.'

'But all those years?'

'It must be as we said, Sam — he found out about Plume's life in London, went to confront him. The old quarrel — not about money, about Rose.'

The shadows deepened round them. Dickens looked along the nave to the chancel where within the grill-gate, white robes could be dimly seen, and the organ sounded faintly, a low, deep murmuring — the voice of Time. They sat, listening, hoping to catch the meaning, but it was obscure, mysterious. Nothing to tell them.

'We have to find him. How far is it to Fort Pitt?'

'Ten minutes walk.'

The way into Chatham took them down the High Street, passing the Guildhall with its moon-faced clock where Dickens recalled seeing an Indian swallow a sword.

'I now suppose he wasn't and he didn't, but at the time, well it was a phenomenon.'

'Disillusioning, time.'

'Ain't it just. I once thought the Guildhall the grandest place I'd ever seen.'

They reached Watts's Charity with its lantern over the quaint old door. Jones paused to look at the curious inscription which promised six poor travellers, not being rogues or proctors, bed and board for one night and a gift of fourpence.

'Two poor travellers?' asked Jones. 'Not to be sneezed at — fourpence.'

They walked on down the High Street full of old gables and timbers carved into strange faces and latticed bay windows until Dickens stopped suddenly.

'Chatham,' he said.

'Where?'

'Hereabouts. If anyone knows to a nicety where Rochester ends and Chatham begins, it is more than I do. But, on the high ground there is Fort Pitt where Doctor Piper, we hope, may be found. You can see the Chatham Lines behind where we used to watch the military parades and reviews. Beyond the lines, there was a grim collection of cottages called Tom All Alone's. I was always looking for poor Tom, whoever he was. I had it in my mind that he must be an orphan ghost — I never found him, but he haunted my dreams.'

An inquisitive little boy, I bet he was, thought Jones, as they toiled up the hill. He imagined a bright-eyed lad whose eyes darted this way and that, taking it all in, frightening himself, but unable to resist the lure of Tom All Alone. And, years later, writing it all down.

Doctor Piper consulted his books. Yes, he had a copy of the letter of recommendation he had written for Doctor Frederick Sefton — somewhere. He turned the pages, frowning — somewhere.

'Ah, yes. Here it is —'

'The hospital?' Jones asked, hardly able to restrain his growing impatience.

'Lying-in Hospital — Queen Charlotte's.'

He handed the letter to Jones who scanned its contents. Dickens saw his face change. He had seen something that was significant, but he only said, 'He was a good doctor, you say here.'

'Oh, yes, indeed. A very skilled surgeon. A man of few words — not a sociable man, but I valued him. I was sorry to see him go.'

'Were you surprised at his choice of hospital in London?' Dickens knew that the hospital was for invalid soldiers and that there was an asylum for insane soldiers at Fort Pitt, too.

'Not at all. We are a military hospital, but we do deal with confined women, the wives of soldiers and other workers, too. There are some one hundred and fifty confinements each year. It is difficult in that we have no special wards for lying-in patients — the wives and children are treated in the barrack rooms. Doctor Sefton took a special interest in the lying-in cases, especially where disease took hold after birth. Many of these women are undernourished and weak before they give birth, and after, well — puerperal fever, septicaemia, phthisis... He wanted to save lives, Superintendent, and he very often did so.'

To save lives, thought Dickens, *and yet to be a murderer*. That was Plume's doing — it must have been.

Doctor Piper was still talking. 'And, of course, as far as Queen Charlotte's Hospital is concerned, it was an ideal choice. The wives of soldiers and sailors are considered to have special claims upon the Charity. Doctor Sefton's experience here would have fitted him well for his work there. I said so in my letter.'

'You have not heard of him since his departure?' Jones asked.

'No, I have not. I did not expect to — he was not a man who made friends. In fact, I have not thought about him for years — not until...'

'Until?'

'I heard of Plume's death. It has been the talk of the town. I wondered if Frederick Sefton had met Plume in London —'

'He may have. That's why we wish to find him.' Jones was brisk. Time to go before the doctor put two and two together. 'You have been most helpful, Doctor Piper. I am much obliged to you, and now we must hurry for our train to London. Might I keep the letter for the time being?' The letter would be useful at Queen Charlotte's Hospital — save time.

Outside, Dickens asked immediately, 'What was in that letter. I saw your face — there was something important. What?'

Jones smiled at his urgency. 'See for yourself.'

Dickens took the letter and began to read. *'Dear Doctor Cream, I write to recommend, without reserve, my colleague, Doctor Frederick Willoughby Sefton* — Willoughby — Will. Sam, we've found him. Will!'

34: The River Rises

'The geography's right,' Jones said.

They were on the train. They'd walked back along the High Street, resisting the temptation of a supper of fried soles and broiled fowl at The Bull, past the huge dark shape of the roofless castle, hurrying over the bridge again, aware of the water swirling in the darkness. They had caught the London train with only minutes to spare.

'It is,' Dickens replied. 'Just along the New Road — not that far from Devonshire Terrace.'

'And, more importantly, near enough the workhouse, David Street, Dab Lane, Bones Alley — and Weymouth Street. He was near Plume, he heard of him, found out — somehow — about Plume's activities —'

'And the past which he had thought to escape in London came rushing back. He knew about Rose — that she had been with child.'

'We think,' Jones put in, tempering Dickens's eagerness.

Dickens raised an eloquent eyebrow. 'Well, yes, but for now let's go with the idea. Sefton feared that she had drowned herself on the marshes. Sefton felt guilty — he may have thought he should have done something. It weighed on his mind.'

Jones considered for a few moments, 'I think you're right about the child. Consider the lying-in hospital. It fits — a charity for poor, pregnant women, women from the slums —'

'Unmarried women, too. They take in unmarried women at Queen Charlotte's. He wanted to atone for Rose's death.'

273

'Plume obviously didn't — I would bet he forgot all about her until —'

'Sefton turned up and reminded him. And they quarrelled, and in that quarrel, Plume was killed — somehow.'

'Mm — but, why did Plume turn his back on Sefton?'

'Told him to get out and Sefton, enraged, stabbed him.'

'Yet, no knife was missing — did Sefton use his own? In that case, did he intend to kill Plume?'

They were silent for a while until Dickens began again. 'And, yet, a good doctor...'

'He wanted to save lives — that's what Doctor Piper said. But, he was prepared to let Miranda Deverall suffer for his crime — I can't understand that. He must have known. Why hasn't he come forward to save her life?'

It was another unanswerable question — at least until they found the good doctor.

The train rolled into London Bridge Station. They threaded their way across another bridge — London Bridge, teeming with people — the clerks like so many black beetles, scurrying from their ledgers, their faces grey in the gas light; the fish-women from Billingsgate with rough shawls over their heads; the laundresses; the dock-porters — the cabs, carriages, carts and wagons. It was easier to walk than to be trapped in the solid mass of traffic.

It was raining. A sharp-edged wind was blowing off the river, and they could see the rain slanting across the light shed by the gas lamps. It promised to be a wild and windy night. Down below, the grimy steamers came and went from Old Shades Pier, taking the pinched-faced clerks back under the bridges to their lodgings and cramped houses in Vauxhall, Pimlico and Chelsea. The dome of St Paul's loomed black across to the left.

Beyond that were the dreadful walls of Newgate, and Bow Street where they would go before setting off to Queen Charlotte's Hospital.

At Bow Street, they saw Sergeant Rogers in earnest conversation with a police constable whom Jones did not know — *from Goss's Division*, he wondered. *Something afoot?*

Rogers saw the Superintendent — his glance was one of relief.

'Constable Cleek with a message from Inspector Cuff, sir. They think they've found Kitty Quillian.'

'Dead?'

The young constable spoke. 'Yes, sir. Mr Cuff wants yer to come, sir. He's sent ter Newgate for Mr Brady — to identify the body.'

'Where?'

'In an old privy, back of an old 'ouse, sir — nobody livin' there. Not far from Brady's. Down some steps. I can take yer.'

'Right — we'll get a couple of cabs. Rogers, we'll follow you and Cleek.' Jones turned to Dickens. 'Do you want to?'

'Yes.' Dickens would go — not that he wanted to enter that subterranean world again. Still, Satan was gone — and his myrmidons, excepting Jimmy Brady, of course.

In the cab, they couldn't speak. What was there to say? Poor Kitty. And that put paid to the idea of the good doctor. Good doctor he might have been, but he was a murderer. Plume might have been guilty of appalling deeds, but Arthur Brimstone and Kitty Quillian were innocent of any crime. Dickens rather suspected that Brimstone had been helpless in the matter of the farmed babies in the face of his wife's stronger will. Helpless, weak, cowardly, probably, but he hadn't deserved his death. And Kitty who had been kind to Miranda Deverall, and to little May Brady — what had she done to deserve a death in a foul privy? It was disgusting, unforgivable. Curse the man who had done that.

Bones Alley again. It was quiet as the graves in that miserable burying ground, except that somewhere unseen, the wind like a demented drummer, blew a door or window back and forth which made a hard, banging noise. The policemen's lamps lit up the flaws of stinging rain which whirled around them, soaking their coats and trouser legs. Hideous night.

Cleek led them down the steps into the little court where the rain thickened the darkness and the wind mourned through the dark tunnels before them. Rain was filling up the holes and slopping against the steps. They might have been at the edge of a river — the underground Tyburn River had flowed this way, Dickens remembered. Rising, perhaps, the ghost of the river giving up its dead. What about Mary Brady and May in their cellar? But, there was no time to do anything about that. Sam was walking on and Rogers waited for him. He hurried forward — he had no desire to be lost in the dark again.

They followed Cleek down the alleys which might have been the same alleys through which he had fled with Scrap — impossible to tell. Water sluiced down from the darkness, waterfalls cascaded from gutterless roofs, water sprang up from underground, and there was the putrid stench of excrement and filth. *God*, he thought, *it's like walking through a sewer* — it was walking through a sewer. And people lived in this, washed up and dragged down again by this filthy tide, the flotsam and jetsam of the flood.

They struggled on, going down, then up again. Cleek kept turning to make sure they were with him. Dickens could see his white face streaming in the light of the bull's eye lantern like the face of a drowning man. Jones turned, and Dickens saw how bleak his face looked in the flickering light. *The rain*, *eternal, maledict, and cold and heavy* — so Dante found in Hell's third circle. Down again. Hell again.

At length, Cleek turned into a narrow passage by a tumbledown building. Near the end they stopped, for another policeman came out with a man. It was Paul Brady in manacles. He was bareheaded and heedless of the rain which poured down on him, running down his face. He didn't look at them as he passed, guided by the policeman. He walked like a blind man, and Jones could see that the rain mingled with his tears. It was Kitty then.

They followed Cleek into the yard where Inspector Cuff waited for them by a derelict outhouse.

'In here,' he said. It was too wet to waste words on greeting.

Dickens and Jones went in with him. Cuff held up his lantern and they saw her.

She lay on her back. The rain fell through the broken roof onto her dress, torn at the bodice, and besplattered with mud and black stains which must have been blood. One eye was open, and her long hair was spread in the water that was ankle deep. She seemed to be floating. Ophelia — but a dreadfully wounded one. No willow here, growing aslant a brook, no cornflowers or daisies — just black, muddy water which smelt of excrement and corruption. The half of her face that leant towards them was unmarked. She had been pretty, but — Cuff moved his lamp — they saw that someone had smashed the other half of her face to pulp.

Dickens looked away, sick at heart. Violence and hatred had been at work here — someone had wanted to destroy her beauty. Not the weeping Paul Brady. Not Sefton, surely not Sefton who had given a tramp two shillings — and money to Kitty for her baby. He looked at Sam.

'Sefton didn't do this.' Jones's voice was flat. He thought about a half-brick he had seen at Mrs Brady's, and Stemp who had talked of a boy with a stone ready to bash his head in, and of Paul Brady who had said that the same boy had followed him and Kitty. 'Jimmy Brady's work. He did this.'

Dickens, Jones and Rogers left Inspector Cuff and his men to deal with the body. Cuff would be searching for Jimmy Brady. He was convinced by Jones's evidence. Constable Cleek would show them out of the alleys — he knew a way they could go to Harcourt Street

The rain was not so torrential now. Little squalls were tossed by the wind, and there was a faint edge of silver on the ragged clouds. The moon was waiting.

Cleek walked away, leaving them standing at the junction of Paddington Street and Crawford Street. It was only a step to Harcourt Street and Queen Charlotte's Hospital. Dickens felt wet to his very bones. He shivered.

Jones looked at him. 'You should go home, Charles — you'll catch your death.'

'No, Sam, I'll come. Let's finish it.'

36: The Stars Make No Sign

Doctor Sefton wasn't there.

He had not been there for six weeks. He had intended to sail for Canada on the SS *Helen* on 27 November. Doctor Hawkins, a surgeon at Queen Charlotte's, had agreed to see them.

'I wrote a recommendation for him. He was to take a post at the hospital in Quebec — I do not understand this at all. I can scarce believe what you have told me. He was one of the best surgeons I have ever met. His success in Canada was certain. Good God, Superintendent, are you certain?'

'Certain that I have enough evidence to justify my questioning him — yes.'

Doctor Hawkins had a commanding presence. He was master here, and he had wanted to know why they sought Doctor Sefton. He had looked at Dickens with speculation in his eye — so much so that Dickens had felt obliged to explain his concern in Miranda Deverall's case. Jones had explained that there was no doubt of the accused girl's innocence, that he had sufficient evidence to believe that Frederick Sefton might well have been in contact with Lancelot Plume, and that evidence of a past quarrel had come to light which made Sefton a suspect. He told Doctor Hawkins of the murder of Arthur Brimstone, and that it was his belief that the two murders were connected. More than that, he was not prepared to say, but it was imperative that they find Sefton.

'Why did he leave your hospital weeks before his intended departure for Canada? Did he say?'

'Only that he had affairs to settle before he left. I assumed that he meant family matters — that kind of thing.'

'And you have heard nothing of him since?'

'No, I did not expect to. Sefton was an excellent surgeon, but a solitary man. Not a man with whom one would be intimate. Ours was a professional relationship only.'

'He had no friends here with whom we might speak?' asked Dickens.

'No, I think not. As I say, he was a solitary man. I think we all imagined that he would be on his way to Canada by now.'

'If you do hear anything, you will let me know?' asked Jones.

'I will — should I ask others if they have heard anything?'

'I would be obliged, sir, if you would — discreetly, if you will.'

'I understand, though I am still confounded by what you have told me. I hope that you find him — and that he is able to prove his innocence in this affair.'

Jones didn't answer — he did not believe for a moment that Doctor Sefton would be able to prove his innocence. Moreover, he wanted to be gone. There was much to think about. What if Sefton had sailed to Canada on 27 November, the day after the murder of Arthur Brimstone. What then?

They went out to meet Rogers who had waited in the hall. They walked out down the drive, out of the gardens and onto the New Road. At least it had stopped raining. By unspoken consent, they stopped.

'That's a facer,' Dickens said.

'What?'

Jones explained. 'He's not there, Rogers. He might have sailed for Canada. He'd booked a passage on the *Helen* for twenty-seventh November — the day after Brimstone's murder.'

Rogers whistled. 'What now?'

'I want you to go to back to Bow Street, get Feak and Johnson, or anybody who's about — get down to the shipping agents, find out if Sefton was booked on the *Helen*, which wharf it was sailing from, and get down there to find out if he's gone.'

Dickens had a thought. 'If you can find a paper for twenty-fifth or twenty-sixth November, you might find the announcement of sailing — the *Daily News* publishes times and dates.'

'Good idea, Charles — if you can't find the announcement, then go to the agents — JB Ford in Broad Street deals with ships to Canada and North America. I'll leave it to you. Just find out if he's sailed — any way you can think of.'

Rogers went off in a hurry. He'd seen the Superintendent's face, and the disappointment there. Rogers believed in Jones, believed in him and admired him, and if he, Sergeant Rogers, had anything to do with it, then Sefton would be found and the Superintendent would triumph. If he had to search them ruddy docks all night, he'd find where Sefton had gone. Dickens and Jones stood where they were, looking up at the moon which had made its appearance from behind the rags of cloud. A few stars had appeared. Sefton might be looking up at them from the deck of the *Helen*, sailing away from them on the wide, wide sea. Perhaps he would be looking for a sign in those stars which would tell his fate. *But*, Dickens thought, watching the restless moon contend with the clouds, *there were no signs in the moon, or stars, for their reading.*

'If he's gone?'

'Well, I'll have him followed — just as the police followed Mrs Manning. They thought she might be on board the *Victoria* — she wasn't, but the point holds. If he sailed two days ago,

281

then he's not that far away. The ship will have left Gravesend yesterday. It will pass Plymouth tomorrow. I can telegraph Plymouth and the police can go out with the pilot cutter. The cutter takes off any passengers wanting to stay in England.'

'Or not wanting.'

'Exactly — Sefton could be taken off and brought back to London.'

'And now?'

'I'm going to Bow Street where I shall sit and wait for Rogers — all night, if I must. I need to do something, anything — I shall immerse myself in my papers.'

Dickens sympathised for he, too, hated delay — waiting was as painful as drawn daggers. However, he considered their sodden coats and boots. 'Samivel,' he began.

'Mr Weller — your wisdom?' Jones smiled at him.

'I knows an 'ouse — a good 'ouse — less than half a league hence — in Devonshire Terrace where there is a blazing fire, a decanter of brandy and where we can eats a bowl of giblet broth made from a recipe devised by the lady of the 'ouse — Lady Maria Clutterbuck wot is agoin' ter publish them self-same recipes in a book. Wot does yer say, Samivel, ter that?' It was true — Mrs Dickens was preparing a book of her recipes under the name of Lady Maria.

'I would say aye, Mr Weller, were it not that I should be in Bow Street to wait for Rogers.'

'He'll send a message to your house, Samivel —'

'But I'll be at your house.'

'Ha, but I will send a message to your Elizabeth to send a message to my house should a message come to your house — in short, as Micawber would say, something will turn up. In this case, the amiable Sergeant Rogers.'

'Very well, I am persuaded.'

There was a good fire in Dickens's study at Devonshire Terrace. John, his manservant, had been instructed to send the coachman with a message to Elizabeth, to provide broth, bread, cheese and hot water, to make sure the Superintendent's coat and boots were dried in the kitchen, to provide a pair of house slippers, and to see that they were not disturbed.

All this accomplished with Dickens's bustling energy, Jones and he sat by the fire with two glasses.

'Do you think he's gone?' Jones asked.

'He had affairs to settle, so Doctor Hawkins said. Well, we think we know what they were. Perhaps he wanted to settle the matter of Rose with Plume.'

'That's our theory — but, if it is so, how does he square his delicate conscience with the fact that someone else is accused of his crime?'

'He can't. And that's the sticking point. What kind of man is he?'

'A puzzle — a good doctor who gives money to a tramp, and to Kitty for her baby, yet stabs a man in the back and doesn't give himself up for the poor girl who will hang for his crime.'

'Unless,' Dickens thought for a moment, 'unless we've got it wrong. Perhaps we're making too much of his charity to Kitty. He wanted information. He knew how to get it — by giving her money for her child.'

'But Michael O'Malley?'

'Hm — that is a difficulty... Maybe, the doctor in him — a natural impulse, perhaps. Everyone we have spoken to portrays him as a solitary being. He makes no friends. He's single-minded — what he wants is to do his work. Suppose he thinks that his life is worth more than Miranda's —'

'But, there's all the work he did for those poor women — I can't help but connect it to Rose.'

'He's good at it. He believes he's the best. He is not so concerned with his patients, but with his own skill. He's ambitious —' Dickens warmed to his theme. He understood single-minded ambition — 'perhaps he wanted fame and fortune and thought he might find it in London. Then he found that Plume had it — Plume who was not half the doctor he was.'

'And that's what tipped the balance. As we thought before, he went to Plume for money to fund his ambitions in Canada. A spot of blackmail — pay up, or I will tell what I know about you. Plume refuses, of course.'

'And the new post — he can't give that up. He won't give it up. He's killed for it.'

'You've answered my question. He's gone — and I'll have to go after him.'

Dickens heard a knocking at the front door, then the sound of voices in the hall. John was speaking to somebody.

'A messenger from the gods, I'll be bound — Mercury in policeman's boots.' He had caught the sound of the voice of Sergeant Rogers. 'What did I tell you?'

John tapped at the library door, and opening it, announced the Sergeant.

'Of this earth, undoubtedly — he has it on his boots,' said Dickens, rising to meet Rogers.

'Sorry, sir — should have wiped 'em.'

'No matter, Sergeant — you are as welcome to the Superintendent as spring is to the earth. What news?'

Rogers turned to Jones. 'The ship sailed without him — Sefton wasn't on board.'

36: A Bonnet with a Blue Ribbon

Jones was in his office the next morning; he sat at his desk looking at *The Morning Post* with unseeing eyes. He was thinking about the news Rogers had brought the night before.

'Something,' Dickens had said, apropos of Sefton rather than Rogers, 'will turn up.'

And Jones was waiting — not with the sanguinary feelings of Mr Micawber. For, he thought, nothing might turn up. Sefton might be anywhere, in or out of London. He looked at the newspaper, at the advertisement promising the relief of defective vision: *immediately the newly invented spectacles are placed before imperfect vision, every object becomes clear and distinct…* If only…

He bent his head to the newspaper. It was time he thought about some other cases — successful ones, for a change. He noted that Benjamin Rouse, notorious burglar and thoroughgoing rogue, had been found guilty of a list of thefts, and had been sentenced to transportation for life — *not that he would mend his ways in Australia*, thought Jones, feeling a twinge of pity for Rouse's new hosts, but he would be glad to see the back of him. The learned Judge, so said the newspaper, had commended Police Constable Johnson for: *the meritorious manner in which he had secured the arrest.* Good — the police praised for once. He chuckled at the report of the conduct of one Cornelius Driscoll, an Irish tramp who had stolen three pounds of bacon from a shop in Aldersgate Street. He had been in London a week — he wasn't sure where he'd been before that. He was sentenced to twenty-one days in the House of Correction, to which he had replied, "Thank ye, your honour." Glad to get out of the rain, no doubt, and no need to steal his breakfast for a while.

Rogers came in. 'Visitor, sir. Mr O'Malley.'

Dear God, Jones thought, *Bridie's tossed him out. Sent him back to me, and he's come to haunt me — he'll be my pensioner for life.* He imagined himself condemned to a life sentence of Michael's memoirs of a tramping man, of the old, old days, of that blessed crayture, Bridie, and all their glorious youth. Could he refuse to see him? Say he was busy. No, Michael would wait — until the end of the world, and after.

He looked up. Rogers was staring at him, wondering at the anguish on his face.

'He looks all right.'

Jones's eyes narrowed. 'When you say all right…'

'Decent — clean, shaved, barbered — handsome, ain't 'e?'

'Clothes?'

'Course, sir, e'd hardly —'

'No — I know — how's he dressed?'

'Overcoat — new. Good boots, hat — quite a swell.'

Well, that sounded promising. Perhaps Bridie had provided for him — even if it was with only the means to go away again. *Still*, he thought, *what does he want with me?*

'Shall I send him in?'

'Yes, I suppose so.'

Michael O'Malley was, indeed, transformed. Not exactly a swell, but certainly respectable. And he was a handsome man when cleaned up.

'Michael — good to see you looking better. You found Bridie, then.'

'To be sure, I did — thanks to you.'

'How?'

'Did she take to me turnin' up like the ghost of old Finn MacCool? She screamed like a banshee — sure, she didn't believe it was me at first.'

'She let you stay?'

'For the time being — she'll see, says she. Well, an' all, I'm after thinkin' she might be glad of a man about the place. None of us is getting any younger, Sammy, my boy.'

Sammy doubted very much Bridie's need of a man about the place — she could take care of herself could Bridie O'Malley, the tallest woman he'd ever known. Magnificent in her way and possessed of a formidable left hook — he wondered that Michael hadn't a black eye.

'You didn't tell her that.'

Michael smiled. 'I did not. I told her that she hadn't changed from the beautiful wife who was ever in me head and me heart.'

'Wife was it? You didn't tell her about —'

'Bejasus, Sammy, are ye a madman? Deed, I did not — 'tis not the kind o' truth you tell to a woman. Besides, the other, she might be dead by now — it was a long time ago. Let sleepin' dogs lie — well, cat, in her case.'

'You're probably right. So, what brings you here — a message from Bridie, is it?'

'I came to tell ye, I've seen him.'

'Who?'

'Your murderer — the man who came into me lodgings.'

'You're sure? Where?'

'Old Pye Street.'

'What were you doing down there?'

'I'd a fancy for a walk — there was a deal o' scrubbin' and polishin' at Bridie's. It was a look she gave me — I was in the way. I took meself down The Strand to Whitehall. I thought to go in the Park, but I took a wrong turn. I was standin', lookin' about me, when I sees a couple comin' towards me. I noticed the lady — an' she was a lady, to be sure — smart, in brown with a bonnet that had a bright blue ribbon — 'twas like the flash of a kingfisher's wing in the grey o' the day. That's why I noticed it. And, she was a very pretty woman. Well, they was passin' me an' I looked at the gent. Right in the eye, an' I knew him. 'Twas only a moment. I turned an' walked away quick as a fish in water — but 'twas him, Sammy, sure an' it was.'

It might have been, thought Jones — but, then it might not. What was Sefton doing down in Westminster? Pye Street. Devil's Acre — so it was called in Dickens's *Household Words*. Jones had read the article about the poverty and squalor there and the work of the missionary who'd opened a Ragged School. He'd been down there years ago. It was a filthy, notorious place — and a woman — a lady. Was Sefton married then? Was that why he'd not given himself up?

Michael saw the doubts and questions chasing across Jones's face. 'I'm certain, Sammy. I could swear on the Good Book.'

'You didn't see where they went?'

'No, I didn't look back, didn't want to draw attention to meself.'

'Which way were they going — towards the Abbey?'

'No, the other way. I was standin' outside a little shop. There were some boxes of mangy old vegetables outside.'

'Well, I'm obliged to you, Michael, and I'll follow it up when I've thought about it a bit more. You'll give my best wishes to Bridie?'

'Deed I will, Sammy. I'll bid ye farewell.'

When he had gone, Jones sat and thought. A slender thread — the lightest of gossamer threads — leading, perhaps, to a murderer. But it's a warren down there, a labyrinth of alleys and courts. It'll be the devil's own job. And, he might just have been passing through… But why would you pass through Pye Lane and its environs with a lady? A place of indescribable infamy and pollution — a moral plague spot, the piece in *Household Words* had described it — worse than any other part of town.

How to find Sefton? He'd have to take Rogers and Stemp — in plain clothes. Could he use Scrap? Too dangerous, probably, though Scrap in his disguise as an urchin might be safer than they would be. But, where to look in that maze of alleys? That was the devil of it.

Rogers came in with Dickens who had come to tell Jones that he had made progress with regard to Miranda's future. However, Jones forestalled him.

'Michael O'Malley said he saw Sefton with a lady — a lady in a bonnet with a blue ribbon — like the flash of a kingfisher's wing as the eloquent Mr O'Malley put it.'

'Good Lord! Where was this poetical bonnet?'

'In Old Pye Street.'

'Devil's Acre.'

'The very same. And I wonder what Sefton was doing with a lady in that nest of iniquity.'

'Perhaps she wasn't a lady.'

'Michael assured me that she was. Pretty woman, too — in a brown outfit. Smart, he said.'

'Unusual down there.'

'Could He have a wife?' asked Rogers.

'I wondered if that's why he hasn't given himself up. But it doesn't matter. What matters is that it is a lead — a tenuous one, I admit, but since we have no other notion of where he might be, I had thought of looking. But where to start, other than lurking about Pye Street in disguise?'

'You read that article in *Household Words* last June?' Jones nodded. 'Well, you'll know about the missionary, Andrew Walker, and how he started up the Ragged School in Pye Street — the premises of The Old Tun pub were converted from a kind of Fagin's den to a school. We could start with him. Of course, he might know nothing about Sefton or his lady, but we could ask. Someone might know of a doctor.'

'Right. Now, Rogers, I think you should change out of your uniform — get down to Zeb Scruggs's shop and borrow some suitable clothes. Get a ragged coat with pockets — for this.' He took out of his drawer a flintlock pistol and handed it to Rogers. 'Just in case. I thought you could take Scrap — in his disguise, too. Just a man with a ragged child. Look for a smart lady in brown, and the bonnet. Follow, but don't go in too deep. Keep to the streets. We'll wait for you at the shop and you can follow Mr Dickens and me to the school.'

'Keepin' our distance. Then we hang about.'

'Exactly.'

Rogers left them.

'Charles, I didn't ask — did you come for something special?'

'I did — to tell you that I have a possible place for Miranda.'

On their way to the shop in Crown Street, Dickens told him his news.

'Some time ago, the Bishop of Cape Town, a friend of Miss Coutts, wrote to her about a clergyman who was coming home to England, a man who had provided a home for emigrant girls sent by Miss Coutts. And this is the important bit — their only daughter died out there in the Cape. His wife wanted to come home. Miss Coutts will tell him Miranda's history — they are good people and it is likely they will understand her background. Miss Coutts will ask if they would be willing to give Miranda a home — not as a servant, but as the friendless daughter of a protestant clergyman. I hope to hear from her soon. The Reverend Mr Woodhouse is back now and living in Devon.'

'Good — very good. Out of London. That'll be better. And a home — she must have a home. I hope these good people will take her. Whether or not we find Sefton, it is time I went to the Assistant Commissioner with my evidence. The death of Brimstone by stabbing makes it clear that Miranda did not kill Plume. She must be released.'

'I think so, too, but she will need looking after until I have word from Miss Coutts.'

'Elizabeth has thought of that. Mrs Feak is willing to nurse her. Elizabeth took her to see Miranda. She will know what is best for the girl until you can make arrangements. Now let us find your missionary.'

37: Devil's Acre

From the stationery shop in Crown Street, Dickens and Jones, followed by Rogers and Scrap, made their way down St. Martin's Lane, through Charing Cross, and into Whitehall. They passed behind the Houses of Parliament where night after night the lawmakers sat deliberating, a stone's throw from the degradation of the streets behind them. The towers of the great Abbey of Westminster looked down, indifferently, Dickens thought. *God's Acre* — he remembered the phrase from one of Longfellow's poems. *This is the place where human harvests grow*, the poet had written of some peaceful burial ground where each grave was consecrated by the blessed name. Not here. Not here where the black tide of human misery rolled its filthy waves up to the very walls of the Abbey. A wilderness of dirt, rags and hunger — and crime of every kind. Devil's Acre.

It was but a step from the Abbey walls into Dean Street and then to Old Pye Street. Dickens and Jones found their way to the Ragged School and went in while Rogers and Scrap loitered further down the street in a doorway by the grocer's shop with vegetable boxes outside. A scruffy man with his boy in the hand-me-down trousers of a military man and boots far too big for him. Doing nothing. Nobody noticed. But Scrap's eyes were everywhere, looking for that bonnet with the blue ribbon. There were very few pretty bonnets in Old Pye Street. Ragged shawls; greasy caps; battered bonnets; squashed toppers; billycock hats; the odd wretched straw hat, relic of a long ago summer, mostly the colour of mud, all passed by, but never a glimpse of blue.

Inside the school, Mrs Tudge, the charwoman, informed them that Mr Walker was out.

'Police are ye?' she asked, looking at Jones with knowing eyes.

'Yes, we're looking for a lady.'

'I doubt yer'll find one 'ereabouts.' Mrs Tudge swabbed her floor as far as the Superintendent's shiny boots.

'A smart lady in a brown bonnet with a bright blue ribbon.' Jones refused to move his feet away from the mop.

'Oh, that lady — she is a lady, Gawd bless her.' She stopped mopping and looked up at Jones. Something in her eyes softened.

'You know her name?'

'Mrs Shepherd — Mary Shepherd.'

'Does she live round here?'

'At the 'orspital down Perkins Rent.'

'Hospital?'

''S'wot we call it — free 'orspital for women an' kiddies. Run by Doctor Shepherd an' 'is lady. Saints they 'is, an' no police can say otherwise. What you want 'em fer?' Mrs Tudge was suspicious now.

'Only enquiries. I'm not after them.'

'Oh, awright — Perkins Rent's a step or two back down the street. Right turn.'

They left her to her mopping.

'A lady, certainly, but not his wife,' observed Dickens.

'And a hospital — a charity hospital.'

'The good doctor again?'

'Maybe — let's find out, shall we?'

Over the road they saw Rogers and Scrap. They told them what they had learned and walked down to Perkins Rent. Jones wanted to have a look at the place. How to get in, and, just as important, how to get out. Sefton might be there — he might make a run for it, and that meant Rogers finding a back entrance he could watch. Scrap would wait at the end of the street.

'If he comes out, just watch where he goes. Don't follow him into any alleys, Scrap.'

They found the hospital. There was a sign outside indicating that it was a hospital for women and children as Mrs Tudge had told them. It was established in an old storehouse, and there were shabby looking sheds on either side, hemming it in. Dickens and Scrap melted into a doorway opposite while Jones and Rogers went along the street to see if there was any way round the back.

Jones came back alone and Scrap was sent back down the street to wait in another doorway. Time to go in. Dickens felt his heart jumping — to see Sefton, perhaps, after all this time. To come face to face with the murderer.

The front door opened into a waiting room with a sanded floor, whitewashed walls, and some hard chairs upon which were sitting some women and some poor, starving-looking children — patiently waiting their turn. A comical looking dog sat in the centre of the room, gazing at the patients as if he were assessing their chances. A door opened and out came a pretty, dark-haired woman wearing a white apron.

Jones stepped forward just before she went to speak to one of the patients. 'Mrs Shepherd?'

'Yes. Can I help you?'

'I hope so. I am Superintendent Jones from Bow Street, and this —'

She smiled, a sweet, shy smile, as she looked at Dickens. 'I know who this is. Mr Dickens, is it not? How extraordinary. I have read your books, but I never expected to meet you, and you have come to see our work here, to write about us?'

She looked so eager, so hopeful, that Dickens wished that they had come on any errand but theirs. He could imagine the distress on that sweet, innocent face when they had to tell her what they wanted and why. He glanced at Jones. He didn't want to tell her either.

'Mrs Shepherd,' Jones began. She turned her fine eyes to him. She reminded him of Elizabeth — dark-haired and lovely. It made it harder. 'I am looking for Doctor Sefton — in connection with a — a case I am investigating.' Perhaps he wasn't there, perhaps, she could tell them where he was, and they could leave her in all her innocence. But, no.

'Doctor Sefton — you mean Doctor Will — that's what we call him. Why, he is here, but I cannot get him for you. He is performing an operation. A young woman — her baby. We do not know if either will live, but, if anyone can save them, Doctor Will is the man. Perhaps you might leave a message for him to contact you.'

'It is urgent. I am afraid we must wait. Is there somewhere?'

'Yes, yes, we live upstairs. I'll show you up, but please be very quiet. My husband is sleeping. Let me just get one of the other nurses to see to these patients.'

She came back from another room with a young woman of about twenty, who smiled at them, too.

'Come with me, Poodles,' she said to the dog.

Then they went upstairs past all sorts of winches which must have been used for the hoisting of goods. Heavy feet and heavy weights had trodden these stairs, and there were inconvenient bulks and beams round which to manoeuvre. It was old, but all was airy, sweet and clean. Dickens could hear the scratch of Poodles's claws on the stairs. Mrs Shepherd pointed out the two wards where they could see children in beds. Poodles went in to see his patients.

Mrs Shepherd turned round. 'Poodles is very popular with the children, especially. He understands them — he was a poor, starving orphan once, himself.'

Worse and worse, thought Dickens.

'In there is our small operating room. Doctor Will is in there now.'

There was a window in the door; Dickens looked in as Mrs Shepherd and Jones went on to another door further along the corridor. He saw the woman on the bed, a sheet covering her from the waist. Her legs were bent at the knees. A nurse, another young woman was holding her hand, but the woman was quiet. The doctor was on the other side of the bed, leaning over his patient. As if he sensed that someone was watching, Doctor Will looked up to the window. His eyes were dark, Dickens noticed as they held his for a few seconds. The doctor glanced at his patient, nodded at Dickens, and went back to his work. Dickens noticed the white bandage on his right hand.

What did that nod mean? He was expecting us, thought Dickens. He was telling me that he isn't going to run. He's telling me to wait. So, that was Doctor Sefton — he had gained an impression of dark eyes and a flow of dark hair, a pale, angular face — a suffering face. Not the face of a murderer, but he was. Dickens knew it — by that nod.

He went on through an open door into Mrs Shepherd's sitting room. He noted a piano, drawing materials on a desk, books, some china and glassware on a sideboard. There was a cheerful fire blazing. It might have been the parlour of any lady's house, yet Doctor and Mrs Shepherd had made their home here in Devil's Acre. With every qualification to lure them away, with youth and accomplishments and tastes and habits that could have no response in any breast near them, close begirt by every repulsive circumstance inseparable from such a neighbourhood, here they dwelt. Perhaps he could write about them — tell the world what nobility may be found in the meanest neighbourhood. Those sleek, over-fed deliberators over there in Parliament ought to take note of this.

Mrs Shepherd was offering them tea. Jones declined. Dickens was glad. They couldn't drink her tea while waiting to take away the doctor she so obviously admired — and needed.

'I do not know how long he will be — it's a difficult situation. The poor mother is very weak. So often, our patients are already weakened by hunger and poverty. It makes childbirth more dangerous, but Will is very good. The finest surgeon he has known, so Simon, my husband, says. Doctor Will has cared for her so assiduously — she is so young. Only about sixteen, and unmarried. Not that it makes any difference to us.'

Dickens had a sudden thought. 'What is her name?'

'Rose.'

He wasn't surprised. It fitted. He didn't look at Sam — he didn't need to. So, they had been wrong the other night. It had not been money. But, what about Miranda Deverall? Sefton would have to explain that.

'Has he been here long?' Jones asked, hating himself, knowing he was trapping her just as he had ensnared Amelia Hodson and Martha Brimstone. They were guilty and deserved it, but Mary Shepherd was guileless. She didn't ask about why Jones wanted to speak to Sefton — that's how trusting she was.

'A few weeks. He came suddenly one day to offer his services — for free. A bit like Poodles, I suppose. Just turned up on the doorstep.' She smiled that touching smile again. 'You cannot imagine how glad I was — Simon has been ill with bronchitis, and we so needed a doctor. It was as if Doctor Will had dropped from heaven.'

'How long was he to stay?'

'A few more days, I think. He was going to Canada, but he postponed his voyage for Rose's sake.'

They heard the cry of a new born baby. How often Dickens had heard that cry. *When we are born, we cry that we are come to this great stage of fools.* Sefton had been a fool — he had thrown away his life for Plume.

They waited in silence then. Mrs Shepherd's anxious eyes kept glancing at the door. They could hear the ticking of the clock on the wall. The door opened and Sefton came in. He looked only at Mary Shepherd who had stood up at his entrance.

'Is she?'

'She — they — will live. A breech birth, but the baby is lusty. The chloroform made it easier for her.'

Chloroform, thought Dickens, remembering the bottle in Doctor Plume's surgery. What had he used it for? Not to ease a poor woman's labour. Sefton was a good doctor, no doubt, but, a murderer, too. A mystery yet to be fathomed.

'Oh, Will!' Mary, heedless of the blood on his apron, went to embrace him.

When she had stood away from him, Sefton turned to the visitors for the first time.

'I expected you. I just needed to… But, I am ready to go with you.' He took off his apron.

Mary looked from Will to Jones. Something very grave in the policeman's expression frightened her. She looked at Mr Dickens. She could hardly understand -his eyes were so full of sympathy.

'Shall I come with you, Will? Do you need me?'

'No, Mary, my dear. I must go by myself.'

She was very frightened now. Dickens could have wept for her.

'You'll come back?' she asked, but she was looking at the Superintendent. He made no sign. 'Will?'

'I will write to you.' Sefton's voice was low, the voice of an exhausted man — a man who had come to the end of something.

They went down the worn stairs, past the wards and into the waiting room. Sefton took a coat from a peg and they went out into the crowded street. Dickens looked back to see Mary Shepherd standing at the door, watching. Her face was like a white flower in the darkness. Dickens raised his hand, but she simply stared.

At the doorway where Scrap was waiting, Jones paused.

'You'll find Mr Rogers down the alley next but one to the hospital. Go back to the shop with him. Tell him I'll see him at Bow Street.'

Scrap looked at the man flanked by Mr Jones and Mr Dickens. Goin' quietly then. Dint look like a criminal, an' Mr Jones an' Mr Dickens, they looked, well, as if they'd lost somethin' rather than found wot they wanted. Queer business — a murderer wot looked like a — a good man.

A cab took Dickens and Jones and their prisoner back to Bow Street. Sefton did not speak. He looked directly ahead as they rolled by the great west door of the Abbey, into Princess Street, along great George Street and into Whitehall, past Downing Street, The Treasury, Horse Guards, The Admiralty, turning their backs on grandeur.

All the King's horses and all the King's men — the old rhyme ran through Dickens's head as he looked from Jones's set face to the prisoner's bleak one — *couldn't put Humpty together again.* What was Sefton thinking now — of dead Plume and the Rose who, according to William Drage, had died out there on the marshes? He looked like one with his face turned to the other world. Years ago, he had seen acted in Paris an affecting play called *The Children's Doctor.* He saw now in the black necktie, the loose buttoned black frock-coat, in the flow of the dark hair, in the eyelashes, in the very turn of his moustache, the exact realisation of the Paris artist's ideal as it was presented on the stage. But, this was no romance. Here was tragedy.

Nought's had, all's spent, said the cab horse's hooves, *all's spent.* That's what he felt — spent.

At Bow Street, they took Sefton to a cell. Dickens stood at the door. He was out of it now. Jones looked down at his prisoner, who spoke at last.

'I killed Plume and Mr Brimstone.'

'Are you prepared to tell me? I must have your confession — the whole story. I need to go to Newgate to secure the release of the girl who is accused of your crime.'

Sefton flinched at that. He glanced at Dickens who saw the emptiness in those dark eyes. Sefton knew what he had done.

'Is it possible for me to write it all down?' It was the voice of weariness, hopelessness, despair. Dry and cracked as though he had not spoken for an age. *Like Miranda*, thought Dickens.

'If you will,' said Jones. His voice was neutral — the policeman at his work. Jones went out for paper, pen and ink. He did not look at Dickens. He placed the writing materials on a small table. 'We'll leave you to it.'

The murderer picked up the pen and dipped it in the ink pot. They left him to write his story.

38: Confession

Dickens came back from Wellington Street two hours later. Constable Feak had come with Jones's message: *Sefton has finished.*

Jones handed Dickens the papers. 'This is for you — that is, he addresses his confession to you.'

'Me?'

'Yes. I took the liberty of reading it — while I was waiting.'

Dickens sat down.

Dear Mr Dickens,

If I may be permitted to address you so. I write to you, honoured sir, for I believe, I trust, that you will think on this, and, perhaps, have some pity for my plight, though I know nothing can extenuate my crimes — they are unforgivable. I wish to tell my story to one whose understanding of human nature has made him the loved of all who have read his works.

I do not know you, of course, but you were so often spoken of in Chatham and Rochester where some of your boyhood was spent. I heard Reverend William Drage speak of those days when he lived at Ordnance Terrace; the beadle of Mr Drage's church, Peter Weller, laughed heartily to find that you had used his name in Pickwick; Doctor Steele of Strood talked of your student doctors in Pickwick, Bob Sawyer and Ben Allen. He thought them very like the students he had known. So many remember you that I feel that I may ask for a hearing.

Yet, I know you — in a sense — because you have followed me. An avenging angel. I passed down Weymouth Street. I saw you, Mr Dickens. You gave some money to a little boy standing opposite Plume's house. I gave him a sixpence. I saw you again with the Superintendent. You were in David Street outside a house where I saw Plume and a woman I

301

thought must be his mistress. I knew then that you were on my trail. I knew you would find me. I felt fate weaving its net about my feet. I saw your face in the window at the hospital so I write to you. I owe you — and the Superintendent — my explanation. You have sought justice and justice must be done.

I killed Lancelot Plume — that you and the Superintendent know already. Now I will tell you why, and how that led to the death of the innocent Arthur Brimstone.

Plume and I were partners in the medical practice we had taken over in Chatham. We were in a small way, but hoped for better. Lancelot Plume was a handsome, young man then, and many ladies liked his manner of sympathy and understanding — thus our practice began to grow. The poor people preferred me — I was rougher, I suppose, less forgiving of ladies and their nerves. Plume treated Mrs Brooks of Restoration House in Rochester — of whom more, later. Through her good report, we acquired other ladies.

In our house, we employed a local lady as our cook and cleaner — a hardworking woman with an invalid husband — and a pretty daughter who helped her mother sometimes. I mention no names for these are old wounds which must not be opened by the Superintendent's scalpel — no good would come of your knowing who these people were.

I noticed that the daughter — let us call her Rose, for she had the softness and dewy brightness of that flower — seemed to blush so when Plume addressed her. He was kind to her, I thought — he said we could help the family by giving her extra work. She was about fifteen and her mother kept her protected from the young men. Rose was too young yet for all that nonsense, the brisk and fond mother explained.

One night, I came back late to our house. Plume came from his surgery, his face white and blood on his hands. It was Rose, he told me. She had come to him in desperation for she was with child and she had implored him to help her. Plume was very reluctant, he told me, but his pity for the girl, the knowledge of her certain ruin and her mother's grief made him agree. He told me that she had confessed to having a lover, but she would not tell him the name.

I went into the surgery to see that the girl was dying. Plume should never have attempted the abortion — he was no surgeon. She was bleeding to death and there was nothing to be done. She died. Our horror was great — you know the law, I daresay, Mr Dickens. We were both guilty now. And what were we to say to the distracted mother?

Our decision was to bury her — out on the marshes. Surely, we reasoned, it were better for the mother to believe that her daughter was missing than to know of her disgrace and death. I will not pretend, either, that we did not think of ourselves, our practice, and our future. Plume had meant well — so I believed then.

We took her in a cart, out to the marshes beyond Cooling — you will know that desolate tract of wild land. There is a church there and beyond that the dark, flat wilderness where one sees the grim outline of the hulks lying out in the river. That sight frightened me for I thought of how I might find myself imprisoned there.

You will know very well, Mr Dickens, the thin, cold wind from the east, whistling its mournful tune, the rattling of the reeds, and somewhere out of sight, the harsh cry of some night bird which saw what we were about. You will see with my eyes, the brittle moon shedding its greenish light on the two men digging in the slimy clay, slipping, terrified of sinking; shedding its light on the white face of the girl who lay on the cold mud. Then, the face of the moon looked down as we bundled the poor remains of the innocent girl into the hole. We crawled back, and we hoped, God forgive us, that if we had not buried her deep enough, the flood would carry her away down the river.

Rose was missing — that was the tale. It was thought that she had drowned on her way to visit an aunt who lived beyond the marshes at Hoo. She was never found. Our cook left us — she is dead now and the invalid father, too. No trace of that poor family remains.

Our terror subsided. Young men are resilient, and our consciences were quieted because Rose's story was heard only with pity — we had saved her from scorn, from disgrace — and her mother would know nothing except that her daughter was as innocent in death as in life. This is what I told myself. I now know that Plume felt nothing at all, for I know now that he was the seducer.

About a year after this event, Mr Brooks, the brewer of Restoration House, died and his widow turned more and more for comfort from Lancelot Plume. You will know that he married her, and came into a fortune with which he set up his fashionable practice in London.

He bargained with me — he would pay me something for his leaving, but since he had brought the fashionable patients, I deserved only what he had put in at the beginning. I felt the injury, and the coldness which had grown between us since the night on the marshes hardened into loathing. I was glad to see the back of him. I thought never to see or hear of him again. The practice failed without him, and I went to be a surgeon at the hospital in Fort Pitt above Chatham, but I could not stay. I used to look upon those marshes with terror at what I had done that night.

I came to London and gained my post at the lying-in hospital. Perhaps, by helping all those women in childbirth, I could make amends for Rose. I think I did. You know my reputation now. I did call on Plume, and I wished I had not. He had forgotten poor Rose. I spoke of her and how I could not forget that night. He laughed at my folly. What was the use, he said, of revisiting the past? It was gone. We were respected doctors — surely, we had paid for our youthful indiscretion. Were we to suffer for a mere servant girl whose own vice had brought about her death? It was her own fault. I knew that he lied.

But, I could not forget. I thought to go abroad, to Canada. I left Queen Charlotte's. How could I rise to eminence when I had colluded in a girl's death which brought misery to simple, good folk? But, then I heard of Doctor and Mrs Shepherd who have given up all chance of riches and fame. They needed a doctor to fill in for a short time. I would work for my bread only, at least for the weeks before I was to go to Canada. I was happier than I had ever been, but I knew that I must leave London and England forever.

However, the past came visiting again. On an October night of dreadful rain, I came across a girl on the steps of the hospital. She was soaked, half-dead with cold and fever. When I took her into the ward to examine her, I saw that she had given birth. It was puerperal fever. I knew that she would not live. I asked where was the child. I could not quite understand her. The effects of fever, I thought. First she said he was dead, and then that he was safe with a Mrs Martin. I could not discover more, but she managed to tell me her story. She had been a servant at a milliner's near the workhouse in Marylebone. She had been seduced by a doctor and had become with child. She concealed her pregnancy for six months, but when the doctor found out he sent her to an abortionist whom she called Mother Hubbard. But the girl was too frightened — she had felt her baby quicken. It was alive in her womb and she could not let Mother Hubbard do her work. She lived in the poorest lodgings. Her intention was to find work after the birth and to leave the child to be kept by a woman she knew. I thought she meant Mrs Martin, but she spoke of Mrs Brimstone. She became ill and thought to go home — I don't know where, but she could get no further than our hospital steps. The Doctor's name was Plume. I had to see him again — to stop him.

I stood outside his fine house in Weymouth Street, and I watched. I saw the well-dressed ladies come in their carriages, and I saw him at his door, smiling his reassuring smile as an aristocratic lady got into a carriage with a coat of arms on its door. I found the lane at the back of his house, and one night I saw him come out with his doctor's bag. I followed him to a house in David Street, and, later, in the lamplight I saw a woman bidding him goodbye, and I knew that they were lovers. Again, I followed him and saw a girl come out leaning on her friend. In the same lamplight, I saw the gleam of blood on her dress. I knew what he was doing.

It was near the house in David Street that I met Kitty Quillian. She lived at the house of Mr and Mrs Brimstone. I had heard that name, too, and I recognised Mr Brimstone — I had seen him in the lane behind Plume's house. I had asked him if the door from which he came was Plume's garden door. He saw me with Kitty. It was Kitty who told me all about what happened at David Street. Plume had seduced her, but she had another lover whose child she had borne and she had left the house in David Street. It was Kitty who pointed out the midwife, Mrs Raspin, whom they called Mother Hubbard. I knew that name, too. I knew it all — I would stop him.

On the night of the murder, I saw Kitty in the street, opposite the house. She told me that Plume had a visitor, a friend of hers. I waited in the lane, hidden in a doorway. I heard Plume's garden door open and close, and footsteps hurrying away. When all was quiet again, I went in. I could see him seated at his desk, his fair hair shining in the lamplight. He was holding a paper knife — it is in the desk at my lodging — a fine object, its handle silver, chased with gold — sharp, too.

I knocked on the glass panel of the door. He looked up, surprised, a little apprehensive — perhaps he thought his other visitor had come back. I took off my hat and he saw who it was. My face told him that I had come for a purpose other than to renew our acquaintance again. He might have seen a ghost for his face turned pale. I was, I suppose, a ghost of a kind for, with me, in his memory, was Rose whose ghastly face so often haunted my dreams. I know that she had not haunted him until then.

He let me in. I could not help admire the way he recovered himself, how he tried to feign the welcome of an old friend, how he asked me how I was faring, as if nothing had come between us but time, the innocent time that separates old friends whose lives have taken different paths. I told him all I knew. He listened, unmoved — what could I do to him? Who would believe me?

I challenged him. I would expose him. I would sacrifice my own career to stop him — I would tell the truth about Rose, about his seduction of her and her death and how we disposed of her body. And all those other things I had found out. I almost envied his mastery of himself for he looked at me as a man looks upon a madman. He lit a cigar — so coolly. He asked again, who would believe me. I would be the one confessing to a murder — a murder which he would deny. He would deny all — as would his connections. And as for Kitty Quillian, no one would believe a girl who had a bastard child. Folly, he said, smiling, all folly.

Perhaps it was money I wanted. He supposed he could give me something. I felt only rage at his contempt for me. He felt himself so safe that he even turned from me and took up his cigar. He went to the door and opened it. It was time for me to go. He did not, he said, expect to see me again.

He turned his back on me and I seized the paper knife. Such rage I felt. I plunged it into his back and he fell where, no doubt, he was found. I left him there and slipped away into the lane.

I went back to my lodging, and I lay awake all night. I could not feel sorry for what I had done. It would be an unexplained murder. No one had seen me at Plume's house. He would never have mentioned me to anyone, and I had never spoken of him. But, of course, I read that a young woman had been accused of the murder. I knew I should give myself up — would that I had!

I needed to wait — just for a week, perhaps. I had something that I must do, as I told you, as you saw for yourselves.

I hear you, Mr Dickens. You say that I was deceiving myself — of course, I was. I was no different from the young man who had persuaded himself that Rose's disappearance was for the best. For all my good works, I was still the same weak, self-centred, cowardly man I had been then. And I was arrogant. Only I could save the other Rose. I made myself believe it.

I went to search for Kitty, to find out about the girl in Newgate. I had some idea of writing a letter to the police, telling them that the accused girl was innocent. Then I would have my week. But, I could not find her. I went to the Brimstone house where she lodged. I did not mean to kill Mr Brimstone, only to threaten him with what I knew so that he would tell me where Kitty was.

He was locking the back door of the house when I spoke to him. When he turned, he looked at me in terror. He fought me like a madman. Terror, and that savage instinct for survival made me a beast. I took out the knife to ward him off, and in the struggle, I stabbed him.

That is my story, Mr Dickens. There is no excuse. No forgiveness. The moment I agreed to cover up Rose's death, my fate was sealed, and I deserve my death. It shall come soon, I hope, very soon, that even-handed justice.

Frederick Willoughby Sefton

'This even-handed justice commends the ingredients of our poisoned chalice —' Dickens began, almost completing Macbeth's words.

'What!'

'To our own lips — dear God — no!'

39: Opium

Jones was on the landing before Dickens got to the door. He heard his feet clattering downstairs. He ran after him.

Jones was shouting to the constable he had left outside the cell. 'Where's Pinch?'

'Call o' nature, sir,' a cheerful voice answered. 'Back in a minute.'

'Open the cell door — now!'

Dickens caught up with Jones as the constable opened the door. Sefton lay on his bed — it looked as though he was asleep. But, they saw that his face was pale and ghastly. His breath was hurried. Jones touched his forehead. It was bathed in perspiration. He felt the pulse — small, quick and irregular. He bent down and sniffed at the pale lips.

'Opium.' Jones shouted again. 'Semple get in here — now!'

Semple came in. 'Sir?'

'Get to Brydges Street, bring the doctor — quick as you can.'

Jones turned back to the bed and lifted the blanket. It was there — the vial of opium clasped in Sefton's hands.

Constable Pinch came in. 'Sorry, sir, I just —' then he saw the man on the bed and the vial in his hands. 'Oh, Gawd, sir, what's 'appened — I was only gone a few minutes — oh, Gawd!'

'Never mind all that. Charles, try to rouse him. There might be a chance — speak to him — shake him.'

Dickens shook Sefton's shoulder. 'Sefton, wake up, Sefton —'

'What happened before you went out — how long's he been asleep?'

'About an hour — I dunno exactly — after you'd gone with the letter, sir, 'e said 'e'd like ter sleep. Asked 'im if 'e wanted anything, but 'e sed 'e was tired. I sat outside. 'Eard 'im go off like — breathin' like someone asleep.'

'You didn't see him take anything?'

'No, sir — 'e must 'ave 'ad it 'idden — the bottle. I only went out 'cos I thought 'e was asleep. I 'aven't been gone more than five minutes, sir.'

Pinch looked scared to death, his young face, white. Jones looked thunderous.

'Stay here — I need you to witness what we do. Write down everything that happens.' He saw the young man's terrified face. 'All right, Pinch. Not your fault, I know.'

And, it wasn't, thought Jones — *it was mine*. Sefton wasn't searched well enough. I should have thought — a doctor. But, there wasn't time for blaming now. He turned back to Dickens who was still trying to rouse Sefton.

'Sefton!' Jones shouted. Dickens looked startled. But Jones tried again. 'Got to wake him before coma sets in — if it does, he'll die.'

At the third shout, Sefton's eyes opened. He looked at Dickens. 'Better as it is.' His voice was slurred and his eyes closed again.

Jones looked at the vial and sniffed it. The opium had been dissolved in alcohol. Of course, the doctor had known what he was doing. Opium dissolved that way worked more speedily, and it would be of pharmacopoeial strength — say two drachms. He must have taken it before Pinch went out — must have. Pinch hadn't seen. How long? He'd left Sefton over an hour ago — Pinch said he'd gone to sleep soon after. Death could follow in a few hours — that much he knew. He turned back to the bed. Sefton was breathing stertorously now. Dickens was still trying.

They lifted him to a sitting position, shaking him all the time, but his eyes remained closed. It was no use. They laid him down again and watched as the breathing became slow and hoarse, the lips turned livid. Jones felt the pulse again — much more feeble.

Doctor Luke Strong came in from his practice in Brydges Street. As Divisional Surgeon, he was responsible for the health and welfare of the police, but he had frequently helped out Jones if there were a death in custody. He was shrewd and experienced and had learned his forensic medicine at Guy's Hospital under the tutelage of Alfred Swaine Taylor whose *Manual of Medical Jurisprudence* had first appeared in 1844. Jones trusted Doctor Strong — he would make a good witness at the inquest, authoritative and succinct — and truthful. Not a man to waste words.

Doctor Strong greeted them briefly — he knew Dickens, too. Then he looked at the man on the bed. Jones handed him the vial which had contained the opium.

'He's a doctor — Doctor Frederick Willoughby Sefton — and a murder suspect, too. Plume.'

'Knew him — charlatan.' He sniffed at the little bottle. 'Dissolved in alcohol.' He examined the bottle. 'Hm — a hefty dose. He knew what he was doing.'

'We tried to wake him — he spoke once then relapsed into coma, as you see him now.'

'When did he take it?'

'Over an hour ago — say an hour and twenty minutes. It's quick, though, isn't it?'

Doctor Strong looked at the dying man. 'Unusual, rare, but not impossible — I know of a case where insensibility occurred in fifteen minutes, and there are cases where death followed the consumption of the drug within two hours. There's nothing we can do for him now.'

All three gazed at the man on the bed. Doctor Strong felt the pulse — it was scarcely perceptible now. The hand was cold to his touch. Then came the loud mucous rattle from the throat. The body convulsed slightly and the breathing stopped.

Dickens looked at the white face. Nothing remained of him — he felt Sefton's absence as an almost tangible thing. Over the dark bridge from life to death, he had passed, silently, swiftly, and, before he had said "Better as it is". It was, Dickens believed. Should Sefton have paid for Plume's death on the gallows? To be jeered at by the crowd for whom his death was a holiday, a festival of cruelty, brutal mirth and callousness so odious that a man should feel ashamed of the shape he wore. That's what he had written about the hanging of the Mannings — and Mrs Manning, that chubby, bland-faced Swiss had murdered for gain, had shot her victim and then watched as her husband finished him off with his chiselling tool. Then they'd eaten roast goose, all unknowing that theirs was cooked, as well as Patrick O'Connor's.

But, what did this death mean for Sam? That was an equally vexed question. For Sam whose prisoner had died in his cell.

Jones was speaking to the Doctor. 'He should have been properly searched. It's my responsibility.'

'But, you wouldn't normally strip a man naked. He had hidden it, no doubt.'

Dickens interrupted. 'He knew we were there at the hospital where we found him — he saw me. He said he was expecting us. Perhaps he secreted the opium when he had finished the operation he was performing.'

'Yes, I suppose he could have done, but, still I ought —'

'You couldn't have known,' Doctor Strong stopped Jones. 'He was a doctor, a gentleman — as I say, it is not customary for you to strip such a man. He wasn't violent or dangerous, I suppose.'

'No, certainly not. He was perfectly quiet.'

'Then, I do not see how you could have prevented this.'

'Let's hope the coroner thinks so.'

'I'll give my evidence — and Mr Dickens, here, and your constable. Presumably his pockets were emptied.'

'Yes.'

'There you are then. Now, leave me to finish my examination. I'll get him taken down to the mortuary.'

Jones and Dickens went back upstairs. Sefton's letter lay on the desk. The strange eventful history of a murder.

Jones picked up the papers, straightened them and put them down again.

'Better as it is?' asked Dickens.

'You know I think so, but, I am a policeman —'

'And a good one, too, Samivel.'

'Thank you. But, it shouldn't have happened — not here, not under my nose. A matter of professional pride, I suppose — not really important in matters of life and death.'

'You're not worried about the inquest?'

'You mean that I might be censured? Not really — I'll get over it, promise the Commissioner to be more vigilant in future. No, it's a feeling of unfinished business. What if it had been some really hardened murderer — someone we wanted to see punished by the full weight of the law? We'd feel he'd got away with it — or she. Mrs Manning, for instance.'

'She wasn't a gentleman.' Dickens smiled at him.

'No — she wasn't a lady, either. Strong is probably right — we wouldn't have stripped him — no cause. Well, I daresay, I'll settle to it, but it all seems such a dreadful waste.'

'It is. Streaky bacon — life, I mean.'

Jones smiled back. 'Oh, yes, what you said about your books — what Scrap said.'

'Yer gotter 'ave the good and bad bits. Philosopher, is Scrap.'

'So, he is. Would that I could understand what it's all about.'

'There's a destiny that shapes our ends, rough-hew them how we will. Leave it to Heaven, Sam. For now we see through a glass darkly.'

Jones thought about the advertisement for spectacles which had promised that every object would become clear and distinct. He had not believed it. Dickens was right. Imperfect vision — he'd have to be content with that.

40: Star Witness

At the inquest on Frederick Willoughby Sefton, Charles Dickens stole the show, as it were — for which Superintendent Sam Jones was much obliged. It took the heat off him.

The coroner's jury, the witnesses, the spectators, the coroner himself, listened with open-eyed curiosity and admiration as the celebrated writer explained his part in the case of the two doctors, Sefton and Plume, for it emerged — to sensational effect — that the man who had died of opium poisoning in a cell in Bow Street Police Station was the man who had murdered the fashionable Doctor Plume.

Mr Dickens, dressed in sober black, delivered his evidence without flourish, though he had been tempted to employ all his dramatic flair when he saw the audience before him, waiting for him to begin. What power that was — to hold an audience in the palm of your hand. He could have made theatre of it — the miserable cell, the flaring gas lamp, the hoarse breathing of the dying man, the policeman's strained face, the discovery of the vial of poison, the sickly smell of opium, then the breathing slowing, the last convulsion, the rattle in the throat. What a story. Then, he caught sight of Sam Jones, the white face of Mary Shepherd, the stern countenance of Doctor Hawkins.

He spoke quietly and simply, but his audience was still mesmerised. His eyes held them. Each member of the jury felt certain that Charles Dickens meant him to understand particularly the pathos of the story of the young girl who had been falsely accused of murder. They heard about his conviction that she was innocent — they were convi

Charles Dickens described the death of the young doctor — how he and the Bow Street Superintendent had tried to save him, but they were too late.

Doctor Strong gave his evidence — his terseness and confidence brooked no opposition. The Coroner asked about the search of the prisoner. Why had the opium not been found — surely some dereliction of duty on the part of the police? Doctor Strong gave him a look. The Coroner seemed to shrivel.

The dead man might have been a suspected murderer, but he was a gentleman. It was Doctor Strong's experience that such prisoners were not stripped naked. The Coroner opened his mouth like a sheep about to bleat, but Doctor Strong was too quick for him. He had examined the prisoner, he went on, and had discovered a pocket in the waistband of the trousers. It was his opinion that the accused had secreted the opium there. Doctor Strong closed his lips like a man who felt he had said more than enough.

Had he grounds for that suspicion? The Coroner dared. His voice was a little hoarse — *an asthmatic sheep*, thought Dickens, but he admired his courage. The sheep-dog, however, seemed to growl.

'Smelt it.'

The Coroner thanked Doctor Strong, who then stood down.

Superintendent Jones came to the witness box to give his evidence. He confirmed Mr Dickens's testimony regarding their attempts to rouse the prisoner. Constable Pinch would be able to support their evidence. He had been present and had m?˙ ˑs in his book.

The Coroner, disarmed by the humble demeanour of the Superintendent, returned to the matter of the search. The Superintendent explained. The accused had been made to empty his pockets. His manner had been quiet; he had confessed to the murder of Doctor Plume and another man, Arthur Brimstone. He had requested that he should be able to write down his story — the Superintendent had agreed, given him paper and pencil, and left him under the eye of Constable Pinch. The Superintendent had returned to the cell when the prisoner had completed his statement. He had noticed nothing about the prisoner which would have made him think that he was about to take his own life. Pinch had offered him tea or water; the prisoner had declined, expressing his desire to sleep. Pinch had heard the prisoner's breathing. Something in the statement that the prisoner had written made the Superintendent suspicious. He and Mr Dickens had rushed down to the cell, but they were too late.

The Coroner explained to the jury that he would read only portions of the letter written by the dead man. Some of the contents were evidence that would be given at the inquest into the death of Doctor Lancelot Plume — the earlier inquest having been adjourned while the police gathered their evidence. Before they reached their verdict, they must consider the moral history of the deceased, his worldly condition, whether he had met with losses, whether he had been solitary in his habits, his disposition of mind. He read the confession of the dead man. Then he recalled Mr Dickens to the witness box.

'You recognised some words at the end of the letter?'

'I did. They were from Shakespeare's play, *Macbeth*. The prisoner used the words: *this even-handed justice* —' he allowed himself a pause. Might as well bow out with a flourish — 'I knew the rest —' another pause — just enough: *this even-handed justice commends the ingredients of our poison'd chalice to our own lips.* He didn't bow — he heard Jones's voice in his head. 'No need to overdo it.' He simply stood still.

There was silence. His audience was spell-bound — as good as Mr Macready. Jones wanted to applaud. And, it was enough for the jury. Suicide.

41: Towards the Future

November went out like the last guttering of a candle — the cheapest of tallow ones. Dickens was glad to see it go. December days came in, burnt at both ends, nights at odds with mornings, which was which.

Dickens looked out onto the bleak, raw day. The garden looked sodden, the bare trees dripping after a night of wind and rain. The house felt damp. Even his study fire had an apologetic look, a woebegone thing spluttering in the grate. About the house, children honked like disconsolate geese — at least half a dozen noses were blocked and more eyes streamed.

'Oh, bisery, bisery in de dose,' he had remarked to Frank. Nearly seven, *but*, Dickens thought, *looking a little elderly that morning with a shawl round his shoulders*. Frank managed a watery smile. Little Sydney frowned. The Ocean Spectre's far-seeing eyes seemed to have shrunk into his head, but his look was reproachful — clearly such snufflings and wheezings and sneezings were not matter for levity. Sydney's look had suggested that Pa might be better employed finding a cure for all their ailments rather than mocking them.

Dickens gave the fire a vigorous poke — it looked hurt, sighed a little, and made up its mind to a few tremulous flames. He went to his desk. There were letters to be answered — always ramparts of letters bristling on his desk, whether at his office in Wellington Street or here, at home. He couldn't normally bear to leave anything unanswered. But, he recognised the writing of his brother Fred — he didn't want to open it. It would be about money. Fred — in debt — wanted Dickens to be his guarantor for a loan. He had refused once —

back in October or September. Why was it that refusing made him feel immediately guilty? He wasn't in debt, but he had to pay everybody else's debts, it seemed. But Fred had a way — like their father — of wounded reproach which somehow put you in the wrong.

In any case, he hadn't felt well himself — some sort of bilious attack which had made his eyes feel like yellow bullets. It came on after the inquests on Sefton and Plume. Sam had looked at him anxiously, thinking that two appearances as the star witness had been too much for him. And it had, in a way. They both felt the waste of all those young lives. But, it was over. That strange, eventful history ended.

Dickens looked down at his letters. It had begun with a letter — the letter from Lady Pirie. But, no — in truth, it had begun on a foggy day when he had found himself in Weymouth Street giving a sixpence to a boy with a birthmark like a teardrop and he had seen a man in a low-crowned hat bend over the child.

He hadn't known either of them, but they had been there, already part of his life without his even knowing it. In his letter, Sefton had referred to fate — fate weaving its net about his feet. Well, Dickens had thought often that we were all connected by fate without knowing it. Perhaps fate had brought them together on a foggy evening: perhaps he had been Sefton's nemesis. Sefton wasn't the shadow — he was. Shadow of his shadow.

He closed his eyes. His mind ran on — inconsequential scraps, as if he were dreaming. A man dying in a police cell; two figures under the moon, digging; a baby's cry; a girl with a stove-in face; a devil's face lit by scarlet flames; a knife swishing through the dark; a boy with an angel's face; a woman with a parcel in a midnight graveyard; a bloody lump in a bucket; a beetle-browed boy with his fists curled; a girl with a gaunt white face on a mortuary slab; a wretched boy sweeping a crossing — odd, how that boy had got in; a portrait in a tarnished frame; a flower in the mud; a speechless girl with a waxen face.

Miranda. He had done his best for her. She had gone, speechless again, with the Reverend Hugh Woodhouse and his wife, Dorothea. Dickens had hopes of them. Hugh Woodhouse was a mild-faced, gentle man, *but with far-seeing eyes*, Dickens had thought. He had looked at Miranda Deverall with such compassion. Dorothea Woodhouse was tall like her husband. She looked intelligent and wise. It would take time, she had told Dickens, but they had plenty of that. Miranda had looked at him, but she had not spoken. Yet, he had seen something — a tiny light. Perhaps it was hope. *It wanted Time*, he thought — all wounds want time — wounds of the heart and mind most of all

And for him? We are here to work, he had told someone once. Our business is to use life well. Time for action — that refuge from gloomy thoughts. Take your own advice.

Answer your letters; deal with Fred; write to Henry Austin about the Sanitary Board — light and air, that's what was needed for places like Bones Alley — go to see Doctor Fuller about Mary Brady and May — do something for that child; go to the stationery shop, see Mog Chips and ask him to take a letter to Captain Pierce in Devon; go down to Wellington Street; set about the Christmas number of *Household Words*; finish the article on the Christmas tree. Brighten it, brighten it.

He walked — that quick, light walk — down to his office, caught up in the surging, wheeling, roaring life of the city, swept along, observing it all with his bright glance, hardly stopping until he came to the junction of Hanover Street and Long Acre.

There was a band playing — an unmusical affair of a couple of cornets, a piccolo and a trombone. No one was listening, but Dickens stopped to put a penny in the hat. However, he wasn't alone. The boy was there. The crossing-sweeper — that very muddy, very ragged, very slouching boy who had popped into his dream. Dickens watched him sweep the pavement for him. Two pairs of eyes met, one muddy brown, one a bright searching blue. Something understood. Dickens gave the boy a coin. The boy watched him walk swiftly across the road. 'Where's 'e agoin' in such a tearin'?'

'To meet the future,' murmured Dickens to himself, 'if I have one.' He stepped smartly out of the way of an oncoming cab.

HISTORICAL NOTE

By 1850, Dickens had nine children, three girls and six boys. Dora, his third daughter, was born in August 1850, but died in April 1851. He gave them the most extraordinary nicknames – Sydney's nickname actually was the Ocean Spectre which was abbreviated to Hoshen Speck. Henry Fielding Dickens was born in on January 15th, 1849. The birth of Sydney Dickens in 1846 had been a difficult one. Dickens had learned about the use of chloroform in childbirth, and promised his wife that she should have it. He wrote that 'the doctors were dead against it, but I stood my ground... It spared her all pain ... and saved the child all mutilation.' According to Professor Alfred Swaine Taylor's Manual of Medical Jurisprudence (first published in 1844), ether and chloroform were used criminally in cases of rape. He cites the cases of a dentist in France and a doctor in America who were convicted of the crime. Professor Taylor also quotes 'an eminent judicial authority' whose opinion was that a victim might be unable to defend herself from attack 'from terror, or from an overpowering feeling of helplessness as well as horror.' Taylor also refers to 'magnetic sleep' and a case in which the seducer was accused of hypnotising or mesmerising his victim into a sleep then carrying out his attack. Moreover, he states that it was perfectly possible for a young woman to be entirely ignorant of 'the nature of the act'. I drew on these ideas when creating Miranda Deverall's circumstances.

William Thackeray, author of *Vanity Fair*, met Dickens in 1836 when he offered Dickens some sketches for Pickwick Papers which Dickens turned down. They became friends, but not always easy ones, though their daughters played together. The friendship of Thackeray's daughter, Annie, and Dickens's daughter, Katey, lasted until Annie's death in 1918. Katey Dickens died in 1929 at the age of ninety.

Dickens's article *A December Vision* appeared in his magazine *Household Words* on December 14th, 1850, and is a powerful expression of his concern for the poor and his anger at the way in which their suffering is ignored by those who have the power to do something about it.

In 1847, Dickens set up a home for fallen women with Miss Angela Burdett-Coutts, the banking heiress. He wrote the letter to the young women to be read to them by prison governors in the hope that some would take the opportunity of applying for refuge when they came out of prison. Some young women were recommended by clergymen or others concerned for the welfare of girls who had drifted into crime through poverty or being orphaned or simply abandoned by their families like Mrs Gaskell's poor Miss Pasley.

The poem *An Old Haunting* did appear in *Household Words*, but I couldn't find who had written it. Contributions to the magazine were always anonymous, but research has been carried out attribute many of the essays, stories or poems. However, the poet I found remains unknown so I borrowed it for poor Edward Lawson – it seemed to fit his circumstances and, of course, gave Dickens the excuse for visiting him about the murder of Doctor Plume.

A NOTE TO THE READER

Dear Reader,

The inspiration for this story came from a letter that Mrs Gaskell wrote to Dickens in January 1850. Dickens had asked her for a contribution to his new magazine *Household Words*. Mrs Gaskell knew that Dickens had established a home for fallen women with Miss Angela Burdett-Coutts so she wrote asking his advice about a young girl whom she had visited in the New Bayley Prison. The girl, aged sixteen, had been imprisoned for theft. Mrs Gaskell told Dickens the tragic story of her abandonment by her mother and her apprenticeship with an Irish dressmaker who placed her with another woman who connived at the girls's secuction by a surgeon in the neighbourhood. Dickens helped Mrs Gaskell to contact the right people and the girl was sent out tp the Cape with an emigrant family.

Another research tool, I use frequently is the *British Newspaper Archive*. I found a similar story there. In February 1851, a seemingly respectable surgeon was charged with assaulting a thirteen year old girl. The evidence showed that he used prostitutes to bring him young girls whom he plied with drink inorder to seduce them. The newspaper article referred to seven or eight girls whom the surgeon had 'succeeded to ruin.'

These two stories created Doctor Lancelot Plume. I also found the case of a homeopathic doctor who was prosecuted for manslaughter. Doctors were a mixed lot in the mid nineteenth century – some were quacks and took up fashionable cures like homeothapy. The coroner at the inquest on the dead patient observed that 'such was the state of the law, as regarded medical practice, a man might write himself a sugeon, practice as one … without having passed any examination.'

There were plenty of stories about doctors procuring illegal abortions, and stories about baby farming – the practice of farming out children to minders in whose care they often died, disappeared, or were sold.

All grim tales, but of interest to Dickens who cared about children and the poor and wrote about them in his novels and articles in *Household Words*, and who set up his home for fallen women with Miss Coutts in 1847.

Reviews are really important to authors, and if you enjoyed the novel, it would be great if you could spare a little time to post a review on **Amazon** and **Goodreads.** Readers can connect with me online, on **Facebook (JCBriggsBooks)**, **Twitter (@JeanCBriggs)**, and you can find out more about the books and Charles Dickens via my website: **jcbriggsbooks.com**

Thank you!

Jean Briggs

Sapere Books is an exciting new publisher of brilliant fiction and popular history.

To find out more about our latest releases and our monthly bargain books visit our website: **saperebooks.com**

20626594R00194

Printed in Great Britain
by Amazon